REVERE ME

FLEEING FROM THE FAE KING

LINA JUBILEE

Crimson Fox
PUBLISHING

Revere Me: Fleeing from the Fae King by Lina Jubilee

Published by Crimson Fox Publishing and Lina Jubilee.

Crimson Fox Publishing, Turner, OR

www.crimsonfoxpublishing.com

Cover by Ali Lawson.

ISBN: 978-1-952667-77-0

✾ Created with Vellum

CHAPTER
ONE
EDONY

I sought refuge beneath the starlit sky. The burst of chilled air seeped gently into my lungs, allowing my first calm, even breaths of the evening despite the tight lacing of my bodice.

The murmurs of conversation threaded through the music in the air behind me, settling over me heavily, a reminder that this would be but a short respite and there were two choices before me.

Return back to the ballroom, finish out what my grand-mother had promised to be my final ball, this last time as chaperone to my cousin, who was still eligible to be a fae bride.

Or venture out into the labyrinth surrounding the Fae King's castle, never to be heard of again.

Glancing over my shoulder in both directions, I found that no one had followed me, and I dared to shift my mask partway up my face to rest on my forehead. My fingers brushed the worn leather of the front of the hand-me-down mask, the brown beads missing in places like jagged, haphazard reminders that my family had seen better days. The thick material of the mask was dotted with my sweat, the cool night air like a balm to my opened pores.

Surely, for a moment, I could be relieved of my duty. Neela had her friends. No one would notice my absence.

Stepping farther into the darkness, I gripped the white marble balustrade and looked out over the view before me.

The labyrinth keeping the Fae King safe from human eyes eleven months of the year was vast. Though almost certainly built by fae hands long, long ago, it seemed to have grown organically upon the rolling hills and dipping valleys between here and our town of Westbridge in the distance, like sprouting vines coiling up and worming their way through the landscape. Stone walls loomed perilously high above any who found themselves trapped inside its paths, but from here, I gazed over it all, able to watch for any movement from far above, as if to revel in the sport of the maze's danger.

Despite the tall weeds that broke through the stone paths, the clusters of overgrown bushes, and the hunched trees thick with foliage, there were creatures that lived within those walls. No human could survive for long. I, as well as my grandmother, knew that too well. But the ones steeped in magic, they had ways to whisper to the labyrinth, to tame its angry impulses, to stay safe in a disorienting place where even the fae themselves were known to leave well enough alone.

I could go downstairs, slip back outside, and lose myself in those walls.

My hand reached out over the balcony. Almost as if I could

touch the twists and turns of the maze, as if it were my plaything.

Of course, I knew this was but a fraction of it. The thatch roofs, the smoking chimneys, the lit street torches of West-bridge beyond the maze was just one such town, the one to the west. North, east, and south of the castle, the labyrinth roamed on and on and on, edging up against our closest neighboring human towns.

North's Glen and Southwold took our traders and travelers three days each to visit, going the long way around the exterior labyrinth walls. From either of those places, it was another three days to Eastmeet.

The fae could guide us on a special roadway, straight through the maze and past the castle at its center to any desti-nation in less than a day.

But the king allowed such passage so rarely. And for just one month per year, the fae deigned to give each village one week to send their eligible young residents to dance their nights away here, at the castle.

To try to attract a groom or bride among the fae.

Each eligible villager was permitted one older escort. Grandmother had been mine, but she'd complained the six nights of noise and dancing were too much for her old bones to take. This year, with my cousin becoming eligible at age eigh-teen just as I became no longer eligible at age twenty-five, Grandmother had asked me to take her place.

"Next year, your aunt should be back from her travels across the sea," Grandmother had told me. *"She'll be her daughter's escort thereafter. Assuming our young Neela doesn't secure a marriage at*

this fete. She's quite a beauty, sure to stand out even behind the mask, wouldn't you say?"

I shifted, leaning my elbows atop the balustrade and looking back into the warm glow of the candlelit ballroom. Neela was easy enough to spot, her thick, dark hair fluttering out behind her as a rather tall, lean man spun her around the dance floor amidst the other couples. The upturned smile of her rosy lips was dazzling even beneath our family's finest beaded mask, the golden color of ovals over her eyes and nose only diminished by the occasional pockmark of a lost bead in the pattern. Whereas the color had washed out my fair complexion, Neela's smooth, brown skin made it sparkle and gave her a mischievous look that was actually quite suited to her character. Still, mischievous and ill-mannered were not the same, and I knew she could be trusted to remain cordial and remember herself amidst these would-be suitors. Amiable to all and mindful of Grandmother's weak heart, she'd told our grandparent she'd looked forward to this week, but I knew that was only because she was always up for an adventure.

She'd been too young to remember the loss of my parents. She couldn't remember her uncle, my father, who'd died chasing after my mother when I'd been eight.

Her own parents were alive and well but home in West-bridge only a few months per year. My aunt was a sailor who had met Neela's father on one of her adventures across the globe. It was only worry for Neela's safety that had led them to leave her with my grandmother to be raised.

If Neela found no groom or bride this year, she'd be free to travel the world with her parents in a few months when they returned for their visit. So long as she made it back for the fete every year until she was no longer of age, there'd be no reason for her to otherwise stay.

Every child born in one of the four villages of the Fae King's rule had to keep to that law.

At least until the Fae King himself found a bride to wed.

But he'd been searching and searching since before my grandmother's time, so I had reason to doubt he'd ever find such a woman to tempt him.

He was here, said the whispers, among us now. Perhaps he was the tall fae man dancing with Neela. He certainly commanded the dance floor, other couples subtly shifting away to allow him and my cousin room. I frowned, taking in the man. Long, silky white hair that reached the small of his back. It hid his pointed ears, no doubt, as we weren't supposed to know who was fae and who was human during the fete.

But even we humans could tell. The fae carried themselves more stiffly, yet also more gracefully. This man's lithe limbs were almost statue-straight, one at my cousin's back, the other holding her hand to the side of them. Together, they glided across the room like swans. The dark eyes behind his impeccable pure-ivory mask did not so much as flinch as they met my cousin's. Her own dark gaze, though more obviously human, more frequently blinking, was similarly drawn to his.

But no one in our Grandmother's bloodline had ever been picked for a fae bride or groom. No one. Neela had to be safe. My legs grew a bit unsteady as the thought hit me that maybe she wasn't.

I'd been prepared to see my cousin off with her parents for most of the year, content to stay behind with Grandmother and take care of her, to put aside all thought of having a life of adventure like my cousin sought and lock it all away.

But if she became the bride of a fae... If that was the Fae *King* especially... I'd never see her again.

Never.

"I imagine the chill air would feel such a relief against my face," said someone from the shadows to the side of the doorway leading back into the ballroom. The voice was deep, the figure tall, broad-shouldered. A man. "But I would be terrified His Majesty should catch me without my mask during his fete. Even such a lovely face as yours would be no exemption for the law."

My stomach rock hard, my racing heartbeat almost drowning out whatever else the man had to say, I spun back to face the labyrinth, yanking my mask back down over my eyes and nose.

If he reported me, the guards would scratch deep grooves diagonally down my face with the shorn scissor claw hoof of the minotaur. The creature roamed the labyrinth, lost forever to the maze.

But that would only be the start of it. I would grow mad, like the minotaur had. Like my mother had.

I'd hear the call of the labyrinth and someday—maybe minutes from now, maybe years—be driven to wander inside it.

Swift execution would be kinder.

CHAPTER

TWO

EDONY

"I didn't mean you any threat," said the man as he drew closer. My palms were cold against the stone balustrade, and I slapped one over my mouth to keep a startled whimper from escaping my throat. "I only wished to warn you."

A softer edge entered his voice, but his hovering presence over my shoulder still lifted the hairs on my neck.

"Do you know what becomes of those who break the law of the mask during fete?" he asked. His breath was warm, and it carried in the air to my ear. He was so close behind me.

I spun away, putting more space between us. "I-I do," I said, my voice quavering even as I clenched my hands into fists to tame the shakiness threatening to invade my limbs. "Better than most." The words were cracked. Quiet.

The man lifted both hands in the air as if in surrender. I got my first good look at him in the silvery moonlight.

He was a head taller than I, as broad as I'd discerned from

the shadows. His muscles strained against a fine white linen shirt, its ruffles and his fine dark chest hair on a creamy complexion bursting out over the embroidered earthy colors of his tunic. Dark leather pants hugged his thick calf muscles, his sturdy hips ending in a prominent bulge between his legs. My eyes darted rapidly upward, the skin on my neck and cheeks flushing, as I focused on his mask. It was simple but still reeked of opulence, sleekly covering his eyes and nose in a dark, shimmering silk, his square jaw and stubble drawing my gaze to the thin, red line of his lips. His dark hair looked to have recently had hands run through it, tumbling over the edge of his mask, over the tips of his ears, even though it was shorn rather close to his scalp for a fae.

For there was no doubt in my mind that despite his ruggedness, he was a fae. No one in Westbridge matched both his build and his apparent affluence at once. And there was the stiffness in his limbs. The unimpeachable straight line of his back.

My hands practically sopping, I clutched at my tan dress. Both to wipe my palms and for support. Suddenly aware of how threadbare the gown my grandmother had worn as a chaperone looked on me, I felt my heart sink. It had bagged at my chest, so my grandmother had altered it and run leather straps through the back of the bodice. But now it strained too tightly against my torso, the exposed tops of my breasts squeezed together and heaving with every breath, the fabric still gathering unflatteringly all over my upper body. The skirt was three inches too short, my ankles clearly on display, the material tugging on my backside and lifting up even higher in the back.

It hadn't mattered. I wasn't going to dance.

Neela wore the golden dress I'd worn for my eligible years at the balls. A hand-me-down from her mother, and Grandmother before her, it had never looked so vivid and gorgeous as it did on her today.

But even that had been more flattering on me than this chaperone's gown I found myself in now. I hadn't cared—not until this man's pale gray eyes began to roam over me.

I couldn't stand the thought of him forming an opinion of me. I knew what it would be—poor, rejected, worthless—but he didn't know me. He never would.

I'd do anything to make him go away. Anything to get those discerning eyes off of me.

But he'd seen me without my mask.

"Will you tell?" I asked, clutching the thick material of my skirt harder.

It took him a moment to reply. His eyebrow arched and he let out a small gasp, almost as if he hadn't expected me to speak again and my question had surprised him.

A smile cracked his lips beneath his sleek mask. "You think I'd wish the marring of such beauty?"

Fae were flirtatious. That was another thing that set them apart, at least at the fete. Humans of any gender were typically more demure at the event. Our fates weighed too heavily on our shoulders for most of us to have much fun.

Though so far, Neela had certainly seemed an exception. I glanced over my shoulder to make sure she was still all right. The dance ended and she and her partner stepped back from one another, he bowing slightly, she curtseying as her mother had taught her. I'd been so clumsy the few times I'd been asked to dance during my years of eligibility. Not her. Not my cousin. Whom I could lose forever due to her amiable, mischievous nature and her grace and beauty.

"Whatever could have your attention?" the man before me asked.

I snapped back to the moment. To the threat he posed, even if he claimed he meant none.

"I'm... I'm looking for fae guards," I lied. There hadn't been any approaching, but the last thing I wanted to do was to draw this fae's attention to my desirable cousin. She had clearly already caught someone's eye, and the prospect of one suitor after her was terrible enough. I couldn't shake the thought that it was the king who'd danced with her, either, and I didn't know what that could mean—the king at last selecting a bride. And that bride being my cousin. No. It would change things, and I didn't think favorably for *my* family, whatever sweet promises danced on these faefolk's tongues. Nothing was worth the loss of her. "I didn't know if you'd alerted them to my transgression," I said, the words tumbling out of me.

It was as real a fear as losing my cousin. But for some reason, less so.

No one but her and Grandmother would miss me if I lost myself to the labyrinth. And Grandmother had survived losing her son and good-daughter to it. Neela was even stronger, with a brighter future promised to her. She would do all right without me.

My aunt and uncle—my entire village—would feel the loss of Neela, even if it were to less tragic circumstances.

"I haven't left this balcony since before you arrived on it,"

he said, putting a broad hand on his hip. A tan leather bracer was on his wrist.

"You could have signaled to them." Now my eyes were darting around for the bringers of my punishment, my stomach growing queasy at the realization that the risk to my safety was so great. Even if I'd choose to sacrifice myself over Neela any day, that didn't mean I was so noble as to truly walk happily, willingly into my demise. Such thoughts before had only been the symptoms of a heart weighed down and heavy. "I didn't know you were here. Otherwise, I would not have—"

"Broken the law of the mask at fete?" He cocked his head slightly. I bit my lips together. "So you admit you would have broken it. It was only the fact that you were *caught* that makes you regret your actions."

Why did he have to spin my words so? Fae were infuriating. The elders said they could not tell lies, but we were to watch ourselves around them anyway. Not being able to tell a lie and being compelled to speak the truth were two different matters entirely, in the mouths of clever wordsmiths.

Despite the pounding of my heart, I straightened as best as a human could and tossed my head back. "If only the stars and the maze were my witnesses, I would argue I'd broken no laws."

The man's lips clamped together, his gray eyes sparkling for a moment before he spoke. "I don't recall an exemption being made for lack of breathing witnesses."

"'The connection of two souls being more essential to an effective union than the sight of a beautiful face doomed to fade with time and age,'" I quoted, citing the law of the mask at fete without missing a word, "'masks shall be worn by all at the fete—human or fae—so that no one shall be led astray by the urges of their inner beasts.'"

He smirked. "Those words sound so dispassionate passing through those lips."

It was my turn to arch a brow beneath the coarse material of my mask as I tried to steady my shaking knees by grabbing the balustrade with one hand. "Are laws ever meant to be anything but?"

Another song began behind us in the ballroom, another dance. I could not spare a moment to check on my cousin just yet.

"Some laws, yes." He took a step closer to me, guiding one hand atop the balustrade beside us as he neared. His fingers danced lightly across the stone as if stroking a beloved pet. "Like those that center on the *urges* of our inner beasts."

I swallowed as his fingers drew nearer to my own. I would not flinch, though. He *liked* to see me rattled. I could tell that much. "You miss my point. The stars and the maze—they have no *inner beasts* to lead astray."

"Oh, I think you underestimate the labyrinth." His hand let go of the stone surface to run through his hair. The moonlight sparkled among his dark tresses, like his own form of starlight.

"I'd do no such thing," I said, quieter. I stared down at it. Some distance away, what might have been half a day's walk if one knew how to get there without becoming lost in the maze, a bonfire lit up, small sparks of light dancing up to meet the sky. A sure sign of a creature of the maze or even a group of them. I couldn't make out their forms from here, but it had to be someone confident in their ability to tame the labyrinth to make themselves such obvious targets.

Besides, news traveled between villages, and there'd been no humans lost to the maze since my mother. Seventeen years ago now.

She hadn't been the first. And now, on this stranger's whims, I might personally ensure she wouldn't be the last.

"You speak as if you have personal experience," said the man.

He leaned on the balustrade beside me, his elbows on the stone and his hands clenched together as he joined me in watching the jubilant flames.

"Do not tease me." I swallowed. "If I must pay, let it be done. I can't... I cannot..."

"Shh." His finger brushed the edge of my jaw, where a single tear had escaped from behind my mask to drip down and catch on the edge of my skin. He studied the tear on his finger a moment in the moonlight before flicking it down below us into the garden I found to be a gentle mockery of the labyrinth beyond it. Well-trimmed hedges and rhododendron bushes grew in orderly lines flush against the stone wall.

"I promised you I meant you no harm, and I do not." His finger returned to my cheek before I could stop it, traveling down to my chin and tilting it up so my eyes had to meet his. "Do you not believe a fae?"

So he admitted it. I'd never met one who had at the fete. Not that I ever met any outside of it, other than the guards who came to deliver us directly through the maze to the castle for the duration.

"Where is your chaperone, sweet one?" he asked. "Who would let you be out here all alone with such disregard for your safety?"

I turned away. If I were an eligible maiden still, I would have had a chaperone cautioning me to stay amidst the crowd, to never fiddle with my mask. Grandmother certainly wouldn't have abided me removing it.

It was supposed to be a pleasure known to me only this year. Only this time when *I* was a chaperone.

He shouldn't have been wasting his flirtations on me. He was a year too late—I'd had my seven years of eligibility and where had he been then?

Despite myself, I studied him again, his broad form, his thick, powerful legs.

Where *had* he been? The fae weren't required to attend the fete, as far as I knew. Only those in search of a bride or groom needed to attend. They had a village somewhere safe deep within the labyrinth and they so rarely set foot out of it, despite the inviting opulence of this castle that held the fete.

They didn't marry each other, as far as anyone knew. And I'd never seen a fae child. But human lives were fragile, short, and wherever the fae village to which they took their stolen spouses was, the human spouses were not here at the castle for the fete. The fae had all the time in the world to find a mate— and then others in lifetimes after those mates turned to dust.

Human lives were far too short for such nonchalance.

I opened my mouth to tell him I was here as a chaperone. Would that make him less likely to care about my supposedly lovely face, and the fate owed to me in punishment? But even if not, then he would surely ask whom I chaperoned. I didn't want to draw even more attention to her. My gaze darted back into the ballroom, expecting to find Neela in the arms of another fae.

She was with that same one again. The regal one I expected might be king. I didn't recognize him from other fetes, either.

No! My hand clutched my chest, all thought of admissions forgotten.

"Do you find him attractive?" the fae sharing the balcony with me asked.

I turned back to him, my eyes widened. The act, thanks to my mask, was like scuffing a coarse rag against my brow.

"I've noticed your gaze dart to him," he said, his voice clipped.

Yes, but only because he can't keep his hands off my cousin!

I chewed my bottom lip. I didn't know how much to tell him. I didn't know what would keep me safe—and keep Neela away from the likes of this overconfident fae. But did that matter? Another fae—a new fae, a regal fae—was already enamored with her.

"I thought the masks kept anyone from feeling *attraction*," I said, tapping the brown beads of my own.

He shook his head slightly down at me, almost admonishingly. "They are not as effective at that as one might hope."

"Foolish king," I blurted out. My hand flew to my mouth even as I'd said it, but it was too late.

"Pardon?" the fae asked, his back, if possible, even more rigid.

"I just meant... He made the law of the mask at fete and... You said yourself, it doesn't seem to stop anyone from feeling attraction." My voice quavered even as I looked over my shoulder to keep my cousin in my sight. She was smiling, laughing, even. Something the fae had told her had *amused* her.

Didn't she know what she was risking? What of her dreams of world travel?

What of Grandmother? Her parents?

Me?

"I suppose I cannot fault you the truth of that," he said. I'd almost forgotten he was standing here with me, lost to thoughts of the danger my cousin was putting herself in. He had *two* things to report me to the guards for, two terrible infractions that could easily seal my fate. There was no *law* against speaking ill of the king, but frankly, it was common sense.

Something I was certainly lacking this evening.

"Nonetheless, I'm positive attraction of the souls can count for every match made at fete—"

"Excuse me," I said, no longer able to stand here and let him flirt with me in the hopes he wouldn't grow bored with me and seal my fate.

I was Neela's chaperone. And I needed to remind her. Subtly. Somehow, without getting the king's attention. He could not know I planned to *interfere* with his potential match.

That was the whole point of this fete.

The melancholy music wormed its way through the swelling conversations as I entered the warmly lit ballroom again. The melody was beautiful in a way, but it was also haunting, settling deep inside my flesh and seeming to weigh down my bones.

"Take me, my sweet fae," crooned the bard leading the musicians on his lute. He had to be fae—no one knew of such a bard in any of our own villages. *"I know not what I give, but I give it anyway. Away, away, take me away."*

Dread weighed me down, my feet trapped as if in iron sabatons.

"Excuse me," I kept muttering to people gathered around me. I wove through dancing couples, drawing as near to my cousin and her suitor as I dared.

And then I froze to the spot.

The regal fae I suspected of being king...

He threw back his head and laughed.

CHAPTER
THREE

EDONY

"No!" I shouted, my voice carrying louder than the bard's, louder than the murmur of conversations around me.

The smile on Neela's face dropped and she turned to face me.

But I could only spare her a glance. The fae I suspected of being king had laughed.

The rumors were that the king would only select a bride who made him laugh.

"I was made for thee, my sweet fae. Now take me, take me far away."

The music went quiet, the song over.

"F-Friend!" said Neela quickly, curtseying at the fae whose grip on her hand and back only reluctantly loosened as she made her way to me. She didn't call my name because names were a commodity in crowds during the fete; even calling me "cousin" might give too much away, though those from Westbridge would surely recognize me regardless. While it was true that the fae wouldn't know us by our names if we called one another by them, the gift of a name during fete indicated a serious interest.

Chaperones were supposed to stay nameless entirely, unremarkable to the fae searching for brides and grooms.

Around us, people spoke in hushed whispers to their neighbors, many hiding their lips behind their hands. Both the fae left standing by his lonesome, rather reluctantly gathering his hands behind his back and tilting his nose into the air, as well as I were the objects of everyone's attention.

"Why would you shout so?" whispered Neela in my ear. She leaned away from me and smiled broadly—at the people around us. At that regal fae.

He softened somewhat at her friendly expression, as clear as day even with the mask.

I threaded my arm through hers and tugged her away, making my tepid apologies as I dragged her through the crowd and into a darkened hallway. The music started up as we rounded the last corner, the heavy, judging silence left in its brief absence a weight lifted off my shoulders.

"What are you *doing*?" Neela asked, tugging her arm out of my grip. The lit torch above her bathed her in a harsh, orange glow that highlighted the pinched expression on her lips. I hadn't seen it in over a decade, not since her last tantrum as a child. That had been about me eating the last of Grandmother's blancmange.

"What are *you* doing?" I asked her.

Her eyes squinted even through the holes in the mask.

"What do you think? I'm enjoying myself. It's fete! I'm an eligible maiden!"

I grabbed her by the shoulders. "You didn't *care* about any of this, not really! You wanted to travel with your mother and father—"

"That was before..." She bit her lip and looked away. Her voice was quieter now, hoarser. "No one in our family has ever been picked as a bride or groom. I didn't think it would be *an option* for me. I imagined I would spend year after year here, just waiting, waiting to turn twenty-five so I could find a human man to marry. If I didn't find one sooner and desire to be expelled from home entirely."

She winced as her shoulders hunched beneath my hands, an unspoken apology. I'd not sought out a human mate, as was my right after my last birthday.

I'd never been tempted to become ineligible and be exiled from the four villages by becoming a parent before the age of twenty-five. Some did. Some left willingly then, their children their ticket to early release from the king's law of fete.

Perhaps Neela, like her mother, could have found a mate on her worldly travels, waited until she'd turned twenty-five to marry and have a child, and never looked back.

Perhaps that child could have been born in its father's homeland, far away from the law of fete here.

Was that... Was that what truly bothered me? Letting my hands slip from Neela's shoulders, I realized with a start that I'd planned her future out for her. She'd supplied the desire to travel with her parents, they'd promised to take her after her first fete. But I'd supplied the rest for her.

Grandmother had predicted Neela would be back next year

in time for fete again. But I'd seen her traveling as her path to freedom. For her and any future children she bore.

Because Neela was different than I was. She would find a mate.

But I'd never imagined it'd be a fae one.

How could I have been so foolish? And I'd dared to accuse the king of being so?

"What is it?" Neela asked, concern overpowering any annoyance in her voice now.

"It's... It's... Never mind," I said, pressing the tips of my fingers to the scratchy beads of the mask over my temple. "You're right. I should be happy for you. You've made the Fae King laugh."

Neela cocked her head and then burst into a fit of giggles herself. "You think Favian is the Fae King?"

So they'd exchanged names? That didn't bode well. It indicated he was serious about pursuing her. "If that's the name of that rather regal, tightly-wound fae you were continuously dancing with..."

She rolled her eyes. "He's a perfect gentleman. And he's... He's very sweet." She clutched the front of her yellow skirt with both hands. "I can't imagine him as a king."

"So you don't *know* he's not the king."

She embraced me, and I hugged her back. Then she pushed me away at arm's length. "Is that what you were worried about? That I would woo the Fae King and put an end to fete?"

"The end of fete is *hardly* something I'd be *worried* about."

She prattled on, not hearing me. "If no one has won the Fae King's heart in all of these years, what would be the chances of the first to do so being from *our* family, from a bloodline who's never once turned a single fae's head? Oh. I mean no offense." Her smile dropped, but I knew she'd meant none.

"I don't care about that. Neela, I... I don't want to lose you."

She hugged me again. "Grandmother always dreamed that one of us would become a fae bride. Only a handful of humans are chosen each year—from all four villages." She pulled back and swirled in a little dance, her skirt swishing outward. "And you know how those families are honored! You and Grandmother won't want for food for your whole lives!"

A yearly tithe of grains and fruits was presented to the family of any bride or groom taken at fete. At least until the family member taken died. That was when the gifting stopped, though by then, there usually weren't too many family members left to receive them. More than one family had grown to rely on an uncle or even great-aunt's tithes for years, though, never having met the lost family member themselves, before the gift had ended.

That wasn't the same as losing the cousin who was like the only sister I had in the world.

"We don't care about that," I said. "We do fine washing clothes and selling what grows in the garden and helping out whenever shopkeepers hit their busy seasons—"

"Edony, you know very well it's hard work. And Grandmother is getting too old for it. I want her to enjoy her last years in comfort." She fluffed her hair over her shoulder, her back straight.

Her mind determined.

My throat grew dry. "Your parents!" I pleaded. "They take care of us. They always bring us back things."

"They don't visit often enough," she said softly. She blinked hard, her eyes glistening just slightly. "Not enough to keep Grandmother comfortable."

"But you... If you're chosen as a fae bride, you'll never see them again. You won't be able to say goodbye."

Neela took both my hands in hers and squeezed. "You'll have to convey my love for me. They'll understand, Edony. I know they will."

I wasn't sure about that. Aunt Millicent had probably hoped her daughter would follow in her own footsteps. She'd probably imagined a life of adventure with her child, visiting grandbabies once Neela had settled somewhere... Anywhere far from here. From this place. From the labyrinth.

"Neela, *I* will miss you." The words were so quiet, the buzz of the ballroom nearly drowned them out entirely. "Isn't that enough?"

She let go to wipe both her eyes of unshed tears. "I'll miss you all. But stop acting like I might *die*. I won't. I'd just... go somewhere with my fae husband."

"But where? And why do the brides and grooms never return? How do you know they... They..." I couldn't say it. That they didn't die right away? We only had the faefolk's word to go on that they lived full lives.

And fae couldn't lie.

But that didn't mean they had to tell the truth.

Neela leaned closer, her voice a harsh whisper. "Edony, the only *danger* is denying a proposal once given. As you, of all people, should know."

She walked away before I could respond, her worn leather shoes squeaking on the stone floor. She excused her way past the crowd gathered and vanished from my sight.

She'd been too young to see my mother lost to the labyrinth.

But she knew the story. Grandmother had told us.

Before I'd been born, before my mother had married my father when he'd turned twenty-five, a fae man had asked my mother to marry him.

And she'd refused.

FOUR

EDONY

My mother and father had fallen in love in their youth. Grandmother had counseled her son that it was a terrible idea, that both were promised to fete during their eligible years as citizens of Westbridge, and they'd kept their promise not to risk pregnancy before their first fete.

If they'd had a child after that, they'd have been exiled, which would have been painful for them, to be separated from friends and family, but they could have borne it.

They'd just needed to attend that first fete, give the fae a chance to meet them, and then no one would pursue them if they left the villages and sought a life elsewhere.

But my mother had secured a proposal her first and only fete.

Her refusal had resulted in the mask being torn from her face, and then the gashes across her visage from the shorn scissor claw hoof of the minotaur that would compel her into the labyrinth.

Her stubbornness—her desire for a life with my father, despite that hope being ripped away—had made her hold on.

She couldn't leave. She was drawn to the labyrinth and needed to stay at its borders. My father had watched her in agony, knowing he couldn't comfort her, couldn't begin a family with her despite the limited time she'd had left, until he was twenty-five. Doing so earlier would have meant he and she would have been banished from the villages, and he could not leave her. She could not leave the villages.

So he'd waited. Year after year. Until finally, free from the fete, unchosen as everyone in that side of my family had been, he and my mother had wed.

Though she'd always been drawn to the labyrinth, some kind of providence had given her almost nine years after that. Sixteen years after her face had been marked with the jagged hoof of the minotaur. Until the pull of the labyrinth had finally been too much for her.

So yes, I knew very well Neela couldn't refuse a proposal from a fae. But did she *have to* be so charming? Encouraging? There was still time. He hadn't asked her yet.

I clutched at the front of my bodice, as if I could tame my heart through my flesh and bones to stop beating so wildly.

No. It *was* too late. We had five more nights of fete and she wouldn't avoid him. Whether or not she was right about him not being the king and his laughter not signifying anything particularly remarkable, he would not go five days without asking her.

He just wouldn't. He'd be foolish to let her walk away.

I followed after her into the ballroom, making my excuses to those I brushed against. I was stopped by a stout woman with streaked gray hair I knew even with a bird-shaped mask upon her face to be Mistress Baker, the mother of one of Neela's closest friends. And almost half the eligible Westbridge residents at the ball. A slight exaggeration, to be sure, but just barely.

"Edony?" Mistress Baker whispered, covering her mouth with a short-fingered hand.

I winced. There was no disguising residents from one another, even in our finest clothes. Then again, most families could only afford so many fine clothes, so we got used to seeing the same outfits for each family year after year.

"Pardon me, mistress, but I'm looking for…" I stopped myself. There weren't other cousins raised as sisters in our village. I couldn't be overheard openly identifying either of us, despite Mistress Baker's hushed confession that she knew my identity.

"She's fine," said Mistress Baker, flapping at her masked face with her hand. The olive skin around it was edged with perspiration. "She's with my Gl—" She cut herself short as a couple—the woman walking stiffly and elegant this time, the man rather cowed to hold her hand—walked past us to head to the dance floor.

Her Gloriana. Sure enough, I spotted Neela in our family's bright golden gown next to three other young women, all her friends from the village. Gloriana was particularly noticeable with her cascading brown curls, her heaving olive bosom centered atop her rose bodice. They were whispering to one another, laughing, their gazes darting every so often to the dance floor.

"Your... *dear one*," said Mistress Baker, "is doing very well for herself, I must say. What a regal gentleman!"

The edges of my vision grew dark as my eyes scanned the ballroom for him. The lithe man I suspected could be the genuine Fae King.

"Yes..." I found myself saying. I found him.

Favian, Neela had called him.

He was talking to... the fae who held my life in his hands. My secret keeper.

"My dear ones, well, some have been doing better than others." She tugged on my arm, demanding my attention, and nodded toward a dancing couple. A man I recognized to be Lief, her eldest son, whirled a woman around the dance floor with all the confidence of a fae himself. It was the slight stoop to his back, the way his right arm muscles bulged just slightly more than the left from his years of pounding bread dough, that gave him away as human. You couldn't tell from the way the golden-haired fae in his arms smiled, though. Her eyes seemed locked on him, as if she'd never seen such perfection.

"I told him he needed to be bolder. No need to approach any of them, to be sure, but with the right smile, the right posture... You'll make them *come to you*." She nudged me, winking her brown eye through her mask. "But your dear one didn't even have to try now, did she? She's just naturally like that."

I stared at Neela, the way her eyes just wouldn't stop veering to the left, toward the fae across the ballroom floor in conversation with my secret keeper. Even when one of her friends said something and she looked back to give them her full attention, it wasn't long before her eyes wandered once more.

Her line of sight was blocked by a tall woman who approached the group, wearing an opulent silver gown with ruffles at the cuffs, the neckline, and the hem of the skirt. Her oak-colored hair was swept up into a perfect bun atop her head, her mask a swooping, elegant silver design to match her dress.

"Oh!" Mistress Baker clutched my arm. My eyes popped as I felt the flow of blood grow strained. "Do you think...?"

The fae woman spoke directly to Gloriana, who startled and curtseyed, her gaze affixed to the woman's feet. The fae held out her hand and Gloriana accepted it, locking eyes with her dance partner and allowing herself to be dragged onto the floor. Neela clutched on to Loreena, who held similarly to Maria, the girls bouncing in place as they watched their friend join the others dancing.

Mistress Baker let go of my arm to wipe a tear that had stuck to the eyehole of her mask. "Somehow they know. They know my Gloriana is sweet on other girls. Oh, I might have *two* children wed to fae by the end of the fete. I can't believe it."

Though her expression was hidden beneath her rather large mask, there was no doubting the light in her eyes as she watched her eligible children dance. Somewhere amidst the crowd were two more of her eligible children, leaving only one at home with their father. I wondered how many of them she could stand to lose. To give up even one child to the fae—that would be enough to keep the family fed. Not that the bakers had any worry about that regardless. They were among the most comfortable merchants in Westbridge.

"Pardon me," I said, the darkness at the edge of my vision spreading outward. My heart was thumping so loudly, I had difficulty telling it from the beating rhythm of the band's snare drum.

Mistress Baker didn't notice as I turned on my heel, heading back to the dimly lit hallway leading to the guest bedrooms. I checked one more time to be sure Neela was enjoying herself, safe amidst her friends and in sight of countless witnesses.

Favian broke away from my secret keeper and made his way around the edge of the dancers, heading in my direction. No doubt on his way to take hold of Neela once more.

If he were the Fae King, surely, he would have announced she'd captured his heart when she'd made him laugh.

But did it matter? Either way, she was bound to be his bride. Whether or not she ended the fete when she wed, Neela would be gone from my life forever.

Favian was growing closer now, his white brow drawn together in a narrowed line. It seemed almost as if he were... looking at me.

I *had* made a spectacle of myself and drawn Neela away earlier.

Too tired, too nauseous to allow him to discuss the matter with me, I retreated down the hallway, putting the soft echo of the music and the voices all behind me as I made my way to the room Neela and I shared for the week.

As my hand reached the door, I heard the distant echo of a footfall stopping short just a moment after mine.

"Hello?" I called down into the darkness. No one replied. No one came forth to make themselves known.

I might have imagined it.

Still, an ache pervaded the back of my throat as I turned the handle and stepped inside.

FIVE

EDONY

"Jarin! She's gone! You have to let her go. To chase after her is madness!" Grandmother took hold of Father by the elbow, but he barely seemed to notice it as he stuffed his satchel with clothing and blankets and food.

"Mother, I have to go," he said.

I curled up beside Neela's crib, rocking her back and forth with one hand, clutching my leg to me with my other, afraid to say a word in case... in case my words made it real.

"She'll never come back," said Grandmother, using her apron to wipe her tears. "I'll miss her, too. We were all the family she had after her mother passed. But she's gone, Son."

Mother. I knew they were talking about Mother, but I didn't want to believe it. Beside me, Neela let out a soft sigh, her stubby brown fist rubbing an eyelid with long, delicate lashes.

"She's not gone." Father swirled on Grandmother. The two were so obviously mother and son, Father almost a taller, broader version of Grandmother. Though Grandmother's brown hair was dotted with gray, they shared the same sharp nose, the same rounded cheeks. The same wide, hazel green eyes. The same features they'd shared with me.

"She needs me," he added softly.

"*We* need you." Grandmother gestured behind her at Neela and me, though she didn't tear her eyes from my father. "Your child needs you!"

"She has you." Father's head tilted slightly toward me, his gaze quickly retreating back to his satchel, which he tied closed and slung over his shoulder. "And Millicent is here half the year."

"She's here less and less as time goes on." Grandmother wrung her hands and stared at Neela and me. "Jarin, I can't... I can't do this alone."

Father grabbed her and took her into a hug, resting his chin atop her head. "I won't be gone long. I'll get her back. I always do."

"She got inside," Grandmother whispered. "You'll never get her back from inside."

Father stepped back and held Grandmother out at arm's length. "I will. I have to."

He turned and stopped in the doorway, then rushed back across the room, fell to his knees, and threw his arms around me. His satchel slid down his arm and bumped up against my hip. My leg strained in the awkward grip, my arms pinned and unable to return the embrace.

When he pulled back, his eyes brimmed with tears. "I love you," he said. "Mother loves you, too. Promise me. Promise me you will never seek a fae's favor."

Grandmother scoffed behind him. "She'd be the first in this family to manage that."

I didn't understand what they were talking about. But I looked to her, then to him, and nodded. Still afraid to speak my words.

Afraid that would make him leave.

He stood, ruffled my hair, and collected his satchel.

I never said goodbye. And still, my father left.

I bolted upright, the ray of sunlight flooding into the room through the carved, circular hole in the window shutters hitting my eyes as they fluttered.

I'd dreamed of Father's farewell again. I couldn't remember the last time I'd seen Mother. She'd just... disappeared. I hadn't expected it. She'd been there in my life one minute, then gone the next.

Neela.

I turned to the bed beside mine. The luxurious feather-down mattress was unblemished, the earth-tone quilt as tightly clung to the bed as it'd been when we'd arrived.

"Neela!" I cried out loud, flinging my own matching quilt aside. I never should have left her alone. I was here as her chaperone!

She'd never come back to go to sleep last night. What a fool I'd been! No. It was too soon. She couldn't marry him and be taken away from me with five more days of Westbridge at fete. I wouldn't allow it.

I ripped open the door leading to the hallway and stumbled

forward, my foot coming into contact with something cold and hard that clattered loudly as I lost my balance. Hopping to right myself, my foot caught again on something softer this time, but I couldn't manage to look with the opposite wall headed right for my face.

I caught myself against the stone, wincing as a jolt of pain shot through my wrists.

"Edony?" Neela's voice, though harshly whispered, still carried down the hall. "What in faekind's name are you doing out here? Without your mask? In your *shift*?"

I blinked, Neela in her golden dress and mask coming into focus. The hall was still dark, devoid of windows, but the light from our bedroom window shone through the open door.

Her hair was limp, the edges of her dress at her exposed clavicle somewhat damp with sweat. Her mask was just slightly askew, one of the ties to bind it caught awkwardly in a knot in her hair.

She bent down as I righted myself and before I could ask her if she was just *now* returning from the ballroom, she shoved something large and soft in my hand and slapped a mask over my face. Doors down either side of the hallway opened and curious masked faces peered out. Neela offered them a smile— Mistress Baker and Lief were among them—then bent down to pick up what appeared to be a shiny, silver tray and a pair of silk shoes from the ground as I awkwardly cradled whatever mask she'd shoved onto my face. It was soft, the insides like a silken caress against the bridge of my nose and my cheeks, my fingers resting on the front's velvety, down feathers to keep it in place.

Neela grabbed my arm and tugged me back into our room,

slamming the door closed behind us and leaning her back against it. "What was *that* about?"

Blinking, I let the fog of my brain catch back up to my surroundings. I lowered the mask, wherever she'd gotten it. It was sky blue and covered, as I'd suspected, in feathers. Whether it was from a blue bird or the feathers had been dyed this sky color, I couldn't say. It was certainly expensive. "I was looking for you," I said simply. I cocked my head at the fine mask but found it unimportant at the moment, tossing it onto my bed. Then I stared at the soft mass of silk Neela had shoved into my arms. It was pale blue, too. I unfolded it to get a better look at it. A luscious ballgown, complete with beads woven into the very fabric of the skirt that shimmered as it caught the sunlight.

A sudden dread of this being some sort of gift from *Favian* to Neela filled me and I tossed it alongside the mask on the bed.

"If you were so concerned, you needed only stay for the duration of the night's ball as *my chaperone,*" she stated. She crossed the room and placed the shiny, silver tray and blue slippers she carried on the vanity and sat down, carefully untying the strings holding her mask on her face and removing it. She blinked hard and stretched her facial muscles as she looked into the mirror, dipping her fingers in one of the jars of cream provided by our fae hosts and working it into the smooth skin over her rounded cheeks.

"I... I didn't feel well," I said by way of excuse. "And I thought you were soon to bed."

She spun around and quirked a brow at me. "We're here *for the fete.* My friends and I agreed we'd just sleep during the day." She fluffed her hair out, pulling a lock of it that had lodged beneath the back of her bodice and tapped the back of her shoulder. "Untie me?"

It hadn't been easy to remove my own dress, but maybe because I'd been practically bursting out of it at the seams, the leather ties had caved easily enough to my slight pulls.

I took greater care with Neela's ties, and she let out an audible sigh of relief as I helped her out of the top of her dress.

"Whatever the reason, don't go wandering the halls without a mask." She stood and kicked off her shoes, then stepped out of the skirt, leaving only her coarse, white shift to match my own on her body. "You know we're only allowed to remove them in our rooms during fete."

We'd even worn them—and our finest clothing—to be picked up and escorted through the straight path through the labyrinth from Westbridge to the castle at the center of it.

"I know, I just... wasn't thinking." I bent to lift up Neela's dress, once mine, once her mother's, and once Grandmother's even before her. It looked drabber in the light of day, off Neela's body and in my hands, my nails short, my callouses prominent from years of working odds and ends. "I suppose you won't need this anymore," I said, folding it and putting it neatly atop the trunk at the foot of Neela's bed.

Neela threw herself on the bed, practically allowing the quilt and down to swallow her whole. "Why wouldn't I need it?" Her eyes shut as she let out a deep, gratifying sigh. "Just air it out on the windowsill." Her lips smacked together as she curled on her side, tucking her clasped hands under her face against her pillow.

I did as she asked, cracking the shutter open just slightly, allowing more sunlight to pour in.

Neela threw an arm over her face and then rolled around, her back to the window.

"You'll obviously have to wear this other dress," I said. "It's so much finer." Back at my bed, I picked it up and felt the sheer silkiness beneath my fingers. For a moment, my stomach hardened and I was filled with an inexplicable sense of envy. She already wore the finer gown in the family and had breathed new life into it. Now she was destined for even finer things. Then, sickened with myself, I folded it up, about to lay it across Neela's trunk.

She sat up on the bed, watching me fold it. I failed the first time and had to try again.

"That's not mine," she said simply. She watched me, a curious expression on her face.

"Well, where did you get it?" I asked, letting the dress unfurl again and holding it in front of me.

"From the floor. Around your feet." She gestured to the tray across the room at the vanity. "It was in front of our room on that tray and you kicked it clear across the hallway."

"It was?" The clattering sound, the coldness and then the softness at my feet during my tumble made so much more sense now. I shrugged. "Well, it was obviously meant for you."

"Obviously?" Neela stood, then shifted herself to stand behind the dress, as if I were holding it out to size her. The dress's shoulders came up a few inches above her own. The skirt would drag on the ground if she tried it on.

"Well, your lord fae was probably a poor judge of size," I said. "Perhaps you can ask to have it fitted before tonight."

"It wasn't from Favian. I'm sure he would have told me." Neela yawned and frowned, staring at the gown. She took it from my hands and flipped it around. It lined up against my body perfectly. "And it looks like it was made for you."

I laughed. "Why would your Favian make a dress for me?"

"I didn't say *my Favian* would make a dress for anybody." She shuffled aside and opened my trunk, finding the tan dress Grandmother had used as chaperone and bringing it out, holding it up against the dress in my hands as if to compare the sizes. Her brow narrowed. "Edony. You broke it."

"I—what?" I tossed aside the fine gown on my bed and took the coarse brown dress from her. Sure enough, one of the leather strings threaded through the bodice had snapped, fraying at the edge several holes down. It was hard enough to keep the thing on when it had *had* functional fasteners.

"Drat," I swore. "Perhaps I can find more." I looked to the fancy dress. Its back was threaded through with what appeared to be fine ribbons.

"Don't be ridiculous," Neela said. She picked up the finer dress and swapped it for the tan one in my hands, snatching it away from me. "Just wear the nicer one."

"I *can't*," I said, reaching for the tan dress to take it back.

"You can and you have to." Neela padded her bare feet across the room to the window. I expected her to position the dress next to the golden one at the sill, but she pushed open the shutter farther and tossed the tan dress out of it.

"*Neela!*"

She smiled, a gleam settling over her dark eyes. "You can't wear mine—the law of fete says no one may swap dresses with another attendee, in case it causes confusion—so just wear that one."

I frowned. "For all I know, this is someone else's dress and

I'd be breaking the law either way." As if my secret keeper needed another reason to threaten me.

My secret keeper. Could he have…?

"I'd have noticed *that* dress on anyone," Neela said. "You're allowed to change your dresses, so long as no one else wore it during the same fete before you. Maria brought *six* dresses, one for each dance."

My thoughts were too focused on the idea I'd had. A gift from the secret keeper? But why? I was a chaperone, not an eligible maiden.

But did he know that? I tapped a finger to my chin, realizing that in all the hubbub, I'd never made that clear.

Drat, I thought again.

This couldn't be good.

I slipped into the fine dress, and Neela fell in line behind me. "Get some breakfast," she said. "Gloriana, Maria, Loreena, and I got some before we returned to our rooms. Well, Gloriana was going to take a walk in the garden with her suitor first." An edge of playfulness danced on her words and I frowned.

She and her friends were too excited about this. My years as an eligible maiden had filled me with dread. All I could imagine was getting a proposal and rejecting it, my face marked with the deformed hoof of the minotaur…

Neela fluffed my hair over the shoulders of the dress and I realized with a start she'd finished tying up the bodice as she snatched the silken blue shoes off the tray and handed them to me. The dress was so comfortable, I hadn't even noticed it was already on. Slipping into the shoes, I gave the outfit a spin, aching at the thought of having to exchange this for that ill-fitting broken tan one. But I'd fetch it from the gardens below. I'd have it mended. Then I'd return this dress with my apologies—and an explanation that his kindness stretched too far.

Neela returned with a brush and worked it through my hair, collecting it into a single braid at one side, tying it with a green ribbon she'd procured from amidst the jars of creams on the vanity. She handed me the silk mask from where it lay on the bed. "Relax, Edony. Enjoy yourself."

"I can't," I said, staring down at the fine, feathered mask. "How can you be *happy* here?" My voice was quieter, a whisper.

Neela chewed her lip, then took the mask from me, spinning me around gently to affix it in place, tying it behind my head.

"Why are you lying to yourself and thinking you're so happy at home?" she asked.

I didn't have an answer to that. I wanted to tell her I was happy, but for some reason, I couldn't find the words.

She spun me back and nodded, looking me over. "A fae must have noticed the poor state of your clothes. This was definitely *made* for you."

I didn't tell her my theory. About my secret keeper, about our conversation on the balcony. About how I'd broken a law of the fete—and only his whim kept me safe.

"I'll see if I can get the other dress mended," I said.

"*Edony*," Neela chastised. But I was already out of the room. I shut it softly behind me, leaning back against it for a moment as if to get my bearings.

No one else appeared out from their rooms. Perhaps Neela and her friends were far from oddities. I'd always gone to bed before the sun rose at the fete, but many of the others, who'd actually *wanted* to be spouses of fae, had slept in far later than I had.

There'd be fewer people to see me in this dress, then.

I headed down the darkened hallway, following dwindling torchlight until I reached the staircase leading downward, the morning brightness filtering upward from below. Clutching the bannister, I realized with a start how silent my shoes were on the stone floor as I descended. It was as if I were walking on air.

The broad, wooden door leading to the garden was open, the guests free to come and go as they pleased. I'd spent many a quiet morning in these gardens during my years of eligibility.

Now it was just a matter of following the hedge trails until I lined up with my bedroom's window, searching for the tan dress.

I encountered no one for a few moments as I shuffled through stone gravel along the edge of a hedge bursting with colorful rhododendron. My fingers grazed the soft petals as I walked, the towering stone wall of the labyrinth peeking out even at this distance from atop the greenery.

Keeping my hand to the hedge, I made a series of left turns until I thought I was in the right area. I looked up. The shutters on one of the windows was wide open. Yes, that had to be it.

I searched the ground for any sign of color among the white and gray pebbles, my heart freezing as I realized there were other footfalls approaching.

"Breadmaking is so fascinating," cried a cheery, soothing alto voice. "My dear Gloriana, I could listen to you talk about it forever."

"You flatter me, Lady Elspeth." That was Gloriana.

The voices carried from the other side of the hedge my

hand traced. They wouldn't see me. It wasn't so easy to get from one side to the other.

"Please, just call me 'Elspeth,'" said the fae woman. "My dear, I... I know we've just met..."

"I feel it, too!" cried Gloriana.

No. My fingers clutched around one of the blossoms, crushing it in my grip. *Don't seek this,* I willed my Neela's friend.

"Will you be my bride?" asked the fae.

"I will!" shouted Gloriana.

The fae woman laughed. "You delight me, my dear Gloriana. How happy you make me. So please. Let us go."

There was something faltering in Gloriana's next breath. Pushing aside the flower as quietly as I dared, I peered through. Green edged my vision, but I could just make out the both of them, still dressed as they'd been the night before.

"Right now?" Gloriana asked. "Not at the end of the fete?"

"My sweet thing." The fae woman cupped Gloriana's face, using her other hand to untie the ribbons keeping her mask secure and letting it fall to the ground. Without removing her own mask, she took Gloriana's rosy cheeks in both hands and moved her lips to hers. Gloriana sighed, a visible sense of relief weaving its way through her muscles.

"You've already accepted my proposal," said the woman. "Your new life awaits."

"I'm... I'm so glad," Gloriana said. "I just thought..." She took a step back and clutched her pink dress with both hands. "I just wanted to say goodbye. My mother and sisters and brother. My friends."

"You said goodbye to them the moment you entered fete," said Elspeth. She slipped her arm through Gloriana's and guided her away. "If not in so many words, then in your heart. You're mine and mine alone now."

"Of course, but..." Gloriana gazed over her shoulder. The two of them walked down the path, their feet disrupting the gravel. "Not even just one more day?"

They stopped, their backs to my peeping hole, and Elspeth waved her hand in front of the hedges. They parted and a gasp escaped my lips. I covered my mouth to hide it, but it wouldn't have been heard over the rustling of the branches as they groaned backward and gave way.

In front of them stood the towering stone wall to the labyrinth. The real one.

I thought even fae did not tread lightly within those walls.

A wooden door opened, an endless tunnel of darkness waiting beyond the sunlight of the garden.

"What are we...? Elspeth, is that the labyrinth?" Gloriana asked.

"Yes, my dear." Elspeth patted her hand simply, then pressed a kiss to her cheek. "Our new home awaits."

"But isn't it—"

Elspeth grew sterner, louder. "Do you reject me?"

"Of course not!" sputtered Gloriana. "I just thought—"

Elspeth took a step into the darkness, holding out her hand. "Then come. I promise I will keep you safe. No spouse of fae is ever harmed within these walls if with their wife or husband."

Gloriana turned around, searching for something—for someone, perhaps, to tell her what to do.

There was only me.

We weren't close, but there was only me.

"Gloriana!" I cried out.

She looked. She couldn't see me. I rattled the hedge as best as I could.

"Don't—"

But Elspeth spoke louder. "Gloriana, dear. You promised yourself to me." She shook her extended hand, as if to remind her it was being held out for her.

Taking a deep breath, Gloriana ignored my cries and took her future wife's hand.

She vanished into the darkness, the wooden door slamming shut, the hedges growing and groaning back into place to hide the wall right beyond it.

CHAPTER

SIX

BRECC

"Oh, divine. Divine. These sea creatures caught in Eastmeet... It should be a crime that such delicacies are confined to a human village." Adelaide smacked her lips, putting the empty shell of a crustacean on her plate to join the other hollow refuse as she sucked the juices off of her long, bony fingers. Still in her red gown from the night before, she was a contrast of elegance and vulgarity, the pile of her long, golden hair jutting out from above the beaded mask I knew to be covering her sharp nose and jutting cheekbones.

Beside me, Favian stared at her, his nose wrinkling as he pushed his own plate, heaping with late summer bounty, forward on the long banquet table. "What nature grants to humans, they grant to our king," he said simply. "Is that not why we venture from our stronghold to make trade with such lesser beings?"

His words, far more jarring than Adelaide's mindless decadence, cut me sharply. "Did I not have to *pry* you away from a singular human woman several times last night?"

My bare-faced beauty had an interest in him.

I was torn between wanting to see her interest in another man rewarded and knowing I was the better choice for her.

I wished for her happiness, but her happiness lay with me.

If only I was ready to commit to that.

Favian grew flustered, his words no longer deep and sure. "Of-Of course. But she is a rare jewel, surely, any number of you could tell?" He gestured around at the table. In the mid-morning hour, our human guests had all gone to bed, leaving those of us for whom sleep was but a pastime at the table to finish our breakfast.

"I couldn't say," said Carac, a member of the Fae Guard taking time for himself to potentially choose a human spouse this fete. Rather tall and with sharp muscles that made him more bulky than lithe, he was probably the closest to my own size and shape. Though he, like many others, kept his raven tresses long, two sections pulled on either side to meet in a twist at the back of his head. "You monopolized her time so thoroughly, the rest of us hadn't a chance to get to know her."

Favian's fist clenched on his lap, though it was hidden, perhaps, from Carac's view. "I have felt my soul calling to her—"

Adelaide snorted, picking up another crab leg. "You have said that before."

"And *you*, dear Adelaide, have said that at least half a dozen times." Below his mask, Favian's lips pinched into a straight line.

"You exaggerate," she said. "But I have married every one of those to whom I have felt my soul call, have I not? I do not tarry and deliberate when I lose one husband and am in need of another." Her pale-lashed eyes blinked rapidly in the small holes of her mask as her gaze found me. "Forgive me, if I offended—"

"Enough." I rested my elbows on the table, my hands threaded together in front of me. Half-eaten tubers and a beady-eyed lobster missing its core stared up at me from my plate. I'd needed to eat, but I'd kept waiting to finish.

Waiting for her to enter. To have found my gift. To have discerned it was from me.

To turn those stunning green eyes toward me.

When I'd had it sent, selecting the colors myself, I'd told myself I was merely improving her chances of catching Favian's favor. I'd sent him to her to ask her to dance—had seen the way her ill-fitting dress had turned his nose, though that was hardly the reaction *I'd* had to the way the overly tight bodice had plumped up her breasts—and she'd fled.

I'd thought she'd found her state unworthy of the object of her interest's affections. Perhaps she'd noticed something about the grim set of his lips.

My gift, I'd told myself, was merely an attempt to aid her.

She couldn't be meant for me. No one ever had been.

Only now, as I waited, my leg bouncing beneath the table, I realized I couldn't stand for her to be anyone else's.

"I shall ask the golden beauty to be my bride," said Favian bluntly, snapping me from my thoughts.

I stared at him. His head held high, his shoulders stiffer than anyone else's at this table.

"It is too soon," I said, brooking no argument.

A twitch of Favian's finger gave way to smooth composure as he reached out to grab his goblet. "As you wish."

He knew I'd asked him to dance with my bare-faced beauty. Could he not even bother to give her the smallest chance to win his favor?

Did I want her to succeed in that endeavor? Of course not. But if she did, perhaps I'd forget these nonsensical thoughts floating through my head.

No potential bride had ever earned my affection.

I studied him, his careful, deliberate movements as he sipped his wine. I grabbed my own goblet and slammed back the half-glass in one gulp. It was sweet on my tongue and it sent my senses pulsating.

"*I shall not ask my baker for his hand until the end of fete*," said Adelaide around mouthfuls of white filament.

"And why is it you always find the husband most skilled with food?" Carac asked, biting into a tuber.

Favian cracked a smile at that. Even I had to stifle a chuckle.

"That's not true," Adelaide said. "Or I would have found a husband among one of the fishermen from last week. Oh! This is so divine!"

"A fisherman couldn't fish where we'd take our spouses," muttered Carac under his breath. "So the baker still proves my argument."

I left the two of them to their sniping and looked again. But there was no sign of any human approach.

She hadn't stayed at the ball, hadn't joined us with so many other eligible villagers for an early breakfast. Surely, her hunger should have been drawing her near by now.

"Was the gown to your liking?" Kaylein, who hadn't said a

word in at least an hour, dabbed her cloth napkin to her dark lips. Her large, round brown eyes were looking directly at me from behind her green feathered mask.

"Yes, thank you," I told her, suddenly eager to hide behind another drink of wine. Only I'd emptied my goblet, and it sat airily in my grasp.

"Is your cup empty?" she ventured, standing and making her way to the carafe at the end of the table. She was skilled in both cooking and tailoring, and even during her time off in order to seek out a spouse, she seemed to find it difficult to leave those habits behind.

Then again, *I* was the one holding my goblet out to her as she hovered behind me. I was the one who'd asked her to make a dress, pantomiming the bare-faced beauty's specific measurements. Time would tell how precise my observations of her figure had been.

"Gown?" Carac asked. His eyes and Adelaide's were on me, their sparring put aside.

"I just asked her to improve a candidate's attire, that's all." I hid behind another sip of the sweet nectar.

Kaylein made her way back to her spot beside Carac on the other side of the table. "Was it to be a secret?" she asked, as soft-spoken and demure as ever, but a fiery glint to her eye. "I apologize."

Carac's fork clattered to his plate. "You can't have found someone who's sparked your interest."

I tossed back the full glass and slammed the empty goblet atop the table. "You cannot be asking me that." I'd meant to speak it a little more jovially, as if to point out he was asking the impossible.

Of course he was asking the impossible. I could not ask my people to sacrifice their only chances at securing spouses because I had finally found someone to spark my interest.

"I merely thought... to offer her a better chance to catch Favian's eye."

"Oh, please." Favian let out a deep breath. "Tell me this is not for that awkward girl squeezed into her dress. I told you, I have no interest in anyone who shouts out to disturb me in the midst of a dance, eager to catch my attention—"

"Or the attention of the girl you danced with," said Adelaide smugly, bringing her goblet to her lips. Favian glared at her. She shrugged one shoulder slightly. "That's what it appeared to be to me."

"*Brecc* told me himself that feckless girl had an interest in me," said Favian, as if my word on the matter were law. Not on *that* matter anyway. I wouldn't force Favian to pick a bride I chose for him. I only wished to save her the heartbreak of never once having a chance with him.

Perhaps after she danced with him once, her attentions would migrate elsewhere.

Still, the way he referred to her left a sour taste in my mouth and my fist clenched on my lap.

But what Adelaide had said... lit a spark inside of me. I pictured my beauty in my own arms, twirling across the polished dance floor. Her giant green eyes, fluttering beneath long, dark lashes. The corner of her red lips twerking up as she made some foolish remark.

As she called me a fool but softened beneath my firm grip on her waist and let me guide her across the dance floor anyway.

"It was the golden girl who got her attention?" I asked.

"I don't know what either of you is talking about," said Carac.

"How could you have missed it?" Adelaide laughed and set down her goblet. "That awkward young child, shouting, 'No!' and getting all the attention for herself."

"Ah, that." Carac pushed his plate in front of him and stood. "I wondered what that was about." He dipped his head at Kaylein beside him, who nodded back, her mouth firm. It was time for him to go on duty for the day, Kaylein as well, as she stood and started collecting the plates of those around us.

Favian bristled. "Jealousy over my lack of attentions."

"You convince yourself of that," said Carac.

Kaylein leaned between Favian and me, so I could not see his reaction. Whatever she saw must have spurred her to speak, though, a change in topic a necessity before fae devolved to fighting fae.

"Where's Elspeth?" she asked.

Adelaide stacked her plates for her, her own time in service long behind her since she hardly went a year between securing human husbands. "She went for a walk in the gardens. With the candidate she sought to make her bride."

"So soon in the fete?" I asked. At least, so early in Westbridge's time at the fete.

More than half of the fae were back home already. It only made sense that those who'd stuck out the longest, delayed claiming a spouse—though it was of course not required of them—would be irritable.

"When you know, you know," said Favian softly, taking a

last sip from his goblet before piling it atop the plates in Kaylein's arms.

My bare-faced beauty had no chance with him. She needed to see that for herself.

She needed to be as glad of that as I was.

All of us went still as the labyrinth shifted. It was a quiet sound the humans in the castle were unlikely to hear unless near the site of the movement, but the stone walls and unbridled brambles sang to faekind's blood.

"Elspeth…?" Adelaide ventured.

I did a quick check of the fae gathered here. Of all those left behind for Westbridge's turn at fete, she was the only one of us missing.

I clicked my tongue and stood. "I will make sure they departed safely."

"Brecc—" started Favian, halfway to standing. I'd rarely known titles from those whom I considered my equals.

It was only my family line that made me who I was. Only my human and creature subjects who should venerate me as their king.

"I'll go alone," I said, stopping Favian. "The labyrinth speaks to me like no other."

Not waiting for any others to voice their objections, I swept from the room and exited out into the garden.

SEVEN

EDONY

I had to tell Neela. I had to *warn* Neela. Mistress Baker would want to know what had become of her daughter, and Neela's friends should be counseled against rashly throwing themselves at fae as well, but Neela first. There was no running from the fete early, but I would tell her of my tricks to go unnoticed. Flitting around the edges of the crowd. Staring at the ground. Dancing as if possessed of two left feet.

Hiding from that *Favian* for the rest of the week.

Blast. There was no hiding from such a determined fae.

Maybe if I convinced her to play ill—

I turned the corner around a hedge of rhododendron, stumbling over my feet as they kicked up gravel, and smacked straight into a broad chest.

As I backed away, I looked up. A blue feather from my mask had stuck in a ruffled, open white shirt, above which was the broad smile and smooth, square jaw of my secret keeper.

"Good morning," he said, his voice deeper than it had any

right to be outside of a bedchamber in the darkness of night. A strange, appalling thought for me to have all of a sudden. "I waited for you at breakfast." He picked the feather out of his shirt and let it fall to the stones at our feet.

My throat grew dry and I took several steps back, putting space between us and the heady, grassy musk he exuded at such a close distance. "I... I'm not hungry," I said, my voice cracking. "If you'll excuse me."

I couldn't let myself be distracted. Neela was sure to be sleeping still, but she had to know.

"Wait," he said. His voice was commanding, and I found my feet stopping as I was about to brush past him. "Have I offended you somehow?" He seemed disbelieving, but he was asking nonetheless.

I couldn't let a fae—particularly one who held my fate in his hands—think *I* had offended *him*.

There was no law against it at fete, but it seemed to be a given. Like not insulting the Fae King.

Smoothing the skirt of the blue dress out, I clasped my hands together and did my best to seem contrite, my eyes drawn to the pebbles at his feet. "Of course not, my lord. In fact, it is probably you I have to thank for this fine gown—"

There was mirth in his voice. "You knew."

He'd confirmed it. It had still seemed so ludicrous in my mind, I hadn't fully embraced the thought. "You are most skilled with needle and thread," I ventured.

He let out a snort that drew my attention back to his face. His lips were clamped tightly together before he spoke again. "Alas, I cannot claim such talent. I had a friend complete my vision for you."

His vision for me. A flurrying sensation traveled up from my stomach at the thought of him taking me in with those eyes, pinpointing the precise curves of my body with such stunning accuracy.

I cleared my throat, clutching the smooth, sparkling skirt with one hand. "Your friend is quite the talent, then."

"She is. But she is quite aware of her talents, and why do I feel for all the world you are unaware of how *stunning* you look? I have good taste."

My voice caught in my throat, my response halted by the idea that it might be his *taste in human companions* rather than dress design to which he was referring. But either way... "And I see you are entirely lacking in self-doubt."

His eyes widened under the mask, his brows disappearing behind the silken fabric. "You are entirely lacking in propriety at times."

"You're right," I said, my palms growing moist. "I apologize. I just can't seem to help myself around..." I cut myself short.

I couldn't help myself around him. And that was a problem for so many reasons. Not least of which was he held my fate in his hands.

If I upset him now, if I told him I was a chaperone, would he have the guards drag me to the labyrinth before I had a chance to warn Neela?

I couldn't chance it.

I would just have to rebuff him. The thought had me squirming, crossing one fine-slippered foot over the other. "I am unworthy of such a gift, and so I am afraid I cannot possibly accept it."

He looked me up and down, and I found myself staggering under his assessing stare. "And yet you're wearing it."

"So... So I am." I took a deep breath. My mind was racing, trying to remember why I was even out here, when there was a far more important task at hand. "I... I lost my dress. In the garden. As soon as I retrieve it, I'll—"

My secret keeper held up a hand. "You lost your dress. In the garden."

It did sound awfully salacious when spoken aloud like that.

I pointed above us, at the windows of all the guest chambers. "An accident." My tongue was babbling faster than I could figure out what to say. "My cou—my friend... It fell out of the window."

"Ah." My secret keeper clasped his hands behind his back and paced a few steps. "I forget how your kind may perspire. Airing it out? We could call my gift a most timely one, then, I'd say."

"My kind?" I said, not letting his faux pas slip. Perhaps if I had some evidence of him breaking the laws of fete, I might not fear his reprisal.

I knew he was fae. There was never a doubt in my mind. But he wasn't supposed to acknowledge it so openly.

The corner of his lip twitched. "The mischievous, adventurous kind."

Damn. I would not catch him that way.

"Those words are the last I'd use to describe myself."

"Then maybe you don't see yourself as I do." He drew his hand over the row of hedge, letting the rhododendron petals flutter through his fingers.

"I'm not like... I'm not like this. Usually. I'm afraid I'm a very dull person."

"A dull person who loses her dress in a garden *on accident*."

"Blundering and interesting are not one and the same."

"No, perhaps not." His hand stopped on the hedge just to the side of my head. His breath grew warm and misty as he leaned over, his voice lowering to a whisper. "But it is not merely your *blundering* I find so endearing."

I jumped back away. This was it. His expressed interest. His fury when he found me to be a chaperone would spell my doom.

But if even a candidate following the law and happy to wed was not given a chance to tell her loved ones farewell, well... What hope was there of me seeing Neela once more if I told him now?

I would tell him. As soon as I dared.

But until then... His interest in me could save one more candidate from sharing Gloriana's fate.

My shallow breath came a little easier at my resignation, a weight almost lifted from my chest.

I had done too much, seen too much to make it home after this. But Neela must. And, if I was to doom myself either way, perhaps I could use this fae's interest to my advantage.

Taking a play out of his repertoire, I allowed my finger to trace a light and airy line across the ruffle of his shirt. "I fear for anyone who falls for one such as you," I said, careful how to word it. Careful not to expressly say that I was an option for him, careful not to differentiate him as fae. "As I have just witnessed a human accepting a fae's proposal... and the fright of the young woman who was swallowed by the labyrinth."

Growing stiff, my secret keeper stood straight. "Elspeth. Damn her." He turned his head, as if to spit her name to the ground. "There are to be no witnesses to such a moment."

Suddenly feeling the sting of rejection, even if I'd felt awkward playing with his ruffles, I clutched my hand to my side. "Another law of fete I have broken?"

Sighing, he shook his head. "What shall I do with you?"

"That's what I keep asking *you*." Darkness crept in on the edges of my vision and I curtseyed, my gaze back on the ground. "My fate rests in your hands."

A finger on my chin tilted it upward, and I found myself overwhelmed with a musk like morning dew on a grassy field. "How strange you should say that when I think the same."

That my fate rested in his hands? We were in agreement on that.

His long lashes fluttering, he looked away, dropping his gentle grip on my chin. "What you witnessed was not your fault—it was Elspeth's." He used a name so wantonly, but I supposed she was done with the fete and he felt no need to protect her. "I cannot let you suffer for that. But you must tell *no one else* what you have witnessed." His lips grew thin. "I will not chance your punishment resting on the whims of the less.... open-minded."

Could I still tell Neela? There was no doubt in my mind she needed to know. She needed to understand the *consequences* of what she was after.

But would doing so put her in greater danger?

"I have to... I have to tell my friends."

He closed the short distance between us in the blink of an eye. "You tell *no one*. No human, no fae."

My slipper kicked up gravel as I stumbled back from him, finding myself pressed against the hedge. The branches stuck into my hair and my back like poking, accusatory fingers.

In that moment, the fate I'd resigned myself to seemed far too real... And far too frightening.

"They'll want to know what became of the bride," I protested.

"They'll *know*," he said, standing straighter and smoothing his hair back. "Any disappearance of a candidate during the fete can only mean one thing. A successful union."

That was how it'd been before, that was true. But no one had ever known—or at least no one had ever *admitted* to knowing—just what that had entailed.

"You take your spouses into the labyrinth," I said, my voice growing hoarse. I'd known that. I just hadn't thought the experience to be so... terrifying. I'd assumed the fae village was a more welcoming part of the maze. I clutched on to a flower in an attempt to grab the hedge for purchase, the sickeningly sweet and spicy scent filling the air.

My secret keeper crossed his arms. "You need not be so frightened."

Of Gloriana's fate? Or of him?

Taking a deep breath, I let go of the hedge and did my best to smooth my skirt.

"It's no secret we take our spouses with us to our village inside the labyrinth."

I froze, my eyes meeting his once more. He was all but admitting he was fae.

He smiled falteringly, as if acknowledging the slip-up, the

peace offering he was extending to me. "What about witnessing it has scared you so?"

"What about telling others what I saw scares *you* so?"

He'd said it himself. The fae took their spouses home to their hidden village in the labyrinth.

But I knew the answer to his question—and perhaps, then, I knew the answer to my own.

It was the strangeness, the brutality I'd felt emanating from the open door to the maze beyond. It was the ease with which that Elspeth had called it open, creating a path through the maze.

It was the darkness that had beckoned Gloriana.

There was just something that had seemed so wrong about Gloriana's union. The way her fae bride had pressured her, despite Gloriana's amenability. She'd offered her human bride no boon to tempt her, had brooked no dissent.

"Our spouses are happy in our village," said my secret keeper. His voice was clipped, all sense of humor dropped from his expression, which was normally as plain as day even partially hidden behind his mask. "You have nothing to fear."

He hadn't spoken to my question.

"Then it should not matter if I tell my friends what became of them."

An aura like ice took over the broad man in front of me, making the fae's unnatural stiffness even more profane.

"It does not happen often, but those who've seen—or have heard detailed accounts of—the moment in which a union between fae and human is sealed are ejected into the labyrinth, a slash upon their faces." He gestured across his own, two fingers representing the spliced hoof of the minotaur used to complete the task. "So I would urge you to keep your account to the two of us."

In that moment, he seemed so much like that Elspeth had, calling and calling after Gloriana, that I could not stand to spend a moment more with him.

Kicking up the stones at my feet, I rushed past him, back to the castle, all thoughts of finding my lost dress forgotten.

My foolish heart was grateful for the stark reminder that even if I were eligible, I'd be a fool to ever desire this fae.

EIGHT

BRECC

Borin sang of lost loves and a renewed kindling of souls in someone new, but until now, I had never experienced love such as that. Had never lost anyone outside of my father, the human mother who'd birthed me gone before she could hold me against her breast. And though my father had been a good king, he'd been a distant parent. Not unkind, but not particularly interested in securing my affection.

His passing had been tragic, but my heart had not been irrevocably broken. The pain had not lingered.

Not like it had for my father to lose my mother. For the fete to start up again, in the hopes of the king securing a new human spouse.

He'd never attended another fete. Had not even tried to find a new spouse and end the fete for that woman's lifetime.

The fete had gone on for hundreds of years and then when he'd passed, I'd been reluctant to take the chance away from my people to secure spouses of their own.

It had been so long since the end of fete. My people were unused to the prospect of having to rush and choose a spouse and hope their humans lasted longer than the king's choice.

For there would be no venturing back here to this castle, no fete with eligible human candidates. Not so long as the king was married, the fete's true aim done.

"For who can take your place in my heart? Why, oh, why were we doomed to part? I knew from the start, but I had to have you. Your soul a path to mine did chart."

"I'm a patient man, Brecc, but can you not see how agonizing this evening has been for me?" Favian stood beside me, his hands clasped behind his back, one toe tapping, not in tune to the musicians' music, but rather obviously with impatience. "I have expressed my interest in wedding her, and still, that cur dares to dance with her!"

His gaze was fixed on his golden beauty, who offered Carac a wide smile as he twirled her across the dance floor. I sought my own bare-faced beauty in hopes that Adelaide's theory had proven true and it was this golden-dressed girl who had so garnered her attention, not Favian. But she was still nowhere to be found.

My heart sunk, my mind racing. The thought of my beauty being more concerned with this human girl had lightened the sinking feeling in my stomach for a time. Knowing I had never lost her favor to Favian. But what was her interest in this friend of hers? What if she... could never find me attractive?

What if there was no hope for my foolish, kingly heart?

"How shall I replace you? Who could ever replace you? My fingers still tremble amidst all of this din, with the ghost of my touch on your skin."

"And where is this ill-dressed candidate of yours you were so insistent I dance with?" Favian snapped. "My hesitance only allowed Carac the chance to secure my Neela."

I raised a brow at him, the use of the golden beauty's name enough to pull me back into the moment. "You've exchanged names?"

"We have," said Favian. The lump at his throat bobbed just slightly. "And you know Carac is just dancing with her to irritate me."

I slapped the back of my hand lazily against his chest. "It seems as if you have nothing to worry about. She would not give her name to more than one person at the fete."

"That is not *a law*," Favian said stiffly. "Unless you might make it one?" His voice grew more hopeful.

My chest rumbling with the echoes of a chuckle, I stepped away, eager to see if my beauty had slipped away to the balcony again. "Go to your prospective bride," I told him. Enough of his grumbling. Even if my beauty *had* found him alluring, she deserved so much more devotion than this single-minded fae could ever offer her. I gripped his shoulder as he passed, his eyes positively lit up. "But do not complete the union yet. I may need you..."

Favian raised a brow. "Surely, Adelaide's guess that someone has caught your favor cannot be...?" He did not sound alarmed. Or judgmental. Or entirely skeptical. There was a thread of joy beneath his words, as if he could not possibly wish anything less than happiness for a friend.

I appreciated it. It gave me the conviction to hint at my own burgeoning truth. "I shall claim no union before you have yours," I told him. "Fret not on that account." Perhaps the *only* thing Favian couldn't excuse me for would be to end fete before he claimed this golden-dressed Neela who captivated him so.

I understood. He had never had a bride before in all of the years of fete. He, like me, was a fae of distinct taste.

There could be no stopping that. I'd been foolish to even try to give my beauty a chance with him.

Favian's smile was contagious. He bowed curtly and moved through the dancing couples to tap Carac on the shoulder.

Neela grew even more radiant, if that were possible, at the sight of Favian. I'd wondered if her accepting dances from other fae had been mere politeness or if her soul did not call so strongly to Favian's as his did to hers.

But as even Carac could see as he stepped aside, there could be no doubt.

These two were meant for one another.

If only my bare-faced beauty wouldn't be hurt by such a prospect—whatever her reasons for those misgivings might be.

I made my way through the crowd, garnering more than a few lingering looks as fae bowed or curtseyed just slightly and human women looked my way.

They seemed to like what they saw—even those who were clearly here to chaperone the eligible at the event. I wondered which of these gray-haired, overripe ladies or gentlemen was my own beauty's chaperone for the event.

Thank Grandfather whoever it was was remiss in their duties. I wouldn't have had any time alone with her if they weren't.

The crisp night air was startlingly cool on the exposed skin on my chest. Fae did not perspire, but we could feel warmth and chill, just as humans did. If we could not, we wouldn't feel the wild thumping of our hearts when faced with the prospect of finding a mate.

My hand clutched against my chest, the wild, thumping rhythm unlike anything I'd ever felt before. I leaned over the balustrade, the vast labyrinth spread widely before me.

Could I do it? Could I choose a bride this year and end the fete, so long as my beloved human lived?

Would I be like Father and never choose another bride again?

The magic Grandfather had cast to form the grueling maze surrounding this castle did not require me to select a bride. It was expected I sire a child someday, but fae had all the time in the world for that.

So long as our sole enemy remained lost and locked away.

Which he would. Until the end of time. The magic of fae and humans mating, it fed into the labyrinth. Grew our kind in number and in strength.

There was but one way to break the enchantment, and that was too frivolous to even concern myself with.

As if any of those wrinkled, antiquated humans halfway to the grave could sway my heart.

No. A king would strengthen the enchantment keeping the minotaur locked away. His choice in human bride would be a strong one, a fertile woman likely to birth a royal heir as full of life and magic as the royals before him.

My heart paused, my throat constricting at the thought of losing my bride the way Father had lost my human mother. Giving birth to such a fae so full of magic that bound the place, well... That could be hard on a human body.

But my grandmother had given birth to Father and lived to

a ripe, old age. Too short for a fae, of course, but plenty long for a human. That had been long before my time, but Father had spoken of her. It had been one of the few times I'd seen a semblance of what could be thought of as *fondness* across his face.

He would not speak of my mother. He could never speak of her.

But his own mother… Yes. It was possible for a human bride to live out her days long after birthing a fae king.

My bare-faced beauty would be no different. For how could I dare to ever think she had not the strength?

She had strength and confidence and humor in abundance.

She had not made me laugh… But she'd been close at times. So very close. I'd only stopped myself until now because I hadn't yet decided. Decided to have her, to end the fete.

But I would be indecisive no longer.

My heart rang true. Her soul called to mine, as surely as any mate's.

She would be mine.

She *was* mine.

She just didn't know it yet.

I thought briefly of what would happen should she refuse me.

It was an impossible future. But think of it I must.

I had kept so many of her secrets… I would not doom her to wander the labyrinth. I wouldn't dare gouge the features on that pristine, alluring face.

She could go home unscathed. I'd not tell any whom I had chosen as my bride if she refused me, so no one would know.

It was a law of fete that she could not refuse me, but what

was one more broken law in my beauty's life of feisty vivaciousness?

Still, that didn't matter. I wouldn't let it happen. I was her king. She had no choice but to love me. Revere me.

I wouldn't hold myself back from laughter, and if she kept those devastatingly plump lips tight and refused to elicit so much as a chuckle from me, it wouldn't matter.

Grandfather had instructed Father, who'd instructed me that the human who made a royal laugh was the one most fit to be queen.

But it was not a law of fete, regardless of what rumors swirled amongst my people and our human guests.

It was just a sign that... she was the one.

And I knew that much already.

But where in the long, dark nights had my beauty run off to?

She was avoiding me.

Perhaps I'd scared her.

I hadn't wanted any human to be frightened of accepting a fae's proposal. The journey could seem a bit intimidating to those who weren't certain of the way home, and I would not have another take my beauty's hysterics to heart and reject a fae suitor, dooming that human to be marred by the minotaur's hoof and live in misery inside the labyrinth.

It was not a law of fete that those who spoke of a fae and human's union would be doomed to wander the labyrinth, but in that moment, I couldn't think of anything else that would guarantee my beauty's silence around the others.

Best the humans not think of the acceptance of a union as anything but the momentous, happy occasion it ought to be.

In my haste to prevent others punished, perhaps I'd pushed too hard. She hid from me now, refusing to make herself known at the ball. She was nowhere to be found on the balcony on which I'd first spied her.

The snorting grumble echoing out into the night was unmistakable.

Only one creature trapped inside the labyrinth walls ever made such a sound.

Flinching, I checked on my people remaining in the castle, but over the docile music, no one seemed to have heard the sound.

Of course. He was still trapped inside. Our enemy would not break free. Would never escape the magic walls keeping it confined.

But he was there... I could hear him from where I stood.

The snorting, groaning, grumbling grew louder.

And then I spotted her.

My beauty, below me, in the garden. Her left hand on a hedge as she probed the growth flush up against one of the maze's walls.

And just on the other side of that stone wall was the steaming, rising breath of the minotaur, mere feet from my beauty.

Separated only by stone and enchantment.

The beast howled into the night.

And my bare-faced beauty screamed.

CHAPTER
NINE

EDONY

Even this far from the ball at fete, the haunting melody of the music echoed out into the air, though I was too far to hear the bard's voice sing of fae and their strange, obsessive forms of human love.

Despite the tragedy that my mother's fate had been, I wondered if she'd been right to spurn a fae's proposal of marriage. Not just to be with my father, but to escape whatever the fae had had planned for her.

No. It couldn't have possibly been worse than where she'd ended up, lost and lonely in the labyrinth until her flesh had faded to bones.

Still. Was it too much to hope for a simple life back home?

What could I do to stop Neela? How could I avoid my secret keeper's eye? The answer to the first, I'd decided was: Nothing. Not until I gave myself time to think. There had to be a way to convince her without explaining in detail what I'd seen.

She and her friends, as my secret keeper had assumed, felt certain Gloriana had escaped off to a better place.

Perhaps they were right. What did I know? All I had to go off of was the feeling in my gut that told me something was wrong.

As far as avoiding my secret keeper, I was doing an excellent job of that alone here in the garden. I couldn't even escape to the balcony—he'd think to look for me there. He knew which room I slept in.

Ever moving, hiding behind the hedges, I'd avoid his gaze.

I kept my left hand on the hedge, a voice softly speaking in my memories.

"You'll always be lost," my mother said. A wild lock of her fair red hair swung down over her shoulder, tickling my forehead. "But take hold of the wall." She put her palm to my left one, her delicate fingers twice the length of my own. "Keep turning, left, and left, and left, and you won't be trapped in one place."

I froze where I was, my hand hitting leaves and branches that sunk sharply against the stone wall of the outer maze.

Threading through Mother's pale, freckled features had been two long, red scars. She'd let me reach up and trace them sometimes, though only when Father and Grandmother hadn't been looking.

Even though the scars hadn't been tender for her, they had been jagged, like winding rivers running through the landscape of her flesh.

They had been cold to the touch.

I shivered. The sensation was now muddled with the feeling in my gut, the one that had warned me that Gloriana's departure had not been all happiness and joy.

Only that feeling was growing thicker now, the chill raising gooseflesh on my arms from the world outside of my memories.

A grumbling, growling snort broke through the silence. Far louder than the soft music of the fete.

The hedge hummed beneath my fingers, almost as if the stone itself beyond the flora were warming.

The creature—for it was no human or fae—snorted again, a scrape, scrape, scrape like a hard stone dug through dirt following the heavy cadence of its breath.

A hard stone or a hefty hoof.

The creature moaned, its throat producing a howl a thousand times more melancholy than that of a coyote's cry.

The heat from the stone turned the hedge beneath my palm to ash.

I screamed, the intense temperature searing my flesh.

Backing away from the wall, I cradled my tender hand against my chest, my breath coming in shaking, heaving gasps. The wall was eating away at the plant life, the creature's cries sending stabbing sensations straight to my heart. But I found I couldn't flee. It was like... there was nowhere to go.

I couldn't say how long I stood there, staring. The air was marred by a sickening scent, like sulfur. The stone was growing red now, as if a hole were about to be burnt through the masonry. This wasn't the dark and simple parting of the wall the fae Elspeth had conjured to take her bride inside.

My tender hand extended toward the burning wall, the heat drawing the flesh it had touched.

"Stop!"

A deep, stern voice.

Between the wall and me leaped my secret keeper, facing the molten stone. His broad form towered over me, the sulfuric air mixing with his bolder, lush musk.

"Be gone, beast!" he shouted to the glow of the wall.

The moaning howl was cut short, replaced by the scrape, scrape of hoof against dirt.

The fae placed his hand against the orange, molten stone and I cried out on his behalf—but though his mouth twisted into a grimace beneath his mask, he did not let up, the place where his palm hit glowing stone rising with steam.

"You cannot escape!" he cried. "Never shall these walls weaken!"

The orange glow grew softer, the light retreating.

With a final snort, the creature's heavy breathing grew fainter, the wall turning gray once more. In front of it, as the fae man pulled his hand back, the rhododendron hedges grew in again, flowers blooming out of season from buds in mere moments.

"What did you—" he started, but his words fell silent as I took his hand in mine, examining it for burns.

"It's fine," I said, turning it this way and that. I let go with my left hand to examine my own flesh. It was hard to tell in the faint light—it still stung slightly, like the result of a quick touch to a hot iron pot handle. The skin might have been red. It was tender. But it wasn't scarred or puckering.

My secret keeper took hold of my right wrist and tugged. "Come."

I stumbled after him, though my feet gave me no choice but to follow. "Where are you taking me?"

"Away from here," he snapped, not looking back. The

moonlight cast his masked profile in sharp relief. It was as flawless as if carved from stone.

He dragged me through the hedges without hesitation, though from time to time, his free hand reached out to graze one of the hedge walls.

"How did you find me?" I asked as the entrance to the castle came into sight.

"You mean, other than the bloodcurdling scream you let out into the night?"

We reached the downstairs corridor now, and my secret keeper led me into a side corridor our fae guards had told us we'd never have cause to enter.

It was a kitchen, the ball upstairs sending tremors of movement from dancing feet above the ceiling.

Four people looked up. Masked, even wearing nice attire. I thought I recognized some of those dresses from the ball previously.

"We need some water," my secret keeper said.

The fae—for they were stiff and precise in their tasks, washing dishes, chopping food—went back to work. My secret keeper let go of me beside a water pump—here in the kitchen, instead of at a well outside—and went to work himself.

His biceps bulged, but he didn't let out so much as a grunt as he pumped the copper. Fresh, sparkling water poured forth into a basin beneath it.

He stopped pumping and rubbed the crook of his elbow across his brow to shift aside a short lock of dark hair that had crossed over his mask. "Well?"

The clink of plates behind me, the feel of stares upon my back jolted me into action. In the lantern light that illuminated the kitchen, I saw my palm better. It was slightly red with the faintest wisps of peeling skin.

I dunked it into the basin.

An audible sigh escaped my lips.

Only outdone by the rumble in my stomach at even the smell of nothing more than chopped potatoes.

"Did you never eat, you foolish girl?"

Girl. Compared to a fae, I supposed it wasn't inaccurate.

"I... I had something last night before the ball." I wiped the hand across my sparkly skirt, then remembered it wasn't the same as the apron I often wore at home and touched the hand tightly to my side.

"Lilibet, please bring our guest something to eat," my secret keeper said. "Something light will do."

"Oh, no, I couldn't trouble you—" I started.

But the fae he'd spoken to, a pallid one with yellow hair tinged ever so slightly in green, appeared before me, handing me a platter, complete with rolls and fruit and cheeses.

"Thank you," I said quietly, but the fae did no more than stare hard at me, stiffly walking back to the table and picking up her knife to resume her chopping.

"After starving yourself and what you've just been through, it's best not to eat anything too heavy," my secret keeper told me. "Come." He grabbed me by the elbow and directed me away.

All four heads turned to watch me go, though none said anything. They weren't particularly friendly like the ones who flirted with anything that moved upstairs at the ball, but I wouldn't say they were angry, either. More curious.

I would be, too, at a chaperone getting such personal attention.

My stomach grew heavy as he directed me into the dining hall, empty but for a long table. Of course. Everyone else was dancing away upstairs. I'd missed dinner, had told Neela I'd felt ill and wished to rest before the dance. It hadn't been a lie.

Though she didn't know I hadn't had breakfast, either.

My secret keeper pulled out a chair for me. "Sit. Eat."

With the shaking sensation invading my fatigued limbs, I hardly had room to argue with him.

"Thank you," I said, putting the platter down and adjusting my skirt to sit in the chair behind which he hovered. I let out a little gasp as he pushed the chair forward for me, settling me closer to the table.

He leaned over, his grassy scent strong as he took my left hand in both of his.

His arms wrapped around me as if in embrace, the hard wood back of the chair the only thing between his body and mine.

"Does this feel better?" he asked.

I swallowed, the lump in my chest about to burst out of my mouth.

"It... It does," I said, then with a start, I realized he had to have been referring to my singed palm specifically.

As opposed to... his body cradling mine.

He traced a feather-soft finger across the palm, and I didn't wince. I didn't flinch. His skin was so much smoother than mine, his finger so much larger.

"It doesn't appear to have left a mark." He stood stiffly, the lack of him so close behind me inviting a chill in the space between us. "Eat. We have much to discuss."

We did?

That only served to lessen my meager appetite.

Still, my stomach proved demanding.

I tore off a chunk of bread and went to work on the meal. The food was an immediate relief to my whole body, like a warm fire after a day chopping wood in the cold.

He paced to the side of me.

"What happened? At the edge of the labyrinth?" He stood at a table beside the dining table, pouring a liquid into a goblet from a carafe.

My mouth grew dry and I realized I was thirsty. "I... I don't know." I was being entirely honest.

He handed me the goblet and our fingers touched again. I stared at his gray eyes before redirecting my attention to the platter in front of me, bringing the goblet to my lips with a shaky hand.

He hovered beside me as I ate. "That's never happened before." I chanced a look to find him biting his bottom lip.

A startling thought soared through my mind. I wished it were *my* lips he nibbled on.

I nearly choked on a grape but covered it quickly with another sip of sweet wine, just enough to quench my thirst. I'd never drink enough to feel giddy like some others did. Too much wine had only made people like my father and grandmother sad either way.

My secret keeper slammed both hands on the table next to my platter. "You truly have no idea what was on the other side of that wall! Whatever you did was dangerous!"

"I didn't *do* anything!" I told him. I shifted in my chair and looked up at him in earnest. "And I know what was on the other side of the wall." Because I did. Without even seeing it, I knew. My voice grew quieter, harsher. "The minotaur."

My secret keeper's brow furrowed. "It so rarely finds itself at the labyrinth's outer edge." His own voice was quieter now, though it had lost none of its gravitas. "It was as if it were trying to get to you." He looked at me straight then, his eyes narrowing. "Or call you to it."

I pushed aside my mask, lifting it up to the top of my head. "I have no marks. You know as well as anyone."

He took a step closer and took hold of the fine, feathered mask he'd gifted to me. Before he did anything with it, though, he brushed his fingers over my cheek and down to my mouth, adding pressure as they dragged across my lips.

I closed my eyes and leaned into it. It didn't hurt. My lips parted, just the edges suckling over the tips of his fingers.

The mask dragged back down over my face. My secret keeper took a step back.

"Be cautious," he said. "I will not have any other know you removed your mask outside of your chambers. There can be no question of your obedience."

My eyes flittered open to find my secret keeper adjusting the leather armband at his cuff.

"My obedience?" I echoed back to him.

He didn't reply.

What was I to do? I wanted to explain about my mother. Was it her blood in my veins that had called the minotaur?

But I had walked the garden a dozen times during my years

of eligibility and never before had I had such a strange encounter.

My secret keeper *tsked*, though he was not looking at me. Instead, he cradled one elbow and stared off at the wall. Behind that wall was the garden and beyond that, the maze. It was almost as if he were willing himself to see through all of the obstacles in his path. He stood there in silence a while as I ate my fill, watching his profile.

His jaw set in a hard line, he glanced down at the table as I pushed my plate away. "Are you finished eating?" he asked.

"Yes."

He nodded, then took me by the wrist again, yanking me to my feet. I stumbled, but he caught me, his arm gripping me around the waist. My heart thundered, my hand spread flat against his chest, coiling amidst the fine hairs peeking out through the open collar of his shirt.

His next words were stern. He was not asking.

"Then you shall dance with me."

CHAPTER
TEN

BRECC

She let out a gasp as I tugged her closer. Her abdomen ground against my pelvis, stirring life into my too-long neglected loins. The music in the ballroom above us was muted, like the cry of someone lost, hidden behind walls and walls of the maze.

But it was enough for her and me, in this dining room we'd found ourselves in alone.

Our footfalls echoed out against the empty space.

Her head kept turning, that wretched mask keeping me from looking upon her face whirling this way and that, as if looking for an exit.

The thought like a vise in my chest, I twirled her on a turn and leaned her backward, bending down so that my own mask hovered mere inches from hers. Her aroma, sweet and sour like the rhododendron, flooded my lungs.

That move got her attention.

"My lord, I..."

"My name," I said firmly, "is Brecc."

A chortled cry came from her lips as I righted her back on her feet.

I waited, gripping her waist with one hand, clutching her back with the other.

I waited for her name.

She owed it to me.

I was her king—though I could not tell her that—and I had just gifted her my name.

No human had been gifted *my* name.

"Br-Brecc," she said, and the sound of my name on her sweet, red lips was almost enough to soften the blow that she hadn't immediately given me her own name. Almost. "You honor me greatly." Her head turned away.

I dropped the grip on her waist to take her chin into my hands, redirecting those vibrant green eyes back to my masked face. An effervescent garden worked its way like molten pools into those irises.

"It *is* an honor," I said, emphasizing her own point. "You have to know what it means for me to tell you. No human has ever known my name."

"None ever?" Her eyes widened as she took a step back, putting space between us.

I realized my mistake. The humans seemed to think that only the king refrained from taking a bride so easily.

"Years hold less weight for a fae," I said. "Not all of us choose a new human spouse as quick as we lose a previous one. Some of us never choose a spouse at all." My voice grew lower, the confession slipping out before I could stop myself. "It is not so terrible to be alone, I thought. There is more to life than a human by my side, a child in my arms." I took another step and ran my thumb under her mask, brushing the soft silkiness of her cheekbone. "But that was before. Before I knew what it was to feel my soul call to yours."

She gasped and stepped back, out of my grip entirely. Her slippered feet echoed once. Twice. Several more steps putting this cold and empty space between us.

She was doing the *opposite* of what she needed to do. Clenching my fist at my side, I waited for her reply.

I would have her, but I would make her *beg*. We had time yet before fete's end.

She'd have to get over this shyness, though. Her discomfiture, her occasional ungainliness, sent a throbbing ache to my core, but I'd abide it only so long.

"I have to… I have to get back to the dance." She twirled on her feet, lifted up the edges of her skirt, and *sprinted* from the room.

I blinked. It was impossible that I'd seen what I'd just seen.

My muscles stiffened before I relaxed them.

No. This was unacceptable. I couldn't—after all of these years—find a bride at last and have *this* for an answer.

Had I been so wrong? I'd entertained the thought of her rejection, but it had been merely that: rational thought. Objective, logical calculation. Not what I'd *known* in my heart to be true.

She felt it, too.

She loved me.

And I would make her admit she was mine before the night was through.

My steps were quick, light. I was up the stairs and down the hall toward the warm, candlelit glow of the ballroom before I could think on it more beyond grinding my teeth.

Her little chase-and-catch-me game was charming. But my heart was too exposed, my soul too vulnerable to put up with it for long.

There. The little creature had summoned almost-fae-like speed to arrive here before I had. Even with her head start, she should not have been able to outrun me.

She was just now at the end of the hall, her masked face turning over her shoulder, her feet moving *faster* if possible, as she retreated into the crowd of onlookers gathered at the side of the dance floor.

My stomach hardened as I imagined grabbing hold of her and tossing her over my shoulder to stop her retreat.

"Pardon me," I said to one of the chaperones, a rather small, portly woman, who stepped out between me and my heart's desire.

"Oh, *excuse* me," she said, giving me a onceover before slipping to the woman at her side. "Gloriana worked so quickly to secure her bride! Now it's just up to Lief—"

I had no time to listen to this prattle.

Squeezing between human and fae, I kept my eyes on my beauty, who managed with her slim, if long, physique, to thread around and through the crowd with far more ease than I. A song ended and she pulled up beside Favian and his golden-outfitted Neela.

I frowned, my feet stilling. She was talking to them both, and Favian—the vexing fae I currently found him to be—he fulfilled a promise to me.

With a slight bow, he let his golden soulmate go and, apparently, asked my beauty for the next dance.

And though I'd convinced myself her attention had been focused more on the human girl than Favian, she, with a single look over her shoulder at me, accepted.

The golden-dressed Neela looked as I felt, stumbling backward with her hands clutched to either side of her skirt.

Murmurs erupted from all around me.

"What does she think she's doing?" a man beside me asked the woman on his other side.

"I haven't the faintest idea," she replied.

So others had been so certain of this Neela's match with Favian, too. And now my beauty was there, acting as usurper, all in a bid to irk me.

Neela retreated to a couple of other human girls, their hunched heads and whispering lips giving away their humanity even if I hadn't recognized all of my fae, even masked, at a glance.

Neela slumped most of all, turning to watch the dancers and quickly looking away. Until she could abide it no longer. She and two of her companions retreated to the balcony.

My nails digging into the inside of my palm, I realized that *I* could abide it no longer. Favian kept my beauty at a respectable distance, their movements across the floor stiff and without passion. His own gaze soared over her head to follow the path of the golden dress amidst the crowd as it retreated out of the ballroom.

My beauty could not look up at his face, either. I caught her staring at me every so often, but she looked down at the floor whenever our eyes met.

So she thought to incite my passions further with jealousy? She was exasperating! This was not how finding my bride was supposed to go.

But if she were not so different, not so quick to rile my passions, would I have even found my soul pulled toward her?

I shoved my way out onto the dance floor, ignoring the stiffly turning heads, the quiet murmurs as I wove my way through dancing couples to Favian's shoulder. I tapped it.

"May I have this dance?" I asked.

Favian arched a brow. I knew what he was thinking. Hadn't I asked him to give my beauty a dance? But hadn't I also told him to chase after his Neela?

I'd decided my beauty was *mine.*

And though I had no doubt that his heart would not have wavered from his preferred bride, I could not abide this.

I didn't care if I'd *asked* it of him. He could not have her. Not for one second longer.

Favian bowed slightly and dropped my beauty's hand, his other hand falling from her waist. "Of course."

My beauty's jaw dropped and she looked over her shoulder but didn't find what she was looking for.

She curtseyed quickly to me, then to Favian. "If you'll excuse me. I'm not feeling well enough to keep up the dance."

Then she wove around Favian and through the dancing couples. I watched her, my stomach leaden, as she pushed through the crowd and retreated from their watchful eyes to the darkness of the hallways leading to the guest bedrooms.

She'd retired early the night before, too.

But not so brazenly disrespectfully as this.

Favian spoke. "I only asked her because I thought—"

My jaw stinging from the clenching of my teeth, I cut him off. "I know. You have nothing to apologize for." Still, I stared him down. "But you can leave her be. I know where your interest lies."

Favian clasped his hands behind his back. "And yours lies... with that one?"

He referred to her not with the sense of disgust he'd once had, but more a mere tone of curiosity. For some reason, the slight improvement in his evaluation of her irritated me.

I couldn't lie. But I wouldn't admit it to him. Not until I secured her name and made her bend on her knees to apologize for vexing me so.

"Go," I told him. "Ask your Neela tonight. You do not have to tarry any longer."

Favian's eyelids fluttered, and a smile broke out on the corner of his mouth. "Thank you." He bowed just slightly.

The sooner he put a salve to the wounded heart of his little human, the better. I'd not have anyone else feel as I did, the sharp pain seeping into my chest.

No more games, not even at fete.

She would admit she was mine now or she would tell me outright she'd never be.

She wanted to run? I would chase her.

Wherever she went, I'd find her.

CHAPTER

ELEVEN

EDONY

Inside my guest room, I tore my mask off and tossed it on the bed. With shaky hands, I struck the flint and lit both lamps in the room before pacing at the foot of the bed. My breaths were shallow and even pressing a hand hard against my breast couldn't even them out.

My legs trembled beneath me as I leaned my back against the door. In and out. Deep breaths.

What was the matter with me?

My mind racing, I'd acted an idiot. Instead of admitting I was a chaperone when we'd been alone in the dining room, I'd found my tongue tied and I'd fled.

To the safety of the ballroom, I'd thought. The eyes on us. Surely, I could retreat into the crowd.

But with the speed of a coyote after its prey, he'd appeared behind me and I'd panicked. I'd rushed to Neela, begging her to retreat with me to our room but careful not to give too much of my reasons away. She'd been reluctant, naturally, and then her Favian had surprised us both.

He'd asked me to dance.

Not joyfully, per se, I could tell it was as if he were asking if I'd yank a swollen tooth out of his jaw. But before Neela could explain I was her chaperone, before I could bring myself to refuse, I'd checked for my secret keeper... for... for *Brecc* and found him approaching.

I'd told Favian I'd accept his offer.

There was no law of fete that chaperones could not dance during the ball. None did, but there was no law.

There *was* the law that only those eligible could become a fae's spouse, and the dancing was part of the courtship, so perhaps the Fae King had thought the law needn't have been said.

But that was what I'd been running from. In Favian's cold, stiff grasp, I'd been safe from Brecc's own grip—warm, tender, *unyielding*.

Favian had had nothing to say as we'd danced in stilted, gliding movements. Were I in a better frame of mind, I could perhaps ask about his intentions with my cousin—without giving too much away—but I knew what his intentions were. He'd given her his name.

Just as my secret keeper—Brecc—had given me his.

I'd... I'd been happy to hear it.

Like a fool, I realized that despite what I'd seen with Gloriana, I wished... A part of me wished... he'd given me his name just one year earlier. Surely, Gloriana would indeed be happy. Perhaps my misgivings over her departure had just been due to the abruptness of it all.

Oh, why had he never come to the fete when I'd been eligible? He'd claimed to never have felt the need for a spouse—for a child, my skin flushed at the thought—but I wished he had. If he was going to come this year and meet me, it was too late.

A knock on the door behind me snapped me back into the moment. I spun around, turning the handle. "Neela, I'm sorry, but I just had to—"

It wasn't Neela on the other side of the door.

"A name is a precious thing at fete," said Brecc. My secret keeper loomed tall in the dark of the hallway. "Be mindful of your tongue. Fortunately, for you, I already knew your friend's name." He arched a brow again. "And I've already seen your bare face."

My throat constricting, I backed up into my room, whirling around to find my mask again. He knew Neela's name? How? And why... why had he followed me so far as my room? I was allowed to be bare-faced in my room. I wasn't allowed to open the door without a mask, but...

With shaking fingers, I went to grab the mask and tie it behind my head.

"I suppose many must know Neela's name now," I said, testing the waters. "If... If that fae she's spent so much time dancing with is who I think he is. It's only natural he may have told others of his interest in her."

The door shut behind me and I stiffened. The musk of a meadow after a fresh rain, of fresh cut wood, spread throughout the space.

He hadn't shut the door and waited for me in the hallway. He was in here. With me. Alone.

"And who, pray tell, do you think he is?"

My hands stilled at the back of my head. "The Fae King," I said softly.

I wasn't certain I was right. But I hoped he would let me know whether or not I was.

"Ah," he said. "The king. You imagine him to be your king. I suppose he *is* rather regal." His voice resounded in the dark, and my heart soared just slightly at his affirmation that Favian was not the Fae King. The man was mythical at this point. I hadn't expected to ever see him here at the fete, least of all showing an interest in my cousin. "There's no need for you to wear this here." Warm fingers brushed against my own at the back of my head, untying the bow I'd started to make with the ribbons threading through my mask.

He took the mask and tossed it, farther across the room to Neela's bed.

I turned around slowly, my breaths coming out shakily, to find him a few steps behind me, removing his own mask and tossing it beside the feather-blue one.

His gray eyes were even more piercing in the relief of his face. And that face. I lost track of my deep, steadying breaths as I took in his sharp jaw melding into defined cheeks. The angle of his nose, without flaw, lent a sense of strength to his expression. His short, thick hair fell languidly across his wide brow.

I didn't realize until my breathing kicked in again that I was tracing my fingers across those features.

He gripped my hand in his, pulling it away.

Keeping it from what I wanted to touch.

"You want me." It wasn't a question.

A gurgled cry escaped my throat. I'd never understood how

anyone could fall for anyone so quickly. Not fae. My parents' deep and abiding love had seemed earned and long-fought-for.

I shouldn't have felt anything for this fae man. But I did.

My fae. My other hand reached up to brush his hair aside. Beneath the dark locks, his tanned ear ended in a pointed tip.

Not that there was ever any doubt.

"You're crying." He let go of me to brush the top edge of a finger along my lower eyelid.

He pulled it back, his skin moist.

So I was.

Panting, I turned away.

"Don't," he said sharply, gripping me by the shoulders. "Don't look away."

I did as bidden, my breath coming in rapidly as I stared up at his face.

"What do you need to settle your nerves?" he asked, softer this time. "I'll give you all of me."

"You can't!" I said, louder than him. *Just say it,* I told myself. *He needs to know.* But I couldn't. I couldn't say goodbye to him.

Not yet. Could I at least have the fete?

The fete. My fingers traced his jaw, the fine, bristly hairs gathered there. He could be mine for the fete.

I'd already doomed myself to wander inside the labyrinth. For breaking the law of mask at fete. For calling the Fae King a fool. For any number of reasons...

And now, for leading this fae man astray.

If he asked for my hand, I'd explain and refuse—and accept my fate. If Neela was no doubt leaving me for her fae groom, that was already another price I would pay.

Could I not have him before the end? Before my wretched fate?

With a quick apology to my grandmother for my impetuousness that had led me here and would keep me from ever returning to her, I pushed all thoughts of others aside. I pushed all thoughts of *everything* aside. Everything but him.

"If only I could..." I said. "I wish I could give you my everything."

"You can." He took my face in his hands and pressed his lips to mine. "You will," he said as he came up for air between kisses.

I'd kissed boys before, but so rarely, so reluctantly. I'd never risk what my parents had during my years of eligibility and since then... It hadn't mattered.

As Brecc had said, I found life fulfilling enough without a partner at my side, a child in my arms.

But now... I was grateful the labyrinth awaited me. I would never feel fulfilled again without him.

His mouth searched hungrily, greedily, his tongue pushing between my lips. My jaw slackened, inviting in the sweet and salty taste, my tongue responding as if in dance to his probing touch.

His hands slid up from my cheeks to the back of my head, winding through my hair, tugging on its roots, but the slight pain sending a wild tingle down to my toes. He was drawing me closer with every tug, every push of his lips. Our teeth clashed, but just so, his hands working the angle of my head again to find a softer entry. No less forceful, but more certain, his tongue retreating and his grip slacking so I could toss my head back and struggle for breath. But his mouth did not stop moving.

It shifted to my cheek, threading sweet kisses along my brow. It came up for air and moved hungrily to my throat, the ticklish, warming sensation stirring a vibration deep within my groin.

"You have not had a man before," he said. Firmly. Resolutely. As if he truly knew.

If he thought me an eligible maiden, well... There was no law against a tumble in the bed that didn't result in pregnancy. I was not among those who'd risked it. The consequences of such an encounter had been too great.

I laughed at the thought that I'd been so worried about expulsion from my village when I'd doomed myself to a far worse fate since fete had begun this year.

Brecc's hands, sliding down my back now, stiffened at the slight chuckle that had escaped my throat. "Tell me," he said, his eyes connecting with mine. "I won't be angry with you."

If only that were true.

But for this, I could tell him the truth.

"I have not," I said, cupping his cheek with my palm.

A low, guttural growl escaped his lips and he yanked me closer again, his hands reaching my buttocks and lifting me up so his mouth could bite an exposed patch of skin at my shoulder. He slammed me against the wall—firmly, but without causing me pain—and my hands flailed out for purchase, wrapping loosely around his shoulders.

I let out a startled cry at the pinch on my skin, but even the bite—his *marking*—had invigorated my core. The area between my legs tingled as if my fingers had caressed the sweet spot in the front. His hands, even through the layers of my dress and shift, were resting on my rear.

So close. I wanted them much closer.

"You will have me," he said, coming up for air. A command. But he was pausing now, leaning in to tilt his head over mine, but giving me room.

Room to object. As a part of me knew I should have been doing.

Time to tell him to leave. To say goodbye to the prospect of this fae's flesh on mine—*in* mine—forever.

"I will have you," I said so quietly, my voice catching in my throat.

He jostled me and yanked me closer, wrapping my legs around his thighs and grinding my sweet spot against his hard, broad abdomen.

A soft, mewling sound escaped my mouth.

"I could barely hear you," he said. "Say it again."

"I... I will have you," I said, louder. My heart thumped wildly, still swallowing up my words.

His mouth seized my bottom lip and bit it playfully between his teeth, nibbling before pulling away.

My head lolled backward.

"Louder."

He jostled me again, grinding my sweet spot even harder.

Moisture beckoned beneath my shift, my groin throbbing and swollen, begging to be touched.

"I will have you," I said, the tremble in my voice still present, though I fought it. Whatever it took for him to stop teasing me so, for him to help me find the release my swollen loins so desperately wanted. "I want you!" I shouted, louder, my head lolling backward.

Brecc chuckled then, and something changed in the air. A chill threaded between us, like a great release of something holding him back. The air grew warmer again. His smile grew wide and he threw back his head and laughed.

I bit my bottom lip. "You mock me."

His smile grew softer. "No, beauty." His head darted forward, the tip of his nose brushing against the side of my neck. "I laugh because I am exultant." His voice was a sweet whisper in my ear. "Because *you* have made me that way. And because your stubborn little games crumbled when I had you in the palm of my hand."

He jostled me again, my head lolling back to roll against the wall as he lowered me. I cried out as my rear end slid, caught only by the bulge in his pants that ground itself with bobbing movements against the apex between my legs.

I mewed again, like a little lost cat, gripping harder to his back. I tried pulling myself up, if only because I knew if he kept grinding against me there, I might burst.

Brecc pushed me harder against the stone surface and angled upward, his hardness practically driving up against my soaking slit.

I let a hand fall and tried to push it between us, my trembling fingers sliding down the exposed skin at his chest, fumbling for the end of my skirts. These endless skirts, twisted around his torso every which way. There was no end to them, no hope of sliding my own fingers in for any form of release.

I cried then, just a few soft tears over the groan releasing from my throat, because I couldn't stand it. I needed release and I was trapped here, and he was teasing me, and I would not have it soon enough.

Brecc kissed me on the lips, grinding harder.

"Please," I gasped between kisses, my palm fighting to reach my sweet spot, settling for splaying across his abdomen instead.

"Please what?" he asked, nibbling on my ear.

"Please take me," I said, my voice shaky. "I need you. I need *release*."

He pulled back and smiled, arching his spine.

"I've been waiting for you to beg me."

I didn't have a chance to ask why before he tossed me on my bed.

CHAPTER

TWELVE

BRECC

There was no law against a tumble in the bed at fete. Yes, our masks were supposed to remain in place, but I was above caring about such a thing.

I *made* law. I could unmake this one, a relic of my grandfather's.

At least when it came to my beauty.

Most fae waited to ask for a human's hand. Most would rather save their first tumble for the softer, warmer beds of home.

I could not wait. I would not. And my beauty had *begged* me, as I'd known she would.

Seizing her lips once more, I pushed my ravenous kisses along her jaw, down her neck. She ground against the mattress, her eyes closed, her neck exposed as her head tossed back. She often bore that long, graceful neck to me during our kisses, I'd found.

I would not pass up the temptation. As I pecked her all

along her throat, her soft mewling was more delightful to my ears than any other melody. Her legs spread wider beneath me as I hovered over her body, her hand slipping downward along the bodice of her dress to clutch at her skirts.

She was bringing them up, eager to get access to the soft, pulsating pleasure I knew waited inside the layers of silky cloth.

I stood beside the bed and snatched her wrist. "No." It was a simple command.

Her eyes shot open as she heaved in and out through throaty breaths. "Please," she said, her eyes widening. "I cannot bare it."

"You shall have to." I took her wrist and directed it over her head, leaning a knee on the quilt beside her to snatch her other one and bind them together beneath my grip at the headboard.

She *writhed* beneath me, beneath my heady, heavy breaths. "I cannot!" she screamed. "Please! I've never felt... I've never..." She locked her eyes with mine. "I'll burst without release."

I chuckled again. My laughter was like a warm, heady ale, spreading out and bringing a vibrating prickle to my whole body. My erection positively strained against the leather of my pants, but I had something important to take care of first.

My bare-faced beauty was about *to burst*.

Letting go of her wrists, I took hold of her skirts and slipped them up, shoving aside the endless, vexing layers until left with her bare flesh.

My heart thundered in my chest as I gazed down. Her pale thighs begged to be gripped, the supple flesh too thick and inviting. Perhaps feeling my stare, she bent her knees together.

I took hold of them a second before they touched, prying them apart.

She let out a little gasp but didn't fight back.

I checked on her to find her biting her knuckle, turned to the side, her dark hair fanned out around her head, clashing with the white of the pillow beneath her.

I let go of her knees to slide to the side of the bed and take hold of her face. My finger latched under her chin, rolling her gaze to look up.

"I can grant you release," I said.

Her eyelids fluttered. Long. Delicate. "I know," she said softly. "But I... I'm embarrassed. To have you see me."

Without thinking, I tore out of my tunic, pulling my shirt up over my head and tossing it to the floor. Her mouth curled into a little circle, her breathing growing heavier as her gaze roamed my exposed torso.

I wouldn't stop there.

Kicking off my boots, I put my hands on the hem of my pants. Then I stopped, a smile curling my face.

"See me," I told her.

She sat up on her elbow, her hair falling across her cheeks.

"My beauty, you have nothing to be embarrassed about." I took a step closer and moved the hair back into place. "The sight of you..." I blinked, remembering the soft, dark curls that had awaited me at the end of her thighs, sleek with moisture and plump with blood. A groan escaped my lips. "I will have you," I said. "But you will see me first."

She shot up, then, her fingers digging into the hem of my pants. She slid them down, slowing as she reached the bulge, hesitating as she looked up at me, as if afraid she might hurt me. I chuckled again, the sensation so true and freeing. She was the one. No doubt lingered in my mind.

The humans themselves would agree, if they saw their Fae King laugh.

But she did not seem to know. She'd suspected Favian was king. I laughed.

"Am I doing something wrong?" she asked.

"No, sweet one." I brushed her brow, and she continued yanking my pants down.

My engorged shaft sprang free and, as her jaw hung slack, her fingers dropped back to the bed, I finished the job for her, stepping out of my pants entirely.

I wanted to laugh, but the fact was, to use my beauty's terms, I was about to burst, too.

Her fingers reached out to touch it, the slightest feathery sensation around the very tip, and I snatched her wrist, stopping her.

"There will be time for that," I said. "This night, I want *you* between my lips. It must be now. Let me *see* you."

She blinked and looked down, but she did not hesitate to reach behind her and fumble for the ribbons at the back of her bodice. I swept in behind her, yanking at the vexing strings and *ripping* the knot undone. Kaylein could be annoyed with me later.

"Oh!" she cried, but I was already lowering her sleeves, exposing more of her shoulder. I kissed the fresh, sweet new skin as I yanked downward, pushing the bodice off of her breasts.

Her mouth gaped, and she moved her arms upward, as if to cover the plump, round, sweet flesh, but she saw my hand reach for her wrist and stopped, lowering her shaky palms to the bed on either side of her.

"Good, sweet one." I leaned forward and took a rosy, round nipple into my mouth, nibbling on the pebbled tip. She moaned, her hands sliding to my shoulder blades as if to steady herself. "You're learning," I said as I came up for air.

I thrust her down, running my tongue over the other yielding, inviting nipple, sucking as the skin grew more rigid beneath my lips.

Her moan was so *riotous* to my ears, her body writhing.

My hands went to work even as I made a feast of her bosom, sucking and nibbling and trailing my tongue between her breasts and down.

I stood back and tugged the skirts down off her legs.

Her heaving breast glistened with the moisture of perspiration and I regretted ever teasing her about that human tendency. I wanted to lick it all off of her flesh. And I would enjoy every salty moment of it.

But now... those curls beckoned me.

I took my place over her, one leg on either side of her thighs, her groans in time with the writhing of her body as her pelvis twitched upward in a vain attempt to meet my own.

I chuckled and put my lips to her belly button, peppering her abdomen with soft kisses and trailing my mouth down into those curls.

Wet, waiting for me.

My tongue did a little dance around the nub welcoming me at the entrance.

She groaned, grinding her hips. I suckled on her nib, saltier, harder, and sweeter than even those pebbled nipples.

She clutched the top of my head now, her fingers squeezing into my hair. The flesh beneath the curls was engorged.

I slid my tongue between her lower lips.

She gasped.

I trailed it back up again, and down, finding the hole I longed to come home to and pushing up against the muscles there to slide inside her.

The muscles caved easily to my whims.

I chuckled.

She was growing louder now, her gasps growing shorter, her moans like music as I worked back up to her nub. She was bucking, growing wilder beneath me, so I sat up and held her thighs down, taking firm grip of her thick, lovely flesh.

She looked up at me, unable to speak, the gasps building in number as if she were well and truly about to burst.

I flipped a finger inside her entrance. It took me willingly. I wriggled it inside, warming up her tender flesh for my grand entrance, adding a second, and then a third finger.

She cried out, tossing her head back, and I knew from all my lessons, from my occasions with fae women for merely a tumble to pass the time, I might have hurt her.

Pulling it out, slowly, I listened, gauging her response.

Her head snapped back at my absence, her breaths still short.

I licked my fingers, savoring the taste of her.

"Does it hurt?" I asked.

She bit her lip before answering, her words short and shallow. "A little. I... I like it. Please."

I kissed her nub again, letting her groan one more time

before adjusting myself and settling the tip of my erection to nudge up against her nub in my tongue's place.

"Accept me," I told her. "Take what I give you, and the pain will lessen," I explained. I rubbed my erection against her nub and she screamed, a joyous, rapturous kind of sound.

I didn't give her a chance to recover, sliding the tip along her folds, up and down, bathing it in her moisture.

"Please!" she shouted. She was reaching the peak now.

I slid into *my woman*'s inner cave, pressing into the sleek, welcoming muscles and filling her, filling her with all of me.

She arched her back, letting out a rapturous squeal.

And that was just with one, forceful thrust.

I pulled out again and she gasped, digging her hands into my back.

Before she could protest, I slammed back in.

She buckled but pulled against my lower back, raising her hips up to meet me.

I put my hands on either side of her head on the mattress and started grinding in tune with her, our bodies a perfect match. She bit her lip as we rocked and as the friction grew, I fought the urge to bite her lip for her.

Her groans started up again, her shallow breaths growing shorter with each thrust.

And then my own incessant need for release came to a head as I spilled inside her.

Her muscles spasmed, clenching me tightly as a satiated grunt escaped my mouth. Her fingers raked into my back.

Our breaths both shallow, I lowered my face toward hers.

"My sweet one." I kissed her cheek. "My beauty." I kissed her chin.

My face hovered over hers once more.

Waiting. Waiting for my next offering.

It was time she gave me her name.

"Brecc..." she whispered, decorating my lips with small, sweet, delicate kisses.

Her eyes shut and she leaned her head back again, exposing that beautiful throat.

Very well. I'd forgive her this oversight.

Tonight, I would explore every part of her body.

Tomorrow, she would let me into her mind.

CHAPTER

THIRTEEN

EDONY

The light trickling into the room nudged my body awake, though I kept my eyes closed just a while longer. I was warm, my cheek pressed against something soft and supple that elicited the tiniest tickle on my nose. I breathed in the refreshing, grassy aroma, reaching out to caress the blades beneath my fingers.

Only it wasn't grass. My eyes popped open. My fae—Brecc—slept beneath my cheek, my arm thrown across his broad, bare chest.

I blinked, remembering the previous night with a flush on my face, only not recalling how it had ended. My mind had been so consumed, my body soaring on a tingling sort of pleasure. I'd collapsed from the sheer sort of frenetic exhaustion of it.

And somehow, I'd found my way here, into the cozy, secure grip of his embrace.

A pit grew in my stomach as I watched the steady rise and fall of his chest in the trickle of light.

Last night I had treated myself. Today I would face the consequences. Only I'd *meant* to end our tumble before Neela got back—

Neela!

Careful not to disturb him—I wasn't ready to receive my punishment, not before I told Neela farewell—I shifted in place to look at her bed.

Empty. Unmade.

But it would have been stranger to find her in here, with me brazenly naked with a fae.

Perhaps she'd crept in and left after spotting us.

Perhaps she was waiting for me in the hallway so I could explain myself. First stealing a dance with the fae who had caught her eye despite me being a chaperone, and now this.

I had no explanation. I clutched my chest as I gazed at his sharply defined face. I wanted to brush my knuckles over his stubbled cheeks, kiss his brow and nose and lips. Watch his eyelids flutter awake.

But I had sinned beyond measure and only heartbreak awaited. Perhaps for him and me both.

I could not wake him.

Quietly getting up and slipping out of bed, I made my way to the pile on the floor where he'd tossed the pale blue dress. Even wearing that as long as I had had been a foolish action, me reveling in a luxury I hadn't truly deserved.

Slipping into my shift, I hesitated at the dress. I had no others, and though the ribbons were ripped, I couldn't very well exit out into the hall in nothing but my shift.

I cleaned myself up with the chamber pot and washbasin, careful not to cry out at the chill of the water against my skin.

I was quiet, but I thought for certain my every move would wake him. He slept on, undisturbed.

Then I slipped into the dress. It hung loosely around the bodice but not disastrously so. I padded my feet, slid into my slippers, and headed over to Neela's bed, taking hold of my feathered mask and affixing it to my face.

I let my fingers brush the top of his silken dark mask on the comforter, soaking my mind one last time in the weight of his name.

Brecc. A fae who'd wanted me... and whom I'd wanted as well.

If it were just me facing the prospect of the union, the strange, demanding way the fae had of taking their spouses through the labyrinth, would I have cared so much that the open doorway had caused a feeling of dread inside me?

Perhaps not.

Do as I say, not as I do. The old saying Grandmother would sometimes toss about when sneaking the last bite of cake or sleeping in a moment too long popped into my head just then.

I'd have gone willingly into the labyrinth as his bride if I could have.

Perhaps I shouldn't have been so worried at the prospect of Neela doing the same. Only the thought of her never seeing her parents or Grandmother again, never traveling the world...

I still didn't like it. But it wasn't for me to stop her.

Still, I owed her an explanation. For the ballroom and... for last night if she'd stumbled upon Brecc and me in bed.

It was morning and she and her friends were surely ready to rest before the next ball.

As quiet as could be, I creaked the door open and stepped into the hallway.

Neela wasn't waiting there. But of course she wouldn't have been. Her hovering outside of our room would have raised questions.

Then again, so would her retreating to one of her friends' rooms for the evening.

I frowned. Still, I had no other leads.

I knocked on Mistress Baker's room, knowing that with Gloriana gone, they'd have a spare bed.

Mistress Baker herself answered the door in her shift, her mask, though crooked, not forgotten on her face.

"Ed... Miss, can I help you?" she asked, trying and failing to rub at one of her eyes through her mask's peephole.

I peered behind her in the dark room. Two figures in two beds. Of course. With the size of the Baker family, they wouldn't have had spare room even after one had been wed to a fae.

But two...? Mistress Baker had come here with four eligible children.

"Have you seen Neela?" I whispered, glancing over my shoulder before uttering her name.

Mistress Baker frowned. "Aren't *you* supposed to know where she is?"

As Neela's chaperone, that was very true.

I'd failed her, myself, and... and Brecc in so many ways.

"I went to bed early." I cleared my throat. "And she hasn't returned."

Mistress Baker looked over her shoulder at her young adult children then stepped out into the hallway, pulling the door shut behind her.

"Can I be frank with you, dear?" she said.

An unyielding sense of dread pervaded my body. "Yes...?" It sounded more like a question. Like I was hoping she wouldn't be.

"Your behavior as a chaperone has been atrocious!" she hissed, keeping her voice quiet but stern. "You're rarely in the ballroom or where your candidate is, and when you are, you're stealing the poor girl's potential fae spouse for yourself!"

"That was..." I clutched my shiny skirt, my tongue growing leaden.

"And that!" Mistress Baker's voice grew louder now. "What is with that dress? I *know* your grandmother couldn't afford that, and if she could, for Fae King's sake, why wouldn't she have provided it to her candidate grandchild?"

I smoothed out my dress and clutched my hands together. "There was an accident with my dress. The fae provided—"

The arch of Mistress Baker's eyebrow was apparent even through her mask. "Was there an *accident* again?" Her gaze darted to the back of my bodice, the torn ribbon.

I gripped my hand over the fabric at the small of my back to pull the bodice tighter.

"Yes, but look, I won't be a chaperone again next year—"

"I should *say*," Mistress Baker said. "Were it not for the prospect of one of her parents returning for fete or the fact that there won't be a need for her to have a chaperone next year at all, I would speak to your grandmother about coming again herself. She always entertained the rest of us chaperones with her jovial manner, and she kept a careful eye on her charge from the edge of the ballroom. Not that *you* ever spent much time on the dance floor. At least until this year."

"Wait," I said, unable to keep up with the rapid pace of her diatribe. I hadn't meant any of those reasons for me not returning as a chaperone, of course. I'd meant I'd be doomed to the labyrinth once Brecc found out what I'd done. "What do you mean, there won't be a *need* for her to have a chaperone next year?"

"What do you think, girl?" Mistress Baker slapped the back of her hand against my chest.

"She's been doing very well in gaining a fae's favor," I admitted. Mistress Baker was right. There was no way this fete would end without Neela securing a proposal.

Mistress Baker *tsked* and put a hand on the handle leading to her room. "Now you take these lessons you've learned this year to heart. By the time you settle down, have a few children of your own, and they grow to attend fete, you'll have to be—"

The door beside Mistress Baker's flew open and out popped, as far as I could tell, Maria in her gown and mask, followed by her mother as her chaperone.

Mistress Baker jumped, all thought of lecturing me forgotten as she watched the tavernkeeper's wife guide her daughter past us and toward the staircase leading down.

"Whatever is the rush?" Mistress Baker's voice echoed after the retreating figures.

Maria's mother's eyes widened as she spun. She bit her lip a moment, as if considering what to say, then checked to see if anyone else was in the hallway, settled her eyes a moment glaringly on me, and decided to speak anyway. "My daughter tells me the fae are whispering amongst themselves. Their king has found himself a bride."

"*What?*" Mistress Baker practically screamed, getting an instant hush from Mistress Tavernkeeper in return.

"Now, the fewer people who know, the better, but we're running out of time," she said. "Our candidates need to find fae spouses *at once* before the Fae King proposes and the fete is at an end for years to come."

Mistress Baker let out a little yelp and screamed, "My younger girls!" before heading back inside to her room with a slam.

Bags were visible under Maria's eyes as she yawned and stretched an arm above her head.

Her mother knocked it down. "Unseemly," she snapped. "I don't care if you've been up all night. You're running out of time."

Maria pouted. "But, Mother, I'm tired, and I'm clearly not going to catch a fae's eye this year—"

"There won't be a *next year* for another chance!" Mistress Tavernkeeper shouted, far too loudly.

Another door down the hallway opened and Maria's mother nudged her daughter forward again with a huff.

"Wait!" I said, my breaths growing shallow. "The Fae King? He's here?"

Brecc had assured me Favian was *not* the king. But what if he'd *had to* say that? What if it was some kind of fae law to protect their king's identity?

But no. A fae couldn't lie.

Could they?

Or was that a lie too?

Mistress Tavernkeeper's lips pinched.

"Maria, where's Neela?" I asked, taking hold of the younger woman's elbow.

"I'll *thank you* not to mention names!" shouted Mistress Tavernkeeper.

The hallway was a buzz now, doors opening, fully dressed candidates piling out, adjusting their wilting attire in an attempt to get a second wind after the night's festivities.

My secret keeper, my Brecc, would follow too shortly at this rate.

Maria yawned. "She and Lief and Loreena stayed behind in the garden after breakfast."

Mistress Tavernkeeper rolled her eyes and shoved her daughter forward. "*Wake up* and keep names to yourself, you foolish girl! You should have stayed with them to snag a spouse!"

But I was already pulling up my skirts, rushing past them, past...

My open bedroom door.

Brecc leaned against the doorjamb, dressed once more, his mask back upon his face, a smirk on his lips.

I froze.

Mistress Baker burst out of her room, her two remaining daughters being shoved along in front of her as they squeezed in amidst the crowd headed back downstairs.

"Fuss with that ribbon later, dear," she said, then she sighed and drew her other daughter to a stop, adjusting the young woman's mask ties, which had gotten caught in her hair. "You've tied your curls right into your mask. If the Fae King has found a bride, we have *hours*, not years, not even *days* to see you wedded. You have to look your best."

"No one is interested in me, Mama," the young woman said.

Mistress Baker tugged on the curl and her daughter let out a soft cry. "If the fete is to be over for years now, they may no longer be so picky." She took hold of the ribbons at the back of her daughter's bodice and pulled them tighter, causing her daughter to let out a cry. "So shape up and do your best."

Brecc arched a brow at me, clearly waiting for me to approach him.

I wanted to ask Brecc if what he'd told me had been a lie.

What had he said? *"You imagine him to be your king. I suppose he is rather regal."* He'd said it as if the thought had amused him, and I'd taken that to mean Favian wasn't, in fact, the king. But Brecc hadn't actually *said* that Favian wasn't, had he?

Brecc opened his mouth, but the last thing I wanted was for Mistress Baker to turn her head and notice he was standing there. The daughter not being fussed with, Gisella, I thought, was already looking him up and down, noticing where he was, probably not recalling whose *room* he was standing in, but nonetheless, taking in his stiff gait, his unfamiliar figure. Identifying him as a fae.

This couldn't wait. I couldn't tell him now. I had to see Neela first.

Though if there was one thought that calmed my heart as I threaded through the crowd and headed down the stairway, it was that if Neela was indeed about to get a proposal from the Fae King himself, there was a chance he might delay in order to allow the rest of the fae one last chance at securing spouses.

Unless, of course, he couldn't bear to be apart from her a moment longer.

The memory of the two of them dancing... There was a chance his need to have her would outweigh any of his sense of duty to his kind. There was a chance he'd end the fete as early as today.

And I might never tell my cousin goodbye. I might never make sure she was certain that she wanted to give up everything to marry that fae, king or not. She had things to lose. Family. Friends. A world that awaited her. I didn't stand to lose that much if I never went home again.

FOURTEEN

BRECC

She was playing chase-and-catch-me again, rushing down the stairs amidst the growing crowd of human guests making their way to the dining hall and garden.

Someone—no doubt Favian—had let it slip that the Fae King was about to propose to his bride. That would mean the end of fete for years—I hoped decades—to come, so all of the fae who were taking their time, wondering if next year might bring a spouse who stirred their souls more meaningfully, might be willing to settle for a charming figure. A bit of grace. Any human candidate any of these fussing chaperones shoved in their direction.

Decades may not have been a lot of time for us when we were fulfilled and content. But alone... Once we'd tasted the sweet charm of human companionship, those years could drag on endlessly without a partner.

I understood that now better than I'd ever thought I might. I understood a fraction of what Father had felt to lose my human mother. The thought struck me sharply that someday I'd lose my beauty, too.

But that would be many decades from now. I had to hope it would be. And by then, if we had an heir to take my place... Perhaps my heart would break like my father's and I'd soon join her.

Outside, the air shifted, revealing that a fae was opening the labyrinth, pulling their new spouse inside as the stone made way to craft a safe path home.

I took a deep breath, filling my lungs with the steamy, raw scent of her in this room where she'd first been mine. Giving it one last glance over my shoulder, I stepped out into the tail end of the crowd, behind a rather gangly male child and his bald, stern companion. They spared me a glance as if to wonder who I might be, then the boy stiffened awkwardly and gave me a bow.

Somehow these humans could always tell which of us were fae, even with our masks. Then again, their villages were so small as to no doubt make identifying each other as simple as it was for fae.

The law of masks at fete seemed truly pointless.

Offering the pair a smile, I slipped my black mask off my head and tossed it atop the post above the handrail.

The chaperone let out a grunting gasp.

I started walking down the stairs backward, my arms out on either side of me, watching the pair of humans as the chaperone held the candidate at bay. As if walking too close might make them accessories to the sin.

"Report me to the guards," I said. "They will not throw your king into the labyrinth."

The candidate scrambled to offer me a sweeping bow, more elaborate than the last, but the chaperone's mouth puckered beneath his mask, as if to call my assertion into question.

I knew I made for more of an imposing figure than the majority of my people. Perhaps I was not so clearly a fae.

I was done with these subjects, though. Let the rumors swirl, the tongues wag. I had a beauty to whom to propose.

And just now, I felt the labyrinth open again. My people were working quickly.

A mass of humans gathered around the castle entryway, chaperones poking their heads into the dining room, no doubt looking for fae to charm. I wondered if any of these humans knew we rarely slept or thought we might be off in our own rooms someplace.

My beauty hadn't seemed aware of the fact when she'd tiptoed around the room this morning. Amused, I'd watched her through slitted eyes to see what she'd do.

Run again. As usual.

I'd thought we were beyond that.

Still... I had slept briefly after our tumble last night. Sleep had proved refreshing. *Invigorating.* I was ready for this new day. Ready for round two.

The murmurs turned to gasps and whispers as I reached the bottom of the stairs, making my way past the crowd of humans with my face on full display. I offered them all a nod and a wink and headed outside. Despite what had happened at the garden last night, I figured that was where my beauty had gone. She'd seemed in a hurry after her friend had mentioned something about the garden. And it offered so many places for her to hide from me.

Wholly too tempting for this vixen of a beauty.

My fingers grazed a hedge of rhododendron, my lungs inhaling the crisp morning air and the enticing sweet and sour of the flowers' scent. She smelled of these flowers.

Footfalls disturbed the gravel around the corner. I hesitated, listening, unwilling to disturb another fae who might be proposing a union at this very moment.

But then I heard her voice.

"Loreena!" my beauty cried.

Careless with a name again. Luckily for her, the laws of fete wouldn't apply much longer.

I shifted aside some of the branches to find my beauty running after a straw-haired girl on her own.

"Where's Neela?" my beauty asked.

The girl jumped. "Are you daft? Keep your voice down."

I bristled at the accusation, though I couldn't fault a human guest for being cautious about a law of fete. It was only my beauty who was so brazen about wantonly breaking them.

My beauty frowned, then bit her lip. "Sorry. I just need to find her."

The girl, Loreena, crossed her arms across her chest. "She asked for some privacy. With her suitor."

"So she's here?" My beauty gripped her by the upper arms. "Which way?"

Loreena slipped out of her grip and pointed behind her. "That way. But not for long."

My beauty stilled. "What do you mean?"

"She said her goodbyes." Loreena sniffled. "We didn't get to say goodbye to Gloriana, so we thought it best. If you'll excuse me, Neela's fae told us our time to make a match is running out. I have to... I have to find someone. And check in with my mother."

My beauty took hold of her skirts and brushed past the other girl, but she stopped again, her feet kicking up a few pebbles. "I don't suppose you'll listen to me when I counsel you not to rush into a marriage?"

Loreena stiffened and sneered. "I *won't* be the only one of my friends who doesn't find a spouse at fete! Just because *you* didn't find anyone—"

If only this girl knew.

"It's not that!" my beauty protested. She held a fist up in front of her breast as she gazed at the hedges, in the direction of the labyrinth walls. "Something... Something just feels off about the labyrinth right now. It doesn't feel safe to enter. For anyone."

Loreena let a *tsk* escape her lips and wandered in the direction opposite of my beauty.

I studied her a moment, wondering what my dear one could have meant. Was this why witnessing a union had frightened her so?

But she turned the corner, kicking up pebbles.

In the distance, a howl pierced the air, my kind's true foe growling at her approach.

Why? Why did she affect the labyrinth so?

Enough of her games. They had no place amidst such strange occurrences. With a commanding wave of my hand, the hedges shifted aside to allow me passage to where my beauty and the other girl had just been.

I commanded the next layer. And the next.

I came upon Adelaide and a rather tall, thick-shouldered candidate at the wall's edge.

"Bre—uh, you, you startled me!" said Adelaide, gripping to her newest human conquest's broad bicep. His neck flushed at her touch and he offered her a steady grip around her back. She blinked hard, looking up at him through her mask.

Baker or not, her love of food perhaps a motivator, there was no denying that there was a connection between their souls.

"Your mask!" she said.

My eyes met the human's, as if daring him to question me. He said nothing.

"Ask him quickly," I said, ignoring her comment as I took a left turn and brushed another cluster of branches aside. Behind me, the hole I'd made in the other hedge was already closing up.

"So it's... it's true?" Adelaide asked. "But I never even saw you dance!"

"Just hurry," I said. "I make no promises the fete will last another night."

She gasped, but the sound was drowned out by another howl in the distance. Her eyes went wide as she looked back at the wall. Her human instinctively gripped her tighter and looked with her.

"Is it... safe?" she asked.

"Of course it's safe," I snapped. My beauty's worries were getting to me. I massaged a temple and muttered an apology before stepping through to the next row.

A distinct scent like grilled meat assaulted my nostrils then, and I followed it, running so far down the path toward an edge of the labyrinth wall that I desecrated the gravel beneath my feet, exposing the dirt and sand below.

She hovered beside the wall again at the end of this path, her hand reaching out toward a singed section of brambles, the orange light calling to her like a moth to a flame.

Not again!

"Fool!" I cried after her, closing the distance between us and smacking her hand away.

She blinked wildly, as if she hadn't heard my approach, and let me take her in my arms, standing between her and the fiery glow of the stone.

Sulfur in the air and the burning of flesh. I pulled her back and examined her palm but found no further damage to it.

"It's... It's just there," she said quietly, beneath her breath.

I followed her gaze and looked over my shoulder. Could that odor have been the minotaur burning its flesh as it pressed against the stone?

High above the wall, the snorts and grunts of the creature echoed out into the sky.

"Come," I said, taking her by the hand.

She stumbled after me, and we stepped away from the wall, down the dirt and gravel path.

Her head kept turning back toward the creature.

"Stop," I said, gripping her by the shoulders as most of the wall fell out of sight.

Already, the odor began to dissipate, the grunts and groans of the beast growing quieter.

"Stop... what?" she asked, stepping back. She nibbled on her lip and looked down. I realized her dress, the ties broken, was loose, and had begun to slip sideways off her shoulder.

"Stop tempting that *monster*, whatever you're doing!"

"I'm not *doing* anything!" She clenched her fists at her sides, turning back to me.

"You have to be!" I tossed my hands up. "It's never done that before, traveled so close to the edge of the labyrinth, *burned* the stone like that!" Taking a deep breath, I rubbed my hands through my hair. How would I propose near the labyrinth wall, how would we open it up and take a safe path back home, if that thing was hovering on the other side whenever she showed up? "It can't escape. It knows that. But it seems damn well determined to try."

"Because of me," she said softly. It was only half a question.

What was I to do? Father had never mentioned such a possibility. But I was suddenly overcome with the thought that we could tarry here no longer, that I couldn't give my people the chance they needed to secure spouses. My senses tingled as the labyrinth shifted. Adelaide and her man, no doubt. Good for them. I could only hope the others worked as quickly.

Everything in me told me my beauty would be safest there, back home, in the stronghold of the labyrinth.

"Tell me," I said. "You're keeping something from me."

She laughed. One sour, *angry* laugh. I bristled at the disrespect. It was a confirmation that she still held secrets, a wry hint that I had no idea. That I might never find out.

Instead of taking her over my knee and spanking her, as I found myself staggeringly overwhelmed with the thought of doing for a moment, I settled for taking hold of her face and ripping her mask off. Tossing it to the ground, I pushed my lips to hers.

"Tell me," I whispered, my lips hovering over hers.

She sighed, closing her eyes and tipping up on her toes, as if hungry for a kiss.

This one time, I would deny her my lips.

"You know why that creature calls to you," I said softly. To tempt that stubborn tongue to loosen up, I pressed a kiss to her temple. "Tell me why."

A tear fell from each of those round eyes and I kissed those away, too.

Her eyelids fluttered open and she took a step back, filling her lungs with air. "My mother," she said. "It has to be."

I frowned. Her mother? Was her mother here with her, the chaperone so remiss at her task?

"What of her?" I asked.

My beauty paced, wringing her ashen hands. "She was lost... to the labyrinth."

A flare of energy coursed inside me, spurring my brain to think. A human hadn't been fated to the labyrinth in years. I'd heard tales of the last one, how she'd evaded the call of the labyrinth for years after... She'd given birth to a child?

When? When she'd already been marked for lost?

My throat went dry. "Your mother had the mark of the minotaur's hoof on her face when she birthed you."

My beauty nodded. "Maybe... Maybe that's why my blood sings to that... that thing."

Father hadn't spoken of such a situation. There was but one bit of magic that could break the minotaur's cage once and for all, and it had nothing to do with a Fae King being denied a lost soul's child.

Yes. I'd have her. I'd protect her back home and keep her away from the monster.

Her mother. The last human lost to the labyrinth, for breaking a law of fete. In her case, for rejecting a proposal.

I hadn't been at fete that year, but I knew the story well.

I swallowed. What was more important? To get her home and at my side? But here I was, demanding her truth, and now I'd be keeping something from her.

Something she might loathe me for keeping from her if she found out too late. If she discovered I'd dared imagined her attracted to him, that I'd encouraged him to take that golden-dressed friend of hers she fretted over so.

"My beauty," I said, just as her own mouth opened. It shut then. Rather than inviting me to learn her name, she seemed awestruck by the name I'd chosen to address her as. "I promise to protect you." I took both her hands in my own. "No matter what. You mustn't be frightened."

The tears grew stronger in her eyes. "Oh, Brecc," she said, my name still like warm sunshine on her tongue. "I don't doubt you want to. But I... I don't deserve your protection. I don't deserve you." Her hands trembled in my grip.

I took her in my arms. She felt so right in my embrace, the tip of her head coming to rest beneath my chin. "It's not your fault, what your mother did. I won't let you pay for her sin."

She stiffened, pushing herself backward from me, stumbling. Her tear-streaked eyes were shining now as she looked up at me. "My mother didn't *sin*! She loved my father. That was all." She practically choked on the words.

I clenched my fist at my side. I hadn't meant to upset her. I wasn't a fan of the law myself—and I'd vowed never to use it on her, even if she rejected me—but the fact was... "Your mother rejected Favian. My friend."

Her skin lost all semblance of color, and her feet stumbled. Backward. Sideways. She didn't seem to know where she was going.

I reached out to steady her. But it was clear she was going anywhere but toward me.

I expected her to rail at me. To scream at me. I was prepared to apologize, to tell her I didn't think what her mother had done had warranted her punishment, that I was sorry I'd never changed the laws in time, that I hadn't fully understood what my friend's wounded pride had led to. Not until I felt my beauty's pain seep right out of her in front of me.

But instead of whirling on me, her eyes grew wider as she looked up at me.

"Neela," she whispered.

And she slipped from my grasp, staggering back toward the labyrinth wall.

CHAPTER

FIFTEEN

EDONY

Neela was going to marry the Fae King—and the Fae King was the one who'd asked my mother to marry him?

The news was a jumble in my mind, of shock, anger, betrayal—but what did it matter? Mother might have lived as the Fae Queen and given birth to some other child. She'd chosen love over such a life. If she'd even realized what she'd been offered at all.

The most pressing thought in my mind was stopping Neela. A cruel fae who would do that to a woman... didn't deserve her.

And I shuddered to think of what he might do to her if she ever displeased him.

Of course, I had to stop him before he proposed or—

"Wait!" Brecc yanked me by the elbow, pulling me back. "You're running in circles! What are you looking for?"

I blinked, attempting to get my bearings. He was right. I had no idea where I was in the maze of hedges. It was but a lesser echo of the true labyrinth that awaited me and I couldn't get my bearings.

"Take hold of the wall."

My left hand reached out for the nearest hedge and I almost collapsed on it. Brecc caught me before I sank.

Part of me wanted to just accept it, to crumble into his arms. But he'd called Favian his friend and that fae had done harm to my mother. May harm Neela yet.

"I have to find her," I said, shoving at him.

"Who?" he asked as I straightened. "Neela?"

"Yes!" I stumbled away, clutching to the hedge this time.

Brecc smiled, his hand on his hip. "I know where she is."

I stilled.

"And I know how you can see her again," he said.

I stared at him, breathless, waiting. The way he'd phrased it...

"Accept a proposal and become a fae's spouse."

I fell to my knees, my breath coming out in gasps. It was done, then? Well and truly done? My Neela was gone?

But...

Brecc crouched beside me, his feet kicking up the stones beside my knees. "My beauty—"

I shoved at his chest and stood on shaky legs, gripping to the hedge for support. "She can't have accepted his proposal," I said, my voice shaking. "Or the fete would be over."

Brecc cocked his head as he stood to his feet. "You still think Favian the king?"

"*Don't* say his name to me," I spat, surprised at the venom coating my words. All I could think about was my father's face as he'd left me that one last time. My mother's scars as she'd sung to me.

He frowned. "All right. We can discuss that later. I know you must be grieved to know that he was the one—"

"How can you be his *friend*?" I swirled on Brecc. "After he committed a woman—*any* woman—to that fate!"

Brecc's jaw clenched. "I'm sorry."

He was fae. He couldn't understand.

I turned away from him, feeling the gaping hole in my chest as I put more space between us, but he caught my wrist once more and forced me to look up at him.

"I'm sorry, my beauty," he said, the lump at his throat bobbing. "But she's gone. I've felt fae after fae take their new spouses home, ever since this morning. He would not have tarried. I told him not to."

I gasped. "You *told* him to ask Neela to marry him?"

"I told him not to *delay*." He lowered my wrist but didn't let it go, that twitch in his jaw visible once again. "I didn't put the idea in his head to marry the girl."

"But you... But he..." I tottered again and Brecc caught me. My arms were weak now, his grip tighter, allowing only the smallest of space between us. "If he were the Fae King, the fete would be over."

"Why are you so insistent in thinking he's king?" Brecc whispered. "My beauty, *I* am the Fae King. Your sovereign. Your ruler."

My breath caught in my throat as the world spun around me. My knees weakened, Brecc stopped me from collapsing, and, bending over, picked me up in his arms. Walking us forward, he didn't say a word, just watched me, one hand tight around my shoulders, the other under my knees.

He offered me a small smile. "Is the news so shocking?"

My voice cracked as I rested my numb, tingling palm against his chest. "It's... too much..."

I'd stolen the Fae King's heart somehow. And he'd taken mine as well.

Our union would spell doom for everyone I'd ever known. Even Neela. Even if she was beyond my reach, in the fae village, wife to the man who'd murdered her aunt.

No one survived the collapse of the labyrinth and the minotaur's freedom. As if the creature knew the freedom and bedlam I could offer it, it hunted me even now. Even before Brecc had put it all into words.

He did not lie. So it was the Fae King who held me in his arms, who'd taken me to heights I'd never imagined.

We reached a section of brambles that grew over an outer wall and he set me down, sliding my feet to the gravel below.

He got down on his knees.

My insides were about to tumble out of my throat.

"My beauty—"

"Don't." I sobbed. "Don't say it."

He misunderstood me and quirked the corner of his lips. "Then give me your name."

I sobbed again. "That's... all. That's all I can give you."

He took both of my hands in his. They trembled so, he had to grip with some pressure to steady me. "Don't be so frightened. I'll protect you, beauty."

"Edony. My name is Edony."

The look on his face. His forehead shot up, his smile grew wider. He brought my hands to his lips and kissed them.

"Edony. My beauty. My dear one. *Edony*."

He kissed each knuckle between words. My plain name was like a rare jewel from his lips.

For him to reach such heights of happiness... and to crush it.

How had I gotten everything so wrong? How had I been so foolish? So *selfish*?

"Edony, will you be my wife?" he asked me.

"No," I said quickly, the word scratching at my throat. "I cannot."

The maze seemed to rumble beside us at his words—or at mine. Whatever magic kept it in place was in tune to his proposal, and what it might mean for me to accept it.

I felt that to be true.

His face went stony, his lips curling into a bitter smile.

"I will protect you—" he started.

"It's not that," I said, taking my hands from his own. He offered no resistance. "I know the fate that awaits me. Proclaim it. I will... I will do as my mother did and wander the labyrinth."

He blinked at me, his bitter smile deepening into a frown. Launching himself to his feet, he sent some of the gravel flying. "Wander the labyrinth? *Wander the labyrinth*? You would rather *die* in the *labyrinth* than become my queen?"

His voice carried out into the air, a hollow echo of the sweetness his voice had exhibited in the stillness of night.

"I'm sorry," I choked out. "I am."

He flung his arms out to either side of him. "Well, *I* am sorry, too, because I won't do it. I won't compel you to such a fate." He crossed his arms, his jaw tight. "So even if I cannot have you, you cannot have this punishment you seek."

My knees grew shaky. He would... He would set me free, even after a rejection? He'd show me the mercy Favian had not shown my mother?

But how...? Why?

Could I...? Could I accept him?

The maze grew shakier beside me, almost as if it were reading my mind.

The king could not choose a bride from those humans no longer eligible. I could not say why, but that law seemed irrefutable, nothing a mischievous secret keeper might let slide.

The walls themselves were built on it.

"You must," I told him hoarsely, unable to look him in the eye. "You must let me wander the labyrinth. For I have sinned greater than any other."

He scoffed. "I was wrong to call your mother's rejection a sin. I will not have you fear the same just for rejecting me, even if I am your king. Tell no one you were the candidate I proposed to and—"

"That's just it," I told him, ready to lay it all bare. "I'm not a candidate."

Brecc's eyes widened, his hands falling to his sides.

Against my better judgment, I reached out to caress his face, to feel the stubble of his cheek beneath my palm one last time.

"I'm twenty-five. I'm here as a chaperone."

Brecc stumbled backward, leaving my hand clutching nothing but empty space.

It was his turn to clutch on to the hedge. A rhododendron

blossom snapped off beneath his hold, the petals scattering to the ground.

"You lied to me," he said, the words like fire on his tongue.

"I... I didn't mean... I never said..."

He laughed. Long and hard and hollow, and I realized he'd laughed last night in such a different way. In an exultant way, he'd told me. I'd sealed our fates then and I'd been a fool not to realize it.

"You have cursed me," he said as he dragged in a gasping breath. "You have cursed us all."

I shook my head. "No. Just choose someone else. I'll head into the maze. Or if you won't let me, I'll leave. I'll never come back—"

He swallowed, the lump at his throat bobbing as his eyes glistened with unshed tears.

"I love you," he said, and I caught the words like daggers at my breast.

The labyrinth rumbled beside us, the bleating groan of the creature rising up to meet us. It was sniffing the air, I could sense it, feel the heat singe my flesh. It had found me. It had found the wall's weakness.

The Fae King's love for me.

"I love you, too," I said back before slapping a hand over my mouth.

The ground beneath us shook as the hedge beside us decayed away, the finest grains of dust crumbling from the stone wall beyond it.

CHAPTER

SIXTEEN

BRECC

The ground itself was fighting against our union.

But she loved me. My beauty—Edony—felt the call of our souls, too.

Why? Why had this happened? Why was this supposed to be so wrong?

What made a human who had lived twenty-five years less worthy of being my queen, of keeping this magic labyrinth intact than one who had seen just one year less of life?

What were single years to a man who'd come of age long before any human alive today had been born?

My father had never explained my grandfather's design, nor the reasons why we determined a human's years of eligibility. I'd just assumed it had something to do with a human woman's most fertile years, but if those humans never selected to be a spouse of fae went home and had human children of their own... They could clearly still bear a fae king's child long after their years of eligibility.

So why? Why were my lungs constricting as I gazed on her grimacing face, her throat swallowing as her wide eyes stared up at me?

In the distance, the snorting grunts of the creature that was our foe rose up over the rumble of the maze's walls.

That was why. Somehow, the minotaur knew. It had let Edony's mother free long enough to bear a child who would tempt me—and curses! Why hadn't I come at any point over the past seven years? Why had I come at all this year if she was to be thrown in front of me, only to be ripped away?

I staggered as the hedge beside me curled to ash.

Somehow, the creature had kept my interest in fete waning —I hadn't been in over two decades—all for this day. For my downfall. For the destruction of the cage keeping it tethered.

Edony let out a cry and lost her balance under the rumble beneath her feet, and my hands shot out to steady her. I caught her under her elbows, inhaled the sweet and sour spice of her aroma. The flowers beside us had crumpled to dust, so I knew it was not them, but her. My beauty. My dear one.

"Let me go," she whispered, her eyes falling to the ground.

It seemed so simple. Deny our love. Let her grow old and die without me.

Choose another bride someday or don't. Let this curse end with me so there would be no Fae King to be born to take my place. No one else need suffer as Father had. As I would. I could live forever, keeping the beast at bay from my people, from the humans...

The rumbling grew softer beside me, as if it sensed that I could do it. I could do the right thing.

My hands fell from her body.

Her long eyelashes fluttered as she looked at the wall beside us, at the growth of vines as the garden's hedges took shape once more.

And then those eyes caught mine.

My body grew hot, a roaring fire building up and out from the center of my core. My groin stirred at the sight of her perfect skin, the bare, exposed shoulder.

The feel of being inside her... The memory of her beneath me, of her fingers clawing into my back... I shuddered with pleasure.

"No," I said taking a step toward her. Toward my beauty. "No. You won't leave me. I won't allow it."

She gasped and took a careful step back. The creature's groans grew louder, the foul beast seeming to have picked up on our scent, zeroing in on our location.

"You can't... I won't..." she said.

"I am your *king*," I reiterated, straightening and swelling up to my full height. "You gave me your love—"

"But I—"

"Don't deny it." I cut a hand across the air, ignoring the scent of ash and fire and death that emanated from the crumbling edges beside me, the new growth dying before it had even bloomed. "You gave your love to your king, and I will accept it."

She whirled around and I surmounted the distance between us, grabbing her by the arm and pulling her close, her back to my chest.

Her breaths were ragged, shallow, as the grumbling moan of the creature grew louder. Just ahead, the stone began to sizzle and glow.

My hand grasped her breast, first through the dress, then

shifting aside the loose bodice to caress the cool, pebbled flesh beneath my palm.

She moaned, almost as loud as the beast just beyond the wall.

I lowered my lips to her ear, kissing the lobe before speaking softly.

"Tell me you don't want me and I'll let you go."

My breath grew still, my heart wild.

Despite the rumbling of the ground, the heat surging from the stone beyond the fallen hedges, my cock grew hard, pushing through my pants to the small of her back.

She let out a little mewling yelp and fell back, her weight slamming against me.

My beauty wanted me. Humans could lie, but she would not tell me the words I needed to hear to end this.

That she didn't want me.

"I am your king," I said again, softly, between kisses on her ear, her cheek, her brow. "You—and you alone—are my queen."

She choked out a sob, her cheeks wet with tears.

I didn't care if the world crumbled. *My* world would crumble without her in it.

Why should all of my people have their humans and not I?

Why should I alone suffer? I, their king?

Ahead of us, a molten piece of stone slipped to the gravel below as the snorting breaths of the minotaur echoed out into the sky.

What would it take for the wall to completely collapse? Our formal union?

It had withstood our joining of souls last night, and I could not imagine simple words exchanged could *begin* to compare to our union of bodies.

We could do this. We could be together.

The maze could crumble, the creature set free—I'd kill it if I had to. I'd do what my grandfather could not.

"I'm sorry," she said, spinning fully around. Before my body could ache at the absence of hers, she took my face in her hands and set a short, sweet kiss to my mouth.

My eyes closed at the feel of her flesh on mine.

I went to grab her, but my hands found only air.

The disturbing of gravel echoed out in my ears below the snorting breaths of the minotaur.

With a bolt of adrenaline, I opened my eyes.

Edony was at the end of the path before me, turning a corner, faster than I had ever seen her. Faster than she had any right to be.

The creature groaned from the wall beside me and the sizzling of stone died out to mere embers.

With a snort, the beast gave chase from the other side of the wall.

It wanted her. But did it not crave its freedom? Did it not want me to have her?

What if, instead of being our destruction, my beauty was our salvation?

What had my grandfather known of the magic he'd cast?

Edony had been born of the maze in her own way. Perhaps that made her different.

I didn't care. I would risk destruction. I would risk it all. She would be mine.

In the culmination of all of our chase-and-catch-me games,

I brought the summation of my speed to my legs, barreling down the gravel path and kicking stones every which way.

The creature kept pace along the wall, its snorts hitting the air, the hedges decaying and growing back as it passed by on the other side.

I didn't know what she had planned, but I had to stop the beast from claiming her. She would not be safe until she was back in my arms.

I turned the corner. She was already disappearing around another corner ahead, her left hand clutching the hedge not growing against the wall.

Yes, away from the wall. From this creature. *Run where it cannot find you.*

I barreled after her, my breaths growing shorter, the excursion unlike any other I'd ever felt, even taking my beauty over and over in the dark of night.

The minotaur's scraping hooves screeched like nails against stone and it let out a deep, guttural grunt.

It could go no farther after her. Not so long as the walls held.

Edony was nowhere in sight as I turned the corner, and I cursed. The hedges got shorter away from the wall, and there were more places for her to duck.

"Edony!" I shouted, the law of fete to keep names a secret as unimportant to me as the law of masks. As the whole damn setup to my crushing lust. "Edony! Don't run from me!"

Half-aware that I sounded mad, a villain instead of her true love, I stumbled onward, the edges of my vision growing dark so I could remain focused. On her. On her returning my love.

She hadn't refused me and left. I could bide the pain I felt now if that were the case. She was mine, and she stayed away out of some sense of sin.

Blast the world. Blast *sin*. We were meant to be together.

The whispers reaching my ears were mere murmurs, figments of my imagination. No more threat than the diminishing grunts of the beast left without his prey behind me.

It was the strong, baritone voice, the simple strung of a lute's strings, that wormed its way into my consciousness, giving voice to the whispers.

"And so it's at an end, for you and for I. We'll not make it through if the beast passes by. Love was our salvation, and love will see us fall. Oh, watch it crumble, tumble shall the wall."

Turning the corner, I came upon a gathering. Musicians. Other fae. Kaylein among them, Carac as well.

They'd removed their masks, though I wouldn't have been impeded by those when it came to identifying them. My people.

All gathered in a circle in a wide, open space in the garden, their expressions dour, their hands wrung, pacing. All except my musicians, who sat on large stones, playing their music as if they couldn't bear to do anything else as the world fell around them.

Somehow, they sensed it. What I may do.

"Brecc," said Kaylein. She reached a hand toward me and flinched. At what? The sight of me?

The ragged breaths escaping from my lips.

The way my shoulders sagged slightly, my legs parted, ready to continue on my trek to track my true love down.

"Where is she?" My voice was raw on my throat.

"Who?" Carac asked. "Brecc, what has gotten into you—"

"*The woman!* The human woman! She must have come this way!"

Carac and Kaylein exchanged a look, the few others gathered around tense as well. Even Borin stopped in his vexing song, the music growing quiet, leaving only the faint rumbles of the wall beyond the hedges.

The quieting of the labyrinth... Because she was getting away.

"Brecc, what's happened? What's wrong?" Kaylein asked, taking a careful step closer.

"Take your spouses," I snapped. "Now. Or be at peace to have none." I continued down the gravel path.

I ignored the sound of footfalls disturbing the stones behind me.

"Brecc!" shouted Carac.

I didn't respond, gripping for the hedge, turning left.

"She's that way!" His voice carried around the corner.

I froze.

Turned around.

Carac joined me at the hedge, his lips in a thin line. "The human girl without a mask. I saw her running past. I stepped out and watched her. She headed that way." He pointed in the direction opposite of where I'd been headed. Closer once more to the wall.

In the air beyond him, a great big grunting groan echoed out, the minotaur picking up the scent of his prey once more.

I shoved forward, meeting Carac's firm hand against my chest.

"What happened, Brecc?" He studied me and swallowed. "You look... crazed."

I ground my teeth as heat flushed my body. "I am *your king*," I said. "And you will respect me."

Carac frowned but stepped aside as I pushed past him.

I'd just made it to the end of the path before the labyrinth vibrated. Not crumbling. Yielding. Opening a way through.

The minotaur's grunts and groans were still a distance away. It was not the beast's forceful burning through the stone.

I turned the corner then again, drawn to a place nearby where the maze had called out its intentions.

A space had opened in the wall, my Edony hovering in front of it.

Beyond was darkness, the shallow hoots of an owl making it seem as if nightfall beckoned beyond its path.

Edony's head was turned over her shoulder, her bodice and sleeve askew, her skirts gripped in her hands.

She hesitated.

She saw me.

Her jaw slackened, the muscles in her arms growing limp.

Somewhere beyond the maze, the minotaur groaned out into the overcast sky, like a brewing storm.

"I'm sorry," she said again.

"Edony!" I shouted, reaching out for her, my feet moving forward.

She stepped through, the walls closing in behind her.

"No!" My fist touched wall, the hedges growing back in place around it as I pounded the hard stone.

I beat and beat the stone, the brambles, until my fist came

back red. And still I beat, the muscles growing corded in my neck.

"Brecc!" shouted Carac. "Your Majesty!"

I fell to my knees, the gravel digging into my shins.

She was gone. And the labyrinth had taken her from me.

SEVENTEEN

EDONY

Darkness. Daylight died as soon as I'd stepped inside the labyrinth walls. Died along with all hope in my heart.

But that was fine.

I deserved this.

Like a fool, I'd set off into the labyrinth without so much as a bite to eat, a sip of water. A warmer set of clothes to keep the chill off my shoulders.

Shivering, I dragged my fallen sleeve back up my shoulder and soldiered on. At first, it was as if treading without sight, but eventually, my eyes had grown adjusted to the false night.

Everything was shadows and brambles and decay, but it was coming into focus, my steps slowing as I realized most of my stumbling had been due to the fact that the ground was uneven, the detritus of a dying forest clogging the path everywhere at my feet.

My breaths were shallow, my eyes welling with tears. Was

there nothing but dead and decayed forest, an endless night beyond these labyrinth walls?

How had my mother and father born it, being lost to this place?

My foot caught on an upturned root, and I cried out, sailing forward, landing hard on my wrists.

Sobbing, I sat myself up, brushing bits of twigs and dirt from my face and hair and hugging my legs to my chest, being careful not to bend my sore wrists any further. Somewhere beneath these wretched layers of sparkle and skirt, my knee was scuffed and stinging.

I sobbed for I didn't know how long, the air dotted with the hooting of owls. Somewhere farther away were the snorts and grunts to which I'd become accustomed in the garden. The minotaur was prowling, and here I was, where it lived.

With no hope of going back.

No hope of seeing him. No hope of seeing Neela or Grandmother or my aunt or uncle again.

The sound of him calling my name, the echo of his "No!" as I'd fled from him, still hung heavily on my heart.

"I loved him," I said out loud in a whisper, with only the owls to bear witness. "I love him."

And it was for that love that I'd plunged into the labyrinth, just like Father had for Mother.

I understood it now. Why he'd left me behind to save her.

Though he'd had hope. He'd had to have had hope he could bring her back again.

I didn't know how, but I would believe that.

I scoffed at myself, wiping my eyes as I thought of Father's last words to me. He'd warned me to never give myself to a fae. I hadn't gone off to marry one, but I'd given myself and more.

The fae—Favian—had done that to Mother. I didn't think my Brecc would have acted the same. I believed him that he would have let me go if I'd only just been able to lie and tell him I didn't love him.

A human could lie... So why hadn't I just done it?

I'd *deceived* him enough already.

It was all due to the mad, wild pounding of my heart. Our night together... It had been sinful of me to accept it, knowing I couldn't be with him. I'd fooled myself to think he wouldn't love me as I loved him, that he could let me go...

Nonetheless, I would treasure it. I clutched the front of my bodice so hard, I practically tore a hole in it.

Our night of love would sustain me. It was more than I deserved.

I wondered what Grandmother would think when neither of her granddaughters returned to her. She might be overjoyed at the thought of Neela securing a fae groom—because no one would know just *which* groom had claimed her. But I? I was supposed to be there, to make things easier for her as she aged.

Now she would be alone.

I could only hope my aunt and uncle thought perhaps to take her with them on their next voyage.

Would they mourn the loss of Neela? Or imagine her happy?

Neela... She couldn't have known.

Rubbing the base of my palms against my eyes, I took a deep breath. Without food or water or shelter, I wouldn't last long. If the minotaur didn't find me and kill me first. Which would mean I had even less time.

Somewhere in this maze was a fae village, safe from the roving monster.

In that village was my cousin.

Before I died, could I find her? Tell her goodbye? Warn her to be wary of her wretched fae husband?

Would he... Would Brecc retreat there? Would I lay eyes on him one last time?

Surely, the labyrinth could grant me that. It had granted me a night of passion without collapsing.

Yes.

I stood to my feet, my limbs shaky. My wrists and knee still stung.

I stumbled forward, my dress catching on the thorny brambles that grew upward far above my head.

But I had a destination. A place to go before I gave up.

And if I never found it, I would at least keep trying.

There wasn't a lot one could do without hope.

This small piece... was what I would cling to.

I walked on and on, hungry for the sky, for a slit of sunlight, even if masked behind a cloud.

But there was nothing but dark and dim and decay.

I didn't know how long I wandered. Every so often, the snort of the minotaur startled me wider awake, but it was distant. Disappointed.

Perhaps I was safer inside the labyrinth than I'd been outside of it.

Nothing was growing. All was death. I wondered how any creature made its home within these walls, least of all the beast. I knew there were beings touched by magic here somewhere. How did they survive in this bleak place?

It just kept going and going and going.

With a gasp and a cry, I tripped again, stumbling, my hand reaching out and falling through a collection of bitter, thorn-covered brambles to hit a solid stone wall.

I cried out as the thorns cut into my flesh and pulled my arm away. But then I blinked, staring at the wall. There were stone walls hidden beneath these boundless brambles and decaying trees all around me. I hadn't even noticed.

Then my heart sunk as I caught sight of a bit of ribbon ensnared on the thorn ahead of me.

I tore it off. It was blue. The same thickness and shade, as best as I could tell in the dim light, as the fraying ribbon at the back of my bodice.

I'd been here before.

I'd thought I'd been making progress, moving forward, but I'd been going round and round somehow.

Letting out a hollow scream, I squeezed the frayed ribbon in my scratched hand, the slightly oozing blood dyeing the fabric.

I tossed it to the ground.

"Take hold of the wall."

What a fool I'd been! Mother had told me this not to help me find my way around some fancy castle garden.

But because somehow she'd known the maze would call for me. She'd known I'd end up trapped in this place.

Mother had spent a few bouts in the labyrinth and made her way back home.

I could make my way to Neela.

To Brecc, if only to see him from afar.

Bundling my left hand into a portion of my skirts, I dragged the makeshift glove across the brambles, gritting my teeth and moving forward.

I'd gotten only a little bit farther before my hand shot out, into the bush.

Because behind it, the wall turned.

If I hadn't been looking for the gap, I never would have found it.

Squeezing myself in the gap, the sharp, dry sticks and thorns catching on my skirt, my bodice, my hair, scraping against my skin, I made my way through.

The view before me wasn't that much better than it had been at the edge of the labyrinth.

But there was something akin to moonlight in this place.

And there was sound beyond the distant owl's hoot.

Gurgling. Like a stream.

I ran forward, stopped, and stuck my hand out again. I couldn't make the same mistake. The walls here were covered in softer brush, the drying, decaying plant life scraping against my skin but not drawing blood.

I grinned, though I knew no one would see it. I felt like I had gained a leg up on the maze somehow.

I headed toward the gurgling sound, my dry throat desperate for relief. The air filled with something unpleasant, just one short note of outright foul. Like table scraps gone bad as compost, mixed just slightly with manure.

I found another hole between the brush and stepped through.

There was water here, all right. Swampy, poisonous water.

Hearing voices, I froze. My heart thumping wildly, I dove for an overturned tree trunk, hollowed out into a log.

"Get in there, you git!"

"Yeah, in there!"

A series of splashes sounded like someone walking in shallow water. Shallow, swampy water.

"I'm in here. That's good enough, innit?"

"No, Gob! In with you. All the way."

On my chest, I used my elbows to crawl through the hollow log, wincing as moss and mud and the slightest bit of swamp water slid over the front of my bodice.

There was more splashing, and moonlight trickling in through a hole in the log. I crawled there and looked through.

There were three small men—or they appeared to be men, I thought, though they were only as big as toddlers.

Perhaps the wan light was tricking my eyes, but they all had green skin. Pointed ears stuck out from mucky, murky pointed caps. They wore thin rags that dangled off their bodies, as if they'd hoped to one day grow into them.

"Now look," said the one who was standing waist-deep in the grimy waters. "I'm in far enough. I'm wet and I'm gross and I'm in so deep, one more step and I may drown. So you've had your fun. Now leave!"

His voice wasn't at all childlike, entirely deep in tone and firm, despite the wavering of his syllables.

"Then drown," said one of the others at the swamp's edge. He crossed his arms, a big stick clutched in one hand.

The other one waved a stick around wildly, jumping up and shouting, "Drown, Gob! Drown!"

The one in the water—Gob—let out a little growl and

barked at his tormentors. "Come in here and *push* me in then, you cowards!" He growled. "Just try it! I'll bite you!"

The tormentors both swung their sticks, one whacking poor Gob upside the head.

Gasping as the green man stumbled, landing in the water backward with a mighty splash, I made a decision.

I didn't know what was going on or what these creatures were, but one was clearly outnumbered.

I crawled faster out the other side of the log, turning around to let my feet land first on the edges of the murky water. From the side of the log dangled a long, mighty branch, and I ripped it off, the dry wood cracking easily at my touch.

Letting out a roar, I ran at the two green men on the sandy bank, pleased to see Gob stand up again, spitting out swamp water and taking in a mighty breath.

"Go away, you bullies!" I swung the stick in their direction as I ran.

The smallest one dropped his stick and cried out, jumping in the air and hiding behind his companion.

The companion laughed and dug his feet into the murky swamp mud. "What's this? You rely on feeble women to aid you, Gobble?"

"Do not," spat Gob—Gobble, whatever his name was. "I've never seen her before in my—"

I swung the stick at the bullies' faces. "Go away!" I shouted. I was fully aware I was just outside the range of hitting them. I hoped my size would be enough to scare them off. "Get back!" I threatened.

The littlest one squealed, but his companion didn't move.

"Weak," he said, and he swung his stick back, knocking my own right out from my hands.

He chuckled.

"Weak," echoed Gob.

I bit my lip and growled. I didn't know what else to do. Charge them? Start punching them?

That one still clutching his stick looked eager for me to try.

"Just shove off, old lady," said Gob from the swamp. "I didn't ask for you to come here."

I blinked, staring the little man down. "*Old lady*? Didn't ask me? I thought—"

But my words were lost beneath the howl of the minotaur somewhere behind me.

Somewhere no longer that far behind me.

The air grew humid and the littlest man was trembling, words turning to mush on his lips as he pointed above my head.

The determined bully companion looked up and his furrowed brow loosened, his jaw growing slack.

The stick he'd been clutching clattered to the mud at our feet with a squishy *thud*.

They both screamed and ran, retreating to climb up the muddy hill.

"What was—" I started, turning back to look at what had scared them so.

The air had grown humid, sticking with mist. Somewhere nearby, right beyond those brambles and trees there, steam lifted into the air. And the dried, fallen detritus was catching fire. Smoke and orange glow and sulfur all swirled into the night.

"Now you've gone and done it," said Gob beside me, splashing his way nearer.

I turned to him, about to ask him what our options were, but the little man was baring his teeth and leaping at me.

He bit me. His sharp, little incisors dug into my forearm with twice the strength of an irritated cat, drawing blood.

EIGHTEEN

EDONY

I yowled in pain, but the sound was soon cut off by the snort of the approaching minotaur.

"Why would you do that?"

But there was no hope of reply. The tiny green man had fled, leaving a few drops of blood trickling down my forearm onto the once-beautiful dirty, ripped remnants of my silky blue sleeve.

"Wait!" I lurched after him, the pain of his bite mark already lessening. Just a few more scratches I'd earned since entering this place. "I... I don't know where to go!" Though stumbling up the hillside every few steps, my long legs allowed me to catch up to the retreating figure.

"Away from *that!*" Gob threw over his shoulder, his mouth a thin, harsh line.

As if in reply, the minotaur let out a growl—and then the smell of sulfur struck the air, overpowering any sour scent from the swamp nearby.

Despite myself, despite hearing the creature's calls for over a day now, feeling in my gut that what it wanted most of all right now was me, my legs trembled on the uneven surface.

I wasn't ready to wait here for my fate.

"Jumping eggflies!" Gob screamed, looking back.

I turned as well. In the distance, more and more of the rotted trees were catching fire, the flames spreading quickly.

"Why did you bite me?" I snapped.

Gob cocked his head and gestured wildly with both hands toward the burning dead trees. "Why did I...? Old woman, we've got more pressing things to worry about!"

"It's not 'old woman'!" I shouted. "My name is Edony."

"Well, I'd prefer to think of you as bait." Gob rushed over to a nearby bush, its leaves brown and wilting. Mumbling to himself, he shoved the stems aside, revealing a log.

Flies darted around the entrance, a smell like decaying waste causing me to recoil and hold an arm—the less injured arm—in front of my nose.

Gob didn't hesitate, though, getting on hands and knees and crawling through the rotted space.

I looked over my shoulder, at the bits of flame piercing up into the shadowy labyrinth sky. Taking a deep breath—though the air already scratched against my lungs—I got on my hands and knees and followed him in there.

Gob was muttering unintelligibly ahead of me in the log. There was no light at the end to guide us, just endless darkness.

My knee stuck in something thick and squishy and I cried out.

"Quiet, bait!" Gobble said, ceasing his muttering. "Bait's job is to stay back there—be the bait."

"Is that why you bit me?" I cried. It was difficult pushing forward in my long skirt, even after I'd carefully extricated my leg from the pile. "To make me weaker so I'd stay behind and face that-that *thing* alone?"

"Ah, so you're not stupid bait, at least," Gob said.

Huffing, I fought against a sudden urge to retch. The irritation growing inside me at least made me *feel*. Something. Anything. "Well, one little arm bite wasn't going to do that."

"Had to try," he muttered.

"No, you didn't, you ungrateful thing! When I tried to *help* you—"

"I didn't ask for your help," Gob said. "And I'm not a *thing*."

"Well, a goblin or whatever you are."

"I'm not a goblin, either!"

The dimmest of shaded light finally appeared ahead of us, casting Gob's crawling figure into better clarity. My head banged against the top of the log and I yelped.

"Quiet, human!" he said.

At least the insults were getting better.

"So you know what I am," I said, keeping my voice even. "What are you?"

Gob let out a little grunt and popped out at the end of the log, standing up and putting both hands on his back in order to stretch. I soon followed, finding it difficult to untangle myself in the long dress to get to my knees. I had to grab for a branch—a live, healthy branch this time, so long on the towering weeping willow beside me that it nearly dusted the ground.

The bough was strong enough to support me, though my feet still tripped a bit on the hem of my skirt as I stood.

My jaw dropped and I inhaled fresher air as I took a look around me.

A forest of weeping willows as far as I could see. Moonlight—whether it was truly night by now or not—filtered in through the trees, shedding its light on a ground covered with leaves and shimmering green moss.

There was no sulfur scent in the air, no sign of anything burning. Nothing decayed and rotten.

This place looked livable. This place was *alive*.

Gob slid in behind me, muttering, dragging some long, fallen branches to cover the entrance to the log.

"Doesn't seem like the proper getup to be exploring the labyrinth in."

I turned around. Even the beauty of this place hadn't moved his stony heart.

"I didn't exactly *plan* the excursion." I clutched my skirt with both hands, wiping away more of the muck my palms had accumulated. The gorgeous gown my Brecc had gifted me... Tattered. Destroyed. Just threadbare cloth between me and the elements.

It was all I deserved of the gift he'd given me.

"Hmm," said Gob, shuffling past me and heading down the path ahead. Trees bent like an arch over a path.

I scrambled after him, looking this way and that. Far, far to my left, there appeared to be a stone wall.

Gob swirled around. I almost ran into him, my gaze stuck on that reminder that this was, truly, still a stone maze beyond the façade of the forest.

"Are you going to be stalking me all day?" he asked.

"I'm not..." I looked around. Though the beauty of this area of the labyrinth brought me comfort, there was no sign of any other life.

Gob was my only hope of finding anything—food, shelter.... A path forward through the maze.

"I need your help," I said, straightening my back.

Gob tossed a hand in my direction. "Do I look like I care?"

I ignored that biting comment. "Are you headed back to your people—your... elves?" I ventured.

He scoffed, his eyes blinking rapidly. "Do I look like a bloody *elf*, woman? I'm twice as big at least."

"It's Edony," I said. "And you're Gobble."

Gob *tsked*. "Spy, you are. Stalking, sneaking spy."

"No," I said quickly. "I just came across you. I'm... I'm lost."

"Well, you're headed in the opposite direction of the exit, I'll tell you that much. The nicer the place gets, the deeper in you are. The maze likes to keep creatures trapped in it that way."

"I'm not trying to leave," I said. My stomach rumbled, and I put a dirty, stinging hand over it to calm it. My throat was dry, too. I felt as if I'd been lost for days instead of hours.

Gob laughed. Short, snappy, and not very mirthful. "You're dressed like *that*, wandering around the labyrinth... You don't have those slashes across your face... And you're *not* trying to leave the labyrinth?"

"I'm trying to..." I started, but something he'd said caught up to me. "You've seen humans with slash marks across their faces before?" I pretended to scratch over my own face with two fingers in echo of the jagged hoof of the minotaur.

Gob waved a hand. "I haven't. But Ma has. While ago."

I took hold of his waving hand and ignored his little chortle of surprise. "You have to take me to her!"

"I'll do no such thing. Now let go, will you?" Gob tugged and tugged.

I thought about letting go. But where would that leave me? Chasing after an unwilling creature.

Holding him against his will would do me no favors and he might leave me for good as soon as I let him go, but I'd get some answers first.

"Why not?" I asked. "Please, I... I want to get to the fae village, wherever it is. And if not there... Well, I'd also like to know what happened to a woman with marks across her face."

"How would I know? Now lemme go!"

"No, please, *listen*! You've got to take me to your village—"

"I can't go back, all right? You happy?" He turned his head and spat.

But beneath his scrunched brow, his taut mouth, a sheen of tears clung to his eyes.

I let go, and he rubbed his wrist indignantly.

"Those bullies by the swamp..." I started.

"They were just finishing the job the rest of the trolls started."

"Is that what you are? A troll?" I examined him closer. Though he was smaller than a human boy, his whole demeanor aged him, sank him with the weight of responsibility. I'd pictured trolls as larger, uglier, with fangs and bulbous skin. He'd look all right if he ever stopped scowling.

"I'm sorry," I said.

"Beh. They can rot, the lot of them. Even my own ma."

I chewed my lip, thinking of my own. Of the grandmother

I'd left behind. But I couldn't force him to face the people who'd been cruel to him.

"Don't look at me like that," he snapped, staring downward and cradling one arm against himself.

"Like what?"

"Like I need your pity..." His voice grew quieter. "Like I deserve it."

My stomach rumbled again and I leaned against a nearby tree trunk. "Well, whatever your past, you're all I've got."

"You don't *have* me," he said. "I'm just trying to survive out here." He looked up at the trunk behind me, then scurried over, sliding the patchworked knees of his pants into the dirt. He started picking mushrooms growing off the trunk, hoarding them greedily in the crook of his arm.

"I am, too," I said, my throat growing drier as what little moisture I had left was used in salivating. "At least for a little while longer. Are you sure those are safe to eat?"

Gob settled back on his bum and stuffed his mouth full of the white fungus. I wondered if that was where he'd gotten his "Gobble" name. "Do I look like I was born yesterday? I know what I'm doing. Been eating these since I was a kid. Though usually only as a snack."

On shaky legs, I slid down to the ground beside him, peering around the trunk for a sign of any more. There were none. I looked to the trees on either side of us. None that I could see.

My stomach rumbled again.

Gobble sighed and handed over two round, juicy mushrooms. "Here."

"Really?" My stomach fluttered at his display of kindness. "Thank you!" I took them from him and ate them greedily.

His green face turned a darker shade, as deep as the moss all around us. "All right, all right. No need to get sappy. You just looked like... you could use a little pity yourself."

Tears streamed down my cheeks as I chewed, the spongy material that by all rights should have tasted bland like a salve to my stomach.

I swallowed the last of the mushrooms he'd handed me.

"I don't know if I deserve pity, either."

Gob frowned, then reached into his pile and handed me half of what was left.

"Thank you," I said, quieter this time.

We ate the rest of the mushrooms in silence. After a while, the minotaur's growl echoed across the air, but it was distant this time.

Even melancholy.

"I don't know what's wrong with the thing," Gob said.

"The minotaur?" I asked, my voice hushed.

"No, my stubbed left pinky toe! *Of course* the bloody minotaur!" Gob *tsked* and shook his head.

"What do you mean?" My hands were caked with the dirt that had clung to the fungi on top of everything else. "What's different about it?" My heart sunk. I may have had an idea.

"Well, he's always been awful," he said after a moment's silence. "But he tends to stick to the deadlands, roaming at the edge of the maze."

"What does it eat?" I asked, thinking of the barren, decayed areas I'd fought my way past to get here.

Gob scoffed. "He doesn't have to—part of the problem with

the blasted thing. He kills just for *sport*. Likes chasing things. Like your humans with his mark on them. And no, I've never seen one," he added quickly.

"There hasn't been one in over seventeen years," I said.

"Hmm..." Gob studied me. "And yet, here you are. Not too long after the creature started growing restless. Burning his own favorite hunting grounds to ash?" He shook his head. "This whole labyrinth is going to hell. More than it ever has."

I looked around, at the shining light of the moss and the slightly swaying boughs of the gentle willows. "It doesn't look like hell to me—not past those outer layers."

"Yeah, well, you're new here, aren't you?" He scoffed as I nodded. "Don't you know anything about this place's history?"

I shook my head. "I thought I did..."

"I reckon not, if you're aiming to head to that fae village."

"What do you mean by that?"

Gob shrugged. "The Fae King. He's responsible for this whole mess."

As the minotaur's lonely, harrowed cry resounded out into the air and faded into nothingness, my stomach felt leaden, a chill skittering down my back.

"I'm running from the Fae King," I admitted. I didn't say more. I couldn't just yet. My tongue was so dry, I thought it might crumble to ashes.

Gob let out a harsh chuckle. "Then I guess I don't blame you, woman. Run far, far away."

NINETEEN

EDONY

"No, you're wrong." I shook my head. "The Fae King isn't to blame. It was his ancestor who created the labyrinth. I don't know how old the current king is, but I know there have been human Fae Queen brides at least twice in history—"

"I didn't say he *created* the dang thing." Gob gestured around him. "Yeah, it was his grandfather." It struck me then, how old Brecc must have been, for the Fae King who'd created the labyrinth had done so long, long ago, before any human living's grandparents had even been born. "Who flipping cares? It's his domain now. He has the power to end this hell, and he chooses instead to hide away outside of his little sheltered visits, his people kidnapping humans—"

"They come willingly," I said sharply. Despite everything I'd seen. Gloriana had only come somewhat willingly. And Neela... Neela didn't really know the fae man for whom she'd chosen to give up her life.

"Oh, I'm sure it's *very hard* to decide to go with a fae who wants you for a spouse when the alternative is being tossed in here to rot." Gob licked his lips and examined me closer, as if wondering if I was hiding my own minotaur hoof marks somehow.

"They're not all... like that." My filthy hands clutched at my shredded, stained skirt.

"And yet you run from the Fae King. Why?"

I didn't answer.

Sighing, Gob leaned back against the tree trunk, settling in right beside me.

"Let me tell you something, human. This Fae King you're defending—despite running from him into this hellscape without an ounce of plan and foresight, I might add—he takes the best of what the maze has to offer. At the center, he channels all of the strongest magic to his village."

"The castle is at the center," I said. "I've... been there."

"Imagine that. You in that fancy dress. I'd assumed you'd come straight from toiling in the fields." He rolled his eyes. "That's not the center, woman. It's close—of course it is, he and his kind have a straight, safe path right to where it's safest —but the true center is somewhat north of that."

"I... I see." So the farther I went from the castle, the farther I may be from my destination? Unless I was headed north. Only I was so turned around, I couldn't tell where I was if my life had depended on it. And in many ways, it did. I looked up and gazed at the moonlit sky. Only I couldn't actually see the moon itself. "Does the sun ever shine here?"

"Only in the fae village. Only where *his people* are."

"You speak as if you've seen it."

Gob hesitated a moment, then tossed his hand in the air. "My people sometimes do trades there—get *cheated there*, mind you. No fae deals with *lesser creatures* fairly. And that includes *your kind.*"

I frowned. There'd been a hesitance in his answer. What if he'd been there himself? He certainly spoke like someone who'd had personal dealings with the fae.

Gob pulled his floppy cap down a bit, over his eyes.

"Are you really going to sleep?" I asked.

"Quiet. Been a long day."

"It's not even..." I had no idea what time it was. But I wasn't tired. Not like that, anyway. I squeezed my legs up against my chest and wrung my hands around my knees.

"Tell me," I said. "The true history of this labyrinth."

If I was about to die, I wanted to know what the creatures who lived inside it thought. I wanted to know what had colored his opinion so—if it went deeper than cheating merchants. That seemed like something I could bring up to Neela if I saw her. She would care, if she knew.

If she was indeed trapped here for life, despite what the fae man she'd chosen had hidden from her.

I sighed.

"Well," said Gob, almost startling me. I'd thought for sure he would have dismissed me with an insult. "In the days before history, that beast wandered the land. Freely. Hunting down every creature he came across—not for nourishment, but for sport."

"It killed the fae, I know."

"But humans and trolls and beasts of all manner, too."

I laughed, short and sharp. Gob shifted his cap to peek one eye out from under it up at me.

"But there weren't trolls and other creatures just living out there with the likes of humans," I said. "All magical creatures live—"

"Inside these labyrinth walls." He gestured around him. "Yes, but the maze didn't exist back then, genius. Where did you think we were? The clouds?"

"I..." I wet my dry, cracked lips with some of the last of my moisture. "I don't know. Where did the minotaur come from?"

"He was born here... in these lands. Some say from a fae who mated with a creature it ought not to have. Others say from pure energy, the malice of the fae themselves."

I shuddered at the thought of the act or dark energy that could have birthed *that*. "Either way, you blame the fae?"

"Of course I do." He shot up, straightening his hat. "They all tried to fight the beast with normal means—swords and magic and pure brute strength." He flexed his small arm, as if to stress his point. "They harmed him once, and once only, taking away as a trophy one cloven hoof." He twisted two fingers together to make his point. "So the Fae King, then, he came up with this plan. Trap all manner of magic creatures in here—along with the wretched beast that was their creation—and keep him locked away. The walls, the trees, the bushes, the swamps—it's all to confuse the creature. Send him spiraling and spiraling, around and around, never ending in his search for prey, but finding obstacle after obstacle in his path."

That much at least aligned with what I knew. Mostly. "The king trapped your people *inside*? On purpose?"

"Didn't even ask if we'd prefer to cross the seas first." Gob shook his head. "Yes, he put his own people in the heart of the place, their magic is strongest, after all, but they're hardly *trapped*, are they?"

"You can't leave?"

Gob shrugged. "Not until the minotaur himself may, or so the rumors say. The magic we creatures feed the walls just by living, by existing—we're tethered to the place."

"But the fae aren't. They don't venture to the human villages often, and it's usually only a few guards—"

"They keep their connection to the outer world by breeding with you lot." He nodded at me, taking a strange, lingering look at my belly. As if there'd be a bump to see there. I shifted my legs to cover it from his sight better. "Fae always had trouble mating. Then the Fae King who'd done this deed discovered it was far easier to have children with humans. Before or after he hatched the plan to erect the labyrinth, I couldn't say. The human blood diluted their tethering to this place just enough, without taking away any of their majesty." He turned his head and spat.

"I always wondered why they bothered to marry humans when surely, they'd find each other far more attractive." I still couldn't say how I'd been special enough to earn Brecc's attention.

"Oh, I'm sure they like you. The same way a hunter likes his little dog." He chuckled darkly.

But Brecc... He'd felt something deeper for me. I was sure of it.

"And despite their guilt, they go on hoarding the safest place, the best resources—even getting you humans to farm and cook and bake for them. They leave the rest of us to fend for ourselves. That"—he looked hard at me now, his brow narrowing—"is why your current Fae King is wicked."

He wasn't entirely wrong if that was true, though I had to admit I felt relief to know Brecc himself wasn't responsible for more, the way Gob had spoken of him. Still, the fae owed the trolls and whoever else lived in here more help. If only I could plead their case to Brecc... But I could never let him see me again.

Never.

"But the world will end if the maze falls," I said.

"*Your* world, maybe." He crossed his arms tightly across his chest. "The faes' world, too, though they hardly deserve to hoard everything forever. But *my* world may just begin."

"You can't believe that," I whispered. "If the maze crumbles, that beast will be set free. He'll hurt not just humans and fae—but your kind, too."

"Well, I'm not exactly endeared to my kind at the moment," he grumbled. "Me, I'd make for the seas. Sail away on a ship to lands far and distant."

"My aunt and uncle travel the seas," I said. "My aunt met my uncle in another land. I'm not sure they even *have* magical creatures in those lands."

"Good," muttered Gob. "Then maybe I can earn my keep showing off my adorable green face."

I snickered. "Adorable, huh?"

"Yeah, yeah..."

"I don't think it's *not* adorable, mind you. But if you want to entertain people, you'd have to learn to... I don't know. Smile more? Stop looking like the entire world is your enemy?"

"Maybe then I'd actually *feel* like it isn't." His voice grew quieter. "Your aunt's a sailor?"

"Well, she travels." I tried pointing east but wasn't sure where it was. "You're looking for Eastmeet. That's where the ships sail away." I picked a direction and pointed to it.

"And you're from...?" Gob asked.

"Westbridge." I pointed in the direction opposite.

"Weird for these towns to be named after the opposite direction, but okay," he said. "If the walls ever collapse in this place, I'll make my way to Eastmeet."

"Wait." I shuffled over to him on sodden knees. "You can tell which direction is which?"

"You can't?"

"No." I chewed my lip. "Gob, if you can't take me to your village to speak with your mother—"

"You think she'd care a sod about talking to *you* even if I could?"

I put that aside.

"If you can't, then, can you at least take me to the fae village?"

"*Why?*" He shook his head, tugging at his large, green earlobe. "You think they'll take pity on you? If you're in here, you've been cast away."

"I chose to come inside the labyrinth."

"Right. Because the Fae King was after you..." He frowned, studying me up and down.

He hadn't said he *couldn't* take me to the fae village.

"What's in it for me?" he asked.

My jaw dropped open. "I... I don't know. Adventure?"

"I'm only interested in the kind outside of the labyrinth."

"The satisfaction you feel when you're being nice?"

"Pft. Like that fills my belly."

"I don't know!" I tossed my hands up in the air. "Just the chance for something to do? What else are you going to do in this place? You can't go home. Well, neither can I. At least let me have some peace before I resign myself to wandering the labyrinth until I die."

Gob chewed the inside of his cheek as he stared my way. "You don't hope to live there? In the fae village?"

"*No*," I said quickly. "Absolutely not. I just want to see my cousin one more time. I'm fairly certain I'll find her there."

"Hmm..."

"Please, Gobble. I have no one. No one but you now. My life is in your hands." Despite myself, tears were welling up in my eyes.

I couldn't convey strength. Not here. Not after the maze and the muck and the minotaur.

He'd given me hope, despite his clear dislike for me.

"How about you *owe* me one," he said.

"You'll help?" My voice grew higher.

"Hush," he snapped. "Do you want to wake half the labyrinth? I said you'd *owe* me one and—"

He grew quiet, his ear tilting up.

"What?" I looked behind me, upward. Something skittered in the trees overhead. Someone—*something*—else was here. "What is it?"

Footfalls ploughed through the woods. I turned around, finding Gob running off down the path, moving so fast, I thought for sure the minotaur itself were on his heels.

"Wait!" I cried, hiccupping out tears. He couldn't leave me.

He'd *promised*. Stumbling to my feet, I tripped over my long hem and fell flat back on the moss again. My forehead was sore and scratched as I looked up. "Please! Don't leave me!" But Gob was gone from view.

Just like that. I'd worn down the grumpy little troll and he'd agreed to help me and then...

He'd left me.

Alone again.

He'd given me hope, only to snatch it away.

A branch cracked like lightning overhead.

I rolled onto my back to get a better look.

Just as a giant, willowy, knotted tree bough fell down, down, straight toward me.

CHAPTER

TWENTY

BRECC

There was a comfort in the night as the sun retreated past the far-off mountains on the horizon. Not because I was any closer to finding my Edony, but because I was shrouded now, as I knew she must have been inside the labyrinth. In the darkness. In obscurity.

The sunlight had been a mockery of the ache inside me.

On the dining table at which I sat in the shadows, there was a plate full of food, untouched, to the side of me. Instead, I focused on the cloven hoof of the beast. It always came with the fae to the castle for fete, in case it was ever needed. I laughed at the thought of that. As if I would have slashed this sharp, jagged keratin across that lovely, soft face.

I dragged it now across the table, the scraping sound as it tore through the wood heavy in my ears, cold, rotten flesh like raw meat in my hands.

Carac's voice carried out into the empty dining room. "Brecc, I've found someone—"

I stood, my heart thundering in my ears as the dinner plate clattered to the ground at the sweep of the hoof in my hand.

"*Where?*"

In the single lit torch of the dining room, near its entrance, Carac's brow quirked just slightly, a hand on the sword hilt at his belt. A charade. What fae had drawn a sword in all of my lifetime?

What fae could handle what our forefathers had, taking on the immortal creature in battle?

If even *they* hadn't been able to defeat it...

Spotting the uneaten food at my feet, a formless shadowed mass in the depths of the dark, I reached without thinking, my hand trembling slightly, for the tip of my ear. It was rounded, smooth, not unlike my Edony's...

I was growing weaker, to be sure. Our human blood grew stronger the more stress we went through.

But what did a fae of today know of stress? Other than what I knew... What I knew better than any of them.

"I'm your king," I snapped, my voice gruff against my throat.

Carac let my words hang in the air between us a long moment, but then he said, "Yes, Your Majesty. I've found a chaperone willing to speak of her. You may enter now."

The last part was for the human with shallow breaths who stepped into the dim light. A short, rounded woman, with long, gray-and-straw hair. Her ballgown drooped on her form, her hands clasped together at her abdomen.

She said nothing. Just stood there, breathing shallowly behind her mask, a plain leather thing, worn with age.

"Oh, confound it, woman, take off that mask!" I shouted,

ruffling my hair in the dark to hide my rounded ears, the outside sign of my weakness. My shame.

The woman's little twittering gasp echoed out into the grand space. "But it's the fete. I can't—"

"*I am your king!*" I shouted, crossing the room with hard, fast steps that resounded against the stone like the minotaur's hooves invading my waking nightmare. The minotaur's own flesh remained glacial in my grip. "If I say to take off your mask, you do as bidden!"

The woman's little gurgling gasp was quickly bitten down as she scrambled to take off her mask. She clutched it tightly against her chest, as if it would save her, her beady, dark eyes flittering back and forth as I reached the edge of the torch's glow.

"Fete is over," I said, drawing to a halt just outside of the light's reach. I must have looked a monstrous, hazy figure to this wan-faced woman. Complete with jagged, cloven hoof.

Carac, who'd removed his mask already as I'd bidden all my fae to do, opened his mouth, shut it, and then spoke again. "There are a few days left in Westbridge's time at fete—"

"Fete is over," I said, brooking no argument.

The human woman let out a little, chittering chuckle, her smile growing wider. "Has Your Majesty chosen a bride, then? If not, I have two remaining daughters at fete. My youngest daughter—at her first fete—found a bride and my son is nowhere to be found, so I have to assume he did as well. The Bakers are a fine family, as you can see, perfect for Your Majesty—"

"Spare me your self-flattery, and speak not of which you know *nothing*, pitiful woman!"

The volume of my voice surprised even me.

But I had not the heart to care at the moment, not even as the woman shirked back, her tongue tied as it endeavored to make some kind of coherent sound.

"You were fetched to speak of Edony," I said flatly.

Her eyes darted to Carac beside her, as if he would explain what she was to do. He looked straight ahead, ignoring her, his gaze focused on the darkness—at the pathetic creature that was I.

"Speak, woman!" I barked, my stance growing unsteady, my legs eager to run and run until I could find my beauty again.

"Yes! Edony! Is there... Is she... Is she in some sort of trouble? It's only her first year as a chaperone." The woman known as "Baker" leaned forward conspiratorially. "Between you and me, I could tell she did an awful job at it. But her grandmother's health has been failing, and she seemed to think she could do the job for Nee..." She stopped, covering her mouth with her palm.

"*Go on,*" I barked.

Her hand fell back to the mask. She was practically wringing it between her sweaty palms. "But we're not supposed to speak names at fete, are we?"

"Oh, confound it, woman!" I tossed my hand clutching the hoof in the air. "I am your king. *I* make the laws, and I'm telling you: Fete is over, and you're about to be sent home with your *two remaining daughters.* Speak plainly and tell me what I want to hear or I can't guarantee I won't throw the lot of you into the labyrinth instead!"

She let out a little squeal, her mouth blubbering.

Carac's brow arched again, his lips pinched, but he said nothing.

Blast it all, his slight reveal of emotion was more maddening than this woman's efforts to imitate a fish. She did rather resemble the kind of sea creature Adelaide in particular might have found delicious.

"Well, yes, yes, Your Majesty. Um, Neela. Sweet Neela, Edony's cousin. My Gloriana's good friend. I'm so glad the both of them found fae spouses. They should be happy together, don't you think? In their new lives." Her eyes glistened, and a slight ache in the back of my throat brought my boiling anger to a standstill.

It was cruel, tearing people from their loved ones forever. I knew that now.

"Her cousin," I said plainly. Edony had never made it clear what this Neela was to her.

"Yes, but as good as sisters, the two of them. Raised largely by their grandmother. Neela's mother likes to sail, you see. She travels and is hardly ever home—"

"And Edony's parents?" What did I care about the cousin's mother?

I clenched my hand tightly around the hoof at my side. I did care, though, that this woman had described them as sisters. So Favian, the fae who had doomed Edony's mother, had then taken someone as good as a sibling to my beauty. That explained some of the depth of her anger.

"Well, they... Her... Her mother was marked." The Baker woman's voice grew quieter, more timid. Carac's breath hitched just a beat. Not enough for a human to notice, but I could tell he found the news surprising. "Quite some time ago, actually. Before Edony was born. But she held on, bless her, resisting the call—well, mostly. We'd hear about Jarin, that's Edony's father, he'd have to go pull her back from time to time. And then... Oh, it had to be just shy of twenty years ago now... They never came back. Either of them."

My beauty had spoken of her mother, and I'd known it had had to have been Favian who'd marked her, as had been his right, upon rejection. But all I could see was the trembling chin, the watery eyes, the hanging head of my Edony as she'd spoken to me. Of the pain the minotaur's mark had caused them all. Of her life without her mother—without her father, too, evidently.

If her mother hadn't been strong enough to resist the call for all those additional years... My Edony would never have been born.

I blinked quickly, the lump in the pit of my stomach suddenly growing heavier as I thought of Favian. I'd been so quick to excuse his actions as his right as a fae rejected and yet... And yet...

"It was seventeen years ago," Carac said. The Baker woman shuddered, almost as if she'd forgotten the fae guard could talk. "The last time a human was lost to the labyrinth."

"Until tonight," I added.

"Oh, dear," said the Baker woman. "Is that what this is about? Has poor Edony lost herself inside? Foolish girl! Or *woman*, I should say. Difficult for me to remember she fully came of age this year, what with her youthful appearance and her lack of maturity—"

"Silence!" I barked, spots growing at the edge of my vision. Yes, I'd mistaken Edony for a younger woman, too.

That was what had led to this mess.

"But what can you *tell me* of her? Her as a person? She cares for her cousin, whom she sees as a sister, I see that. But what else? Her wit? Her stubborn streak? What does she want from this life? What can I do for her?"

The Baker woman looked at Carac, as if expecting him to answer, to intervene and save her from having to comment further.

It was clearer than ever that she didn't know Edony. Not really. I'd learned all I could from her.

Leaning over the edge of the long dining table, I slammed the minotaur's hoof against it.

I could not have stopped myself from feeling as I did for Edony even if I'd known.

Like a fool, I may have even still *bed* her had I known.

But she still deserved so much of the blame! She hadn't told me. She hadn't let me make the choice for myself to throw the world into chaos so that I could hold her close.

My mind flashed to the thought of her running, running down past the hedges, past me. I wanted to reach out and grab her, throw her over my shoulder, and toss her onto her bed again. Never to let her go.

I could still smell the sweet and sour scent of rhododendron blossoms as I ran my lips across her skin.

"Edony is lost to the labyrinth," I said, swallowing hard so as not to lose myself in the dream. I wouldn't settle for the dream. I needed her in my arms again. "But she is also to be my bride."

The Baker woman gasped, and even Carac let out a small, punctuated puff of air.

"But, Your Majesty, she is no longer eligible! She's twenty-five!" the Baker woman cried. She clutched her mask to one cheek, the other gripping her hair as her whole body trembled.

"I know." My voice was deep, quiet. It silenced her trembling almost instantly. "Go back. Tell your human people. Warn them. Once I find my bride, the walls will fall—and the minotaur will roam wild again."

The Baker woman grew faint, letting out a frenzied, tittering cry as she stumbled to find support from the nearby wall.

"But, Brecc!" shouted Carac, his shoulders growing tense as his grip tightened on the hilt of his sword. Yes, he'd need to learn to actually wield that—and soon. "You can't! The law forbids it."

"*I* am the law!" I slammed a fist on the table. "And I will have the bride I desire!"

"But she… she can reject you…" The Baker woman tried to straighten herself. As if to present a challenge. To *me*.

"She could and she refused to," I said. "She wants me, as I want her."

"Then why did she run from you into the labyrinth?" Carac's voice dripped with venom.

I crossed the space between us and stepped into the flickering light, towering over him.

The human woman gasped again but didn't move. I supposed I looked mad to her, even more clearly in the torchlight.

"Give me your sword, Carac," I said, holding my hand out to him.

He swallowed. "Brecc—"

"Do not speak to me as if you were my friend," I snapped. "Hand me. Your sword."

The slink of the metal against the scabbard prompted me to take a step back.

For a moment, Carac stood there, his sword's hilt in his hand, the blade at his side but pointed toward me. Toward his king.

"Your Majesty," he said then, taking a knee and holding the sword up with both hands.

I took it from him, slowly, hesitating for a moment, and then holding it up with my free hand. The torch's flames danced off the gleaming metal as I turned it to and fro in the night.

I'd never worn a sword of my own.

My lessons in the arts as a child had been mere diversions.

It was *I* who was not fit to slay a minotaur, far more even than my guards.

Edony was out there—and with every moment I tarried, she could be at death's door. That thing... It sought her with greater fervor than even I did.

But I could do nothing to save her. Nothing to save my people if the wall fell.

Hold tightly, I thought to my beloved. There was one place I needed to go—one place that may have answers on how to defeat the beast. The foul, dead flesh of the creature grew heavier in my hand. Grandfather had cleaved off that wretched hoof, had he not?

It could be maimed. Why could it not be killed?

"Brecc!" Kaylein's voice echoed down the hall and she skittered to a stop. "The maze—it's on fire!"

A tingling sensation pricked at my skin as her words sank in, my heart growing louder than the nervous sobs of the human woman, the clink of Carac's chain mail as he leaped to his feet.

Edony was in greater danger than I'd even imagined. Answers would have to wait. I had to find her.

CHAPTER

TWENTY-ONE

EDONY

I rolled as far as I could, as fast as I could, the moss far gentler on my aching, bruised, and scratched skin than I thought possible, but I found myself stuck.

The bough crashed to the ground where I'd been, my dress's long skirt stuffed beneath it. A moment slower and that would have crashed right on top of me.

As it was, I was stuck.

"Help!" I called out, tugging harder and trying to rip the dress. It was beyond salvaging entirely now, even though it was all of Brecc I carried with me. "Gob!"

It was hopeless. The dress wouldn't tear. The brambles could make small cuts in the thing, but not my own sheer strength.

Gasping, I lay back, resting a forearm against my forehead. Then again, I was exhausted. The mushrooms had filled my belly, but they were settling a little alarmingly in my stomach, and my throat was still so dry.

The place where Gob had bitten me stung on my arm as it rested against my forehead.

"Please!" I cried out. "Gob, please!"

My voice echoed out into the twinkling moonlight. There was no reply.

I choked out a laugh, my body shaking. That was what I got for having even an ounce of hope.

I'd chosen this place.

It wouldn't be so bad... to wither away here. It was nicer than those outer layers of the maze at least.

I lay there, thinking.

Of Neela, who'd never know what her fae husband was capable of—not without me.

Of Brecc, his grassy scent as his rough cheek brushed against my neck. My groin throbbed at just the thought of him.

I could shimmy out of this dress. I still had a slip on underneath it. And if that was pinned, too, well... I'd figure it out.

I couldn't just give up here. I needed to speak to Neela—and I would see Brecc somehow.

And then, I would discover what had become of my mother.

Only then could I lie back and wait for my end to claim me.

Something feather-light tickled my arm cradling my face.

A spider or something creepier crawling over me.

I gasped and whapped my arm out, shaking it, only for it to bump up against something soft and fuzzy. Something that flew back a bit and hissed.

A tiny, not-very-frightening hiss.

I leaned up on my arm, wincing at the wound digging into the moss beneath me, and stared at what I'd hit.

A little kitten. Gray with darker gray stripes. Its back was arched, its tail straight up and its ears pointed stiffly. Its little whiskers—perhaps the "spider" I'd felt on my arm—were straight back as its maw stretched into a snarl.

An adorable, tiny-toothed snarl.

"Shh, shh, I'm sorry." I reached out for it, but it was just beyond my grip. Like everything now. I chuckled darkly, a tear escaping my eye. "I didn't know you were there."

The kitten's stance eased, slowly, as if wary of letting down its guard. With more relaxed ears, it sniffed at my finger. I went to scratch it under its chin and it flinched, jumping back.

"No, it's okay!" I called. "I just wanted to pet you. You seem so sweet. And this place has been lacking in sweetness."

The kitten sat up, just outside of my reach. But no longer in a defensive position. Just... observing.

Then its mouth moved. "What are you?"

I blinked. My eyes darted around for a sign of the little girl I'd heard speaking to me.

The kitten cocked its head. "Can you understand me?"

"Oh, it's... You can speak?" I asked.

The kitten dug its—her—paws into the moss beneath her. "Of course I can. I'm an elf, aren't I?"

"You're a... an elf?"

"Yeah." She paced back and forth, in echo of how a larger barn cat back home might pace around a cornered rat before pouncing, but hardly half as intimidating. "Of course I am. What do I look like?"

"A cat," I said. "I thought elves were..." What had I thought elves were like? Like Gob, I supposed. Smaller people. Pointy ears.

"Well, I'm a little small yet," she said, though her back

puffed up and her tail went up straight, as if to make her seem larger. "But I'm halfway to full-grown."

Twice this elf-cat's size would still be very small indeed.

"I apologize," I said, remembering how insulted Gob had been when I'd mistaken him for an elf. For a little, furry cat-like creature, apparently. The closer I looked, the slighter the differences I saw between this kitten and a barn cat. Its ears ended in little tufts barn cats didn't have back home. Its muzzle was slightly sharper, too.

"S'all right," she said, drawing to a stop just outside of reach again. "I don't know what you are, either."

"Human."

She bounced, launching back up onto four feet. "No way!"

I laughed. "Yes. Have you heard of us?"

"Mama has!" she cried. "And Papa! They were both adventurers before they had me and my siblings. They've seen them before!" She pounded her feet up and down, looking for all the world as if she were frolicking. "I never thought I'd see one myself!"

"They've seen humans?" I asked. "Where? When?"

The little elf-cat was frolicking toward the fallen tree bough now, making her way down the log and closer to my face. "Oh, long, long ago. They don't leave the colony now."

"Colony?" I asked.

Her little kitten nose popped out around a bunch of leaves on the fallen bough, lining up closer to my face. I knew better than to reach out and try to touch her, but I had a feeling that if I did, she would consider herself safe enough to hide amidst the leaves and out of reach.

"Yeah, the elf colony," she said. She cocked her head. "Not too far from here."

"Can you take me there?"

"I don't know..." She looked around, at the bough trapping my skirt, which fanned out around me. "Aren't you squashed now? Can you walk?"

Chuckling, I kicked up my feet, though the material of the skirt tugged and gave them only limited motion. Still, it was enough to make her jump and spin rapidly, digging her claws into the bark.

"Those are my feet," I explained. "This other stuff..." I licked my dry lips. "It's my clothes."

"Clothes..." The little elf-kitten slowly let herself relax, sitting on top of the bough. "Good. I thought I'd hurt you."

"You?"

She licked her forearm and then used the wet fur to rub behind her ear. "Yeah. I was watching you and that little troll man up there in the trees. I guess I leaped onto a diseased bough. Boom!" She tossed both of her front paws out to either side of her in a distinctly non-cat, human-like gesture. "I only just managed to leap to the next bough myself."

"So you didn't mean to attack us?"

"Of course not!" She rolled her eyes.

"It's just... The way Gob ran out of here..."

"I'm sure he didn't even get a good look at me." She shrugged, then scratched her cheek, dangerously close to her eye, with the claws on one back leg. "Haven't you ever heard the insult 'scaredy-tro'?"

"No, I can't say that I have."

"Short for 'scaredy-troll'?"

"We have 'scaredy-*cat*' where I come from..."

The kitten huffed and jumped down onto my trapped skirt. "I have never met a cat-like creature who was scared, thank you very much. It's trolls who flee at the smallest disturbance. They're *too* scared of that big, mean cow. Elves, we just hide from it."

"The minotaur?" I decided not to mention I'd seen this very elf-cat be scared several times since I'd met her. She'd been scared of *me*, even.

She dug her paws under the bough and tried pulling at the caught material. "Yeah, that thing. He howls and grunts and snorts a lot? Doesn't come this far in, usually." She sniffed the air. "But Mama sent me out here to see if I could learn anything. Said she smells the sulfur spreading."

"The minotaur set the dried brush and trees at the outer edge of the maze on fire," I admitted.

"Hmm." The elf-cat kneaded at my skirt again, looking out toward the edge of the willow forest, where the slightest hint of the stone walls poked through. "Mama and Papa need to know about that. But first..." She held up a paw and unsheathed a single claw. "Can I rip out this part of your fur? Will it hurt?"

I laughed. "No, it won't. I can take it off if I need to." I squirmed a bit. The back of my bodice was loose, but pinned as I was, I couldn't quite get entirely out of it.

"*Take your fur off?*" she echoed. "Do you know how long it takes for fur to grow back? Do you *want* to be cold and shivering for months and months?" She sniffed the skirt, then picked up her back foot and shook it, as if she found stepping on the skirt to be a strange sensation. "Smells funny. Feels funny. Weird fur. What was it you called it? Closed?" Then she shook her head. "You humans are certainly surprising."

She went to work ripping at the dress with her paw, the tear of the fabric the only sound in the little forest until her work was done.

"There!" she said proudly. She stood up on her hindlegs, bending her front legs like no barn cat ever could to place her hands on her hips in a very human-like manner.

An elf indeed.

I sat up, tugging at the skirt. She'd managed to just rip a bit of the hem off. As I stood to my feet, wincing as I bumped cuts and bruises even so, I gave her a beaming smile. The dress was a mess, sure, but it still nearly reached my ankles. "Thank you!"

"Chip," she said.

"Pardon?"

"'Thank you, Chip,' you should say. Best everyone knows my name." She licked one paw and then ran it behind her ear again. "Everyone will want to know it once they tell of my great adventure."

"Well, I'm Edony, Chip. And thank you... Chip." I added the last part when she'd squinted one eye at me, as if clearly expecting it. "What kind of adventure are you planning?"

"Don't know yet." She snickered. It sounded almost musical. "To be honest... When I saw you, in your pretty blue fur, speaking to that troll like he was anything but a fleeing, grumpy old coward like the rest of them, I thought maybe... you could tell me?"

"Me? Tell you?"

She sat back down, more like a cat, her front paws straight in front of her as her back legs curled. "I thought maybe you were a fae. Mama and Papa have told me about them. They're said to be beautiful."

I felt my face flushing, then pulled back some of my tangled mess of hair to show off my ear. "No, I'm not a fae. Fae have sharp ears—kind of like yours."

Chip ran a paw over one of the pointed tufts atop her ear, almost absentmindedly.

"But I... I am hoping to go to the fae village. Secretly," I added, appealing to her better nature. "I need to talk to my cousin there."

"Why's your cousin there?"

"She got married." My stomach felt like lead. "To a fae."

Chip's bright, orange eyes grew wide—another sign she was no ordinary cat, as if I hadn't been inundated with a countless number of those. "Wow! She's lucky, then, isn't she?"

"Not really..." My voice grew quiet as I looked over my shoulder. For sign of what, I didn't know. The fae village to see Neela. The minotaur closing in on me.

Brecc, hunting me down, ready to sweep me back into his arms again.

"Come with me." Chip tapped, tapped, tapped at the back of my hand. I turned around to find her standing like a human again. She came up only to just below my knee, even standing like that. Her maw turned into a frown as she got a look at the place where Gob had bit me. It was flaming red, worse than I'd seen it last. The puncture marks were oozing. "We should talk to my parents. They may know the way... Are you feeling okay?" she asked.

"Yes," I said, though suddenly, I felt woozy. "I've just... I've been walking so long and I'm thirsty and tired and..."

There were two of Chip as I swayed. The trees themselves had doubled, each growing fuzzy. I blinked, but the moonlight brightened, everything else blurry.

"Did that troll bite you?" Chip's voice carried out over the pounding in my head. "Oh, I hope not! Troll bites are poisonous! Bit slow to kick in, but once they do—"

But before I could tell her he *had*, the little treacherous creature, I fell, slamming my head against a thick curtain of moss.

TWENTY-TWO

EDONY

The fire crackled, and an aroma of meat, potatoes, carrots, and celery wove through the air.

Grandmother must have let me take a nap. My muscles ached and my eyelids felt heavy. Too heavy to open them just yet.

"Grandmother..." My voice croaked. Breathing was like pushing through glass in my airway.

"She's up! Hello, young human." Soft fur brushed up against my cheek. "Can you sit up? You need to drink."

I blinked. In front of me was a cat—a lithe one, standing up on its hindlegs with both front paws wrapped around a small wooden cup. Steam poured off the cup.

I sat up, then let out a groan as my vision clouded with black.

"Not so fast," said a deeper voice. Though there was still a bit of levity to it. "Chipper, help me steady her."

"Of course, Papa."

Two sets of furry paws took hold of my arms on either side, the little pads like icicles against my warm skin, and I let the dizziness wash over me as they directed me to lean back against a tree trunk. The hard, rough surface dug into my back, the edges of my slip catching on the bark. My dry lips smacked together as the cat-elf holding the wooden cup stepped forward, placing the cup in my open hand.

"Thank-Thank you," I said, looking down.

Clear broth, though it smelled of meat and vegetables, carefully strained from the pot boiling over the nearby fire. The wooden cup was likely a bowl for these little creatures, who were all staring up at me.

Behind the svelte, pointed-ear cat-elf who'd handed me the cup, nearer the fire, were three tiny kittens. Each no bigger than the palm of my hand, they huddled against one another, their lips moving in hushed whispers as their wide, orange eyes stared at me.

"You rest your voice, dear," the second-biggest cat-elf said. "You've been regurgitating in your sleep."

That explained the scratchy throat. Though whatever I'd been doing, I likely wouldn't have called it *regurgitating*.

The little cook still didn't come much higher than the top of my knee standing up. She walked on all fours toward the fire, then stood up on her hindlegs and grabbed some more wooden cups, spooning stew into them and passing them out to the three kittens.

"Must not have gotten a lot of poison," said Chip, scurrying into view and staring up at me from my feet. The warm broth was like a balm to my hoarse throat, just warm enough to soothe without the risk of burning. I wondered what kind of meat these creatures found out here. Perhaps it was best I didn't ask. "Just enough to knock you out after a while," Chip finished.

I held my injured forearm out in front of me to check the wound—less inflamed than I remembered it—and realized I wasn't in my blue dress any longer.

"My wife took the liberty of washing your dress," said the largest of the cats. He, too, would have just come up to my thighs. His face was a bit wider than the others', his pointed ears even larger. He gestured one front paw to a bough of the tree above me. My blue dress sparkled in the flicker of firelight, spread out and damp. Though there were still tears and a piece missing from the hem, it was almost as good as new. Someone had even replaced the broken ribbon at the back, a long, dried vine weaving through the holes instead.

"Thank you," I said again. My throat felt decidedly less raw.

"Do you want to take a bath?" Chip offered, twitching her whiskers.

"I don't know if she'd fit, honey," said the cat I assumed to be Chip's mother as she handed off the last of the little bowls to a kitten.

"I could dump the warm water over her!" Chip cried.

"It's-It's okay," I said. "Please. You've gone to enough trouble."

"Nonsense," said Chip, standing up on her hindlegs and puffing out her furry, white chest. "You have to look your best if you're headed to the fae village." She unsheathed the claws on one paw and started running it through my hair.

I opened my mouth as she tugged on the knots but didn't

dare let out a gasp. It was somewhat soothing, anyway, and I was sure I looked a mess.

The little kittens were a twitter at Chip's declaration.

"Those are my siblings," she said. "Another litter—I'm the only one who made it from mine." Chip tugged on an especially tough knot as she spoke. "Sully, Tea, and Bash. Short for 'Sullen,' 'Tease,' and 'Bashful.' Though if you ask me, they're all rather bashful."

"Are not!" said one of the kittens, standing straighter. He sounded like a little boy.

The other two kittens clung to his sides, belying his point.

"Hush, Tea," said their mother. "Finish your stew." She walked over toward me, slipping beside her husband, who draped a front leg around her back, rather like a human might with an arm.

Chip kept tugging on my hair with her claws. I grabbed a lock she'd already worked through to make sure it was still attached to my scalp and found it soft and smooth.

"Chipper caught us up to speed," said the father elf-cat. "The troll she found you with..." His voice lowered as he tossed a glance over his shoulder at the little kittens drinking their stew. "The minotaur and the fire."

"Did you leave the fae by accident?" the mother asked.

"No..." I admitted. Chip finished with one big, tugging yank and came around to my side. Surprisingly, like a cat, she took a seat on one of my thighs without asking. "I-I came here to get away from them."

The mother frowned. "Well, I'd say they will not help you, but if they're *looking* for you, perhaps they will."

"I don't need their help," I said quickly. I found myself

rubbing Chip's head and cheek with one finger, like I might have with a barn cat. She didn't protest, instead leaning into the pets and letting out a soft, rumbling purr. "I just need to speak to someone who's there—then I'll be on my way."

The father's maw downturned into a frown. "Your way where?"

I remembered what Chip had said, about her parents having seen humans.

"I'm looking for a human—two humans, really," I said. The older elf-cats exchanged a look, their eyes shining with nothing but the flicker of the fire behind them. "Have you seen them?" I asked, undaunted.

"It's been a long time since we've seen humans before you. A long time," said the mother. Her voice was twinged with sadness.

"That's—That's okay," I said. "You still may have seen the people I'm looking for. My parents."

Chip stopped purring and turned around to look at me, her little body sagging. "You lost your parents to the maze?"

The older elf-cats broke away from one another, each taking one side and headbutting me in an affectionate way.

"Humans do not tend to live long in this place," said the mother cat. "Can you not stay here, with us? Let us watch over you?"

"We can bring you back to the fae," said the father. "But that is only a good idea if you think they would want to take care of you. If they truly did cast you in here…"

"No, I… I think the Fae King would want to see me." I chewed my lip, focused on what they'd said, about how humans didn't last long. I'd always assumed my parents had died, for why else had they never returned to me, not even my father? But still... As long as I was destined to follow their fate, I would like to know. Their bones rested somewhere in this place, surely.

But it was something else in my words that had caught the elf-cats' attention. The parents both scrambled to my feet, the mother cat biting Chip by the scruff, and Chip putting up a little fight as her mother dragged her off my lap.

"The Fae King is after you?" the father cat asked. His bright orange eyes traveled up to my dress—my fine fae dress—and then over to the fire and his smaller children.

"Get off me, Mama!" Chip struggled until the mother cat let go of her skin. The younger elf-cat scrambled back up to my side. "She was sent to me for a reason!" The fact that little Chip thought I'd been sent to her instead of the other way around warmed my heart. If only I could offer her anything, like she had me. "I've vowed to help her and I will!"

"I don't want to cause you trouble," I said quickly. "More trouble, that is. But if it's the Fae King you're afraid of, you needn't be—"

The mother cat shook her head. "I wish we could help you more." She turned, and I followed her gaze. Beyond the tree on which I was leaning, there were several more trails of smoke, likely from fires. The path ahead was decorated with burrows and bits and pieces of things I'd have considered clutter, like broken wooden crates and threadbare woven baskets, as far as I could see. Chip had mentioned a colony. "But the others wouldn't let us keep you. Not if the Fae King himself is after you."

A long, lingering grunt echoed out into the silence. The

little kittens by the fire trembled and dropped their bowls, two of them hiding behind the other. The father cat ran over on four feet, walking around them in circles and rubbing them until they calmed.

The mother cat watched them. "And with the strange behavior of the minotaur, the timing of your arrival…"

I knew I couldn't tell her. It was me. I felt safe now, in this softer place, but I didn't know whether or not the creature would come here and put them all in danger.

"I understand. Thank you for the food." I handed Chip the little bowl and got to my feet. I swayed a little but caught the tree trunk for balance before reaching for my dress. It was damp, but it would not be too uncomfortable to wear.

"Mama." Chip skittered over to her and handed her the bowl. "Why don't I take her to see Lyra?"

The mother cat bit her lip as I slipped into the dress. When I struggled to tie the back of the bodice, Chip scurried up the tree trunk, landed on a nearby branch, and took the vine ties into her little paws with finesse.

"Who's Lyra?" I asked her.

"The wisest creature in all the maze—though don't tell a fae that." Chip finished tying the bodice—without tugging too tightly—and spat.

"Chipper, that's farther than you've ever gone on your own," her mother said.

"Good!" Chip put her front paws on her hips. "It's about time I go on an adventure. And I won't be alone." She gave me a onceover. "She may not be much of a fighter, but she's big, and she got this far. She can intimidate any trouble we encounter, surely."

I opened my mouth and shut it, remembering the trolls who'd teased Gob and how one had managed to knock the branch from my hands.

"I... I'd appreciate any help," I said. "And any information you have about the humans."

The mother cat sighed and sat down, sending one quick glance to her husband and other children around the fire. He was gesturing with his front paws, his face transforming wildly from scary to happy to sad as he told them a story, likely as a distraction. They lapped it up, clutching one another, their faces echoing their father's.

The mother cat turned around, the striped fur at her forehead drawing together as she sent Chip a stern look. "Just as far as Lyra's, you hear me? Then you leave her there and come back to us."

"*Yes!*" Chip did a little dance on the bough, then scrambled down the trunk, running toward the fire. "Tea! Sully! Bash! Wait until you hear!" She darted around the three kittens, letting out a wild, exhilarated cry.

"Take care of my girl," the mother cat said.

"Of course..." I replied. "But I have a feeling she'll be taking care of me."

"Yes, she does have a big heart." She looked back at the fire, a gleam in her eyes. Then she turned back to me. "You wanted to know about the humans?" She cocked her head. "It's been so long, but... I remember. A woman with hair like fire, and marks across her face."

"My mother." The words left my lips in a form of reverence.

"She danced," said the mother cat. "She danced and the creature howled, like he does now." She chewed her thin lip, though the minotaur had gone silent. "And there was a human man with her," she said softly. "I don't remember what he looked like. My eyes were drawn to her."

"That had to be my father," I said. My heart was thumping, a sense of warmth spreading throughout my body at the idea that they'd found one another.

"He tried to stop the dance," the mother cat said, turning to lock her eyes with my own. The large, orange irises were like fiery sunrises, the kind my aunt had spoken of as a sailor's nightmare. "So she took out a dagger and killed him."

CHAPTER
TWENTY-THREE
BRECC

"Who else is left at the castle?" Carac cried over his shoulder to Kaylein, the two running behind me as I made my way through the garden maze to the walls of the labyrinth proper.

Fire stung the air, smoke taking root in my throat. I blinked back watery tears and held a forearm to my lips but pressed forward.

"At least ten others," Kaylein said. "Anyone who didn't claim a spouse yet—and there are the humans themselves."

"Send the blasted humans back already!" I shouted, turning around to face them.

"But, Brecc—" started Kaylein.

Carac elbowed her and shook his head.

I pointed to the castle. "Get them out. Tell our people to meet us here. We're going back in."

Kaylein's eyes widened. "Back home, you mean?"

I didn't answer her, instead running through the rhododendron hedges toward the maze. Toward where Edony had left me.

Footfalls kicked up the gravel in the other direction.

"Your Majesty." Carac jogged forward, his eyes darting to his blade in my hand, which I still carried. That, or the severed minotaur hoof I clutched in the other fist.

The wall hadn't opened for me when I'd bidden it to right after it had swallowed up my Edony.

"We have to find her," I snapped.

"Her?" Carac asked. "Bre—Your Majesty, if the maze is on fire, we have to regroup in the village. Make sure it's protected, that the fire hasn't penetrated past the outer layers."

Kaylein pulled up beside me as I turned a corner around a hedge, the smoke and smell of burnt meat filling my nostrils. She clutched her skirt with both hands, lifting up the hem from the gravel as her legs moved rapidly to keep up. "There's the matter of the other creatures in the labyrinth, too. They may need to be evacuated—"

"Hang the other creatures," I spat. "They've lived hidden in the depths of this foul place long enough. They'll survive." I drew to a halt at the wall where I'd seen Edony last. The haze from the fire beyond the wall seeped up and over it, filling my lungs with crackling, burning heat. I coughed, my eyes still watering, but I had no spare hand with which to wipe away the tears.

Kaylein coughed behind me. "Some of those *other creatures* trade with us." Her voice was hoarse, her sentence peppered with hacking sounds.

With a mighty swing, I slashed Carac's sword against the stone wall. It clanged, the sound ringing out even over the crackle of fire, the dead flora in the outer layers of the labyrinth like tinder to the flame. "You'll have to do without whatever useless thing they traded you." I slashed again. Carac winced beside me at the flicker of silver light as metal touched stone. "Assuming they can't save themselves."

I swung another time. The sword ricocheted off the stone, the hilt slipping from my fingers.

Letting out a growl as the metal thudded to the gravel below, I slashed at the wall with the minotaur hoof as Carac darted down beside me, letting out a volley of his own coughs. He stood with his sword, slipping it back into its sheath as I hacked and slashed at the maze again. The hoof made a soft thud against the wall, hardly audible over the crackle of the fire.

"Open!" I screamed at it.

"Your intent..." Kaylein swallowed. "It should respond to your intent."

I swirled on her. "You think I don't know that?"

Carac stepped up beside her, his hand on his hilt. What he waited to withdraw the sword for, I couldn't say.

He, like all of my guards, wouldn't be ready for the fight I knew awaited them.

If I got my way.

As king of this entire kingdom for however long it lasted, I intended to get my way.

Carac and Kaylein looked at one another, and my body tensed at the unspoken conversation between them.

How dare they look at me with those pitying eyes.

"You're thinking that you want to look for her, aren't you?" Carac said.

There was no need to elaborate on whom.

He shifted to Kaylein. "His pick... was no longer eligible to be a bride."

She gasped. Her eyes had the audacity to dart around, her breath growing heavy with the thick, smoky air.

I was ready to shout at her, for looking at me like that. With horror.

I was their king. I thought I'd been their friend. But they cared nothing for me.

"I want," I said, turning back to slice the wall with the tip of the scissor claw hoof, "to slay the beast."

"If even your lord grandfather could not—" started Carac.

Kaylein put a hand on his arm. "Do as he says. Summon the rest of our people," she said, almost too quietly to be heard over the crackle of the fire and the thump of the hoof against the stone wall. "Make sure the humans leave, and gather our own here."

Carac spared one last glance at me in my attempt to tear my way through solid stone and took off, his feet disrupting the gravel path.

I stopped to take shallow breaths, the air heavy in my lungs with every harried, heaving breath.

Kaylein put a hand on my shoulder.

My pulse quickened, and I turned to her.

Then my tense muscles softened, just a little, to see her eyebrows draw together as she locked her gaze with mine. "The maze... It wants to live."

My eyelids fluttered quickly. "The maze is but a tool—"

She shook her head and held her hand out over the stone wall. "Take us home," she said. She could have thought it and it would have worked just as well, but she wanted me to hear. To feel it.

The moment the stones warped and stretched, shifting aside as if retreating into a hidden space.

Though the smoke withdrew into the air on either side of the opening, the way before us was dappled in a warm, orange glow, the last of the evening sunlight. The path straight to the heart of the maze was quiet, peaceful, the trees swaying in a slight breeze, undisturbed by the dying gasps of the dead plant life we should have had to pass through along the maze's edge.

"I can't go back," I said. The husky whisper of my tone surprised even me. "Not until I'm sure she's safe."

Kaylein's hand fell from my shoulder, and she took the minotaur's cloven hoof from my surprisingly feeble fingers.

"Trust in the maze," she said. "It will keep us safe—her, too, if she's precious enough to change you like this."

"I'm not..." I started, but my lungs filled with the sweet, clear air of home. The smoke and darkness blotting out the sky on either side of us couldn't reach the sunlit path before us.

I'd wanted to go there. Home was the only place there might be answers. Answers to defeating the beast.

I spared Kaylein a glance, focusing on the rotting flesh in her delicate brown hand.

As if in answer to my hesitance, a drop of water splashed on my cheek. I looked up as the rain began to pelt my face, forcing my eyes closed.

The cool water was like a balm on my boiling flesh.

"Home," I said, blinking through the rain and locking eyes with Kaylein. "Bring them all home."

She nodded, and I stepped through the path she'd created,

the sizzle of extinguishing flames echoing in my ears, even as I took my first steps through the dry, lush conduit home.

The king's quarters in the fae village were not so opulent as the rooms in the castle in which we held the fete. That place was a façade, an exaggeration necessary to impress the humans come to celebrate the ties that bound them to us once a year.

Ages long before my grandfather had used the magic of the land to grow the labyrinth, we had lived here, away from prying human eyes. And it was here that we'd returned to, swaddled like children, complacent enough to allow that beast free rein all around us for centuries.

Four trees grew like pillars in the corners of my room, some of their boughs hanging overhead, the rest growing outside of these four wooden walls. Stone was the soul of the labyrinth. There was not much of it to be found within the fae village proper, ancient home of our people, somehow both natural and orderly.

Right now, though, my quarters were chaos, every book, every scroll, every tapestry handed down to me through the generations splayed out amidst the furniture.

The bed, often unused, might have been cradling the delicate, soft body of my beauty this night had things gone as planned.

Could it really have been just this morning that I'd held her so close, her flesh against my own?

"Brecc. Oh!" A familiar, deep voice laced with humor

echoed out from behind me. A book I'd just tossed over my shoulder clattered to the floor.

I turned around, two other books held in each of my hands.

Favian smirked from the doorway, his hands clasped behind his back, one long lock of his ivory hair out of place, perhaps from the quick dodge he'd had to endure to avoid the book now by his feet hitting him in the head.

"Carac and Kaylein warned me you were in ill humor, but…" One of Favian's brows arched as he took in the mess, lit only by the flickering flame of a tallow candle at the table beside me. "They did not warn me you had taken to rearranging your quarters."

I stared down at the book in one hand. A collection of poems, written by bards from my father's and grandfather's times as rulers. Borin's mocking song about the end of the maze if I chose my bride wrong echoed foully in my mind. I threw both books on the bed.

"Are the others all back from the castle?" I snapped.

"Yes." Favian took a few steps closer, examining the room. Though he never lost his poise, he glided with smooth steps around the mess on the mossy dirt that formed the floor at our feet. "Fete is well and truly cancelled, the last of the Westbridge humans escorted home. The guards who took them were the last to arrive back, just in time for the moon's highest ascent."

"And the fire?"

"Extinguished. So far as the guards could tell. The smoke died out, the path forward cooled. The only remains of the disaster were the ash of the flora and the lingering, charred scent."

My heart thundered for a moment at the prospect of the charred minotaur. "And the beast?"

"Howling. Agitated, clearly, as any creature, intelligent or base, might be at the loss of their environs." Favian tossed back a section of his hair, smoothing out the anomaly. "Carac thinks to send a scouting party, to see the extent of the damage. But all signs thus far point to the blaze being confined to the outer layer. Nothing to lose there other than detritus to begin with."

A tightness in my chest pulled my thoughts away from Edony. Kaylein's words. "And the others? The creatures?"

His chin tilted just slightly, Favian traced a hand over the book of bards' lyrics I'd so recently tossed from the shelf wedged between two of the tree trunks. "I did not know you cared."

"I am their king." My words were harsh, but Favian didn't flinch.

He took the book and clutched it to his side. "Of course. But your interactions with them have been limited, to say the least—"

"Answer my question or leave me be." I tossed a hand in his direction, turning back to the shelf and flipping through the three remaining books there. They were all on frivolous topics —the preparing of food found in the forest, the history of humanity—what did I care about such things?

Grunting, I pushed the last few books aside and clutched the shelf with both hands, staring downward.

"You are... changed," said Favian. "To think, when I saw you last, you were in such great spirits—"

"That was before," I barked, turning around to face him. "Before I lost everything." My lips pinched into a thin line as I took in my closest friend. He looked bright, as a fae who'd found a human spouse might, his posture impeccable, his pointed ears on display with his long hair pulled behind them. He held the book to his chest as if for wont of something to do, but his murky eyes searched mine, as if looking for a lost soul.

How accurate.

We'd been born around the same time. Had grown as close as brothers. And now, to learn of what he'd done years back, to my beauty's mother...

No. I'd *known* of what he'd done. I hadn't known the details—hadn't *cared* to ask them—but I'd known he'd been rejected, had slashed a human woman's face, as I'd agreed had been his right.

I hadn't thought more on it until.... Until today.

I didn't deserve happiness.

But I craved it.

And I would not be denied it.

"Your bride has settled in?" I asked, clearing my throat to keep the darker urges at bay.

"She has." Favian's lip curled into a smile. "And to think, if I hadn't been rejected, I might not have met her! She is so much greater. So much more refined. And her beauty..." He let out a little gasp. "I could tell even with the masks between us, but even my wildest imaginings could not have put such soft, contoured exquisiteness to her face."

My stomach sunk with the reminder of his rejection. Of what it had done to Edony—how it could have been responsible for the danger she was in now.

Whereas my good friend's face softened, his pale flesh flushed with the thought of the happy love he'd managed to secure for himself, I felt my skin roar with fire, my gut churn with the desire to rip it all away from him.

"Bring her to me," I said, for if I did not know where to look in here, there was still whatever the sister-like cousin of the woman I loved could tell me. Perhaps some clue to my beauty's parents' fate would lead me to where she'd be headed out there in the labyrinth.

"Pardon?" Favian cocked his head. "To-To Neela? She's sleeping, Brecc. It's been a long day, with a spectacular end after our union"—he whimpered with mirth, his expression particularly, *annoyingly* bemused—"and humans do need their rest, so—"

I brushed past him. "Then I'll go to her. And delay the search of the maze to determine the extent of the damage. I'm going with them."

"But, Brecc! You can't! The king never—"

I whirled on him, already out in the hallway of the long, twisted warren that housed those closest to me. "So you remember that I am *your king*. Do not presume to address me by my given name."

The lump at Favian's throat bobbed, his eyes darting about. "But you—"

"Your bride," I snapped. "Bring me to her or so help me, I'll have her dragged out of bed kicking and screaming so the two of you can bow before me in the dirt and moss."

I didn't wait for his reaction, sweeping out and down the darkened hall I knew would lead to the quarters of the closest fae I had to a brother.

To the treacherous, callous fae whose actions had led to this heinous, hideous day.

TWENTY-FOUR

EDONY

Too large for the home Chip and her family had made for themselves in a hollowed-out log that ended in a tipped-over crate, I curled up at the side of the log, a series of four small blankets over my side and a pile of straw the elf-cats used for a mattress under my head.

No other elf-cats had come to see—Chip's mother explained that they all shared a distrust of humans, though they'd seen so few... and now I understood why.

If any of them had seen my mother stab my father with a dagger...

It was a wonder Chip's family welcomed me so readily.

"What were you thinking?" I whispered into the darkness. Chip's father had told me it was night, but I wondered how they knew in this forever moon-speckled part of the maze. My mother was not there beyond the trees to answer me.

I could just make out the stone of the nearest wall, beyond

a layer of trees, reminding me that even this small, quiet, cozy corner was tucked away in the endless labyrinth.

Could I do what they had done, carve out a small place for myself? But these creatures lived as a community, foraging, hunting... I couldn't stay. I had no one who would welcome me for long.

Whoever this Lyra was might have answers for me. And then, once I'd satisfied myself, I could let the monster find me. Perhaps a quick death, terrifying though it may be, would be easier than dying of starvation and dehydration and withering away.

My mother's bones were out there.

I might not have wanted to forgive her, but part of me understood it hadn't been her fault. The maze had driven her mad, led her to take some kind of dagger she'd procured and...

I sat up with a startle. Where had she stabbed my father? Were his bones there? If Chip's mother had witnessed it—

"Can't sleep?"

Chip's voice, quiet though still lyrical, echoed out of the edge of the hollowed-out log. She popped her head around the corner, her whiskers twitching.

"No," I said. "I suppose not." I ran both hands through my hair, the sensation of tugging on my scalp like a sting to remind myself to wake up. To not let the quiet comfort of this place lure me into a false sense of hope.

"We'll be leaving soon," she said softly, coming to rub her cheek against my side. Immediately, the tension in my muscles drained as I scratched her head. "You must be anxious to be on your way."

"It's not that," I said. "I feel... happy here. For the first time since I entered this labyrinth. Thank you for that."

Chip frowned, her whiskers drooping as she settled on my lap and looked up at me. "Well, if you wanted to stay, I wish you could—"

"I understand." I looked over my shoulder. The other burrows and little homes were no longer flicking with light, the entire colony likely gone to bed. They must have come together to decide night and day in this place.

"How did you bring me back here?" I asked. "After I passed out? Surely, you're too small to drag me such a long way."

Chip stood up like a human and patted her chest. "Oh, I'm plenty strong." She slunk back down, her maw twisting up a little sheepishly. "But you're right. You may be just a tad too big for me."

"A *tad?*"

She chuckled. "I found you not too far away. And well, every elf-cat hates a troll. So when I told everyone you'd been poisoned, half the colony agreed to help. Papa and Mama and other adventurers, they each took a part of you on their backs and carried you away."

"The other elves saw me?" My jaw hung down just slightly.

"Yeah. I know they haven't been too welcoming since." Chip rubbed the back of her hand with the pads on one paw. "But they all helped make you the lotion!" She pointed to the faded scars on my forearm from Gob's cruel bite. "Got rid of the poison in your system, that did. 'The right bit of salve sucks out all the venom.'" She nodded sagely. "We learned that from Lyra."

"Well, thank you. Again. For everything. And please tell

everyone else that, too. I don't mind that they hid away after helping me—that makes it all the more amazing they helped me at all."

Chip's expression softened as she sat back down on four paws. "You're real nice. Especially for a human."

Cringing, I thought of how my mother must have formed the elf-cats' opinions of humanity.

"We're not all..." I stopped. How much did she know?

Almost as if reading my mind, she shrugged as she curled up and settled on my thigh. "Mama and Papa don't tell me much about them. But they do tell me to stay away from them."

I pet her little, furry forehead. "And what did you do instead?"

She lifted her chin, sniffing the air. "You don't count. You're my destiny. Hmm..."

"What?"

"Smells like rain's about to come."

"Rain?" I looked up, but I could see nothing of the sky beyond the tree boughs. "How can you—"

But the first few drops fell on my eyelids as I looked up. Chip jumped and snuggled under one of the blankets her family had spared for me, just as the rain fell down in sheets in the clear spaces around us.

The rain caught on the leaves above, filtering down in lilting, hesitating trickles.

"Come on!" Chip shouted. She dragged the little blanket up toward the top of me, running up my chest and forcing me to lie back down. Tucking the blanket carefully around my head, she nestled up beside my cheek in the dark. "This is the best we have to offer you for shelter, I'm afraid."

"You can go back inside the log," I said. The blanket was getting wet now, a chill spreading throughout my body.

"And leave you alone? Never." She rubbed the top of her head against my own, letting out a purr.

Sighing, I pet her as I closed my eyes, drifting off.

"The maze must have wanted to put an end to the fire," Chip said softly. "'Ask the maze and it shall provide.' Another quote from Lyra."

Before I could ask more about this Lyra we were off to see in the morning, I found myself drifting asleep.

"Can you carry more water?" Chip's mother fussed at the satchel she and her husband had put together, packed with nuts and mushrooms and tubers and several small waterskins, too small to offer me more than a couple of gulps.

"If you have the skins to spare," I said. I was on my knees in the dirt beside her as she tied the satchel around and under my shoulders. The satchel, though generous for such small creatures, barely weighed more than a book to me.

"Remember Chip will have to bring it all back by herself," said Chip's father. He stoked the fire they'd built as soon as the rain had stopped from twigs they'd stored in their hallowed-log home. Chip and I had used it to warm up and dry our fur and clothes respectively, while Chip's father had cooked a porridge for breakfast for us all.

Now, full and dry, Chip played swords with two of her siblings, the little Bash sticking to the side and watching.

"*En garde*, foul beast!" Chip said, pointing a stick at Tea. "I shall save the Queen Bash!"

"Not until you beat Sully first!" Tea said, running behind his sister. Sully poked at the dirt with her stick, scuffing one paw as if kicking around the stones.

"You're slain!" Chip poked Sully in the leg, but Sully didn't flinch. Chip leaned over and whispered something to her.

Sully's eyes grew wide and then she lay back, letting out a dramatic moan.

Tea and Bash giggled as Chip started chasing Tea around the trees.

"Careful!" their father shouted. "No running so close to the fire!"

Chip's mother finished tying up the satchel. I checked over my shoulder. More of the colony was out and about, the candles burning brightly in their homes. A few looked over toward us, but no one approached.

"Chip told me how you all saved me," I said. "Will you thank everyone for me?"

Chip's father waved a paw at me. "Of course." He lowered his voice. "But you cannot stay much longer. We initially agreed to see you on your way as soon as you were well again. I imagine they're checking to make sure we're keeping our word."

"Good morning, Tepid!" Chip's mother cried, waving a paw at a rather large elf-cat making his way past their little home. The other cat mumbled something and narrowed one wide, orange eye at me as he passed on his way.

"I'm sorry to ask for one more thing when you've done so

much for me already," I said. "But I... I'd like to know where you saw the woman with fiery hair stab—"

Chip's mother put a paw over my mouth. "The children don't know," she said. "Not even Chip."

Chip's father licked the back of his paw and used it to wipe down the fur at the top of his head. "It's not something we like to talk much about—anything we did while on our adventures exploring the maze. From what little I do tell them, Chip's got her mind full of adventure already. Of course, we should have known at least one of our children would be like that. My name is Pluck."

"And mine is Brava," said Chip's mother.

"Short for 'Plucky' and 'Bravado,'" added Pluck.

"Though I wonder if we've done enough to make sure she realizes the *danger* of the maze..." Brava's voice grew soft, and Pluck gave her a hug.

I could just barely make out his whisper to her. "Our kittens rest easy, my love. The maze cares for them now."

Brava wiped a tear away with her furry forearm and turned to me. "Not to scare you, dear. You're so much bigger than us. And Lyra will help you. She always knows what to do."

"It's all right," I said. "I appreciate it. It's just... The man who... fell... was likely my father. I'd like to see where he may yet rest."

Chip's parents exchanged a look as a flurry of giggles rang out in the air and a series of shiny, orange eyes reflected out from the moonlit darkness beyond the fire. Chip raised Bash above her head, shouting, "The queen is mine!" Bash smiled broadly as she tittered.

"There's no one... at rest," said Pluck finally.

I turned back to them. "What do you mean?"

"The maze, it takes those who die to it." Brava nodded sagely. "Perhaps it's not the same for those of you who live outside of it, but those who *fall* here, inside the walls, they get absorbed rather quickly."

My pulse quickened. "You mean... I won't be able to find my parents' bodies? Say a prayer and lay them to rest?"

Pluck shook his head. "I'm afraid not."

I let out a deep breath. But besides seeing Neela and laying my eyes once more on my Brecc, the only other thing I'd hoped for would have been to find my parents' bones in this place.

Even that sliver of hope would have given me purpose.

"But if there's anything to learn about them, Lyra will know," Brava said quickly. "She gave the fire-haired woman that dagger—and the place where it happened, well, it was there. At Lyra's cabin. In the moonlit garden outside her front door."

Lyra had given my mother the dagger? But why? And why hadn't she stopped her when my father had appeared?

A grunt and a snort shot through the air, and my heart thundered, but I should have known straight away the sound had been too light and high-pitched for it to be the real creature.

Chip scraped her two back paws against the dirt, her nostrils flaring as she waved one front paw in the air, the other bent slightly at her side. "I'm going to get you!"

The three kittens squealed and ran toward their mother.

"Enough, Chip!" she said, patting Tea's and Sully's backs. "Don't scare them!"

Pluck sighed, his eyes glistening as he stared at his eldest daughter beside the fire. Chip rubbed at the back of her head, her "Sorry!" only just louder than the crackle of flame beside her.

"She's too naïve," Pluck said to me. He turned his wide, orange eyes on me. "Promise me you won't let Lyra convince her she has a greater destiny."

I opened my mouth to answer. The way he'd spoken, it was as if he'd already known what this wise woman would say to the little energetic elf-cat when we met her.

"I... I'll do my best," I said.

Considering what I now knew about this woman on whom all my hopes now rested, I *would* try my best to keep Chip from getting entangled in any business the woman would have with me. And my best, well... Judging by the slew of messes I'd gotten myself into during my short time in the maze thus far, my best wasn't much. But it would have to be good enough.

CHAPTER

TWENTY-FIVE

BRECC

I tore open the door leading to Favian's rooms, ignoring my simpering friend's protestations. The room was dark, though morning rays were beginning to trickle through the shutters, which were cracked open, letting in a soft breeze. This deep into the labyrinth, none of the smoke from the fire lingered, the air sickeningly sweet on my lungs.

Like rhododendron petals. Unless that was all just a memory, the thoughts of my beauty swarming in my head.

No. There was a familiar, sweet scent. On Favian's bed, a woman lay beneath his covers, her soft, steady breaths breaking into the quiet.

Favian flew between me and the bed, spreading his arms wide, the book he'd purloined from my mess for reasons unknown still held tightly in one hand. "Brecc, have you gone mad?" His nostrils flared as the form behind him rustled.

"Favian...?" The voice was soft, a slight croak to it.

I flinched at my own intrusion for a moment, but then I

clenched my fist at my side. "Make yourself presentable. I'll wait in the hallway. But then you're speaking to me."

Favian's continued protests did not penetrate the fog in my mind as I stepped out and slammed the door behind me. The soft mumbles of conversation were impossible to hear over the thudding of my bare feet on the dirt floor, the roar of my heartbeat.

After what felt like forever, the door opened again, the dim rays of dawn joined with the warm glow of several candles illuminating the room.

"Enter," said Favian, his voice clipped. He no longer held the book he'd taken.

I stormed inside, brushing past him.

"You would do well to remember I'm your king," I sputtered. I didn't like his tone.

The human woman's dark brown eyes widened, and she took hold of the skirt of the green leather elven dress Favian had no doubt gifted her. It had been crafted by Kaylein, I could tell just at a glance. Favian's bride curtseyed. Her dark hair was thick and wild, perhaps more so than her cousin's. But there was something about it that reminded me of my beauty.

I bit my tongue and turned to look at the ground. I would have no treacherous thoughts in my mind about how other women reminded me of she who could not be matched.

"Yes, *my king*. As you are so quick to remind me since your return." Favian shuffled up beside his wife. I dared to look up and found spots growing in my vision at the picture of the two of them side by side. Favian's lips were in a grim line as he wrapped one arm around his bride. "But I would have thought our long history as friends carried more weight than any... *formality.*"

A sharp pain picked at the back of my throat, but I dug my fingernails into my palms and got straight to the point.

"Your cousin," I said, looking at the human. There was only the faintest echo of her on this woman's soft brown complexion, my beauty also taller and less willowy than this younger woman, but there was still something there. Something that tugged at my heart and loosened my tight fists.

She didn't say a word, didn't respond at all, instead looking to her fae husband.

"He speaks to you, darling," he said.

Her eyes fluttered, her cheeks darkening as she turned back to me, quickly performing another curtsey. "Excuse me, Your Majesty, I didn't realize. My... My cousin?"

"Edony." I started pacing again. "Tell me everything about her."

Out of the corner of my eye, I saw the blissful newlywed exchange a look with her husband, the fae she hardly knew but who took her hand and squeezed it. Offering her comfort. Strength. In the face of her king.

"I don't understand." She swallowed visibly. "I... I left without saying goodbye to her. She was my chaperone. Is she all right? Has she done something? I know she danced with Favian at the fete, but—"

I struck a hand through the air. "She's not in trouble. Not with me." I stopped, boring my gaze into hers. "But she is in danger."

The woman—Neela, I remembered—stumbled backward. "What's... What's happened? Is Grandmother well?"

"I couldn't say. But your cousin never returned home, so this has nothing to do with your other family." I took a deep breath, steeling myself, as if *I* needed the nerve to tell this floundering child a thing. "I asked your cousin to be my bride."

Neela gasped, her free hand flying to her mouth. Her other hand was still clutched aggravatingly in Favian's. "But she's-she's not eligible, Your Majesty!"

I rounded on her. "Do you think I don't know that now?"

She shirked backward, into Favian's arms. I was driving the lovers closer together.

"I apologize," she said softly as Favian rubbed a hand down her hair. "I just... don't understand..."

"I am aware of what choosing a woman who is twenty-five means for this maze. For us all. And Edony is aware, too. That is why she ran from me. Into the labyrinth."

"Like her mother." Neela's voice shook as she stumbled in Favian's grip. Over her head, Favian looked at me curiously.

I locked eyes with him. "Only she was not scarred by the minotaur's hoof. She chose to go willingly. Because she loves me, too." I swallowed. "And she could not bear to just tell me *no* and go home. She ran where she thought I could never find her."

Favian chewed his bottom lip and turned away, patting his wife's back as she attempted to gain her strength to stand on her own two feet. But I knew. He was focused over her head, looking away from the both of us. He had realized it was *he* who had sent his beloved's aunt into the labyrinth. No other fae had been rejected in decades.

"I have to go find her," Neela said.

That got Favian's attention. "No. You cannot."

She slipped out of his grip, tapping his chest gently. "I understand you'll worry about me. But we can go together."

Favian's brow wrinkled.

It was I who spoke for him. "You cannot go," I said. "No human may leave our village. And if it *were* possible, I assume Favian would not dare see you put in danger."

"I... cannot leave?" Neela asked. "Not ever?" She sat down on the foot of the bed, her head tilted slightly. "I knew the spouses never came home, not even for a visit, but I thought... perhaps they were free to stretch their legs elsewhere."

"Where? In the labyrinth?" Favian clicked his tongue. "It's not safe there. Nowhere but the fae village is safe amidst the twists and turns of the walls. Amidst that *monster*." He slid in beside her, cupping her elbow.

"Then all the reason you must go, my love!" Neela's jaw dropped. "If my cousin is out there—"

Favian shook his head, then turned to me. "She is lost. Forget her."

I wasn't sure which of us he spoke to more, but his eyes were on mine.

My voice deepened, my feet grinding into the mossy floor. "Never."

Favian jumped to his feet. "She's lost, Brecc! She's probably dead already! Give up or—"

"Silence that treacherous tongue!" I said. Neela whimpered in the quiet that rolled over the room between us, clutching at the bedspread as her gaze pinned on her feet.

"Brecc," said Favian, taking a step closer and irritating me to no end with the continued casual use of my name, "on the very small chance the woman lives, you will doom us all should you pursue her. Let her go.”

“Can-Can she not be found and brought back home?” Neela asked, her voice shaky. “To our grandmother?”

The way she looked up at her husband, her expression curiously blank, it was as if steeling herself for him to crash all of her hopes.

“She *will* be mine,” I said at the same time Favian turned to her and said, “No.”

His sharp, single word was enough to suck the stiffness out of Neela’s limbs. She looked down again.

But *I* would not be cowed.

I would not walk away from this encounter subdued into submission. Particularly not by him.

And he would feel a fraction of my pain—every ounce of it deserved.

“The last woman sent to the labyrinth—*compelled* there by the minotaur’s magic, slashed across the face by a fae who would not stand for her offense—lived many years.”

“That’s true,” Neela said. “She even gave birth to my cousin after being so cruelly treated.”

Favian flinched, his words measured. “It is a fae’s right to sentence a human who rejected them to—” He cut his own words short.

Neela had swirled on him, her chin high, her nostrils flaring.

“You’re speaking of my aunt!”

“Who died before you were born, by the sound of it!” Favian crossed his arms stiffly.

"And you think *that* matters?" Neela leaned back as if his verbal sling had actually stung her. "My cousin lost both her parents to that fae's actions. I may not have known them, but I know *her*, and she's like a sister to me. Whoever carved those slashes across my aunt's face carved a deep and cutting gash across my dearest's heart." Her eyes watering, she wiped leaking tears away. "Oh, I can't believe I came here! I should have... I should have blended in with the crowd. I shouldn't have drawn your attention. My mother and father expected me to join them sailing the seas, and Grandmother will be alone now, and Edony... Edony..."

"What can you tell me of Edony?" I said as Favian swept in beside his wife. A misbegotten thrill soared through me as Neela drew away from his offered embrace, putting more space between the two of them and crossing her arms tightly.

"If she's... in the labyrinth," Neela said. "All I could guess is she wants to find her parents while she's there."

Of course. I had guessed as much. Did I also picture her running wildly, aimlessly, wherever she could go to get away from me? Perhaps. But as long as she was there, as long as she had resigned herself to this dark fate she didn't deserve... Of course she'd want to know.

"They're dead," Favian said stiffly. "They have to be."

Neela turned pointedly away from him.

"And the dead become a part of the labyrinth," I said. "There may be... *traces* of them. Somewhere. Perhaps they..." Could I dare hope?

"What?" Neela asked, her posture softening. Then she jumped a little in place. "Your Majesty," she added quickly.

I'd be a king to these people yet.

"Perhaps they're watching over her," I said. "I can only hope."

Neela bit her lip and nodded, her gaze downward.

Silence descended amongst us as the room grew brighter and brighter. It was a new day, but that wouldn't help Edony, out there in the eternal darkness.

"I'll accompany the search party," I said. "We'll assess the damage of the fire, see where she may have gone—"

"You'll find no evidence there," said Favian darkly. "The guards said the outer layers are nothing but ash and stone."

A sudden thought struck me. "Then we'll head for the wise woman!" My fingers snapped. "What was her name? The one the other creatures go to?"

"She's daft," said Favian, waving a hand at me. "Delusional."

"She speaks to the maze, they say," I said. "The trolls all swear to it."

"And the trolls are about as intelligent as she is." Favian couldn't see the way his bride turned on him at those words, her eyes narrowing. His insult of trolls had disturbed her? Perhaps it was a step too far after all his callousness toward her cousin.

"If she speaks to the maze, she may know something of Edony's parents," I said. "That'll give us a place to start."

"Oh, come on, Brecc! Part of the maze or not, they're *dead*. And the dead don't speak. You're chasing ghosts. Get a hold of yourself!" He stood, shaking his head.

He looked at me with a mixture of pity and... scorn. As if my actions *sickened* him. Well, he would know what that was like soon enough.

"Tell that to your wife," I said simply. "Tell her, then, how her aunt rejecting *your* offer of marriage led to *you* slashing the woman's face. Led to her *death* and that of your wife's uncle besides."

Neela covered her mouth with both hands, her eyes wild, darting.

Favian's eyes narrowed at me.

"Was it not *your right*, as you said?" I tossed back at him.

"No!" shouted Neela.

Favian softened and turned to her, but she smacked at his hands as they reached down to take hold of her.

"No! Don't touch me!" she screamed.

"Neela, darling—"

"Don't call me that!"

I turned on my heel, headed for Carac and whoever else was on duty. I had a plan now, a destination.

I had never spoken to the wise woman, didn't know if I could set stock in her answers, but the woman heard things at the very least. If Edony met *anyone* in the labyrinth who was willing to lift a finger for her, they would likely direct her there.

Besides, the maze... It spoke to me in some fashion.

I was a king, but who was to say it couldn't speak to this woman as well? Rumors were birthed in partial truths more often than not.

Neela's shouted insults grew only louder as I made my way down the hallway, putting distance between me and the mess I'd left behind. The remnants of Favian's happy marriage.

The human woman was trapped here, that much was true.

It was too late for her to escape—but she had the right to know the fae she'd married.

Besides, if the world would end with Edony at my side, she would not be stuck with him for long. And after the disrespect he'd shown me, Favian didn't deserve for the last few moments of his languid life to be filled with naught but joy and happiness.

Those would be reserved for my Edony. We'd find bliss again—and watch the world crumble together. Hand in hand.

TWENTY-SIX

EDONY

"Well, that's a dead end." Chip stood like a little human in front of the solid wall she'd revealed by brushing back the foliage of the thorny bush with a long, thin twig she'd kept with her even after finishing her games of pretend with her little siblings. In her other paw, she clutched a lantern, its candle lit and the light sweeping over the scene before her. She took a step back, looked at one lane of trees and then another, and then back again. "Mama always says keep your left hand to the wall." She swapped her lantern with her stick and dragged the stick along the bushes on her left side, scraping stone between the leaves, and I followed behind, the satchel full of food and waterskins and blankets making soft clanking sounds as we picked up speed again.

"My mother told me that, too."

Chip sent me a pitying look. "Your mama must have been

real smart. And brave. To remember that much, despite the minotaur's madness in her veins."

Was that what these creatures of the labyrinth called it?

And according to Brava, Chip didn't know the half of what the *madness* had done to my mother.

"Oh, there we go!" Chip's stick dipped deep into the bushes. I'd done something similar, just with my own arm, back in the outer layers of the maze. She let out a little battle cry and hacked and hacked at the bushes until the leaves mostly fell away.

I backed up to give the little elf-cat some space.

The bare branches revealed a small tunnel in the stone, no taller than my waist.

I never would have found such a path without Chip. Bending over, I tried to peer inside, but it was dark, even with the entrance lit up with Chip's light. "Are there many secret paths like this?" I thought of the log Gob had crawled through. My arm stung a bit with phantom pain at the memory of his betrayal. He'd been the first ally I'd thought I'd found in this dismal place.

"Oh, yeah, all sorts. The maze takes care of us who live here, who feed it." Chip looked from the tunnel up to me and back again. "Do you think you can fit, though...?"

I frowned. "I think so. I just need to crawl through." I started slipping out of the satchel as Chip went back to work hacking, making a clearer path for us to get inside the tunnel. "What do you mean when you say 'feed the maze'?"

"Well"—Chip let out a huff as she hacked—"Mama and Papa told you, right? When we die, the maze eats us?"

"They said those who die are absorbed..." A sudden vision

of Father slipping into the ground, swallowed up by dirt and stone and brambles flashed through my head.

"Absorbed, eaten, it's all the same." Chip put down her lantern and wiped her forearm—foreleg—across her fuzzy brow. She examined her work and nodded.

She looked up then, her wide, orange eyes a bit glossy with tears. "My brothers—my littermates... The maze ate them."

I swallowed. Brava and Pluck had hinted as much, but I hadn't wanted to ask them. "What happened? If... If you feel up to sharing."

Chip got on all fours, but not before tucking her stick through the satchel strapped across her own back. "They got curious," was all she said before snatching up the lantern handle in her mouth and taking little bouncy steps into the tunnel ahead.

I got on my own knees, shoving the satchel in front of me after Chip's retreating tail. The tip of her upturned tail scuffed along the top of the tunnel, stirring up little bits of dirt and dust that fell down between us.

Shoving the satchel in front of me, I slipped inside. My head scraped the top of the tunnel as Chip's tail had, knocking down a volley of dirt.

I coughed, blinking my eyes through the mist of filth.

Once it had cleared, I saw Chip ahead, turning around, the lantern still in her mouth. "Moo Mallight?" she asked through her occupied maw.

"Keep going!" I shouted, rolling my back downward and shoving my satchel ahead. "I'm coming."

It took a while—I couldn't be sure how long—but we made careful progress. Though I mostly crawled on my forearms, my cleaned dress now becoming hopelessly dirtied once more, I kept up a rhythm. Shoving the satchel forward, looking up to see Chip's lantern ahead. Looking down as I moved forward, closing my eyes against the volley of dirt that fell as my head inevitably scraped the stone above. Repeat and repeat and repeat. Eventually, Chip's lantern light grew still, set down on the ground, and her chipper voice carried down the length between us. "We're close!" she said. "Goodness me, the maze did provide!"

She spoke as if the maze were sentient, creating new pathways for those in need of a path ahead.

It *had* let me into the maze and shifted its rocks. I supposed perhaps it *was* sentient, and it had shown us mercy. Either because it felt sorry for me or because it felt it owed Chip. Either way, I was glad for her company.

"There you go!" Chip's voice was comfortingly close and she tugged on the satchel between us with her teeth, bringing it out of the tunnel and landing on her rear. I stretched my arm forward as far as it would go, squeezing my shoulders through the very edge of the tunnel.

Come on, Edony. Almost there.

Though my head scraped the stone more than ever, letting down a final volley of dirt from the top of the tunnel above, I got through, Chip doing a little dance of triumph as my torso sprang loose.

"You're far braver than I!" she said. "If I were squeezed through a tunnel like that..." She shuddered. Then, seeing me slowly taking first one and then the other leg out of the tunnel, my skirt getting caught on the tunnel's ceiling, she rushed forward to help, leaping at the puffy skirt with a battle cry and squishing it down so I could slide out.

"Thank you," I said as she landed on the side of one of my thighs.

"No problem." Her little cat-like maw broke into a grin. Then she leaped off and strut around on all fours, taking in the view around us.

I scrambled up to my knees, brushing my hair and dress off best I could.

We'd come out in what could only be described as a field of flowers. Somehow here, within the walls of this labyrinth, there was a seemingly endless field of rainbow blooms darkened with the filter of the sky's endless night. The moon—false or true, as I could not say what time it was here—hung heavily over the place, bathing it all in light.

"Where're the walls?" I asked. I spun around and found that even the tunnel we'd used to get here was covered now, a bush taller than I could see swung back over the opening.

I was tempted to push aside the branches and see if it was still there—the wall with the tunnel. But I needed to move forward, not back. Chip stood on two feet again and slipped her front paw through the lantern's handle. Leaning down over it, she blew out the flame. "Always enough light here," she explained, letting the lantern swing on her arm as she skipped ahead.

I picked up my satchel as I stood, sliding it back over my head and weaving my arms through.

We'd only been away from the elf colony for half a day at most—at least, that was how it felt, the hours speeding by, Chip

filling the quiet with chatter that seemed to keep any other creatures who might have lingered out here at bay. Here, there didn't
seem to be a place for any creature to call home, unless they
wove through the reeds and stems of the grass and the flowers.

As we reached the edge of the growth, Chip stepped right
through, pushing aside the flowers and stems in her path. They
were easily as tall as six of her, towering over even my head. At
least they caved easier to a simple push of the hand, Chip no
longer relying on the stick she kept tied in her satchel at her
back.

"Chip," I said as the elf-cat hummed, our destination
unclear to me, "how many creatures live in the labyrinth?"

"*Creatures*?" Chip stopped and turned back to me, wrinkling her nose.

"Um, well.... What should I call them?"

"Well, you're right. 'Creatures' is fine for most of them, in
my opinion. Trolls are cowards and smelly to boot. And ladydoves are mean, even if they're pretty. You can't always be
fooled by pretty." She looked me up and down and then kept
walking forward.

"I've never heard of ladydoves."

"Well, they like it that way." She whacked at another flower
stem with her paw. "Secretive lot. They only really come out for
the... the dullahans." She spoke that last word hushed, as if
scared someone might overhear her.

I looked around. There wasn't a sign of any other creature.
"What are those?" I hadn't heard tale of such things.

She shuddered. "Best not to speak of them." She whacked a
long reed ahead with rather too much gusto. "Eager and

Humble, they... They were rather fascinated with them. That's why..." She whacked at a reed again.

"And then there's the elves, of course, though too many people call us 'cats.' And there's all sorts of small creatures, like chipmunks and squirrels and owls and mice—they don't talk, so they're good for us carnivores." She tapped her belly with her free hand. "I mean, well, I feel a little bad about it, but an elf's gotta eat, and there's mostly only tubers and mushrooms growing in this place. Lyra grows more vegetables—the moonlight is good for plant growth here—but the cost to trade for them is mighty high. Trolls get most of them, and then they go and trade them to those wretched fae! As if they need them despite getting what they do from you humans, free of this place to grow what you need in the sun! Fae could grow their own crops, of course, but they're a lazy lot."

Lazy? I'd never heard a fae referred to as such. "What of the Fae King?" I asked. "Have you ever met him?"

She stopped and put one paw on her hip. "Why ask me that? Aren't *you* running from him?"

"Well, yes, but..."

"He fancies himself the king of us all, but what king never actually shows himself to most of his *creatures*? Not a king I'd follow, I'll tell you that. Did you know elves aren't even allowed in the fae village? They let those scaredy-tros come trade with them, but not elves? Pft." She took a swinging jump to kick the stem ahead of her, then paused. "Do you smell that?"

"What?" I sniffed the air. There was something faint. Like cooked meat, fragrant vegetables... and a thick, heavy smoke. I started choking.

Chip raced ahead, dropping her lantern to run on all fours. I bent down to grab the lantern for her, then ran onward, the reeds smacking like whips against my skin. "Chip!" I cried. "What is it?"

Somewhere far, far away, the minotaur let out another wretched howl. I turned around. But it was behind us, not where we were running toward.

"Stand down, you tro!"

Chip's voice echoed out as she burst through the edge of the field.

It took me a few long moments to catch up to her, the whack of her stick hitting against something hard with a *thunk*.

"Lay off!" screamed a shaky voice. A familiar, shaky, grumpy voice—Gob. "Lay off, I tell you!"

Chip roared, her high-pitched tone at odds with her fervor.

I burst through the last of the reeds and stems and coughed, my eyes watering.

There was a bonfire going, black smoke lifting into the air, falling back down to coat the area with a thick veil. Behind the fire, some distance away, was a cabin made of wood. An offshoot of flames was making its way toward the front door from the fire.

"Fiend!" Chip's whacking drew my attention. She smacked her weapon against a curled-up figure on the ground some distance away from the bonfire. "What have you done to Lyra?"

The fire was spreading, another offshoot headed toward my only friend in this place.

"Chip, watch out!" I ran toward her.

The door to the cabin burst open.

And someone threw a large basin full of water over our heads, the metal object clattering with a thud to the ground.

TWENTY-SEVEN

EDONY

The grass sizzled around me as I blinked through the drip of water falling from the hair at my forehead. Chip, I presumed, let out a groan before shaking her head so quickly, I could hear her skull rattling.

My vision cleared in time for me to see Gob scrambling to his feet, clutching his arm and glaring at the soaked Chip still shaking water off her fur. He shuffled over to a tall, lanky woman and hid behind her furry, brown leg.

She was, in only some ways, human-like. She stood up on two legs, like Chip often did, that ended in black hooves, but unlike Chip, her arms did resemble human arms, complete with brown, furry human hands. There were white spots throughout her coat, and the clavicle at her neck was also white, though she wore a long, baggy and tattered pale tan dress of some sort that cut off at her upper leg.

Her face was doe-like, complete with the short buddings of antlers between her soft, flexing deer ears. Female deer with antlers were rare, I remembered Father telling me once. Her eyes were huge, round, and dark, blinking slowly as they narrowed on me.

"Well, don't just stand there! Help us put the fire out!" Her voice shook a little, a deep alto with some gravitas woven through it. She was already waving her hands around, stepping forward lightly on black hooves and gesturing at the bonfire.

The other trail of fire was still spreading.

Chip engaged in one last shake, tossing her stick to the ground, and then scrambled up my wet skirt and to the satchel at my back.

"The waterskins!" she cried.

The doe woman was already picking up her large, metal washbasin, barking orders at Gob, whose steps were languid as he made his way over to help her, his eyes never leaving me— or Chip at my back.

I snapped back into the moment as a crackle of flame shot high into the air. Chip leaped off the satchel, a waterskin in her mouth as she raced toward the fire on all fours.

"I don't think that'll be enough," I said, scrambling to slide the satchel off my arms and digging for more waterskins. Half were already depleted. Still, Chip uncorked one and let it fly over the errant trail of fire, causing the flames to sizzle and snap.

I tossed the remaining waterskins on top of the satchel for Chip to work with and then scrambled over to the doe woman and Gob, taking hold of the slightly rusted basin in Gob's place so that the doe woman could move faster.

"Where's your water pump?" I asked.

She frowned, a distinct downturn of the lips on her snout. "No such thing here, human. There's a stream out back."

I grabbed the basin from her—it wasn't too heavy empty—and ran through the open door of the cabin. She'd come this way, after all. Sure enough, another door was wide open at the back, and I stepped around towering piles of baskets and crates cluttering the floor. Some were filled with vegetables, others with straw or dried reeds. Still more dried plants hung from the ceiling. I closed my eyes and let the vegetation whap across my face, darting around the baskets, a table, and some chairs to the open back door. Bright sunlight lit the way, the trickle of a steady stream only now just audible over the crackle of flames somewhere behind me.

I skidded to a stop at the bank of the stream, hardly pausing to take in the marvel of this small body of water snaking its way through the high reeds and flowers blooming on both sides, and dipped the basin under the flowing water. It was cold, my hands growing numb almost instantly.

I pulled up the basin, my arms straining now to find the weight increased at least a dozen-fold.

"Give it here." A coarse, deep voice sounded around my shoulder as Gob bent down to grab one of the handles of the basin.

He stood with it, the weight not seeming to bother him at all. I scrambled to raise the basin by the other handle, though I had to crouch to keep it all from tipping over onto Gob's head. Even so, a bit splashed on top of him and he grunted, but he led the way back through the cluttered house and to the front door, my back sore from walking quickly while hunched by the time we reached the line of flames.

"Now!" he shouted as we came to the flames.

We swung the basin between us, winding it up before showering the bulk of the wild fire with the water.

Chip just narrowly managed to scurry away in time, the doe woman scuffing her hoof along the dirt around the bonfire and dampening the last of the offshoot of the blaze.

We all stood there a moment as the smoke cleared, breathing hard, three of us dripping wet.

Then the quiet was gone, replaced by Chip's roar as she took a running start toward Gob. "You fiend!" Her fangs flashed in the crackle of bonfire light.

"Wait!" I found myself standing between the troll and the elf-cat, sweeping my large dress skirt out to hide the little green man from the closest thing I had to a friend in this place.

I rubbed my forearm, where the faint remnant of the scars from Gob's bite still were. I didn't know why I was protecting him.

But I just felt like Chip had it all wrong.

"Let me at him!" Chip shouted, coming around my dress. She hissed and snarled. I bent down and grabbed her by the scruff of the neck, just as Grandmother had done with barn cats who wouldn't stop rummaging round in our food stores. *"Just something to make them go limp and think twice about things,"* Grandmother had said. *"It won't hurt 'em. Their mamas do it to them, too."*

"Hey!" said Chip, still thrashing in the air. I lifted her up to eye level and she sulkily drooped down. "No fair," she mumbled. "You're too big."

The doe woman took a deep, heaving breath and shuffled

nearer on soft, quiet feet. "But she's right to hold you back, child. Why are you attacking my guest?"

Gob timidly peeked around the fluff of my dress. The blue skirt was cleaner than I'd expected. The water had washed much of the dirt from the tunnel off.

"'Guest'?" Chip crossed her front legs. "I thought *he* caused the fire."

The doe woman fluffed a human-like hand in the air, examining the bonfire. "It was a cooking accident, nothing more."

Chip looked from the doe woman to Gob to me and then nodded. "All right," she said, but then she glared down at Gob. "But don't try anything. I've got an eye on you."

I set her down gently on her back paws.

"A 'sorry' might be called for," mumbled Gob. He'd never been so demure around me.

"*What was that?*" Chip leaned around my dress skirt, the claws on one paw slowly withdrawing.

Gob let out an *eep* and flipped up the back of my skirt, disappearing beneath its folds.

It was my turn to let out a startled yelp, but Gob quickly popped out from the front of the skirt and ran behind the doe woman, clinging to her toned calf.

"*Enough!*" said the doe woman, slicing her hand through the air. She glowered down at Chip, who pulled in her claws and stood sheepishly at my side. "Haven't you come to ask me something?" The doe woman's eyes darted up to me. She studied me, but she didn't seem surprised to see me at all. Perhaps everyone who came here came to ask her something.

"Why is *he* here?" snapped Chip, but she went quiet again as the woman's large, doe eyes rounded on her.

I decided to speak. "Chip was kind enough to guide me here when I was lost." I couldn't help but notice the way Gob's eyes fell to the dirt at his feet. "Are you... Lyra?"

"I am." Lyra's doe head bobbed. "And you..." She narrowed her eyes. "Are human. Not fae."

I went to brush back my sopping hair so she could see my rounded ears more clearly. But I found they were already exposed. "Yes. I figured my ears might give that away."

Lyra waved her hand again. "Then you haven't seen a fae depleted of their strength, I take it. The few who wind up lost in here usually don't manage to get help." She studied Chip, who puffed her fluffy, white chest out quite proudly. "But their human blood comes out. They lose the sharpness to their ears. And to their tongues, for that matter. Metaphorically speaking."

I tried to imagine Brecc with rounded ears. Just another human in the village, a strapping man whom I'd be free to marry, now that I was no longer eligible to be a fae's bride.

Lyra shuffled around the bonfire, picking up her basin and turning it over. Gob hesitated but walked over to the pot suspended over the flames, grabbing a wooden spoon from the ground, shaking it free of dirt, and stirring something in a pot. Sure enough, the doe woman had been cooking.

"You don't have the marks," Lyra said, so quietly as to almost not be heard.

My hand went shakily to my face in echo of the scars I remembered vividly across my mother's pale, freckled features.

Lyra stiffened and stared at me, the empty basin dangling from one hand at her side. "But you've seen them before."

I clutched the soft, torn fabric of my skirt with both hands.

"Chip's parents..." Chip looked curiously up at me at that. "Well, that is, I have reason to believe you may have seen my mother. Years ago. She was marked, and she came here. A human man followed her..." My mouth went dry. I couldn't finish my sentence, my heart squeezing painfully at my chest.

Gob stopped his stirring and stared at me. Had his mother really seen mine as well? Before or after she'd killed my father?

"Ah," said Lyra. "Give me a moment." She stepped inside her cabin without another word.

I shuffled closer to Gob as Chip went to gather the discarded waterskins strewn about the yard, being careful not to dip her paws in any of the charred grass. She kept a watchful, orange eye on me but didn't display any more of her aggression.

"Surprised you're still standing," Gob muttered as I neared, slowly turning the spoon through whatever stew was brewing.

I showed Gob my arm, the inflammation entirely gone, though a patch of darker skin around the puncture marks was still on display. "Why? Because of this? Or because you left me alone back there in the woods?"

He didn't answer, his mouth a thin line, staring pointedly down at the stew. It was a creamy color, and I wondered if somewhere here Lyra kept cows or goats or sheep. Then I wondered if it was weird for a deer woman to drink the milk of other beasts.

I shuddered. But this world was so unlike my own. I didn't know anything. I hadn't known my mother would grow so mad as to kill my father. I hadn't known fae could sometimes appear human. I sat down on the dirt beside Gob, my skirt spread widely over the edges of the charred grass.

"It was Chip," I said. "And she and her colony saved me. From your bite."

He grunted.

"She taught me there really could be kind creatures in this place." The lump at the back of my throat made it hurt to hold back the tears. "But you taught me to stay alert and never assume the best of a friendly face."

Gob's features softened. "I fed you, didn't I?"

I chuckled. "Were they poison, too?"

"No." Gob rubbed a finger under his nose as he kept stirring. "I never bit a human before. I thought maybe, on account of your size, and how long you were up and walking after that... Maybe it wouldn't affect you none."

"But you told me you tried to slow me down. Make me bait for the beast."

"And *you* told me the Fae King was after you, anyway, right? Better a quick death from the beast than a wrathful one from a fae royal, I say."

I pinched my mouth shut. I hadn't told him *why*, exactly, I was on the run. Did he really think so little of the fae? "That doesn't give you permission to poison me."

"Yeah, well, it's every creature for himself, isn't it? Out here?"

I looked over my shoulder to see Chip packing up the satchel again. "No. It isn't. That's just how *you* act."

"That's the troll way," said Gob, his back going stiff.

"And *you* told me you were no longer welcome among the trolls," I pointed out. "What do you care about the way trolls do things anymore?"

He blinked at that, his gaze growing glossy as he stared out into the fields beyond the bonfire. Maybe I'd given him something to think about.

"Jumping eggflies, you act all innocent, but you're harsher than you seem," he mumbled. Then, more quietly, he added, "Sorry."

"What was that?" I cupped my ear.

"I'm sorry, all right?" he snapped, louder this time. "Been regretting leaving you back there. You can ask Lyra. I told her I needed help finding someone. Or where the labyrinth might have eaten a fresh carcass."

"You were looking for me?" My voice grew softer. I wouldn't comment on the part where he'd assumed I might have been dead.

"Had to know for sure," he said simply. "Nothing else to do out here, is there?" He shrugged and kept stirring.

I still wasn't sure he deserved my trust. But Chip was due to go back home and it seemed like this Lyra never ventured beyond her field.

"Will you take me?" I asked again. "To the fae village?"

"You still want to go there?" He *tsked*.

"Curious." Lyra spoke from behind me and I turned around. She approached me, a cloth wrapped around something that dangled over the sides of both palms cupped together. "You seek the fae village? You're unlikely to find the other human woman there."

My chest tightened and I scrambled onto my knees. "You speak as if you know she lives."

Gob muttered something unintelligible and Lyra unwrapped the item in her hands. It was a dagger, and the fire gleamed off the silver, twisted blade. There were dull spots on the blade, too, brown and splattered.

And the hilt was strange. It was covered in coarse, dark fur that ended in a tuft. It resembled the tail of a bovine back home.

"I'd feel it if she had been claimed," Lyra said, turning the dagger back and forth. "The walls speak to me about those with deep connections to it." She stared over the dagger at me. "But it didn't know what to make of you. Not even when I asked."

She rolled up the dagger again and thrusted it toward me with both hands. I didn't know if I should take it. My skin grew cold at the nearness of it, and I broke out into a shiver.

"I gave this to the human marked by the minotaur," she said. "Bits of the creature, left behind after battle, have been woven into its magic. I told her it was her only chance at banishing the darkness that trailed her."

My tongue grew dry as I held out a shaking hand toward the wrapped bundle.

"But she killed my father with it instead," I whispered. Gob dropped the wooden spoon to the ground between us with a *thud*.

"If that was who that man was, then yes," Lyra told me. "Though the maze took him quickly. Too quickly for me to assess his wounds."

"Then he could still be...?" My throat closed up.

Lyra shook her head. "No. He's dead. The walls only take those beyond hope."

Hope. What a choice for a word. My feet grew unsteady. I'd

braced myself for their deaths, but still, to have hope and to have it continually ripped away…

Chip came up beside Lyra, her gaze darting between the wrapped dagger and me, a little paw to her mouth as her orange eyes glazed with tears.

"Her actions are proof her mind is too far gone to do what must be done." Lyra held the dagger closer to me, oblivious to the way it sent a shiver up my spine, practically demanding I take it from her. "So someone will have to do it for her."

My mouth fell open, my lips parted. I found myself reaching for the dagger.

TWENTY-EIGHT

EDONY

"Almost there." Chip reached back in through the window in Lyra's loft, as if her little paw could offer me any stability. I smiled at her and grabbed the open shutter for balance instead, then settled next to her on the thatch roof.

"You sure this will hold me?" I'd sat on my skirt, so it twisted a bit beneath me. I had to wriggle and fix it, tugging at the material.

I really shouldn't have been traversing the labyrinth in such an ornate dress. If I couldn't find anything else to wear, I could at least cut away the skirt to make it more manageable. But it had been gifted to me by Brecc...

"Lyra comes up here all the time. And she's taller than you." Chip stared out ahead, across the long bounty of flowers and reeds.

"But she probably weighs a lot less," I said, thinking of her lithe, deer-like body.

What *was* Lyra? It had seemed rude to ask. This place was full of wonder I'd never seen before setting foot inside of it. Danger, too, of course, and that monster breathing down my back.

But here, in Lyra's quiet cove, all of that bad stuff seemed so far away.

I ran a finger over the scars from Gob's bite, trying hard to forget the wrapped dagger I'd left on Lyra's table on the ground floor below us.

"Have you ever seen the maze from so high?" Chip asked. "It almost looks... beautiful."

I had. I'd seen it from even higher, from the safety of the castle's balcony.

I looked around now, spotted the castle far, far off to my left, farther than I'd imagined having gotten in this place. The rest of the maze was harder to see, Lyra's roof only reaching the very tip of the wall's great height. Still, there were dips and valleys, intermittent trees and small bursts of smoke off into the horizon. I searched around for a spot of light, for the fae village was said to have daylight, the sole location with such in this place. Either I couldn't see it... or maybe it truly was night.

Lyra had suggested we all spend the night in the safety of her cabin. It was rather cramped, so Chip and I were making do in the loft, Gob taking a chair by her fireplace down below.

Tomorrow, I would part ways with Chip and convince Gob to take me to the fae village. He owed me that much.

"What's that?" I asked. To my right, nearly as far back as I could see, jutting somewhere between where I knew Eastmeet and North's Glen would be—the waters to my right orientating me correctly—was some sort of spire. Tall, decrepit... It was hard to make out. Around it looked to be a wide patch of dull, pale sand.

"The Hall of the Obliterated," Chip said, a hint of wistfulness about her voice. "Never go there."

"Why not?" I studied my companion, noticed the droop in her ears, the slouch of her shoulders.

"Back when I was a kitten," she said, "Mama and Papa were still a little more adventurous than they are today. Not so much as they had been in their own youth, but they took us around the maze. To the safer places, mind you. Never to the outer edges, where the minotaur most loves to tread."

My gut wrenched, as I had a feeling I wouldn't like where this story was going.

"We were near the Hall of the Obliterated, surrounded by sand as far as one could see. Humble and Eager had never seen the likes of it. Me, neither. We frolicked and played in the cold, rough sand and Mama panicked, dragging us back one by one. Papa too." She scratched at the back of her neck. "Rather like someone *else* going around grabbing elves by their collars."

"Sorry," I said. "But I didn't want you to keep attacking Gob."

"I'd have taught him a good lesson, too." She sniffed. "And don't tell me he's Lyra's guest—he deserves a good fight for what he did to you. Too bad he couldn't offer me any challenge. I suppose even I have to admit that was hardly a fair fight." She chuckled.

I waited for her to continue her story, the chirp of crickets filling the quiet in the air.

"We saw the ladydoves there, flying overhead. Papa explained that the fallen tower was home to the dullahans, and the ladydoves were their companions." I had a hard time picturing what she meant. Were the doves as small as the ones I knew back home? And they were the companions of what... exactly?

"What are those?" I whispered.

"Headless knights," she said softly. "Fallen fae knights. The labyrinth likes to eat what dies in it, but the warrior fae... It makes them walk around in their armor, forever seeking to end the minotaur, forever unable to keep the beast at bay."

Gooseflesh shot out across my body, and I hugged my arms close. "That's horrible." A dark flash of Brecc in armor appeared in my mind's eye. There was a strike of lightning, then a headless version was staring back at me. "But why?"

"To discourage others from trying to fell the beast is my mama's guess." Chip shook her head. "The maze only exists so long as the minotaur does."

"Which seems to be forever," I pointed out.

"It's forever so long as we allow it to be." Gob's voice, soft and deep, rung out from the open window to my left.

Chip hissed, but I held out a hand to stop her as Gob stuck his head out between the shutters. He took a seat on the ledge and stared out over the maze, ignoring the elf-cat, whose fur was now all on edge.

"Since when does a scaredy-tro seek the fall of the labyrinth?" she spat. "Aren't you all too accustomed to shaking in your pointed boots to even imagine such a thing?"

"I've always wanted out of here." Gob shot a sheepish look my way. "To tell the truth, discovering what had happened to you wasn't my only aim in coming here. I thought maybe the wise woman could show me the way out."

"Of course he wasn't that concerned for you," said Chip. "Even if it *was* his fault you were in danger at all."

"That's not entirely true," I said. "I was the one who willingly came into this place, remember?"

My companions grew quiet.

"If you ask me, maybe those dullahans are key," said Gob, rubbing a finger under his nose and sniffling. "The beast fears them, don't he?"

Chip hissed and raised her hackles, arching her back. "You just try and ask them for a favor! You'll see! They and their companions killed my brothers, brave and courageous and true, so they'll end you before you even open your mouth!"

I swallowed and put a hand on Chip's arched back. She softened her stance, and I pet her gently until she snuffled and curled up into a ball like a small, helpless kitten. Waiting to see if she'd protest, I scooped her up and set her down on my lap, in the middle of my fanned-out dress. She started purring, letting me gently stroke her back.

"Well." Gob *tsked* and crossed his arms. "Didn't mean to bring up bad memories. And yeah, so you're right. I'd be terrified of them. But they're the only ones who'd ever put up a fight with the beast. And that's the only place the thing has never dared to tread."

I chewed my lip, something bothering me about what he'd said. "The minotaur can come even here?" I almost wouldn't have believed it. The creature had chased me in those outer layers of the maze, but the farther in I'd gone, the safer I'd felt. The softer the edges of the maze had been. It was hard to imagine the creature moving through here.

"Oh, yes," said Gob.

"He's been through the colony once before," Chip added, lifting up just her little head. "When I was little. Mama and Papa and the other adventurers chased him off, and he hasn't been back since. Doesn't mean he'll never be."

My breath hitched, my hand pausing in my gentle strokes of my feline companion. But if the colony wasn't safe from the creature... What if I'd led it there? What if it knew I'd been there and followed me?

"Well, I suppose it's never been to the fae village," said Gob. "Scared of fae, living or dead."

"Don't know why," muttered Chip. "Maybe they fought him centuries in the past, but they're layabouts these days."

"The beast remembers," said Gob.

Of course it did. It didn't strike me as a creature that gave up easily.

"But if... my mother is still alive, and the beast can travel just about anywhere here, how has she kept out of its reach for so long?" I gasped. Surely, she wasn't in the fae village. That would make no sense.

Gob blew out a breath. "Tell you the truth, when my ma saw the human woman with the fire hair and the gashes on her face—she was there."

"The fae village?" I asked. He had said his people traded with the fae.

He shook his head. "No. The Hall of the Obliterated. Well, at the edges of it, in the desert. Ma never would have gone so far through the sands to reach the spire."

My back stiffened, and Chip jumped up off my lap.

"Do you think... she's still there?" I asked.

Chip poked at my arm. "You can't go there, Edony. You can't."

"That's my best guess," said Gob at the same time. He quirked an eyebrow at me. "You know, if we went there together—you could check for your ma, I could see if those ghastly beasts might take up arms again. Bring down the walls, win-win for us both?"

Gob was asking *me* to go with him somewhere? After all his talk about not needing anyone's help?

Then again, I'd seen how even little Chip had cowed him into submission.

"After we sneak into the fae village," I said, extending a hand out toward him.

I'd warn Neela.... Maybe see Brecc. And then I would go. Whatever danger awaited me. I had to see my mother. Even if she'd killed my father. I knew she wasn't in her right mind.

Gob eyed the extended hand warily, his eyebrow quirked.

Chip ran over to my arm and jumped up on it, clutching to it with her front two paws, no claws extended. "You can't! It's too dangerous there."

I pet the top of her head with my other hand. "I appreciate your concern, Chip. I do. But I have to do this."

Chip slid down off my arm, her ears drooping. "But I have to go with you. You're here to take me on my big adventure."

"Of course you don't have to go with me. I promised your father I'd see you off back home, that I wouldn't let Lyra convince you to go anywhere dangerous."

Chip's ears perked up at that, and she stood like a human once more. "Papa said that? He thinks Lyra would tell me to go on an adventure?"

"And so I shall." Lyra's shaky voice carried out through the open window, her doe-like head peeking out above Gob. He stared up at the wise woman. "Chipper the Elf, the walls have spoken to me. Your destiny lies with this one." She stuck a thumb toward me. "And, if you'll have a big enough heart to accept it, this one, too." She tossed her thumb toward Gob below her. "Gobble the Troll. Edony the Human. Will you travel together to trap the minotaur once and for all?"

"Trap it?" I asked. Then I thought of all the discussion of how the maze wanted to live—and to live, it needed the minotaur alive, and me far from Brecc, that much was true.

"Aye." Lyra looked out over the maze, nodding softly. "It's scared. Something has shaken the labyrinth to its core. It realizes now that it has to give you something—and that something is the freedom from the beast. So long as the walls themselves never fall."

She stared at me, her giant doe-eye on the nearest half of her face unblinking.

The labyrinth had to give something to *me*?

But of course it did. My love for Brecc threatened its existence.

But if the minotaur was at least trapped forever, unable to wander around this place and terrorize these creatures...

That was something I could live with. If even fae knights had failed to slay the beast, what hope did I have?

"I accept," I said, nodding at Gob. "I'll go with you to the Hall of the Obliterated. But I just want to see my cousin one last time. In case..." I looked to Chip. "In case things don't go as we hope."

"I'm coming too." Chip flexed her paw, her claws coming

out as she stared out over the maze walls toward the decaying spire.

"You can't," I said, in echo of her own words.

"She can," said Lyra, sweeping her ratty dress outward as she spun on her hoof. "Her parents had adventures. They cannot deny her hers. So I suggest you all get some rest." She froze, her nose turning up, sniffing the air.

Something cold and thick wrapped around my insides.

Out in the distance, the minotaur yowled, its groaning almost full of sorrow.

"He comes," she said quietly.

I flinched. "The minotaur?"

Chip jumped up and held her front paws in front of her, as if she would claw the creature into submission. Gob trembled and disappeared back into the loft.

"No," said Lyra, sliding back inside. "The bringer of the maze's doom. The Fae King."

My breath hitched and tears rose unbidden to my eyes. Feeling dizzy, I stared out over the labyrinth, hoping to see him approach somehow.

Hoping to see him.

Despite knowing what the two of us together could do.

The end of the maze. The liberation of the minotaur.

The end of all life as we knew it.

"What was that?" Elspeth swung her bow with notched arrow upward, as if the heaving, bulking minotaur might descend upon us from the trees.

"Stay your hand," I barked. It was impossible for the beast to climb the towering, wispy willows above us. But my Edony... Well, I didn't know if she had the strength to climb a tree, the patience with which to lie in wait atop a thin branch. But I imagined she could. I would not risk an errant arrow flying wherever she might have been.

Elspeth lowered her bow, the tension in her neck muscles easing just slightly, the swaying, speckled shadows of the leaves above her in the moonlight indicating it was just the wind that had startled her so.

But then the real creature—far off but loud enough to be heard across the distance—let out a melancholy cry, his snorts and grunts echoing out through the air.

Elspeth, usually so stoic, so poised, whipped around, her notched bow pointed straight at Carac.

"Easy, sister," he said, holding both palms out in front of him.

She lowered her bow and took a look around her.

"It's far off," I informed her. Were even my guards so unreliable? We had grown soft these past few hundred years. And I had no one to blame but myself since my ascent to the throne.

That didn't make the thought any more tolerable to bear.

"We can't stop." In my hand, I held my grandfather's sword, passed down to my father and collecting dust in the centuries since in a corner of my room. Carac insisting on its sharpening and oiling if I were so intent on using it was but one of many aggravating reasons we'd delayed our departure. I could have insisted on a guard lending me one of their swords, but I knew it was this blade alone that had severed a hoof from the minotaur.

It had to be. It was my grandfather who had done it.

The hoof itself remained behind, in the care of Kaylein. She'd insisted I not take it with me, and it was only her promise to spend the time we were gone examining it for clues on how to defeat the beast that had allowed me to walk away from it.

Even now, my free hand itched for proof that the beast could be maimed.

For years, a guard had transported the shorn scissor claw hoof to the fete and then back again, untouched during the proceedings for the most part. Unless a fae judged a human's feelings wrong and asked for love where it was not returned.

It had been tradition.

There'd been no more to it than that.

But now... Hang tradition. No more would something so useful sit idle, nothing more than a reminder of history long since past. We would *make* history.

My sword struck stone with a clang. The walls were hidden almost imperceivably here, amidst the vines sprouting out and upward, endless vegetation woven amidst the tall, white-barked willows.

My breaths were shallow. If I could sweat, perhaps some of the heat squeezing at my muscles, boiling at my mind, would have somewhere to go.

Letting out a growl, I hacked with my sword again.

"Brecc, enough!" Carac slid in beside me, a hand on my upper arm. "You'll damage the blade."

Those were the few words that would still my hand just then.

"Besides, the walls don't respond well to threats," added Elspeth from behind me.

I narrowed my brows at her as my breaths grew more even.

She shrugged, lowering her bow and releasing the tension in the strings. "It may not speak to the guards as it speaks to some, but we can sense some things, after all the time we've spent here."

Though I often allowed the married guards to take more time to rest than their colleagues, being a guard was one occupation a human spouse could not take over for a fae, as we didn't trust the fragile creatures to make it long out here in the maze.

That was what worried me so about Edony.

Sliding my sword back into the sheath at my waist, I ran a warm hand through the shorn dark locks at my head.

At a glance, I was a frail human for the labyrinth to take. Rather than hide my rounded ears, I'd hacked off the length of my hair, already short for a fae, and made the ears more prominent.

Let my people think I had lost my mind.

It would take a fae who had lost his mind to fight so ardently for the end of the world in any case.

Only I would not be satisfied with a brief reunion with my love. We would defeat the beast.

We'd have to.

I examined the group of six fae guards woven throughout the willows and the vines. All of them, other than Carac, were too tense, a marked rigidity in their already stiff posture only noticeable to the fae eye.

That, I still had.

The human blood boiling through my veins was said to make me weak in moments like these, but the heat, the determination—they only made things sharper for me.

"Should we not be at the edge of the maze, assessing the damage?" Elspeth asked. She looked over her shoulder, at the direction whence we'd come. "Or if not there, then home, enjoying the first few days with our most recent lovely spouses?"

Carac frowned, a slight shake of his head directed at his sister.

Reminders of the human spouses awaiting so many of them back home were not bound to endear me to them at this particular moment.

"You're the only one who's visited the wise woman's cabin," I snapped. Though it had been new information to me.

She shirked slightly under my gaze, and I turned to Carac instead. "Send the others there—see if any creature needs our aid. The two of you, stay with me."

I left them to it, not waiting for their concerns or objections or arguments.

The fae had become nothing but a sluggish collection of disrespectful subjects. They had to be constantly reminded that I was even their king. That their beloved fete was supposed to be about *my* bride, not anyone else's match.

Granted, we wouldn't have many more fae without the other human spouses. Least, no more fae whose blood carried the magic of the labyrinth, said to seep into the four human villages and enter the human children born there.

I barreled ahead in the direction Elspeth had indicated, letting out a growl of frustration as I came to another dead end.

"I know you can hear me!" I shouted to it. It had gone quiet as of late, the abstract messages I'd once received from it when I'd spoken to it nothing more than a dream. "Open the way! You can't keep her from me forever."

Letting out a cry at its stubborn silence, I turned on my heel to double back, stopping just short of barreling into Carac.

He tossed his braid over one shoulder. "They've gone. And Elspeth says you're headed the wrong way."

"I can *see* that," I snapped, brushing aside the bulking man as the long, wispy willows smacked across my face.

His hand caught my shoulder and I whirled on him, brushing it aside.

He held his palms out as he had to his sister, as if to prove his own defenselessness. "I want to help you find this woman."

"Oh?" My shoulders relaxed just somewhat as my gaze

found Elspeth, who took soft, sneaking steps through the maze, her eyes darting in every direction. The other guards were gone, eager to fulfill their task away from me, no doubt. "And here I thought everyone stood against me."

Carac frowned, studying my face. "I think you'll rest easier when the human is free of the labyrinth."

"Yes, I imagine I will. Rest easier with her in my arms. Until the maze crumbles and the danger rips her away."

"See, that's what I don't believe you'll let happen." Carac took slow steps toward his sister, and I followed. "You cannot marry her. It'll be the end of everything."

"I don't care."

"But you do—the end of everything means the end of her, too." Ahead of us, Elspeth slipped her arrow back into its quiver, sliding her bow over her back, and used both hands to shove aside some vines.

I froze, even as Elspeth got on her hands and knees and crawled through the undergrowth.

"I won't let that happen," I said.

"If you marry her, it *will*." Carac narrowed his eyes, which darted furtively to my ear. "Brecc, you're not seeing sense. Your human blood runs too strong—"

"Don't speak to me of human blood." I threw my shoulders back. "I am your king."

"A fae willing to doom us all is no king."

I ground my feet into the dirt. "I don't remember there being any such constraints put upon the position."

"What is wrong with you?" Carac's voice carried out into the quiet stillness of the never-ending night. "You're not like this. It's that woman—"

"That *woman* means everything to me."

"Brecc..." Carac spoke more gently now. "You hardly know her. Is she worth all of this?"

"Yes," I said quickly, without hesitation. "Do any of the fae know their spouses for more than a few days before they decide? Why am I to be held to a different standard?"

"Because you chose wrong."

It was as simple as that.

"I don't believe that." My hand caressed the hilt of my sword. "If you felt what I felt—"

"I've been there before. I've had husbands and wives over the years, each with their own charms." He shook his head. "I understand the *craving*, but, Brecc, if you make love to this woman, the beast will win."

I scoffed. "Then that shows you're wrong. I've already made love to her and these infuriating walls are still standing." I gestured around us to the messy vines, somewhere behind which stood the stone walls.

Carac's eyes widened. "At the fete?"

I nodded, then bit my bottom lip. "I didn't know her age at the time."

"I wonder, then... if that made the difference." Carac paced slowly, leading me to where his sister had disappeared. "If you were to take her now, knowing what you do, would that break the spell?"

"I don't know," I snapped. "It's a risk I'm more than willing to take. Perhaps it is only officially taking her as my bride that will do the deed."

Around us, the ground seemed to rumble, if just faintly.

Carac spun on me. "Then perhaps that's it! Take her as a

lover, but not a bride." He frowned. "But if she should bear you children—"

"No," I said, grabbing hold of the vines and pulling them back.

"No?" Carac echoed as we made our way forward.

"I'll not have her as a plaything and nothing more. She will be my bride." I marched forward, not caring as the plant life scraped against my skin, pushing harder as the growth grew thicker and more unwieldly.

"Brecc! See reason!" Carac's voice was farther behind me, the crunch of our boots over uneven terrain almost louder than his speech. But I would push forward. We hadn't hit a wall yet—perhaps Elspeth did know where she was going.

Even if it was having gotten lost that had led her to stumble upon the wise woman's cabin to begin with.

I saw her, then, the vine growth growing thinner to reveal a vast field beyond, flowers and reeds growing at least head-height. Elspeth stood at the edge of the growth, brushing away the bits of green that clung to her long, brown hair.

"She will be mine again," I said, more to the maze itself than to Carac. "And she will be my wife. The maze may fall and I'll take care of the minotaur myself—once and for all." I used my arm to hack at one last cluster of growth. "And if I should fail, then I'll die as the husband to the woman I love."

I took a step out of the vines, the willows nowhere to be seen in this new environs. I turned over my shoulder to check how near Carac was.

He shouted.

"Brother?" Elspeth spun quickly, arming herself once more.

I reached for my own sword and turned, but my foot caught in the vines in the dirt and I fell.

I let out a small cry myself, reaching toward the fields and digging my hand into the dirt.

"Brecc? Your Majesty!" Elspeth scrambled to get nearer.

Somewhere beyond the tall reeds, a pillar of smoke reached out into the air.

"Edony," I whispered, my gut churning with the thought that I would never find her.

Using all of my strength, I tugged on my leg. The vines snapped and ripped.

My limb was free, Elspeth with her bow notched and ready to shoot behind me. She never let her arrow fly. There was no definable foe to be seen.

And then, from the depths of the dirt itself, the ground rumbled. Stone scraped against stone and a wall birthed up from the dirt and soared high above Elspeth's head, separating my guard from me.

My hand slapped against solid stone.

CHAPTER

THIRTY

BRECC

"No!" I dragged myself to my feet, crushing the dirt between my fingers in order to disentangle my ankle from the vines completely. "No…"

The voice hardly felt like my own. It was quiet. Pitiful.

But as the wall settled in, the last of the rumbling dying off into the thicket of the endless night, it was all I heard but for the harsh exhalation of my own breath.

Carac and Elspeth were lost to me. I couldn't hear even their cries to indicate they were still nearby.

I jumped to my feet. Elspeth had been parted from me by a stone wall, but Carac had been behind me. I had to find him.

I marched back into the worst of the brambles, only to take a single step, push aside a cluster of vivid green vines, and find stone.

Another tall, stone wall.

"You bastard!" I took out my sword and slammed it against

the new stone, each reverberating clank exploding with a spark. "Will you stop at nothing?"

The tip of the sword broke off, the clanging chink startling me only just in time to dodge the ricochet. The piece scraped my cheek and flew off into the brambles, drawing blood.

I thought of Carac warning me not to strike at the walls with swords and collapsed to my knees, laughing.

Laughing darkly out into the quiet all around me.

The sword—my grandfather's sword, my hope of what had maimed the beast standing in my way—slipped from my grip and into the brambles all around me.

"But it's not the creature standing in my way just now," I said aloud, "is it?"

I looked up, waiting for some kind of answer.

The reply wasn't in words so much as a feeling. A wash of *feeling* that hobbled me even further, sitting me on my boots beneath me.

Don't destroy it.

The maze itself didn't want to be destroyed. But why? Grandfather had made it an adaptable thing, tasked with keeping the fae safe from the minotaur and the beast away from the rest of the world around us.

An adaptable thing... was in some senses, a living thing.

"Then why didn't you lead me to fete even just a year earlier?" I whispered. The words scratched against my throat. "I would have married her, sired my heir, and never thought twice about it." It was true, though I knew at least enough to be slightly ashamed. My happiness fulfilled, I would have let the maze stand. My people would have been content that way.

But I'd just pass the problem on to my son. To his sons after him.

The maze had no immediate reply to that, perhaps as flabbergasted as I that it should have messed up so completely. It could have sent me its *feelings* to urge me to attend fete at any point during the seven years Edony had been eligible.

Why had I even gone this year? It was not the maze's prompting, I knew that much.

Boredom. A stray comment from Favian, determined to bring home a bride this year after too many years of "subpar offerings." Since he had been there during those years when my Edony had been eligible, he was a fool for not seeing what a prize she'd been.

Though I wouldn't have wished her mother's fate on her for anything.

"What do you want from me?" I asked aloud. "To waste what time I could have with her doing nothing? To always be chasing the shadow of what I feel for her, finding it nowhere? Would that make you happy?"

When it didn't answer, I got to my feet, my legs burning with the movement after all the walking we'd done since setting out. "If I bear no heir, will you be happy?" I spat out at it, stumbling along, my hand scraping along the surface of the more visible stone wall that I knew blocked me from the fields of reeds and blooms. "Shall I die here, going around in circles, leaving the fae with no king to act as the focus of all the magic that keeps you standing?"

My steps grew faster now, my feet slapping across the uneven terrain with louder, more forceful movements.

"Well, let me tell you something—if she dies here, within

your walls, of anything but old age, in my arms, I *will* follow her! Without an heir, without your sole hope for future existence!" I was running now, my vision growing darker at the edges—from either the lack of the moonlight in this narrow corridor in which I found myself or my own righteous fury.

A scraping of stone halted my steps. The wall on which my hand rested gave at my push, just slightly.

I would not let the maze hesitate, give it pause to think. I dug between the stones, my short nails driving into the dirt and mortar the maze had conjured to keep Edony from me.

The stone I dug at, scraping, grinding, determined to loosen, fell through.

I peered through the hole it unearthed, the narrow, bramble-covered walkway it had left me filling with a single beam of bright moonlight.

Wait here, the maze itself seemed to tell me.

As if I would.

I reached an arm through the hole, trying to signal Elspeth on the other side of it. But she was nowhere to be found.

Gripping the hole as best I could with both hands, I strained my arm muscles to tear at the stones on either side of it.

When my fingers and palms grew sore from the effort, the narrow scratches tearing at my skin, I removed my shirt—unchanged since the fete—and balled my hands up in it, resuming my efforts.

I did this for ages. I could not say how long. But not a single speck more of dirt gave way. My shirt now stained with my own blood, I tossed it to the ground and let out a roar of frustration.

And then, a deer head swooped before me, peering at me through the hole.

"You really can't follow instructions, can you?" It was a woman's voice, deep and with a song-like quality. It reminded me somehow of Borin and his melodies.

I took a step back, and before I could ask her who she was and why she spoke those words to me—as if it had been *her* giving me instructions and not the walls themselves—dirt began to trail down from all the crevices of the new-formed wall before me.

And then it sunk back into the ground, revealing the wide field of reeds and moonlit blossoms. In front of them stood a deer, but on her back two legs as if they were feet. Her hands were more like a fae's, though, but her body was covered in soft, tawny fur speckled with white spots.

Her long snout was like that of a deer, as were those wide, dark, blinking eyes.

"The maze doesn't know how to deal with you," she said, crossing those dexterous hands in front of her pale brown shift.

I straightened, taking the smallest of glances left and right, and found no other living creature in sight. Then I stepped past where the wall had been, standing closer to this creature unlike any I had seen before.

No. Actually, she was far too similar in a strange way to exactly one creature I'd seen before.

The minotaur.

Though that was a beast without a word to say, and his hooves were not replaced by hands, to which the trophy Kaylein kept for me could clearly attest.

Still, there was something about this woman...

"You'll never get anywhere in this place barking orders at the labyrinth," she said. "I should think that much was obvious, considering it can so easily hinder your way."

"You must be the wise woman." The only other I'd known of beside my father who could hear the labyrinth's thoughts, or so the rumors said.

"Wiser than some, maybe." She tapped a finger against her temple, near the budding start of a horn. "I have a name. Lyra."

"I'm—"

"I know who you are." Her eyes were piercing, unyielding. "And I know the threat you and that human pose to this place."

My heart beat wildly. "You speak as if you've met her—"

"She's here."

My breath hitched.

"Here...?" The word was soft, gasping. It couldn't have been true. It couldn't be this easy—

"The maze allows you two to reunite," she said simply. "But remember it is a gift these walls bestow upon you—one that can be taken away as easily as it is given."

I quirked an eyebrow. "Does the *maze* consider itself ruler over me?"

Lyra cut a hand sharply across the air as the ground beneath us rumbled. "The maze may have been crafted by your forefather, but it is not beholden to anyone. Least of all some *boy* with human blood in his veins."

I felt the skin behind my ears flush, the retort on my tongue.

"Humans dilute ancient magic," she said. "As necessary as they may be. So. Will you fight and scream and have this gift taken away, or will you reunite with this human girl to whom you pledge your very existence?"

Clenching my jaw, my gaze flickered to where the wall had been. "My guards—"

"Are safe," she said. "For now. They're being kept from you. The maze assumed you'd like your privacy."

At least on that, the maze and I were agreed.

"Fine," I said. "Lead me to her." Whatever the labyrinth and this shifty wise woman may have had planned, I would not risk walking away. On even the slightest chance they were telling the truth.

I came here to speak to this woman, to have her find Edony for me.

If she had done that already, then I had no complaints.

"She's waiting for you," said Lyra softly, walking straight into the reeds. She let them whack her as she moved, as if they weren't even there to block her path.

I followed after her, my hand reaching for the hilt of my sword—only to find its scabbard empty. Of course. I'd left it behind, chipped and useless.

"I had to give her companions something to encourage them to sleep," said Lyra.

I halted, a particularly noxious flower slapping across my face. "Companions?"

Lyra turned around, her expression unmoved. "Your Edony has a greater destiny than lying leisurely in your bed."

We'd see about that. There would be nothing to put my Edony in danger anymore, not if I could help it—nothing beyond becoming my wife and whatever that might bring.

The ground rumbled beneath me, and somewhere off in the distance, the minotaur howled.

Lyra looked up, as if gauging the direction of the cry. "You're doing it again," she said. "Thinking something that could hurt the labyrinth."

I laughed darkly. "So you mean the maze will let me have Edony, so long as she isn't my wife?"

"That is the key to its doom," Lyra said without emotion. She went back to plunging through the endless reeds. "If you won't live apart from her, you'll have to make do."

"With what?" I asked, pushing aside a bending reed. "I'll have heirs with no other—"

"So you say." Lyra's mouth grew tight.

I scoffed. Was that it? They'd let me treat my Edony as a plaything, then, grateful for the time I'd have with her, someday I'd take another woman to be my queen?

Fine, I thought out to the maze, however it may have been intuiting my thoughts. *Just let me hold her. Give her to me. You owe me that much.*

Lyra stopped and reached forward, bending back a clump of reeds as if pulling back a curtain.

Deep in this field was a clearing, the moss and grass at its edges cut short by a patch of sand. Through the incongruous grains poked out stone tiles, as if the maze were keen to remind me that its reach was expansive, even this far out from the last hint of a wall.

And on a large rock in the midst of it sat my Edony, her hands threaded together, her fingers twitching nervously, her ripped and silky blue skirt spread across the top and side of the smooth stone as she sat there. Waiting for me.

Her bottom lip caught between her teeth, she looked up as I stepped out from the reeds.

The grass swung back into place behind me, Lyra's shuffling footfalls indicating to me that she'd left.

"Brecc." Edony's voice was soft, gasping, her green eyes blinking, as if she couldn't believe I stood before her.

I couldn't say how many seconds passed before I had her on the sand, pinned in place beneath me, never to run away again.

But it was done before I'd managed to take another breath.

CHAPTER

THIRTY-ONE

EDONY

When Lyra had bid me to let Chip and Gob rest—they'd been snoring, the both of them, sleeping as if slumber had been for too long out of reach—and led me to this clearing just beyond her hidden home and told me to wait, I would never have guessed she'd have brought the Fae King to me.

She'd felt his presence, yes, but she'd assured us he wouldn't make his way here, not without her blessing—without the labyrinth itself's permission. *"Have some tea and relax,"* she'd told us, stirring honey into only Gob's and Chip's cups, I'd noticed. *"Rest up for the fight you have ahead of you. I'll keep that meddlesome king from going where he's unneeded."*

But either she—or the maze—had decided he was needed at my side, or it was all some sort of miracle. Because Brecc appeared from between the tall reeds.

The ever-lasting moonlight was strong in these fields, stronger still in this clearing.

275

It caressed him as only a lover's hands should, perfection on his bare skin. If a fae could perspire, the man would have been glistening—but the reflection of the moonlight did the glistening for him.

It was difficult to draw my eyes away from his broad muscles, but he didn't linger long amidst the reeds. He took a step forward.

His name passed my lips. "Brecc."

His dark hair was shorn short—his ears... His ears appeared human. For a moment, my heart sunk at the thought that something had been taken from him, from *my* Brecc.

But his hands were around my body, his cheek brushing against the top of my head, and somehow I was on the ground, his commanding push not to be disobeyed but gentle nonetheless, my landing on the stone and sand beneath us cushioned by his embrace.

But only for a few seconds until he could grip me by the hands and pin me in place beneath him.

"Edony." His voice was a whisper, my name choking him.

No longer were we two lovers who didn't so much as speak one another's name. There could be no more secrets between us, me and my secret keeper.

"I... I..." My throat caught. I braced for the rumble of the stone and sand beneath us, the disapproval of the maze at finding us together.

He didn't wait.

He kissed me, and all thoughts of the labyrinth's wrath floated out of my mind.

Our breath, heaving and warm, was like the loveliest of melodies. The heat of him above me was enough to drive away the cold and damp I'd experienced since recklessly throwing myself into this place.

How long had we been parted? It could not have been so long, but my leg bucked upward, cradling his thigh, my foot trailing over his calf as a fire burned within me. We'd been apart too long. Being together now—I didn't know how I'd ever stood for it.

"Don't leave me." He spoke firmly between soft kisses on my cheeks. His fingers threaded tighter through mine. "Don't leave me," he said, this time more of a plea than command.

My mouth parted to reply.

To assure him I never could. Not again.

But through my mind were flashes of Chip, of Gob, of the dagger that awaited me wrapped in cloth on Lyra's table...

I clutched his hands back, pressing forward to claim his mouth with mine.

His knee settled between my legs, nudging upward and nestling against my groin, stirring a jolt of intensity to an already burgeoning fluttery sensation driving upward from my core. His kisses wouldn't let up, traveling from my mouth to my forehead to my cheeks and neck until he came up for air with a rending gasp.

Letting go of my hands, he kneeled, his legs still straddled over my right leg, his knee pushing upward against my core. He stared down at me, his chest heaving in the silver light, haloed like a man from a dream in the midst of this dark and endless nightmare.

I had to have him, whatever would come.

I shrugged a shoulder out of my sleeve, grinding against the sand to loosen the makeshift tie threading through my bodice.

Brecc put a hand on the shoulder to stop me, his lips hovering near my ear. "You are mine. The maze that so desperately rends us apart is proof of that."

The maze that should have kept the two of us apart. But he was here now, with me.

My hand caressed his ear, the soft curve of the warm flesh there, just an echo of the pointed cartilage that had once been. "What happened to you?"

His hand clasped mine, bringing my knuckles to his lips. "Not now." Each kiss to my fingers brought with it the promise of so much more. "Now, I must have you. And you *must stay*."

I bit my lip, staring into his eyes.

"I am your *king*," he reminded me. "Revere me."

A gasp choked to my throat, his command sending a wild thrill through my bones. But it wasn't like that—a subject before royalty. The fae weren't rulers who inspired fear. Not to us. They were supposed to be our salvation, taking a few fortunate humans away.

But I would worship every inch of his flesh if the world would allow me.

"I love you," I said, and it was true. If it hadn't been, this wouldn't have been so hard—I wouldn't have thrown myself into this place in a desperate scramble for some sort of quick end.

He closed his eyes and tilted his head up. The lump at his throat twitched.

"I'll worship you," he said, snapping back to the moment and dropping another kiss on my throat. "I may be your king, but you are *mine*—in every way a deity who belongs to no other."

His lips met my own and there was no stopping it. I pushed hard into the sand, a rip at the back of my bodice dragging the sleeve off once and for all. Scrambling, I slipped my arm out, the bodice slipping down to reveal one breast before I threaded my hand through his short hair and turned to meet his lips again.

He pulled back, pressing his mouth down upon the exposed flesh, taking hold of the pebbled center and gnawing it gently between his teeth.

I moaned, throwing my head back, letting the sand mix with the messy strands of hair fanning around me.

He came up for air, his hands moving quickly to rip the other sleeve down. The broken ties allowed him quick access, my arm threading through so that we were both bare-chested. He pressed his muscles against my breast, wrapping his arms around my back. We sat there like that for a moment, his cheeks pressed hard against the side of my forehead.

Was he waiting for me to beg, as he had back in the comfort of the castle bedroom?

Or would he have me now, consume me without stopping to think twice about who obeyed whom when it was just the two of us, flesh to flesh?

"I love you," he said softly.

My heart stopped. A dream. This had to be a dream.

Then he was back on his knees, working to tear the skirt down my legs. I squirmed in order to provide access, not even flinching as he tossed the beautiful, shiny blue material aside.

I lay before him, naked, vulnerable in this place of sand and stone and endless vegetation.

He wouldn't let me stay that way alone for long. He stood

and stepped out of his pants, towering over me like the Fae King myth I hadn't thought him to truly be.

Powerful. Unyielding. Blessed by the very sky above him.

And then he crashed to the ground, nothing left between him and me.

His hand went to work first, threading through the moisture cumulating at my core, running between the folds with slick precision. The pressure he applied to the nub had me breathing short and quick, my hands running down my sides to grind out the feeling of desperation swelling within me.

His other hand lifted my right thigh, softly massaging the flesh and directing the leg to bend, my slippered feet grinding into the sand as a foothold.

He switched hands, his left rousing the heat between my folds, his right aligning my left thigh into place.

My breaths were growing louder, warmer, steam rising in the air between us. I stroked my sides as he caressed the place between my legs, first one finger and then another dipping deep inside me.

I closed my eyes and groaned, thrusting my head back.

"Take me inside you," he said, his voice quiet but firm. Unmistakable between his own heaved breaths. "Take all of me."

"Yes," I moaned. "*Yes...*"

His fingers slipped out and in their place, his stiff erection, sliding up and down amidst my slickness.

"Fill me." Words were difficult to get out between the heady sounds of my breath. There was room for nothing now inside me—not inside my mind, not plaguing my thoughts— nothing besides him.

He planted one hand on each hip, lifting me up as if I weighed no more than a feather to him. He collapsed back on his calves as my hands dug into the sand around me in order to brace myself, the grains somehow both soft and scratchy as they wedged up inside my nails.

And then he leaned over me, lining our cores up as one, sliding his thick girth into place. Shuddering, my torso twitched to meet his move, desperate to lodge my flesh against his, to bring him deeper, deeper inside me.

He gasped, leaning into the thrust, tugging hard at my hips to bring me crashing against him.

I shrieked, though the sound could only be described as delight.

He pulled back, the sensation inside me fluttering outward to my stomach, to my chest.

And then he thrust again, bringing me back down against him harder.

We moved faster together, no amount of closeness enough, him plunging fiercer to pit flesh against flesh. He filled me deeper, harder, the friction never enough.

The air was cold as I gasped it down my throat, but the movement kept our bodies warm and glistening despite it. He, with the moonlight, I, with the inferno tearing up with every point of his touch.

And then he shuddered, an animalistic grunt escaping from his mouth as he leaned forward, sweeping me into his arms and pressing his chest against my breasts. I let go of the sand to embrace him back, my roar of ecstasy every bit as primal as his own.

We were meant to be—there could be no doubt. Some

deeper magic wanted the end of this labyrinth, whatever deals the maze may have made to try to keep me away from my king.

The ground trembled beneath us, and in the distance, breaking into our small, sandy paradise, echoed the unrelenting, despondent howl of the wretched beast.

CHAPTER

THIRTY-TWO

EDONY

He was here with me now, beside me, his finely shaped bicep the object of my fingertips' gentle worship. He was solid, warm. Real.

There had to be some reason why he was here. Why Lyra had spoken of his nearness as something to fear and then led me to meet him.

The minotaur's howls had died out minutes ago, our breath quieting so that only the quiet chirp of distant insects joined us in this special retreat.

Our eyes locked for ages, his hands both fastened around my back, gripping me securely, as if afraid I'd slip away.

But even the best of dreams didn't last forever.

And this, as I'd reminded myself over and over, was no dream.

"Who's with you?" Brecc asked, letting go of my back for a moment to brush some of my sand-coated hair behind my ear.

I frowned. How did he know? "Did *you* come alone?"

Now it was his turn to frown as he settled his hand back into place against my spine. "No. But the maze—and that wise woman—contrived to separate me from my guards so I could find you."

The maze had? I bit my lip, thinking over everything Lyra had told me about the bargain with the labyrinth itself. Trap the minotaur, leave the walls standing.

Which meant...

Not letting the Fae King take me as his bride.

And yet here he was, as real as could be.

"Lyra brought you to me?"

"Yes." Brecc sat up on one elbow, shifting one arm out from beneath me. "What troubles you so? We've found each other at last—and you're still keeping secrets from me?"

"Keeping secrets from you?" I shot up, scooting to lean against the large rock I'd used as a chair when waiting here in the clearing. "I didn't tell you everything about me at the fete because I was scared, all right?" I gestured around me. "Scared of being sent here."

It was his turn to sit up. He leaned his back against the stone and hugged one leg to his chest as if stretching. I tried not to stare, kept my eyes on the sand at my bare feet. "And yet you plunged yourself right into this place. Willingly."

"You left me no choice."

"You could have gone home," he snapped. "Rejected me. I made it clear I wouldn't have sent you here for that."

I threaded a careful hand through his beside me, still not looking at him. "I couldn't have done that. Even though I wish it were so simple."

He unhooked his hand from mine. "You *wish* you could reject me?"

"If it would have prevented all of this..." I let go of him and hugged both knees against my chest.

"You would have saved yourself the heartache." Brecc scoffed and stood, snatching his pants off of where they dangled haphazardly from between two tall reeds.

How did I explain? It was my turn to shuffle to my feet, taking hold of my sparkling blue dress and finding it, despite even Brava's best efforts at repairing it, ripped and dirtied and sodden. I stepped through the skirt despite that, left with nothing but a sense of vulnerability without it. Sliding my arms through the sleeves, I found the ties at the back of the bodice ripped once more, the bodice hanging loosely from my body.

I was exhausted. The journey here—the bliss I'd just felt with Brecc moments before—had led to my muscles aching, my energy depleted. My head buzzed with thoughts of taking up that dagger that awaited me, heading to face the minotaur and dullahans in a land of sand and desolation, my hair a sandy mess, this dress a wreck that would not stay on my shoulders. Perhaps the appearance of me could cause the beast to laugh to death.

The ground rumbled beneath my feet, and I steadied myself, digging my bare feet into the sand. When it stopped, I located my slippers and slid my sandy toes inside of them.

Brecc stood, still without his shirt but covered from the waist down.

"Come," he said, his voice clipped. "We'll head back now."

"Back?" I asked.

"To the fae village." He gestured to his left, then, frowning, looked to his right. "We'll go back the way I came and then meet up with Elspeth and Carac—"

"Wait a moment. I can't go back with you."

Brecc's chest hitched and he closed the distance between us, snatching my wrist. "I won't let you go."

"I have Chip and Gob," I explained.

His lips pinched. "Who?"

"Friends." I snatched my wrist out from his grip, and he let it go. "We have a task the maze itself has asked us to complete—"

"The maze itself? Do *you* speak to it now?"

"Well, no…" I cradled my wrist as if to guard him from grabbing it again. "Lyra told us—"

"Ah, yes. Your companions and your destiny. Just as that odd creature spoke of." Brecc shook his head. "Forget it. *I've* made a deal with the labyrinth as well. We can be together." He held both hands out to me. A sword sheath I hadn't noticed before dangled empty at his trim waist. "So come with me. Come *home*."

It was tempting. His face was soft, so inviting. Just a few feet stood between us. After all this time of endless walls and twists and turns and immeasurable distance.

And in the fae village… was my cousin.

"Neela," I whispered. "She needs to know what her husband did to my mother."

Brecc's hands fell and a sharp intake of air passed his lips. "She knows. I told her myself."

I blinked. I hadn't expected that.

But what had I expected? To sneak to a place lodged in this dark maze, full of sunlight and prosperity, to wipe the smile off my blissful cousin's face? Then to leave her there, her whole world dropped out from beneath her feet?

I couldn't take her with Chip and Gob and me. I doubted she *could* leave Favian now—or if she did, he'd be just the brute to mark her face for it, make her a beacon to focus the minotaur's wanderlust.

My knees grew weak at the thought. What was she thinking now, trapped in paradise with this knowledge?

"I'll take you to her," Brecc said. "You can see her for yourself."

Yes... I could comfort Neela. We could carve a life out in the fae village somehow, her trapped in her deceitful marriage, me stuck in this impermanent state with the man—the king—who didn't understand. Didn't understand that there were things more important even than this love that consumed me, consumed us both.

"The maze wants the minotaur trapped," I said. I could not —would not—take Neela with me, but perhaps Brecc himself would have the strength necessary. Perhaps we could do this together. I'd promised Chip's father she'd be safe—I could leave her behind, too. Brecc's guards could show Gob the way to freedom. Neither needed to come with me on this dangerous quest.

"Trapped?" Brecc scoffed. "He *is* trapped now. In the maze itself."

"I know, but don't you see? If the minotaur stops wandering, the maze's inhabitants at least will be free."

"If they leave, the maze loses its magic."

My stomach clenched. Surely, the maze could spare just one little troll, though, if he wanted to be free? "Free of the terror of that-that thing, I mean. Which I hear the fae never have to deal with in your village—”

“Never have to deal with the minotaur?” Brecc’s dark eyebrows shot up. “As if every move we make outside of the village isn’t fraught with danger, as if *we* haven’t been the only ones to fall in an attempt to end that thing!”

“But you’re safe inside the village,” I pointed out. I stepped closer, eager to make him understand. My hand reached for his cheek, my sleeve falling off my shoulder with the movement. “The others out here—are suffering.”

“I take it your Chippengob is one of *them*, then?” He turned to kiss the palm of my hand. “And he’s filled you up with all sorts of ideas about the big, bad fae—”

“*They*’ve told me about their lives in this place, yes. But I’ve seen it with my own eyes, too. This maze—it’s filled with darkness. With suffering. Little pockets of joy, too, they can’t be denied trying to carve out that—but they need food. They need freedom.”

“They’ll never be free so long as this wall stands.” Brecc tossed his head back.

I caressed his ear, his human-shaped ear. “What happened to you?”

He snatched my hand in his. His eyes were wild, a slight darkness to the bags beneath. “I’ve been worried about you. I can’t eat. I don’t rest.”

“And this happened because of that?”

“It’s the human blood in me,” he explained.

The human blood in him was making him weak.

His love for me was dooming not just the world, but even

him. How could he ever be happy with me with things as they stood? Couldn't he see that?

"Help me trap the beast," I pleaded. Beyond that, I could see Neela again. Perhaps I could stay there, with her. With Brecc. Just never allowing myself the title of his bride.

But could he handle this proposal—right now, as he was? His eyes roved my face wildly.

"I'll defeat him," he said simply. "I'll find the way to do what even Grandfather could not do—and I will slay the beast."

Before I could open my mouth to dissuade him, a crack resounded across the air. With a rustle as if the tall grass had been assaulted by a harrowing squall, the reeds nearby cracked outward and snatched Brecc around the waist.

Then they devoured him inside the field, pulling him away from my sight with the force of a tornado wind. My mouth fell open in a silent scream.

THIRTY-THREE

NEELA

"Neela?" Favian's voice carried around the corridor. I snuck into a room with its door ajar. "Neela, my darling?"

My heart thundering, I ducked behind the door, pressing myself against the wood and holding my breath.

"Neela, please, you can't keep running from me!" Favian's voice quavered. I couldn't tell if it was pain or anger that lanced his voice. Perhaps both.

At last, his footfalls echoed down the hallway, my name on his lips growing fainter. I let out a sigh of relief, then slipped back out from behind the door to examine where I was.

A bedroom, similar to the one I'd just escaped. In front of the wide-open window across from me, there was a cushioned seat. And the dappled light filtering in through the window fell on a figure waiting there. Dressed in a soft leather bodice with a flowing, green skirt, she might have been a fae at first glance.

But I'd recognize that heart-shaped face, those chestnut curls anywhere.

"Gloriana!" My hands immediately went to my mouth.

"Neela?" She cocked her head and nodded at me. "Shut the door."

I did as bidden, but slowly, carefully, afraid the sound might draw Favian back.

Favian.

My chest squeezed as I pushed the door into the jamb. I was running from Favian. I could still picture his handsome face, the way his smile hit his eyes, with and without the mask he'd worn at our first meeting.

I'd loved him. I'd known from the moment I'd seen him, he was the one.

All thoughts of a future exploring the world with Mother and Father... All duty to Grandmother and even to Edony gone.

I hadn't expected to be chosen. No one in my mother's side of the family ever was.

Except... that wasn't true at all now, was it?

Edony, what in the world happened?

What could explain the strange human-like Fae King and his even stranger obsession with my cousin?

"I shouldn't be surprised to see you here," said Gloriana. Her voice was missing some of its usual vigor. Tired, though not without its charms. "You and that fae were as one the moment he saw you." She smiled teasingly, the same way she used to whenever she'd caught me staring at her brother for a moment too long. As if I'd risk anything to date a human from the village before my period of eligibility was over. I knew the story too well of what had happened to my aunt and uncle.

"Though I wonder what sort of game you're playing? That was him, wasn't it? Your groom? He looked in here and I nodded politely at him, without giving him any indication I'd just seen you running inside to hide from him. Is this part of your love-making? Some kind of chasing thrill?"

I scrambled across the room to sit beside my dearest friend, throwing my arms around her. She let out a startled cry but soon returned the embrace.

"It's all gone to dust—all of it." I was surprised to find my voice quavering, tears running down my cheeks. I squeezed her harder, clutching to the one thing left I had of my old life, the one thing that still seemed good in all this new existence.

He'd lied to me.

Or worse yet, he hadn't known of my connection to the woman he'd scarred and doomed to wander the labyrinth. She had meant that little to him. Humans were just playthings to him.

And now my cousin was in danger as well—I didn't even understand it. How that man could have been Fae King. How his love could put us all in danger.

At least, apparently, my cousin had had sense enough to run. Run away from her fae. Before she could fall in with him too deep.

Sobbing, I wiped my face with the heels of my hands.

"What's wrong?" Gloriana asked. "Do you miss home, too?" She sighed. "I never thought I'd miss home, least of all so quickly. But Elspeth was called away. She's a guard, you know. Guards don't get to take it easy around here." She spoke of her fae bride with palpable pride, her chest puffing up. "And your husband? What is he?"

"I don't know," I admitted. "We haven't talked about much..." My throat went tight. Nothing much at all before the Fae King had come bursting in. And only about what Favian had done to my aunt since.

Gloriana nudged me on the arm with her elbow. "I see." She winked, but then her smile vanished as she stared at me. "*Are* you homesick?"

"No. Yes. I mean, that's not why..."

Gloriana stood and reached back, holding out a hand. "Let's go explore, shall we? Elspeth said I had free rein of the whole village. The sun is about to set, but I have a feeling this place comes even *more* to life in the evening." She laughed, and the sound was enough to make my hand reach toward hers.

I hesitated.

This wasn't a carefree evening in our own hometown.

"If your husband crosses our paths, we shall hide again, of course." She winked at me.

I took her hand. It was foolish, maybe, but perhaps being amongst people, amid a crowd, would help me to stop thinking about everything...

Gloriana led me across the room and then carefully opened the door, peering left and right. "All clear," she said, giggling, like I was spending the night and we were sneaking past her parents' room to head out past curfew. She'd brightened up considerably in the few minutes I'd been with her. As if home-sickness were indeed the only ailment plaguing her. She'd never liked to be alone, I knew that much. And her wife was out on guard duties... Likely with the king, off to find my cousin.

No. I couldn't think about that now. I wouldn't. My brain needed a break.

The hallways were dark, though lit by torches affixed into stone-and-dirt walls every few yards. Gloriana stifled more giggles as our leather-slipper-clad feet padded over dirt grounds. The place was smaller than the castle, less grand. I hadn't had the awareness to really take it all in when I'd arrived. I'd been so focused on my husband...

No. *Clear your thoughts.*

At last, we broke through the torch-lit darkness, a wide-open door at the end of the hallway letting in the fire-red twilight.

Gloriana's steps grew quicker. We practically burst through the open door and out into the evening air.

It was refreshing against my dampened cheeks.

The quiet of the building we'd been in was replaced by the soft hum of conversations. Off in the distance were the dulcet tunes of musicians' percussion and strings, reminding me starkly of the music at the fete.

No, I told myself, shaking my head clear once more.

I turned around to get a good look at the building we'd withdrawn from. A large tree jutted out of it, wood and stone woven through and around it like branches.

"Come on," said Gloriana, tugging me forward again.

We passed other, smaller buildings—perhaps more like hovels. Various fae gathered around in front of them, talking. My eyes caught sight of a few humans as well. One with his arm around a fae woman, sitting on a bench in front of the hovel I assumed to be their house, just talking. She had a babe swaddled in silk in her arms at her breast. I didn't recognize the man; he seemed at least ten years older than Gloriana and I. Another I spotted through an open window of another hovel.

She stirred something in a pot over a fire. Her hair was streaked with gray.

Several youthful-looking fae sat at the table beside her awaiting dinner, wooden cutlery set in front of them.

They looked happy.

They looked like families.

"It seems like there's a market this way."

Gloriana dragged me down an alleyway, the music growing louder, though it was still drowned out by conversations.

There did appear to be a market in this place. Gloriana dropped my hand to cover her mouth with a gasp.

Stalls overflowed with foods. Produce. Seafood the likes of which I only saw when Mother and Father returned home by way of Eastmeet. Silks and fine fabrics hung from several other stalls. And there was woodwork and all sorts of shiny baubles. Gloriana made a beeline straight for a place with dangling necklaces adorned with jewels. She plucked one down from a stand like an apple from a tree and held it out in front of her bodice. The green jewel sparkled. "What do you think?"

"It's nice." I tried my best to smile as I looked around. Mine was the only sad face in this place. The human woman at the stall at which we found ourselves shot up. She wasn't familiar.

"Why, you're a Baker girl, aren't you?" she said. A streak of gray striped through her auburn hair, and there were wrinkles at the edges of her narrow, brown eyes. "I'd recognize that family anywhere."

"Yes." Gloriana laughed nervously, hanging the necklace back up. "Did you know my parents?"

"Of course." The woman beamed. "Your father and I were good friends once. Though it's been years. Whenever someone new comes, I ask how he's been doing. I only wish I could send word to him about my life. My fae husband taught me how to fashion all of these jewels into ornaments." She beamed and plucked another necklace off of its stand, holding it out in front of Gloriana, who sucked up the attention with relish. "And my children... I never got to tell your father about my own children." Her face fell, the sheen of joy cracking just slightly.

I looked around, but instead of finding her fae children, all I noticed were humans behind other booths. Some distance away, another human consulted with the man selling produce, tasked with doing the shopping.

Where were all the fae? We'd passed some on our way here, to be sure.

"They're listening to music." The woman at the booth with all the jewels thumbed over her shoulder and put her hand on her hip. She must have assumed I was looking for them, too. "You want to listen, dears? You're both so new here. I doubt your spouses have instructed you about your tasks yet."

"Tasks?" I asked.

Gloriana offered a little curtsy, her shoulders bobbing coyly. "*My* wife is a guard," she said. "She said I'd be busy keeping our room clean and doing some cooking when she's not eating with her friends, but that I wouldn't have to lift a finger otherwise. Though, perhaps, if we adopted a baby, then I'd be more busy..." Gloriana's face flushed and she giggled.

So she and her bride had discussed this all already?

Informing her of her tasks?

"Well, aren't you a lucky one?" said the merchant woman. "Yes, guards' spouses don't have to take over their duties. Too dangerous. And none of us can step foot out of this village regardless."

"Take over their duties?" I asked aloud, but the merchant was sliding the necklace she'd selected over Gloriana's head.

"And there are couples who have so many babies, they don't mind spreading them around for others in the village to raise," she said, fussing with Gloriana's long hair so that it wasn't caught in the necklace.

"Spread the babies around...?" I asked.

But neither was paying me any mind.

"Now doesn't that look marvelous?" the merchant said, stepping back. "Why don't you tell me your wife's name? My husband will bill her—you have to get used to what these fae consider currency; sometimes you might be asked to perform a helpful task for another fae. Regardless, he'd sure be happy to be in a guard's good graces."

"Yes, of course." Gloriana fingered the jewel at her neck, checking out her murky reflection in a solid silver tray set up on the booth. "It does look lovely... Oh, but what about some earrings to match with it?" She grabbed a set of sparkling jewels from the table and held one up to one ear, her attention wholly on the silver plate in front of her.

My feet were moving backward before I even realized it, the conversation worming its way like crawling bedbugs into the edges of my mind. I'd worked so hard to keep it clear the past few moments, to push aside the nagging doubts.

Why were there only humans working here?

Sending Gloriana to work for others as payment?

I slipped through the remaining stalls, my feet drawing to a halt as the music grew louder. There was a circular opening, perhaps best likened to a town square, though this place looked more natural, untouched. The chairs and tables consisted of logs and tree stumps. In the center of the large group gathered blazed a warm fire, the flames crackling up into the sky.

The bard from the fete—I recognized his shape, if not his face—sang in the middle of a group of fae. Beside him, a wrinkled, hunched human woman who had to be at least eighty struck a tambourine, swaying to the music. Throughout the square, fae lay languidly, some with eyes closed, others kissing partners—human and fae alike—and still others lying in human partners' laps, humans feeding them slices of fresh fruit, fanning them, stroking their hair.

Only the fae were coddled so. The fae, who were so charming and romantic at the fete in their quests to woo human spouses back home with them.

"'*For king and for fae, we must find a way.' And with a cry, they struck again, they struck again,*" sang the bard, strumming his lute. The melody was harrowing, growing bolder with each note. "*But together they fell, into their ever-lasting hell. To the beast, they lost their heads, lost their heads. But never dead, they're never dead...*"

I blinked hard, the song cutting through the noise and panic in my mind and striking me to my core as if a flint to stone.

And then someone gripped me from behind and whirled me around roughly.

"There you are!" Favian. His trembling lips drew tightly together as his hands dug hard into my shoulders.

THIRTY-FOUR

NEELA

"Come," Favian said, taking hold of my wrist and tugging me far harder than Gloriana had. "There will be time for frivolities another day."

"Will there?" I couldn't stop myself from saying as we left the square and neared the stalls once more.

His voice soaring on the air behind us, the fae bard started up another song, this one with more pep behind it. The crowd broke into rhythmic clapping, in time with the old human woman's instrument.

"Will there what?" Favian spun on me, dropping my arm.

"Be time for frivolities?" I gestured around me, clutching my wrist to my chest and rubbing it, more to keep it safe from his grip than because of any soreness. "Seems to be the human spouses do all the work around here."

Favian arched a pale eyebrow. "And do the humans not work in human villages?"

"We do," I said. "But few get away with doing nothing, unless they have good reason."

"Such as?"

I *tsked*. I didn't want to debate details on this topic with him. I brushed past him. Where was there to run? I couldn't flee into the labyrinth alone. And if the Fae King had taken Gloriana's wife and other guards out into the maze to seek out my cousin... Perhaps it was best I waited for her here.

Anxious and always a bit lost in her own mind, Edony nonetheless always knew what needed doing. She was always there for me if I had an argument with a friend.

She'd help me make sense of this mess somehow together.

Perhaps, if she really was able to navigate the maze, the two of us could then go home together.

Favian let out a sigh loud enough to be heard over the clapping and the melody we were leaving behind us.

He stepped in front of me as we reached the lane between the stalls. Gloriana was still several booths away, an array of trinkets glistening on her person in the early evening moonlight as she twirled in front of the human woman's booth.

"If we are to be happy together, we need to *talk*," Favian said.

I scoffed. "You mean, like you didn't tell me about what you'd done to my aunt?"

"We've been over this and over this—"

"Yes, since I found out all of half a day ago! Do you expect me to be done with the topic already?" My hands curled into fists by my side.

Favian frowned. "Yes. No. That is—"

I threw my hand up and walked back toward the largest

building in the village. Perhaps I could await Edony's return in Gloriana's room, so long as her wife was gone out to find her anyway.

"When would you have had me tell you?" Favian asked, his feet hitting the dirt path loudly with each step as he caught up to me. "I didn't know you were related to her—"

I spun on him. "It wouldn't have mattered! If you'd done that to *anyone*, I'd have the right to know!"

"You *knew*!" Favian's lip curled. "You knew what became of those who rejected a fae's proposal—"

"But it happened so rarely." My nails dug into my palms, my teeth grinding before I spoke again. "I didn't think I'd fall in love with the one who'd actually *done* it!"

I realized my mistake almost as soon as I'd said it.

My confession of love softened the sharp angle of his brow. "It happens so rarely because so few dare to refuse us."

And then all softness, the little crack in my heart's armor hardened.

"Any one of us fae would have done the same," he snapped.

I let out a growl, brushing past Gloriana at the jewelry booth.

"Oh. Your Eminence." The merchant woman held her earthen-tone skirt out to either side and did a little curtsy toward Favian as he passed her, her head bowed.

It was enough to halt my steps. *"Eminence"?*

She looked up and smiled at me. "You didn't tell me your husband was Favian." She stepped back and gestured to her booth. "Please, look around. With your fine complexion, there are so many baubles that would suit you. Don't you agree, Your Eminence?" She dared a look at Favian.

He grunted, clutching his hands behind his back.

Gloriana stood behind the merchantwoman, looking from Favian to me to the other human and back with puzzlement woven into her soft expression.

Favian's jaw twitched as the merchantwoman smiled. "My jewel would look lovely with an array of jewels, of course…" His eye caught sight of Gloriana and he frowned. Perhaps he remembered passing her in her room, how she'd kept me hidden away. More out of confusion than any attempt to aid me, though, to be sure.

Gloriana curtseyed despite knowing no more about Favian than I did—for I had to assume she would have told me anything she'd discovered about him. The moonlight bounced off the silver tray and sparkled against her many, many jewels like fireflies. I was glad to see *she* was so quick to be over her homesickness.

"I need nothing of the sort," I snapped, picking up my feet and heading back down the lane.

Favian was quick to follow me, eager, no doubt, not to let me gain any real distance from him again.

"You needn't have been rude to Mistress Brucie," he said. "And do you know Mistress Elspeth? I thought I saw the two of you together at the fete, but I could not say. My eyes were always drawn toward you—"

"Is that what I am? Mistress Favian? My own name forgotten, reduced to your shadow?" I halted as we reached the entrance to the closest thing there was to a castle or manor in this place.

Where the Fae King may have lived. Where Gloriana's

esteemed guard wife did as well, and where Favian had brought me...

"Why 'Your Eminence'?" I asked.

My question cut the consternation brewing on his face short. "The human spouses treat us all with respect—"

"As *you* were supposed to respect your king," I observed.

He shook his head. "Brecc was never like that before—"

"You speak of him so familiarly."

He shrugged. "He's my dearest friend."

"And yet he's out there, right now, tracking down my cousin, and you stayed here."

His nostrils flared. "I'm no *guard*."

He spoke of the position with distaste.

"Well, what are you?" I leaned forward, raising up on my tiptoes.

"That woman is dead. Brecc is out there on a fool's errand—"

"That *woman* is my cousin!"

"Her death is not on my hands." The corner of his lip twitched slyly. "If she had been born my daughter, she would not even *be* in such danger—"

"She wouldn't have been born had my aunt stayed with you!" My voice grew louder, scraping against my throat. "Though at least I would have been free, I suppose, if you'd been taken up with some other servant, whatever you are, *Your Eminence*!"

"I..." His chin tilted higher. "I don't have to answer you."

"Oh? You're not going to tell me how I can take over your duties? Grovel and serve you and raise your children alone for all of my days?"

"We do *not* ignore our children—"

"Right. Because they're at least born fae." My memories flitted through the happier scenes I'd seen during my tour of the fae village. There'd been that couple—gone upon my return trip—enjoying the sunset on their front step. And that human woman with fae youth. Even human children often waited for their mothers to serve them dinner...

Perhaps there was still much for me to learn about this place. But I'd seen enough to want to run and hide away.

Happiness was out of my reach with this man, and there could be no other for me now.

He stepped forward, caressing my cheek. "I love you."

I flinched, and for a moment, I closed my eyes, losing myself to his touch. To the giddiness that burst out from my core and traveled down to my fingers and toes, engulfing me entirely.

Last night had been the most amazing night of my life.

And then it had all been ripped away.

My hand flew to my stomach nervously and I stepped back, my eyes flitting open.

"You love me, too," he said. "You told me so." His hand shook at his side.

"I loved a lie," I said, still walking backward. "I don't know who you are. I was a fool."

If I were in a more forgiving mood, his expression right then would have broken me.

His stiff shoulders slumped just slightly, the lump at his throat bobbing. His chin trembled, though it still pointed upward haughtily.

I turned on my heel.

Based on the quiet around me, the crackle of the torchlight flames the only sound my ears picked up, he didn't follow me.

By the time I'd wandered back to what I recognized to be the corridor leading to Gloriana's room, I paused. Favian's room was just around the corner, and if he wasn't following me, I could grab my dress.

It was the only thing of home I'd brought with me, and I would not be so childish as to put it on and wander the halls a spectacle in a fine dress to spite him, but I would keep it with me.

It was something of my own.

I turned the corner just as a fae woman stepped out of another room, clutching something to her chest.

"Oh!" she cried. "Good evening."

I nodded at her and bit my lip.

She was beautiful—they all were—her complexion as dark as my own, no doubt the result of some human blood in her veins from the lands overseas from which my father hailed.

"You're Favian's...?" she asked.

I would not confirm it.

I was Favian's wife. His human plaything. His servant. His deceived bride.

My eyes blinked hard as they zeroed in on the item against her chest.

It was mangled and practically rotten. It didn't look at all to fit in with this place of lushness and comfort, even with the edges sanded down by human labor.

The part she clutched was furry. It ended in a twisted, jagged hoof.

She saw where I was looking and gazed down at it. Then

she laughed and brought the hoof to her side. "No need to fear this. You're here, aren't you? You've accepted a fae's proposal."

My eyes widened. It was that thing that had doomed my aunt. The claw of the minotaur, the beast that roamed the labyrinth. Where my aunt and uncle had died. Where Edony, even now, was in danger.

The fae woman kept talking. "I've been doing some research in Brecc's library—though the man has certainly turned it into a sty—trying to find a way to defeat the beast."

That got my attention. "It can be done?"

"Our king wants it so. So we must at least try. Or…"

"Or he may marry my cousin and doom us all," I finished for her.

She looked at me, really studying me for the first time.

"Do you think he's on a fool's errand?" I asked her.

"I… I don't know." She laughed. "I'm primarily a tailor, for maze's sake. And he's asking me to find answers to defeat the beast not even our best warriors in ages past could match?"

"Headless, but never dead…" I said, the lyrics of the bard's melody jumping to the forefront of my mind.

Why, I wasn't sure at first. But then I knew. I hadn't heard the entire song, but it was about those warriors and their last stand against the beast. Before the maze had been created, trapping it away.

The fae woman grimaced. "Yes, that's true."

"It is?" I cocked my head.

Her dark eyes twinkled. "A lot of what Borin sings is steeped in real history. I assume that's where you heard the tale."

"Yes." I cocked my head a moment, thinking. Could the bard hold the answer?

No, it couldn't have been that simple. If he sung of how to defeat the beast, it would have been from a story about the beast's defeat.

And who was I to assume I could find a way that even the fae themselves could not, after all these years of searching?

"I'm Kaylein," she said, extending her hand. The one not clutching the shorn hoof.

"Neela," I said, taking the hand carefully, waiting for her to dismiss my own name in favor of my fae husband's.

"I've never married," she said, dropping our handshake in order to clutch the hoof against her chest again with both hands. "I love my work. I didn't see the point in marriage."

Then again, she reminded me... If most fae married to have someone to do their work, they were probably more often idle than not. They couldn't have been looking for answers all of this time, now could they have?

"And what does Favian do for work?" I asked. If the man himself wouldn't answer me...

"Favian?" She laughed. "I don't know, actually. Read books, perhaps. Keep the king's ear full of the news and gossip of the town. Officially, he assists him in ruling over everything, but the both of them have always just seemed like aimless brothers to me."

I would not be expected to take Favian's place at the Fae King's side, I could be sure. A life like Gloriana's, then? Cleaning and cooking and raising fae babies?

I curtseyed and excused myself, eager to get back to claim my dress before Favian himself retreated to his room.

Kaylein was the first fae in the village I'd met who'd been actively doing anything—other than the bard Borin and his singing, I supposed.

I opened the door to Favian's room quietly, eager not to alert him if he'd taken another route and reached it first.

It was empty, the room lit only by moonlight streaking through the open shutters.

He probably assumed I wouldn't be here. Or if I were, perhaps he had no desire to see me again just yet.

Good. I'd had enough of him today.

I crossed the room and found my dress folded nicely where I'd left it, atop a table. I remembered doing so happily, thinking of it as a memento of a life left behind, my family's best mask discarded and forgotten somewhere back at the castle. My old life would be looked at fondly, I'd thought, but without regret.

I would never feel the bliss of no regrets again.

Clutching the folded fabric against my chest, I brushed past the bed, stopping to stare down at it, my cheeks flushing with the memory of how we'd spent our time here together, just one short day ago.

My hand reached out to caress the soft blanket despite myself.

My fingers jammed against something hard. A book. Favian had brought it in here, shortly before the Fae King himself had stormed in, his eyes wild and manic.

I lifted it up, examining it in the moonlight. Books were treasures my mother and father brought home from lands far away. They were rare and expensive.

But I could read them, thanks to my parents. They'd taught Edony, too, though Grandmother had never wanted to bother, after *"living this long without filling my head with all those letters and words and things."*

It was hard to see in the dim light, but it seemed to be a book of songs.

My heart fluttered. I'd had the idea myself to seek the answer to the beast's defeat in a fae song.

There had to be some reason this book was in my hand now.

And if not, well, I would not speak to Favian about it. If he missed the book and suspected I'd stolen it, he could chase me down again. If he could find me.

THIRTY-FIVE

EDONY

"Brecc!" I shouted. "Brecc!"

Diving into the reeds, I ran in the direction in which he'd been swallowed, the coarse plantlife whapping against my cheeks, stinging the bare skin at my arms. Brecc had kissed the small puncture wound when we'd embraced, had asked me where it had come from.

I hadn't had the heart to explain Gob and his foul bite. It would have just given him another excuse to attempt to steal me away to his village without doing what needed to be done.

There was no sign of Brecc—of anyone—anywhere. How fast had the reeds moved him? The labyrinth. The labyrinth itself had moved him—because he wouldn't budge. He'd sworn he would marry me.

Stubborn fool.

I parted another reed and almost let out a scream; Lyra stood before me, her thin, long fingers threaded together at her abdomen.

"He's gone, child. Separated from you—at least until you accomplish the task the maze has set for you."

I peered around her shoulder, as if I'd find Brecc being held just out of sight behind her.

I wouldn't see him again...

But I'd resigned myself to that before this. And then the maze itself had thrown the two of us together, dangling happiness within reach—or reminding me that the Fae King and I would never see eye-to-eye when our love itself put so much at risk. Brecc hadn't even accepted the maze's terms, to love me but not entwine his soul with mine, to never make me his queen.

He would not give an inch to the labyrinth.

He would not allow me to see the creature captured—he'd sought its end.

With a rumble beneath my feet, I realized that I, too, for a moment, had wished for the creature's end. If there was no minotaur, it wouldn't matter if the maze collapsed. No one would be in danger. In fact, creatures like Gob and Chip—they'd be better off. They'd be free.

Lyra held up a hand, the reeds twisting as if by a forceful gale all around us.

The corner of her lips on her long snout tipped up in a smile. "Thinking traitorous thoughts, are you?"

The maze had offered me a way to coexist peacefully—for everyone inside this place to be safe. I had to take it.

"I'll not put Chip and Gob in danger," I said, straightening.

Lyra let out a little chuckle. "Fancy yourself strong and clever enough to take on the beast yourself, do you?"

I put a hand on my hip, tilting up my chin. "The maze itself is on my side, isn't it? If it can separate the Fae King from me, surely, it can guide me to what needs doing—and help me see it through."

Lyra clucked her tongue and turned on her heel. "If the maze could do more to the beast than keep it lost within its walls, it would have done so long ago. Come. You must rest and wait for your companions to wake." She shuffled forward through the tall stalks, turning left.

I hesitated a moment, staring in the direction I would have kept running had she not barred my way.

But I would not find Brecc if I kept going that way. I had to trust that he was safe and reunited with his guards. And I had to see the task before me done—before the distance between the Fae King and I weakened him further and drove him mad.

Sighing, I turned and followed Lyra, the sleeve on my left arm drooping, the bodice loose.

"You warned us the Fae King was coming," I said. "And then you insisted we stay."

"To rest," Lyra explained. "This may be the last safe place on your quest—though the longer you linger, the more dangerous even my sanctuary becomes." Lyra stopped as we reached the clearing around her cabin. "And I obey the maze's orders. It's kept me safe this long, and I knew it wanted the two of you reunited for a short spell—but your companions would not be particularly welcoming of such a reunion. You'd be wise to keep it from them."

"Would they lose morale?" I asked.

"I imagine they might."

I bit my mouth shut. I wouldn't do anything to distract my

companions—if the maze wouldn't help me, they were the only hope I had of even finding the minotaur.

Still, I wouldn't let them throw themselves into danger when the time came. I'd promised Chip's father. And Gob, well, he'd seen enough suffering, whatever he'd done to earn the trolls' disfavor.

Approaching the cabin from behind, we passed the stream, as well as the garden in which she grew hearty vegetables that could flourish even without the sun. I stumbled, the hem of my dress dragging on the dirt.

Lyra shook her head and grabbed me by the forearm before I lost my footing entirely. "It's high past time you put your days of wandering in glamor behind you."

I looked down at the wreck of the dress—the dress Brecc had had made for me. Back when he'd known even less about me than he did now. When I'd been nothing more than a dream he hadn't known he couldn't have—even if he'd stolen his way into my heart.

"I never meant to wander in this place so woefully unprepared." The admission was soft, almost reluctant, on my tongue.

"Those days are behind you now," Lyra said. "Rest, and when you wake, the maze and I shall have done all we could to prepare you."

Still, the question remained: Would even that be enough?

Chip's parents had done a perfect job of saddling us with enough supplies to reach Lyra's cabin—with a smaller portion for Chip's solo trip home. But now, here we were, shuffling through the remaining items and rearranging them to make more room in the satchels. Lyra had provided Gob with a satchel, too, and he piled waterskins freshly filled from the stream out back with a sour, sullen expression on his face.

"You can still make your way out of here, if you'd prefer," I told him. I flipped the braid I'd twisted my hair into over my shoulder. Lyra had fashioned some attire for me while I'd slept that was more flattering than her own. A homespun cotton shirt was only the slightest bit large for me, particularly flowing at the bottom, and leathers formed a pair of trousers that fit snugly—maybe just a tad too snugly at the waist. My stomach felt bloated. Perhaps I'd gorged myself on Lyra's variety of food, remembering the hunger of my first day in the labyrinth far too well.

"Won't let me leave, will it? Not until we see this through." Gob sniffled and started tying his satchel closed.

"Don't forget this." Chip took the dagger off of Lyra's table and carried it reverently out in front of her with both front paws, the item still wrapped in cloth.

The dagger seemed to bleed its dark aura into the air between us.

I snatched it from her, sliding it into the scabbard Lyra had provided on the belt tied around my waist. Even the hilt felt cold in my hands. I didn't like the weight of it at my hips, either.

But Lyra had insisted this weapon could banish darkness— it had to be necessary to corralling the beast. I could dispose of it and its foul history after that.

"Good, good." Lyra stood in the open back door of the

cabin. "It looks like you're ready."

Chip and I took turns tying each other's arm's through our satchels, Chip using the mantelpiece to reach the top of my shoulders.

"Do you want help?" I asked Gob, who was fiddling with his own knot.

He yanked his satchel back from me, as if I were even close enough to take it from him in the first place. "I'll do it myself."

At least his clipped tone wasn't peppered with insults. Perhaps we had made progress. If I could forgive him for biting me and calling me names, he could forgive me for... daring to exist, I supposed.

"I'm ready." Chip picked up a small, needle-like dagger Lyra had provided for her and slipped it through one of the ties of her satchel. It would do more damage than a stick, but not much.

I had to make sure she stayed back when we found the beast.

"You're certain you don't want a weapon, Gobble?" Lyra asked. "The maze will provide."

"I don't need these stinkin' walls and stones to provide me nothing." Gob flashed his fangs. "I have my own weapons."

I rubbed my arm. That, he did.

"Very well." Lyra stepped back out into her gardens and gestured behind her. "The maze will show the way."

Listening to her speak, the reeds along the edge of the stream parted, as if to widen a path along the waters.

"North," said Chip, scrambling on four legs to lead the way.

I couldn't tell which direction we were headed.

I just knew that I wasn't headed to the fae village. If Neela knew the truth, at least I could rest easy if it turned out I never saw her again.

And Brecc… At least I'd seen him one last time.

Without even a goodbye to Lyra or another word of advice from her, Gob and I followed after Chip. We walked in silence for a while, the trickle of the stream beside us filling up the air.

I got so used to the silence that it was almost a surprise when Gob said, "So, what's the plan exactly?"

Chip hummed from ahead of us, the reeds fading away and thick, foggy forest taking its place. The stream continued onward, no walls to impede our path—unless it was the maze removing them from our way.

"Capture the minotaur," I said, taking my first hesitant step onto the forest floor, covered in fallen leaves. The leather boots Lyra had provided made the uneven ground so much easier to manage.

How had I ever coped in that dress? I must have looked half-mad to anyone who'd lain eyes upon me. Maybe that was why Gob had had such distaste for me from the start.

"I *know* that," snapped Gob. "'Capture the minotaur,'" he muttered. "How? With what? You think no one's ever tried that before?"

"Well, I know the fae *tried* to defeat it," I said. "But they never tried to capture it, did they?"

"Oh, that'll make all of the difference." Gob snorted. "Please, sir, we're not trying to hurt you. If you'd kindly step into this stone cage… And what kind of cage are we putting him in?"

My stomach gnawed at me from the inside. He'd thought more about this than I had. "The maze will provide."

"Oh, yes, let's put all of our faith in this prison of stone and muck," Gob muttered. "Wonder what it needs us for at all, then, eh?"

Before I could retort—or even think of what to say—Chip called out from ahead of us. "Hey! Dead end!"

"Oh, that was faster than expected," muttered Gob. "Thought the bloody thing wanted us to go somewhere."

I hastened my steps, calling out Chip's name and heading for the blurry figure in the mist who called back to us. The elf-cat waved.

"Stay there!" I called after her. "Stay where I can see you!"

"Hold up!" called Gob. "Don't go getting so far ahead of me, I can't—whoa!"

Gob's voice cut short. I spun in the mist, looking for the hobbling troll to appear somewhere behind me. "Gob?"

Chip let out a cat-like yowl.

"Chip!" I whipped around, bolting for the sound up ahead.

Finding myself weighed down, the waterskins and provisions clanking in the satchel at my back, I slipped my arms out of it and started running faster.

"Hands off me, you squirrely-faced fiend!" Chip came into sight, squirming and twisting, her two front paws trapped in the grip of two other small figures. "Tricksters! Thieves!"

One of the other figures was yanking at the satchel at her back.

"Let her go!" I shouted, and without thinking, I reached for the wicked dagger at my hip. Holding it out with both hands, I ground my feet into the dirt.

And found myself face to face with two familiar green-skinned trolls, each with a firm grip on one of Chip's legs.

THIRTY-SIX

EDONY

"Oh, look, it's the big, scary human," said one of the troll men. Sure enough, as Chip had said, there was a tall stone wall behind him—at least on this side of the stream. "Looks like you got an upgrade on weapons, eh? No more big, dull stick?"

"Lemme go!" Chip growled and bit the troll's shoulder through his clothing, her face contorted into a sour expression as she immediately spit. It did the job, though, as the troll yowled and let her go, freeing her to draw her needle blade and poke the other troll holding her down in the cheek.

With the two yowling and cradling their wounds, Chip fixed her satchel at her shoulder and backed up so we stood side by side, our blades drawn.

As if I knew what I could do with it.

Would I stab them? *Could* I stab them? I'd never even done any of the killing for the occasional meat we'd had back home.

My heart thundered. How was I going to face the minotaur if I was frozen to the ground against two trolls?

"I better not have gotten any of your vile poison!" Chip spat again.

"It's in the teeth, you dolt!" said the one she'd bitten, peeling back his lip to show a fang.

"Stinky rat!" said the other, cradling his arm. "Foul cat!"

"That's 'brilliant and brave elf' to you," snapped Chip. She shook her little needle-sword in front of her, taking one jump forward. The troll cowed, moving backward.

"Enough!" said a woman, her voice gravelly and deep. "We've got what we came for."

Chip spun around so her back was to mine, and we both turned our heads slightly, eager not to leave the two trolls who'd attacked her unguarded.

"Lay off, Ma. I said I'd come with you, didn't I?" Gob emerged from the mist, escorted by two women trolls with downturned mouths and brown hair pulled tightly into harsh buns at the napes of their necks. Their threadbare clothes stretched against broad shoulders, and red, pointed caps like Gob's jostled on their heads as Gob kicked and squirmed. Finally, the women looked to one another and let go, Gob stumbling forward toward us and sliding into the dirt at our feet.

The trolls who'd held Chip—the same ones who'd tormented Gob in the swamp—chuckled darkly.

More trolls emerged from the mists. One carried what I realized was Gob's satchel—clearly missing on his back—and several dragged my own.

"Hey!" Chip called. "We need those!"

"Payment," said one of the troll women.

Gob lifted himself up to his hands and knees. I shifted the dagger to my left hand and reached down to offer him a hand up. He slapped it away and stood up on his own stubborn two feet.

"I don't need a filthy human's help."

And here I'd thought we'd been making progress.

Chip hissed at him. I held my free hand out to her to signal she should stay calm.

"We don't mean any harm," I said loudly, just as Chip pulled her lips back as far as they would go and hissed again. I cleared my throat. "Just let us go on our way—"

"*With* our supplies." Chip shook her thin sword at the troll women in front of the group lugging our satchels.

"Oh, no, I don't think so," said the woman who'd spoken before. "Payment for Gobble's crimes demands far more than this."

"Crimes?" Chip asked. "What kind of *crimes* can a troll commit amongst a horde of no-good scaredy-tros? Did he not run fast enough from a little ol' scary bug?"

The trolls murmured amongst themselves at Chip's insult and I hushed her.

The troll woman's eyes narrowed—on me.

"Ignore the little rat," she said, louder to the group around her.

Chip growled. "Call me that one more time!"

"You..." she said, not tearing her eyes from mine. "I've seen you before. Only..."

"My ma," whispered Gob from around my thighs. So he wasn't totally detaching from our merry little group.

I straightened and made a decision, slipping my dagger back into its scabbard. "You've seen my mother," I said. "But she had hair the color of fire—and a face marked with scars."

"Yes." The troll woman stroked her chin. "Marked for the beast, that one. Mother, eh? Doesn't seem likely."

I stiffened. "She and my father—they found a way. Only I lost them both to this place in the end."

"The maze claims all that belongs to it." Gob's mother nodded. "Like you, human."

"I wasn't marked—"

"And yet here you stand." She gestured around her. "Found your way home, didn't you? Fitting for that lout son of mine to be wandering around with the child of a filthy beast's meal."

"I'm not a…" My throat went dry. Was that what she was saying? My mother had been eaten? But everyone told me the creature didn't even need to eat.

"When did you see the human woman?" I asked. "Was she… Why would you call her a 'meal'?"

The troll woman laughed and tapped her temple. "Any human marked for the beast is gorged in the end." She pretended to gobble up an invisible meal, her smile malicious.

I opened my mouth, but Gob hissed.

"She didn't see your mother eaten," he said quietly. "There's no doubt she would have bragged about that before. She said she was dancing and singing and completely out of her wits."

"I think my exact words were 'two beans short of a chili,'" said the troll woman.

The others behind her laughed.

"Keep your filthy son," snapped Chip. "You can even keep his rations. But my companion and I have to go." She puffed her chest proudly. "We have a quest."

Gob slapped a hand over his face.

"A quest?" his mother echoed. "And what, pray tell, might the three of you misfits hope to accomplish?"

"Capturing the—" Chip started.

I spoke louder. "We're not leaving Gob behind." That was enough to make Chip's jaw drop, her sentence forgotten. "We're supposed to do this together."

Gob's brow softened as he looked up at me. I couldn't tell him I still planned to make sure he wasn't in any real danger—not when it was clear that leaving him here amidst his own kind would definitely prove disastrous for him.

"Keep the provisions, if you like," I said. How far had we gone? Lyra's cabin couldn't be much of a hike back. "But let us go."

Almost as if in challenge to my own thought, the ground rumbled and the mists parted behind the crowd of trolls around our dropped satchels, a stone wall birthing up from the dirt itself and working its way around the trees to block our way back.

What was the labyrinth thinking, taking away all hope of returning to stock up once more? Weren't we on a mission it had *agreed* to send us on?

I grit my teeth. Even so. "Just let us go."

Gob shook his head. "They won't..." he whispered.

His mother cackled, and more trolls emerged from beside

the two who had grabbed Chip. We were surrounded now, trolls on three sides, walls on at least two—though that left the stream on the fourth side. The waters were moving faster than they had back at Lyra's clearing—perhaps even faster than they had moments before. The appearance of the new wall, which stretched across the water, leaving only a small tunnel for it to flow through, seemed to have enraged the liquid, hastening its pace.

"Trying to buy us off with things we already have, are you?" She gestured to the satchels. Some of the trolls had untied them and were rummaging around their contents. One held an especially long carrot out and smacked his lips as he turned it in the misty slivers of moonlight.

"Think again," she finished.

"I left your rotten village, didn't I?" Gob bellowed. "What more do you want from me?"

Chip's eyes widened. I also found it surprising to see the troll stand so firm.

"You took from us!" his mother shouted. "You walked to that fae village and traded the goods we'd gathered with our blood, sweat, and tears—and then you took what the fae gave you back, and you ran off to eat it all yourself!"

That was it? Gobble's great crime. It surely sounded selfish of him, but was it worth all of this furor?

Chip growled. "'Gathered with blood, sweat, and tears'? Everyone knows you steal from the rest of us in the labyrinth— and you keep all those nice goods the fae give you to yourself!"

Gob winced at Chip's loud voice. Or maybe it was the contents of her accusation.

His mother continued to ignore her. "Exile isn't enough, you lazy son of mine! Refuse to do your part of the raiding and thieving, do you? Then you fail even the trading assignment I gave you?" She gestured for those around her to line up. They did, leaving the satchels untouched but firmly behind them. Even the ones behind and beside us pushed in closer.

"Any regrets?" his mother asked.

"You try it! You just try it!" Chip snapped her jaws and swung her sword in the air, keeping the trolls nearest her hesitating and slightly at bay.

"Only that I didn't share it," said Gob. "Delicious seafood, from the far-off seafaring place of Westbridge. Divine creatures you can't even imagine."

"The seaport town is Eastmeet," I said—then remembered I'd gotten the two directions mixed up when I'd pointed them out to him.

Gob quirked an eyebrow at me but grunted.

His mother stopped, raising a fist in the air.

"You actually regret not sharing?" she asked.

"Yeah. With the elves and with Lyra and with even the minotaur himself, rather than letting a single, succulent tiny leg of those crabs hit another troll's palate!" Gob puffed out his chest.

Chip cocked her head, examining our troll companion, and the nearest troll used her brief distraction to lunge forward.

"Watch out!" I said, reaching for my dagger.

Chip quickly stabbed the troll in the eye and he screamed.

My hand felt cold on the dagger's hilt. I thought better of it.

Gob bounced on his heels beside me, bringing up his fists.

I grabbed Chip by the scruff of her neck, yanking Gob up by the arm with the other hand.

"What are you—" started Chip.

"Oi!" shouted Gob.

And then I bolted in the one direction I could, my long legs giving me advantage over our pursuers, and jumped straight into the raging stream.

THIRTY-SEVEN

BRECC

"Brecc, we've been going in circles—"

"Then we'll wear a circular path through the dirt and muck of this maze until the ground itself opens up."

I didn't have to turn around to feel Carac and Elspeth's exchanged glance. They'd been begging me to turn back toward the fae village for hours, countless hours, until their incessant whining had muttered off into a welcome silence.

I hacked at a cluster of vines, my grandfather's sword, which Carac had found during his attempts to locate me— during those blessed few hours I'd spent wrapped in Edony's arms—cleaving at the thick foliage. The tip of the blade thudded against stone beyond the visible overgrowth.

"*Again?*" Every direction we went, there was another wall. *Every direction.*

Carac pulled up beside me and put a tentative hand on my shoulder. I lowered my weapon, trying to keep my fist gripping the hilt from trembling with rage. "You saw her. You know she's safe—"

"And how long do you think she'll stay safe in this place?" Grunting, I whapped a particularly aggravating vine away from my temple. "She spoke of some quest, and *companions*, and a desire to *capture the beast*—"

"You know she's not alone, then," said Elspeth stiffly. Her hand rested on the sword hilt at her hip. The sword she'd never drawn outside of training in the courtyard or whacking at these infernal vines and branches.

"And you think she's capable of capturing that *monster*?" I kicked at the nearest cluster of vines for emphasis. "She, a human with no experience in such things—"

"*No one* has experience with such things." Elspeth's mouth formed a grim line. "Even our forefathers, who roamed a wilder landscape, who had raised these swords against more than just branch and vine—they fell to that thing."

In the quiet of the eternal night blanketing this place, the creature's howls rung out in the air. Was it because of Edony? Was she on the move now? How long had it been?

I rotated my arm, unused to the soreness from excessive movement, unused to fatigue of any kind. But oh, did it weigh on me. I paced back and forth in front of the vines, the heaviness in my eyelids, the prickling of my scalp such foreign feelings. Love was a never-ending hunger for me, and the world itself was working against my ability to satisfy it.

"How would *you* capture the beast?" Carac asked. "How would you have us help you, my king?"

I did not miss the harsh look Elspeth sent the man. I had

gone too many years too soft, letting them think us all one jubilant gathering of friends, rather than a king and his subjects.

"I don't know," I snapped. I'd thought to search for a way—but I hadn't had time. I hadn't had a moment's rest to *think*, to reflect on how we might...

I'd left Kaylein with the shorn hoof. She'd promised to carry on the research in my absence. She'd always been more intelligent than I. And she wasn't consumed by this *hunger*. Perhaps she'd found something.

"I know one thing," said Elspeth. "You have no hope of success looking like *that*." Her lip curled in disgust as her gaze grazed my ears.

It would take food, and rest—perhaps even sleep, it had gotten so bad—before I could hope to look like the Fae King again. My free hand grazed an ear; there was the slightest tip protruding. My time with Edony pinned beneath me had been exhausting but exhilarating. Rest had come for the first time since we'd parted, and it had done me some good.

My mind had cleared, the anger swelling up inside me subsided.

And then it had all returned with the whip of the reeds around my waist, the force of the tug as they'd sent me flying back to where Elspeth and Carac had been searching for me.

I was a fool. I had no hope of beating the minotaur as things were, but more importantly, I had no hope of ever finding it—of ever reaching Edony again—opposing the maze itself.

It simply wouldn't let me. I wasn't about to cow the maze into submission.

Growling, I slipped the sword back into its sheath, my

stomach gnawing at the evidence of the damage I'd done hacking it fruitlessly against walls that would always rise up to meet me.

"We return home," I said, fully sliding the sword back into place.

"Thank the ancestors," Elspeth muttered under her breath.

Carac broke into an uneasy smile.

"Rest," I said. "Rest will do me good." I tried to clear my mind, to keep the maze from reading any more than that in my words.

Whatever its intelligence, its ability to tap into the unknowable magic that tied a being's thoughts and energies to the stone and flora of which this place consisted, it had to concede at least this much.

It wanted me out of the way.

And I would think things over better after rest.

To the left, in the direction I sensed would lead to the fae village—our little paradise amidst this dank and depressing place—a wall retreated, fading into the ground as if showing us the way.

Two nights I slept. Two nights those around me let me waste away the time I needed to figure out how to save my love. Two nights they probably gladly stole from me in order to extend their own security and peaceful existence, as I intuited later when I asked how long I'd slept.

Hours they robbed me of feeling the warmth and security of my own loved one in my arms.

But no. The maze would have kept me from her regardless.

Fae did not need sleep. But human blood in our veins was nourished by it, and as mine had proliferated so much the past few days, my human blood had *craved* it.

I woke rejuvenated, my eyelids no longer heavy. My hands reached for my ears—they were pointed, too.

I'd eat. And then I'd force these lethargic creatures around me to prepare themselves for a rescue.

Leaping up from my bed, I sorted through the trunk containing my clothes, pulling out the outfit most conducive to comfort and flexibility—and perhaps most important, protection. Leather pants. Leather vest. Arm guards, but those I'd gone to sleep wearing. Boots that would stand up to long treks.

Clothes made for my grandfather, the warrior.

I stood and looked around—someone had tidied my room in my absence, a fact I'd hardly remarked upon as I'd collapsed upon the soft mattress, giving the maze this one small victory.

It had needed to stop concerning itself with me, to instead focus on Edony and this "mission" it had bestowed upon her. I'd needed to gain strength. And now I would clear my mind and sneak up on it without it even realizing my true intentions.

The maze thought I could be persuaded. Bartered with. It held the power—for now.

It had better protect my Edony.

Bursting out of my room, I headed toward Favian's, knocking on the door. This time of day, he was often in the dining hall, or at someone else's home, enjoying a human-spouse-cooked meal, but with his new bride, I figured he'd be nowhere else.

"Who is it?" Favian's voice was weak, his words cracking.

"Your king." I would not be turned out so he could canoodle his wife.

The door opened with a creak, Favian poking his head out of the door. His long, white hair was untied, hanging messily across either side of his face. His eyes... looked heavy.

"You're awake," he said, a small smile emerging on his lips.

"You look like you ought not to be." I pushed my way inside, and he stood back, slipping out of my way like sediment washed away by water.

I peered around. There was no sign of his bride.

"Is she learning to cook in the kitchens?" I asked. I needn't specify who.

Favian gripped a chunk of his hair, his eyes growing wide and wild as he stroked the lock without purpose. "My wife? Who could say? I haven't seen her since the day you left in search of her cousin."

"You haven't—" I cut myself short. There was no way for a human to exit the fae village undetected. There simply wasn't.

Unless the walls surrounding our village had willed it so. And the maze was quite capable of willing such things, I knew now.

But what could be the advantage of that?

Favian flicked aside his hair over his shoulder, as he often did, and a glimpse of a rounded ear caught my attention as he sat on the edge of his undisturbed bed. "She's likely with her friend from Westbridge. I can't speak to her. Not anymore."

Did I have time to worry about Favian's marriage when my own true love was out there with companions I knew not on an impossible quest?

I sighed.

Then I sat beside him. My mind was clearer now.

"You could use some rest," I said.

"I'll be no help to you either way." He turned to stare at me, intently studying. "You seem calm."

"I'm not," I said. "Calmer, maybe. But I will never be settled until…" Afraid to speak the words, lest it draw the labyrinth's focus to me, I stopped my loquacious tongue.

"Kaylein told me you'd instructed her to research the hoof. The incident that led to its shearing."

I nodded.

"I told her to speak with Borin."

My eyebrow quirked. "The bard?"

He shrugged. "I could have sworn he sang a song once of that day. But only once. His audience found it… too disturbing." Favian wrinkled his nose, then walked over to his bookshelf, which was almost as large as mine. "I thought I grabbed a book of songs from your room the other day—"

A book of songs? Why? "Looking for something with which to woo your wife?"

"Do not tease me now," he barked. "I am not in the mood." His fingers ran over the spines of the collection. "I can't find it. That day… is hazy in my mind." He gestured wildly around his head as if to quantify his lack of clarity.

I knew the feeling.

"Perhaps whoever cleaned my room put it back on the shelf." I stood. We had much to discuss, he and I, but I knew all too well, if he wouldn't rest, he'd be in no mood to hear it. "I'll go look—or see if I can find Borin or Kaylein."

As I reached the doorway, Favian's hand clamped down over my wrist, causing me to pause.

"I understand now," he whispered. "If what I feel is but a fraction of the torment you've faced..."

"Rest," I said simply, putting a hand atop his. "Then wake refreshed and find a way to atone for your sins—save the woman's daughter, save my heart. Win your bride back."

His hand fell. His expression looked haunted in the shadows cast by trickling light. "I don't know if I ever can."

"Love," I said, not even thinking the words before I spoke them. "Love, if it's true—you will find a way."

And find a way I would.

CHAPTER

THIRTY-EIGHT

EDONY

The stream was flowing even more angrily than I'd anticipated, the waters rushing me forward. I couldn't swim with my hands clutching desperately to my companions.

Chip's wet head burst up above the water. "Drowning!" she screamed. Her paw clutched desperately to her needle-like sword even so. "We're drowning!" Water spurt from between her thin lips.

"Hang on," said Gob between heaving gasps. He shook his head, his red cap washed away to reveal wispy, dark-green hair plastered against his broad scalp. His arms moved in smooth motions, unencumbered now by his satchel. He broke free from my grasp before I could even put up a fight.

My head went underwater. I blinked, but there was nothing to see but the indistinct shadows that spun around me. My hand clung to Chip's wet fur, and I put all of my efforts into raising her higher, above the water's surface.

Something dove in, my ears filled with the muffled force of movement even as the stream raged away.

Small. Human-shaped. A troll. Gob took hold of Chip, who wouldn't stop flailing, but he kept on fighting. He slipped an arm through her satchel, wrapping her tightly against him. She stopped moving, poking her sword higher above the surface.

I couldn't tell for certain, but I thought I saw both sets of eyes staring down at me, shining. Sad.

My cramping hand let go of Chip's fur.

My eyes closed.

I sunk.

My last few thoughts, after I'd stopped thinking of Neela, Grandmother, Father, and Mother—after I'd stopped thinking of even Brecc—was that the maze had trapped us with those trolls.

The maze had struck a bargain with us and then it had betrayed us.

A small hand tightened around my wrist.

I lost consciousness.

A fire crackled, the warmth hitting my cheek so welcome with the chill all over my back.

I blinked my eyes open, though the lashes had crusted together, and the movement was a strain. Murmured voices echoed in my ear, as well as someone riffling through a squelching collection of items.

"Ugh, even the *water* is wet!" That was Chip.

"Dry off the skins near the fire. The water's still drinkable. If we've lost any, we can get some more." Gob. They were both safe.

I was safe, too.

"I'm not stepping near that thing again."

"You will if you need to drink. And you're going to need to drink plenty before we go farther."

"The stream *is* tamer here..." Chip scattered on little paws across a hard surface.

My eyes finally opened, and I drew the ones around me into focus. Chip stood on her back legs, her fur a sort of mottled, unkempt look halfway from wet to dry. I wondered, briefly, if elves bathed themselves from head to toes with their tongues like barn cats. I hadn't witnessed one licking their fur for more than a moment during my stay with them.

She walked hesitatingly toward the edge of the stream. The easy trickle hit my ears now, nothing at all like the raging waters it had been. Nearer the fire, Gob was setting out items from Chip's satchel.

The one pack of provisions we had left.

"You're awake!" Chip let out a soft mew and bounded over on all four paws, her tail straight up in the air. She rammed into me, purring, and I chuckled, scratching under her little jaw.

"What happened?" I asked.

Gob took quiet steps as he continued to shuffle around, stacking items in front of the fire—on stone, I realized. Cobblestone covered in sifted sand.

"Gob saved us." Chip let out a little grumble in her throat. "I mean, *you* thought for us to jump into the stream to begin with—which I would have voted against had you *asked*, but I supposed it couldn't be helped, considering." Her voice grew gruffer on the last few words.

"How did we get here?" I looked around. The stream curved off into another direction, traveling deep into an overgrowth of woods. On the other side towered a wall covered in vines, blocking out all other sight. There was forest left in one direction and in the other...

The forest broke into sand. A horizon that seemed to have no end, just sand and sand and...

"The Hall of the Obliterated," I remarked. At the very edge of the dunes, there was something dark and towering that poked out into the sky.

Gob grumbled. "We went where the waters took us. This is it. The edge of the maze. Beyond those sands—and the rotten tower—is another wall, I'm certain, but farther still, one can finally make it to the human world." He looked out at the horizon almost wistfully.

So the maze had taken us here, was that how he saw it?

It had corralled us into having no choice but to follow the stream—and the stream had most definitely taken us here faster than our own feet could have.

Had it worked with the trolls? Guided them to us, knowing they were after Gob?

Had it... not betrayed us, then?

Chip bounded over to where Gob had spread the contents of her satchel—the satchel itself, too—and picked up her needle-like sword. It glinted in the firelight. So that had made it through our swim.

My hand reached for my scabbard at my waist. It was gone. The entire belt and scabbard.

"S'over there." Gob gestured to the farther side of the fire, where a pile of clothes were laid out on the sandy stone, as well as my belt. Gob was almost entirely naked, but for the loincloth around his hips. "Didn't like touching it, but I held it by the belt."

I couldn't blame him. There was something far too strange about the dagger. But perhaps "strange" was what was needed to corral the minotaur.

My own clothes hung limply against my body, the leather reeking as I took in deep breaths. I stood, steadied myself on shaky feet, and began to strip, starting by kicking off my boots.

Gob jumped in place and pointedly turned away.

Chip laughed and nudged him on the shoulder. "I'll never understand you fur-less creatures and these 'clothes.'" She spoke as if she truly had learned the word recently. From me. "I used to think her blue clothes were her fur!"

I chuckled, too. "And you thought cutting them might hurt me." The trousers were particularly difficult to peel off, but I managed. I left my damp, overly-large shirt on and spread my pants beside the fire on the warming stones.

"Yes, well, no wonder you're all often cold." She shook her head rapidly, nearing the fire. "Though this is why we only bathe when necessary. Takes forever for the fur to dry!" She sent my pants and boots on the stones a pointed look. "Though I don't think your *clothes* provide you any advantage there."

This place reminded me of the secret clearing in Lyra's fields, where I'd met with Brecc—for perhaps the very last time. It was like a path had once been inlaid here, whether from the sentient maze itself or from a civilization long since forgotten, I couldn't say. Perhaps it had once run the length of this labyrinth, before the walls had sprung up.

Something on a stone caught my eye. I brushed aside the sand.

"What's this?" I asked.

Chip walked over, dragging the tip of her sword against the sandy stones. Gob came over, too.

It looked like an etching, carved with intent rather than scratched by happenstance. Two shapes. Each was triangular, but they were curved.

"Antenna?" Chip offered, cocking her head. She licked her lips. "Haven't had a good grasshopper in a spell. Might have to catch us some bugs for dinner, considering all of our provisions are ruined."

That would be a new experience.

"Horns," said Gob gruffly.

Horns like the minotaur's.

I shifted aside my boots and kept brushing away the sand. There were a number of stones with the same pattern, but the path—or whatever it had once been—was broken, dirt and sand engulfing places where stones might have been.

"Maybe it's just a sign that the minotaur walks here." Chip shivered and looked around, as if the beast might jump up from behind her.

"Or the boundary where it stops," Gob offered, looking back at the ruins of the tower. "Didn't you say that the minotaur fears the dullahans?"

"That's what my ma and pa said." Chip frowned and scratched behind her ear with a sharp claw. She sighed, then finally looked out at the horizon herself. Her eyes grew glassy.

"I thought perhaps our mission would take us here, but I didn't imagine so soon. I... swore never to go there again."

We all grew silent.

"The place where the dullahans rest," I said, reality finally snapping into place. "The only ones who've taken on the minotaur in earnest."

"Yeah, taken him on and—not survived." Gob waved a hand in the direction of the dunes of sand, then padded back over to the supplies strewn out beside the fire. "But I don't see we have a choice. We have to speak to them. But first, I say we work to replace some of what we lost. Gather food—then make our way to that blasted hall."

"No," Chip whispered. "There has to be another way."

Gob grunted and crouched down on the balls of his feet. "This is where we're meant to be. The maze led us here. Either that or it really wanted to do me in back there, what with sending all of the trolls our way."

"The thing lives in the outer walls mostly, right?" Chip asked. "We can make our way there, take him on in his home turf. We don't need... We don't need *their* help," she whispered.

"There was a fire in the outer walls," I said. "The beast might have moved on. In fact, I think he must have. He's after me."

Gob looked up and stared at me. "You? Right. Your mother." He frowned and studied the array of things laid out beside him. "That's what children do, eh? Take on the sins of their mothers?"

"She didn't sin," I snapped, harsher than I'd meant to. "But..." I frowned. He wasn't talking about me. "Gob, you told me once you didn't deserve pity."

"He *did* bite you," Chip pointed out.

I shushed her.

"You made it seem as if you'd been exiled from the trolls deservedly," I said.

"And?" Gob stood and walked over to his clothes. Picking up his pants, he smelled them. His nose wrinkled, but he slid them on anyway. "You'd think that mob back there would have confirmed that theory."

"But they said you ate all the food you got from the fae," I said. "And *you* said you wished you'd shared it with others in the maze. That it had been some sort of revenge for the other trolls stealing."

Chip crossed her front legs like arms across her chest. "And monopolizing all the trade, I might add."

"Which you seemed to *regret*," I added.

Gob shrugged and put on his shirt. His clothes were dryer than mine. He was still missing his red cap, though, and he ran his hands through his hair, making it messier than even before.

"It was a small act of defiance." The corner of his lip turned up. "But hey, a bit of a selfish one, too." He tapped his stomach. "Had me a feast that day."

"I think you're a nicer person—troll—than you want to admit," I said.

Chip's jaw dropped. But then she frowned. "Thanks for saving me," she muttered.

Gob cocked his head. "What was that?"

She shouted this time. "Thank you! Okay?"

So even Chip was in agreement.

Gob ran a finger under his nose and shrugged. "Couldn't

exactly leave you two to drown, could I? Bet the maze would be too mad at me to let me out if I had."

He could tell himself that was why. If that was what his pride needed.

"Hey, were those horns all lit up before?" Chip asked.

Gob was spreading out the cloth that made up the sole remaining satchel, stuffing the waterskins inside.

"What do you mean?" I turned to find what Chip was pointing her thin sword at.

Sure enough, the etching in the stone was glowing now, a deep red color. All around us, the sand lit up with those symbols, glowing from the stones below.

"I'd get your clothes on, human," Gob said, his voice a harsh whisper. "Don't forget that wretched dagger."

The hairs on the back of my neck prickled as I turned around, looking for whatever it was that had gotten Gob's attention.

The steam was the first thing I noticed, edging out from the forest opposite the sandy dunes. Then the glowing red eyes.

The harsh, heavy breaths.

I ran for my clothes and scooped them all into my arms, taking hold of the dagger and the belt by the scabbard. Gob was tying up the satchel, leaving most of its contents, still sodden, on the ground as he slipped his arms through two loops of fabric.

Chip cried out and swung her sword in the direction of the glowing eyes.

"Chip!" I screamed. "No, Chip, this way!"

The dunes. We had to run for the dunes. If the rumors were

right and the beast wouldn't follow us to where the dullahans lived...

Gob skidded to a stop beside me, just beyond the row of glowing lights below. The sand was soft and cool beneath the soles of my bare feet.

"We might be safe past this line," Gob said, echoing my own thoughts. Why else were these symbols here?

But Chip... Chip was running, growling, heading in the opposite direction.

THIRTY-NINE

EDONY

"Chip!" I flung my pants and boots into the sand, scrambling to pull the dagger out of the sheath, but it dangled in front of me because my hand gripping the belt shook.

"Come back, you blasted fool!" shouted Gob beside me.

Chip let out a cry, and the minotaur snorted, stepping out from the trees. His hooves stamped fallen leaves and twigs with slow, methodical steps, the crinkling sounds as unsettling as bones shattering beneath his hooved feet.

Chip jumped up to a nearby tree with a cry, sliding the hilt of her sword between her teeth and scattering up the bark of the tree with claws extended.

The beast's head turned upward as Chip retreated, but he didn't stop in his progression toward me.

Toward me. Good. Chip wasn't the thing's target, after all.

The dagger, cold in my grip, slipped out of the sheath and I flung the belt to the side, into the sand.

"What's the plan?" asked Gob, his voice trembling.

"You hide," I said. "And keep Chip from doing anything foolish again."

The trees above the minotaur's head shook as presumably Chip moved from one to the next. Only the minotaur was making his way to the fire now.

"Oh, no, I'm not going past that line." Gob pointed to the glowing symbols on stone and beneath sand. "I think the creature can't get past there. Oi, bloody elf! You hear me? Make your way past the glowing line and we'll regroup."

Chip let out a little chittering response, but the minotaur's head didn't so much as budge. He stared straight ahead, his dark irises sparkling with the crackle of fire. I moved through the sand, putting more space between Gob and me. The creature's head shifted to watch me.

So it would be simpler than I'd thought to keep Chip and Gob safe. If Chip hadn't run out to face the thing.

"Come here," I said, wanting to test Gob's theory.

"Then what?" Gob asked.

The dagger shook in my double grip. Stab him? Where would be best? Something told me I'd only have one chance. I glanced around. What would we use to trap him?

My gaze fell down. My toes were lost beneath the grains of sand. We were still inside the labyrinth walls. Could the maze open up the sand beneath our feet?

"I have an idea," I said.

"Spit it out before that furry fool flings herself at the back of the monster's head," said Gob.

"Chip?" My back grew rigid. "Stay put."

The branch nearest the minotaur shook. "On your signal," she called back.

I wouldn't have a signal for her.

The beast trampled through the fire Gob and Chip had fashioned, kicking aside the logs as he headed my way.

"Come on, come on," said Gob quietly. He chewed a thumbnail as he watched the creature headed in a straight line for me.

Flames licked the creature's fur, first one leg and then the other catching fire as logs and twigs rolled outward, sizzling in the sand.

But the minotaur kept moving, his legs smoking as he exited the fire. The flames were vanquished.

"He's not succumbing to fire!" Chip yelled the obvious. "No wonder he didn't mind setting the whole outer edge of the maze ablaze."

Had the creature done that himself, then? But no. He'd been afraid of the fire at the time. Perhaps the difference was the amount.

Steam rose from the minotaur's nostrils. He cradled his single upper hoof against his broad almost-human like chest like an arm.

"Keep coming," I said.

"Testing my theory?" Gob asked.

There was that, but then...

The minotaur lifted one hoof and froze. He put it back down where it had been. Without even looking down, he somehow knew.

At his feet was a stone tile with the glowing carvings of the horns.

"Yes!" Gob shouted, throwing a fist in the air. "Now, come on, furball! Come to our side, where it's safe—"

Chip let out a scream and jumped, practically gliding through the air and landing atop the creature's head. She grabbed on to a horn with the claws of one paw, her other front paw gripping her sword, which she plunged down into the beast's bulbous eye.

He screeched out into the night and turned, whacking his arms wildly as the little elf held on.

"Chip!" I ran forward, ignoring Gob's plea to stop, sending sand scattering as I passed through the glowing barrier, my feet tender on the warmed tiles. "Chip!" I called again, aiming the dagger at one of the beast's shoulders.

I made the swing, putting all my strength into the double-fisted grip, but the minotaur turned to me, moving his shoulder out of my range and sending me tumbling. The monster whipped his head so fast, Chip went flying—over my head, into the dunes behind me.

"Got you!" Gob shouted, and there was a thud, the two rolling through the sands somewhere behind me.

I was too transfixed on the monster's face to look. Chip's sword stuck upward from his eye, the great thing squinted and swollen. He took a heavy, loud breath, tilting his snout toward me.

My guts grew heavy and my knees shook. But I couldn't let this opportunity pass. I still had the dagger between my hands.

It was my turn to cry out, and as I swung this time, the blade caught the creature's forearm—and stuck, like the thing was becoming a pincushion.

The beast turned his head to the skies and yowled, using

his stub of an arm to bat the needle sword in his eye free at the same time his other arm, the one with my dagger inside his bone, flung outward at me. I didn't have time to dodge before he clocked me in the chest and I fell backward, screaming as I landed on a stick still hot with embers.

"Now!" I said to the maze. It could usually just pick up on *thoughts*, it seemed, at least as far as how I understood it. "Take him now! Swallow him up in the sand!"

Only... as the creature flailed around, he could never get past the glowing symbols. There was sand on this side of them, yes, but it was mostly stone and dirt.

"No, no, no," I said, as I dragged myself to my feet. My hand went to the small of my back, but I winced as I touched tender flesh. My idea for trapping the minotaur. The sole weapon I'd been given—the weapon even Chip had been given. Gone. Useless.

My dagger was still stuck in the monster's arm. I had no time to think of how to get it back, or what else I was going to do, before he let out a roar and charged me, bending downward and tilting his head forward.

My feet flew across warm stone, burning embers, as I made my way for the glowing red line.

"Come on!" Chip's voice, joined soon after with Gob's.

"You've got this, Edony!"

Maybe it was the sounds of their voices. Or Gob using my name like that.

I ran, stumbling, but fast enough to cross the glowing red line of symbols and dive into the nearest dune of sand, scrambling around to see if the beast had followed me.

The monster let out a roar behind me as he slammed into an invisible wall, halting his momentum with a crash.

"Ha!" Gob said, buckling over. The satchel was off his shoulders, tossed somewhere behind him. "Ha," he said a second time, slower, clutching his knees and heaving over.

I swallowed. I was safe here—for now—behind this border. But I had no idea what to do from here on out.

The maze had led me here, but if not to swallow the creature up in sand, if not for my disastrous skills with a dagger to do any actual damage, then for what?

Chip bounded up beside me on four legs, kicking up a cloud of sand. "I hear something!"

Gob quirked an eyebrow at her. "Yeah. We all do." He gestured with one thumb at the beast, which was panting and growling.

"No!" Chip held up one toe of her front paw. "Something worse than that," she whispered.

I looked up above us. There couldn't have been anything worse than the minotaur in this place.

A soft, sweet song rung out in the air, its words indistinguishable. The melody was tinny, the voice almost shrill.

And then it was joined by a chorus of similar cries, a warbling song on the surface meant to soothe but doing little beyond filling my gut with a heavy sense of dread.

Gob stood up straight and turned around. "What in the blasted maze...?"

A storm of bright white specks was headed our way from the direction of the Hall of the Obliterated. The horde clung to the sky, like a blizzard of snow being blasted across the horizon.

"The ladydoves," said Chip, her eyes wide, her back pressing up against my side. I winced as she touched one of the sore spots of my flesh.

"Get dressed," hissed Gob, nodding his head toward my pants and boots. I didn't know if I'd have time before the horde arrived.

But I wouldn't find out by just lying there. "And then what?" I asked, slipping a leg into my still-sodden trousers, kicking off sand as I jammed a foot into a boot.

"And then we run," said Chip, her voice a murmur.

My shirt tucked into my pants, my now-useless belt around my hips, I looked left and right. "To where?" Behind us, the minotaur lingered.

Only he squinted his one good eye upward and shirked, as if the sight of the flock of birds disturbed him too.

"Away," said Chip. "Anywhere but here."

She fell on four paws and bolted down the dunes of sand, sticking to the forest edge.

"What are they going to do?" asked Gob. He'd tried to inject levity into the question and added a dry chuckle. "Peck us to death?"

I thought of Chip and her fallen brothers, of the creatures she'd told me were the ladydoves' companions. Creatures we had reason to seek.

The dullahans.

We'd faced off against the minotaur alone and gotten nowhere.

I ground my wet boots into the sand, dying the pale grains darker around the soles of my shoes.

"Go after her," I said. "I have to stay here, come what may."

The flap of the wings grew louder, drowning out the tinny song that neared as the flock descended.

And then the haunting song became an outright screech, the myriad birds swirling in circles together until they came together in a line—a line headed straight for my head.

CHAPTER

FORTY

EDONY

"Watch out!" I screamed, as if Gob and Chip weren't already fully aware of the flock of birds headed straight for our heads.

Chip was already gone—I couldn't see her past the flurry of white.

I shielded my face with a forearm as their wings scuffed the top of my head, their song turned to shrieks in my ears. I waited for the pecks of their beaks, wincing every time one drew near, the flutter of their wings pricking gooseflesh on my skin.

But the birds seemed more concerned with—

"They're after the beast!" Gob shouted. He gripped my wrist. "Come on!"

He tugged and we moved through. I couldn't see past the flock, diving down, whirling up, a flurry of white far denser than even the worst of snowstorms.

But through the white, amidst the pale yellow-silver of the

dunes of sand, were large, dark... figures. Moving closer at a steady pace.

"Don't just gawk. Come on!" Gob tugged again.

I tried focusing on what was right in front of me, on the ground. We passed the satchel Gob had tossed aside. He'd managed to save the waterskins at least, if we were able to go back for it.

Even if we were, though, the supplies wouldn't last long. But we wouldn't, either, at this rate.

We crested one particularly tall dune, Gob kicking up piles of sand that sprayed my face as he ascended the little hill first, and then Gob tripped, tugging me with him. Hard, packed sand was like stone beneath my ribs as we tumbled. Gob's hand dropped my wrist at some point and I found myself wrapping my arms around my abdomen until I rolled to a stop. My head spun as I tried to sit up, but I fell forward, my hands catching me, the sudden movement hard on my wrists.

Heaving, the nausea overwhelming, I saw a little furry ball beside me, shivering. Chip's eyes were wide, her tufted ears sleeked back.

She was mumbling.

I'd never seen the little brave soul so terrified, not even before the minotaur.

The beast in question howled, the ladydoves' returning song half a melody, half a shriek. I whipped my head around to see—

And then I vomited, all over the sand.

"Edony!" Chip's voice rung hollowly in my ears, as if she were somewhere else entirely.

A small hand clasped on my back, Gob's heavy breaths an anchor for my unsteady head.

Feeling the sickness pass, I leaned back, wiping my lips against my forearm.

"I'm all right," I assured them.

Chip rubbed her head against my side, then stared up at me with trembling whiskers. "I ran," she said, almost as if she couldn't believe it herself.

"I understand." I pet her head gently, my sudden burst of nausea retreating with pointed deep breaths. I cradled my other hand against my stomach. It felt strange. Not pained like it usually would have while ill. But not quite as it should have, either.

The shrieks behind us grew louder, drowning out the minotaur's cry.

I turned around again, but our campfire and the beast were blocked by view of the sand.

"We can't let it leave." I shifted warily, trying to get to my feet. "We have to capture it."

"We need a new plan," said Gob.

I froze. "It has my dagger."

"You can't go back there," Chip said. "They're coming."

It wasn't the minotaur that had her shaking still. It was the line of black figures that neared us now.

They were the size of large, human men—their armor giving the appearance of broad shoulders and thick muscles. The armor was black and uniform, and the closer they moved, the louder the scrape of the different plates grinding at their joints. Only the plates weren't like any metal I'd seen before— they were black, shiny, but rough, formed like rocks.

Their helmets glowed silver at the cracks, as if moonlight itself emanated from within.

They each dragged a black sword at their side, the tips leaving lines behind them in the sand.

There were nine of them. At their center there was one... Its helmet seemed bigger than the others'. Grander, if a helmet fashioned roughly of stone could be referred to in such a way.

A sharp pang at my thigh drew my attention to Chip, who was clawing at my leg without tearing her gaze from the line of armored men approaching from the Hall of the Obliterated.

But they were the dullahans, of course. Which meant there were no men inside that armor—only the souls of the fae who'd fallen in battle against the minotaur.

"We need them," I whispered, patting Chip's head gently. She sheathed her claws, and I stood, letting her hide behind my calf.

I spared a glance over my shoulder. I could barely see just beyond the crest of the dune, but there was smoke from the campfire—and not a sign of the beast.

There went my dagger.

We had no choice but to plea to the dullahans for help.

The birds sang out again, their sound warbled, and scattered backward toward the line of soldiers. The flapping of their wings made even Gob tremble as he walked around me slowly to stand on the other side of Chip, sandwiching the terrified elf between us.

She spared him a quick, questioning glance, the fur at her brow scrunching and then releasing.

We were weaponless, all of us, and we had no supplies but the waterskins dropped somewhere in the sand.

We weren't here to fight them, though. I didn't know how we'd even have a chance.

"Hello," I said, loudly to be heard over the din of fluttering wings and scraping stone. My voice cracked as I spoke. "We-We need your help."

"You're just going to ask them outright? Like *that*?" hissed Chip from my thigh. She sunk her claws in again and I winced.

"Not sure they even speak," added Gob.

"Do you have any better ideas?"

Neither one said a word.

The dullahans froze, but then the one in the center stepped forward on his own, a single bird on the stone pauldron on his shoulder. The bird flapped her wings, her black, beady eyes focused on me.

I gestured for Gob to take a step back. I was the only one tall enough here to even begin to approach the dullahan's height.

"Hello," I said again, my voice shaky. The ladydove tittered from the soldier's shoulder, as if mocking my obvious nerves. I steeled myself and ignored it. "We've been sent on a quest—by the labyrinth itself."

The dullahans stilled just a few yards ahead of me.

He said nothing, though, the light filtering through the stone helmet sparkling.

Still, I took his pause as an acknowledgement of my words —he'd responded to me talking about our mission.

"We must capture the minotaur," I said. "Make it so he no longer wanders freely, endangering those who make their homes here." My eyes darted briefly to the tops of Chip's and Gob's heads.

I cleared my throat when there was no response. "We tried

on our own—just now, before you came. We failed. I... I lost the only weapon I had to use against it." I focused on the dark sword dragging behind the soldier. Could that have been what they'd used in their battles against the beast? Or had it been something crafted for them along with that armor after their spirits had been eaten by the maze?

"Please. You're the only ones who've tried to take on the creature. You're the only ones who've hurt him, if you're the ones who cleaved his hoof from his arm." My stomach spasmed with a sharp pain. I clutched it and did my best to stand steady. "Please. The maze sent us this way—there must be something you can do."

The ladydove at this dullahan's shoulder screeched, flapping her wings rapidly. The ones behind her—scattered across the dunes, some perched on dullahans' shoulders or even heads—flapped their wings in echo, the cold desert filling up with the sounds of these birds once again.

The dullahan before me lifted his free arm, and the birds went quiet, almost instantaneously. A grinding noise replaced the cacophony, the shimmering silver light growing brighter as the soldier's free hand moved to remove the helmet—no, to pry the plates comprising the helmet apart.

They shifted aside, the bright light blinding. Chip, Gob, and I all closed our eyes, blocking our faces with our arms.

"You're like I was. In this place."

A voice, soft and warm and... feminine.

I blinked, my eyes watering in the bright, silvery light, but I lowered my arm, determined to see who was speaking.

The dullahan's armor was open, like a gaping wound, from torso to head. A human hand—pale and covered in dirt—

clutched to the side of it as a human leg climbed out from the armor's legs.

A grimy bare foot, almost as white as the silver light inside the armor, hit into the sand.

As soon as she jumped out of the armor, the stones ground again and shifted into place, the bright white light fading.

"Poor child," said a woman. Wild, matted hair hung over most of her face, all the way down past her waist. She stepped toward me, holding out a rail-thin arm.

"Don't touch her!" growled Chip, leaping in front of me and baring her fangs.

"No, Chip, it's all right..." I swallowed. A fae had been inside the dullahan. They weren't just spirits, they...

My eyes caught sight of an ear poking out from the matted hair. Rounded. Like Brecc's had been when he'd been weak. It made sense, except...

A lock of hair shifted aside to reveal a bright brown eye, and I realized that through the dirt and muck, much of the hair was gray, but some of it... had a fiery tinge to it.

Hair like a fiery blaze.

"Poor child," she said, caressing my cheek. Her hand was rough. And cold.

Tears spilled down my face.

Her touch shifted down from my face and to my abdomen.

"Poor child," she said again. Half her visage was visible now. Scarred gashes ran diagonally across her flesh.

"Mother?" My voice was a rasp.

Chip's growl cut short, her head turning up and cocking. Gob snatched her by the foreleg and pulled her out of the way.

The woman—my mother. It had to be. She laughed and

grabbed hold of the skirt of her dirty dress. It was ripped and muddied and it hung off her bones like it had been made for someone two sizes larger. Or she had withered away inside it for all of these years.

"Come, come." She laughed and danced, the ladydoves all joining in a song to the rhythm of her bare feet across the sand.

"No," Chip whispered beside me. "This is... This is the song I heard before these demons took my brothers."

My jaw dropped, all thoughts lost on my tongue. Mother was humming now to the song, her movements like that of a young maiden's at the fete. It was so clear now how all eyes could have been drawn to her steps that fateful fete.

"Edony, get away!" shouted Chip.

Gob hushed her, but she screamed, fighting against the hold he still had on her front leg.

The birds took to the air, and the dullahans—even the one from which Mother had emerged—moved, lifting their swords from the sand and out in front of them.

Then they charged, Mother weaving her dance through their sudden and quick movements.

CHAPTER

FORTY-ONE

BRECC

There was no sign of a book of songs among the tomes on my shelf, but I hardly spent more than a moment running my hand against the spines before I was eager to move on. My scabbard was strewn across the table in the corner of my bedroom—empty.

Only one person I knew would have taken it. I clipped the belt and empty scabbard around my hips then made my way down the darkened hallways, lit only by the torches and the light trickling in from the doors left ajar with shutters thrust open.

Somewhere out there, Edony was stuck in an eternal darkness. And if I'd only agreed with her infernal plan of *capturing the beast*... What was the maze thinking?

I drew to a stop. Took a deep breath. Closed my eyes.

Don't think of such things. Don't let it plunder your mind.

Opening my eyes, I knocked on Carac's door. There was no

answer. He had no spouse as of late, so there was unlikely to be anyone tending to his room when he was not at home.

He had my sword—and I knew the state it was in. Perhaps he was at the blacksmith's to get it sharpened.

The creak of a hinge drew my attention. Kaylein exited a room a few doors down. It wasn't her own. I couldn't remember whose it was, who lived so close to Carac.

"Brecc," she said as she shut the door behind her. She then gave a little curtsey, though it was hard not to stare at the abomination she kept clutched to her chest.

The beast's shorn hoof I'd entrusted her with.

"You're well now?" She peered up to inspect the sides of my head.

My ears. I was certain they were the talk of the village—when the villagers could bother to speak of anything beyond the next meal or the next bauble to trade for in the market.

"I am." I thrust my shoulders back and rested a hand on the open end of the scabbard, almost forgetting I'd find no hilt to grab. "And we need to talk." I sent a pointed gaze to the hoof. "How have you spent this time I was away?"

"Well, not making any new pieces of clothing, I can tell you that much." She grunted and put her free hand on her hip.

A sharp pang of guilt hit my gut. Kaylein was fond of her work. It was why she hadn't bothered to secure a human spouse—though it wasn't as if one *had to* unload menial tasks on one's human partner. I'd had no intention of making my queen do anything of the sort, but then again, I'd never imagined having a queen at all until recently.

I took a deep breath. *Don't think.*

"Yes, well, I don't imagine any fae is in dire need of another outfit—"

"There's a need in one's soul, too." Kaylein stared down at the hoof in her hand. How she wasn't repulsed at the mere sight of it, I couldn't say. "Something you once understood."

I clutched at my heart. "I think I understand the need of one's soul now more than ever." I frowned. "Tell me. Have you learned anything more?"

Her head tilted tellingly behind her, to the door she'd just exited. "I have a theory..."

"Favian told me of you reaching out to Borin. Asking about one of his songs."

She stiffened at the name "Favian," which I found extraordinary. Why should his name cause a reaction in her of any kind?

She started walking down the hall, and I fell in step beside her.

"Borin did remember what I was talking about," she said. "But he refused to sing it for me."

"*Refused?*" The fae had so little to occupy him. Surely, he could do the one thing he did best and sing a song of importance.

She gestured down the hall in the village. "He didn't think it would go over well with the crowd."

"Go over well with the...?" My lips smacked together. "This isn't a game!"

Kaylein spun on me, clutching the hoof tightly to her chest. "But our lives are, Brecc. Our lives are nothing but games. We've lived within these walls so comfortably—"

"I know that," I snapped. Then I bristled. "I may have, admittedly, been a bit too slow to grasp that fact, but I know it now."

"You can't ask the fae to change their ways now." She spoke softly, almost as if afraid to be overheard.

"We were warriors once. Free. We roamed the *world*—"

"And look where it got us." She stared down at the hoof in her hands. The light of a nearby torch flickered in the shine of her eyes.

I opened my mouth to respond. But I couldn't speak freely of defeating the monster, in case the maze's eyes were on me. Even here. Away from the walls. In a village bathed in the sunlight the maze itself denied to so many out there.

"Bring Borin to me," I said. "With or without his instrument. He'll *write* the damn lyrics down if he won't sing them to me." I turned on my heel to head toward the village and blacksmith.

Kaylein wasn't far behind—at first. But then there was a ruckus somewhere in the halls we'd left behind, an indistinct clamor of voices. Followed by a much nearer set of footfalls.

I whipped around to see Kaylein vanishing around the corner, back the way we'd come.

There weren't often altercations in this hall—or anywhere in the village. But regardless, Kaylein was no guard. What could have spurred her to act so quickly?

At the end of the hall—in front of the room Kaylein had exited, I realized—was Favian, his hands gesturing wildly above his head. The door was open, blocking from sight whomever it was he was speaking to.

"You can't stay angry with me forever!" Favian shouted, the dark circles under his eyes darker than ever in the flickering torchlight. Was this how I had seemed to everyone when I'd been consumed by the gnawing feeling inside me, grown from being apart from my love? "You're my wife!"

That clarified that.

"Hold on," said Kaylein, coming to a stop beside Favian. "She doesn't want to see you."

"The guards are back, and Elspeth has come to see me. She asked I take my bride from *her* room." Favian's face turned into a sneer and he reached forward, grabbing hold of his bride's wrist just as I came to join them. "Enough of this childishness. You have a home—with me!"

"Neela, I'm sorry," said another human bride from within Elspeth's quarters. The bride the guard herself had chosen, no doubt. "I thought Lady Elspeth would understand, but she can't let you stay forever." The little brown-haired thing was wringing the front of her dress. Shiny jewels bobbed along her hand. "And she was already upset with me for all the baubles I purchased without asking her—"

Favian yanked at Neela's wrist and dragged her down a few steps.

Instinctively, I reached for the sword at my hip that wasn't there.

"Enough!" I said. I thought sharply of how I'd pinned Edony beneath me, took command of her whenever we had a moment alone together—but this.... The tears on the girl's face. She wasn't happy with it. "Let her go."

Favian dropped her wrist. "Go where? She's *my* wife."

Kaylein stepped between Neela and Favian. "She can stay

with me." She turned around and nodded at the girl, who nodded sullenly back, rubbing her arm with her newly-freed hand. She was clutching something with the other hand. A book.

"We agree. So come." Kaylein gestured for Neela to follow her down the hall.

Favian's gaze darted wildly all around, falling lastly on Elspeth's bride and taking hold of the room's door, slamming it with brute force in the girl's face. "She is *my* bride!" he shouted.

"Watch yourself, man." I spoke sharply.

His eyes were wild and he ripped the book out from his wife's arm. "And what is this? Did you steal it from my room?" He flipped through it and thrust it toward me. "This was the book I told you about! The one I was looking for!"

"I was just borrowing it," said Neela, the first words I'd heard her speak since my arrival to the scene. "And for good reason—"

"You had no right! No right to take anything of mine—and that includes yourself!" Favian shoved the book at me and I took it clumsily, too taken aback to react as his arm wound back for a slap to his wife's face.

He wouldn't dare.

I reached out to stop him, but as I did, Neela herself snatched what Kaylein had been clutching, then slashed the thing diagonally across her husband's face.

The shorn scissor claw of the minotaur.

Favian froze. He screamed. And he cradled his head.

Blood trickled out from between his fingers, dripping to the floor.

Neela gasped, breathing hard, then looked at the molted,

grotesque hoof in her hand and shrieked. It fell from her grasp, clattering to the floor, and she bolted down the hallway, her footfalls like stampeding hooves as she drew away from us, Kaylein taking only a moment to grab the hoof and start running after her.

CHAPTER
FORTY-TWO

EDONY

The dullahan nearest—the one from which Mother had crawled out—swung its great, big sword, but as I moved to dodge its clumsy, foreshadowed swing, it launched its other hand out and wrapped it around me by the waist where I landed, as if that had been its intended plan all along.

"Lemme go!" Chip's shriek drew my attention even as I kicked and flailed myself. Only there was no budging against the stone-cold grip of the knight's gauntlet.

Gob was attempting to bite the pauldron of the dullahan that had him tucked under his arm. Of course Gob's teeth just thudded against the stone armor, and the poor troll let out a cry as he rubbed his sore lips.

"Haw!" Chip leaped from the helmet of the dullahan with which she tangled and soared through the air to mine as it made slow, steady steps past hers. Using just her claws, she dug into the crevices between the stone plates and twisted and turned, yanking off plates of the helmet entirely. The helmet crumbled to the sand, but the light revealed was blinding, and I had to look away.

"Come on!" Chip grunted, and I could hear her claws scratching fruitlessly against the stone armor.

But the blinding light wasn't affecting anyone but us. Mother's song still rung out. The stone armor scraped against itself as it retreated through the sand. The flapping wings of the birds and their haunting melody still echoed out in unison with Mother's tune.

"Chip, run!" I cried. "Before they catch you, too!"

"I can't... I can't leave you!"

"You have to—" I stopped my words short. Would she run into the minotaur if she went back? Would she take it on again? Alone, this time?

Fur snuggled up beside my arm and I opened my eyes, blinking through tears as I fought to make sense of anything around me but the bright, enduring silver glow of the headless knight. But I saw Chip, a dark form amidst the brightness, and I took her firmly between my arms against my chest. Letting my head loll forward as I shut my eyes once more.

Letting the dullahans hold us at their mercy.

I must have lost consciousness at some point because I woke with a subtle weight across my chest, my back against a hard and cool surface. There was something hard flush up against my side.

I blinked my eyes open. Silver moonlight streamed in from

between broken bricks and stone towering up overhead, but the light wasn't so overwhelming as it had been out in the desert.

Soft, subtle breaths drew my attention. Chip was curled up on top of my chest, Gob on his side against my hip. Their chests rose and fell, and they appeared to be uninjured.

Sitting up and gently repositioning Chip on my lap, I looked at my arms, finding only the faded scars of Gob's bite. I appeared to be uninjured, too. A fact I found surprising, considering I'd just fought the minotaur and then been carried off by a brood of headless knights.

An echoing flutter of wings drew my attention. A ladydove soared overhead, resting atop the ruins of a mantelpiece. The fireplace below it bore scorch marks, soot and broken tinder revealing recent use.

A woman's humming broke out amidst the silence, and I turned my head to find Mother approaching, a tray in her hand.

"Are you hungry, child?" she asked. "You need your strength." Crouching, she set the tray down beside me. It was covered in mushrooms, still dusted with dirt, as well as the occasional nut or berry.

"The ladies gather it for me." Mother put her elbows on her knees and rested her face on her palms, a smile breaking out and shifting the scars into a strangely spookier expression.

I flinched, then quickly moved to cover my reaction, grabbing a mushroom and sniffing it. "The doves?"

Mother nodded and shifted to sit on her thighs, resting the side of her calves across the stones of the floor. Moss and weeds grew out from between the tiles.

I went to rouse Gob up, about to ask him if this mushroom

was safe, when Mother shook her head and put a cold, clammy hand on my wrist. "Let them rest. The true form of the dulla-hans—it can be too much for many creatures of this place to handle."

I looked around for a hint of where they had gone. Even most of the doves were out of sight.

Mother leaned back and nodded, as if judging my concerns by no more than the expression on my face. "They walk the halls," she said. "Keeping it safe. That... That thing won't venture here, but who knows? Perhaps one day it will summon the strength to break the seal and find me."

"The seal?" I put the mushroom down and settled for one nut. My stomach was rumbling, and it still felt heavy. "Those markings in those stones?"

Mother nodded. "My knights... They carved those for me. Or rather, they told the ladydoves to. It alerts us to when the beast is near. And it reminds the beast what it may find should it venture farther into the sand."

"I don't... I don't understand." I finished chewing the nut—it was rich on my tongue—and pet Chip's sleeping back. I had a dozen questions, but I decided to start with the most impor-tant. "Why are you here?"

"Why are *you* here?" she tossed back at me, that unsettling smile across her face. Had she always unsettled me so? No. She'd had those scars my whole life and yet...

She was changed.

"You have no scars," she said, cupping my cheek again. Then her hand fell to my stomach. "Of course, my baby won't have scars. And still, their blood will call to the beast."

Her *baby*? No. She was too old—and besides, with whom

had she sired a new child in this place? The dullahans were but spirits.

She hummed softly, stroking her abdomen.

As I stroked Chip's head, I felt myself doing the same to my own stomach with my other hand. It was soothing.

"My husband wants me to give birth back home in the village," Mother said. Her husband? "But I told him, I'm part of this place now. Our baby is, too. They have to be born here. The maze has willed it." She laughed and stared down at her flat, flat stomach.

"Mother..." I said softly. "Are you talking about me?"

She looked at me, frowned, and then laughed. "You are far too large to be my baby." Then she stared at me. "But you do... look like my husband. Millicent! Yes, Millicent." She remembered my aunt. "It's so good to see you. I almost forgot..." She cocked her head. "You travel the seas, don't you?"

"Mother, it's me." I took her hand from her stomach and held it tightly. "Edony. Your daughter."

"Don't be silly." Mother squeezed my hand, then pulled hers out of my grip, standing up. "I told you I like the name Edony. If it's a boy, we'll name him Jarin, after his father. But Edony..." She patted her stomach and swirled around. "Edony, I think she'll be."

The heaviness in my stomach settled. She didn't know. She didn't remember Father was... dead. She didn't know she'd killed him.

And I could see now how she could. The maze's madness had taken root in her for far too long.

The ladydove that had settled on the mantelpiece responded to my mother's song and landed on a frail index finger Mother held out for her. "These sweet things nest in the dullahans," she said. "They feed off their energy. They all take care of me."

But why?

Weren't these stone soldiers fallen fae?

"Moth... Aldreda," I said, deciding perhaps it best she think of me as my aunt. We had a quest to complete. Trapping the minotaur should free Mother, too. "My friends and I..." I swallowed, looking down at Chip in particular. What would she do when she woke? She was terrified of the creatures here.

"Oh, that poor little thing." Mother allowed the ladydove to fly up and far over our heads to the broken turret above, then crawled down beside me. "May I?" She gestured at Chip.

"She's afraid," I said.

"I imagine she would be." Mother took hold of the sleeping Chip and curled her up in her arms like a baby, though Chip was still in the circular shape she had wound herself into. "I think she's been here before." Mother chewed her lip, as if contemplating.

"To the Hall of the Obliterated?" I looked around me. Chip had never mentioned her and her brothers getting as far as this.

"The Hall of Heroes," chastised Mother. "Faekind's greatest warriors." So she knew that much about the dullahans. "The maze rewarded their bravery by turning them into protectors in the afterlife. Or maybe the maze just wanted something to nurture its ladydoves." She snuggled Chip close to her face, sticking her nose lovingly in her fur. "They don't have babies, you know. They lay eggs, but there are no gentlemen doves to father their children." She hummed and rocked Chip gently, spinning slowly in place.

"Chip and her brothers came out to the dunes, years ago," I said.

"Yes, the poor babies..." Mother shook her head. "I'm afraid the ladydoves thought... Well, they thought I might like to eat them."

My eyes widened.

"Oh, I didn't," she said quickly, patting Chip's back. "But it was too late. The maze took them. I made sure my doves knew —never again. I'll eat nothing breathing. I don't care if it comes walking right up to our front door."

Tears escaped my eyes as I thought of Chip and her brothers.

"I stopped them," Mother said, bouncing Chip like an infant. "I stopped them before they got to her. They don't mean to be cruel, you see. They just care about me." She hummed again.

I stood, sparing a quick touch to Gob's shoulder to make sure he was still sleeping, and offered to take Chip back. "Here. Let me."

She let me take Chip without much of a fuss. Chip's eye opened blearily as I cradled her against my chest, draping her head and front legs over one shoulder. "Wha-What's happened?" she asked, her voice cracking. "Where are we?"

I patted her back, hushing her. "We're safe. I've got you. But be careful—we're in the Hall."

Chip's claws dug into my back and I quickly shifted her, realizing I'd pointed her toward the dove on the mantelpiece.

"Aldreda," I said again. "We-We need to capture the minotaur."

Mother's eyebrow arched and she laughed. "Don't be silly. The maze has it captured, you see." She danced around. "And you're safe here. You can all stay here with me. They'll protect you."

She danced into the dark alcove across the way and when she frolicked back, the grinding of stone footfalls followed after her. The dullahan in which Mother had ridden—inside that blinding light, no less—stepped out from the shadows. It positioned its sword in front of its legs, downward, always the tip dragging against the floor.

"Take hold of the wall," Mother singsonged.

"Keep turning, left, and left, and left," I finished for her.

Mother stopped in her frolicking dance and looked at me. "You know. But of course, you made your way here. Why, I wonder?" She stopped in her dance and cocked her head. "The maze calls to you... But why?"

Chip perked up and crawled up to stand on my shoulder, though she was perhaps just a tad too large for it. "This is your mother, isn't it?" she whispered in my ear.

I nodded. "She doesn't know, though. She's lost..."

"I don't remember seeing her," Chip said, and I realized she'd been awake for at least part of what my mother had said about her brothers. "I just remember... her song. The birds. And the dullahans marching forward."

"Maybe she was inside one," I pointed out.

"I got away," she whispered. "I watched my brothers sink into the sand, but I got away. The birds went back. I thought I'd just run beyond their reach."

"I'm sorry," I murmured, putting a hand over her paw.

Gob moaned, rubbing his eyes as he sat up. "Where in the blazes…?"

"Oh, I know!" Mother slammed one fist against her other palm. "Your child. Millicent, your child was conceived somewhere in this labyrinth. You don't bear the scars that would tie your baby to this maze like mine—but the magic of creation, it was here within this place." She danced and giggled, holding out her ratty skirt.

"Mother, I'm not—" I snapped my lips shut. My hand went to my stomach and I could feel both Chip's and Gob's eyes boring into my abdomen. I was bloated, but surely…

Yet I knew I *could* be pregnant. The castle for the fete—that was in the labyrinth. And most definitely, so was the secret haven amidst Lyra's fields.

But these were the rantings of a madwoman, who thought herself still pregnant with me, twenty-six years after she actually had been.

How would she even know?

"A future king, a future king," Mother sang, dancing all around the room, even around her dullahan.

How did she know *that*?

"The Fae King's son?" Gob asked, his jaw slackened.

"Oh, poor Edony," said Chip. "Why didn't you let us know?"

Let them know…

They didn't know I *loved* the Fae King. Could I tell them?

If I didn't, they'd brand him a monster—even more than they already had.

But right now, with the numbness slinking up from my toes to my head, I needed to be alone. To process these feelings.

But there was nowhere to run. And I wouldn't abandon my friends.

It couldn't be true. Mother was mad. I couldn't be out here, risking my future child's safety as well as my friends' and my own.

I'd resigned myself to maybe never seeing Brecc again.

But this... This, if true, changed everything.

FORTY-THREE

BRECC

"It burns!" screamed Favian, cradling his face in his hands. "And I... I..." He looked up, his eyes wide. The gashes—two long, thin lines—wove jagged paths through his impeccable flesh, dripping rivulets of red that stuck in the dimples of his cheeks. "I must go."

He wasn't looking at me. He looked beyond me, a hunger roving over his distorted features.

This. This was what he'd done to my Edony's mother. And I hadn't been there to stop him. Hadn't thought much of it when he'd told me about it.

Fearing for his wife, I jumped to block him.

"Hold on, Favian. We must seek a healer—"

"No *healer* can stop this." Favian focused beyond me, his gaze darting about frenetically. "I must go. He calls me." His hands shoved against my chest, and I stumbled backward, watching in astonishment as he turned the corner, observing

the haggard steps, the slight dip in his usually rigid posture—
and realizing that could have been me.

"He calls him—the minotaur?" I hadn't known the hoof
would affect him. That it could seep its magic into fae flesh as
well as human.

I had to let Carac know, to seek his help in stopping Favian.

Surely, Kaylein could deal with my beloved's cousin.

I jogged down the hallway, the book of songs tucked under
my arm, looking for anyone who might be of help. Somewhere
far in the distance, an otherworldly howl sent a shiver down
my spine.

It wasn't the creature. It sounded like a fae.

"Hey!" I shouted, hoping Favian would stop for me. I
reached the door leading to the rest of the village, but Favian
was nowhere to be found.

What would the fae do? Head to the gate? The guards there
would stop him as soon as they saw his face.

"Bre—Your Majesty."

I turned to find Elspeth, offering a curt bow.

Perfect.

"Elspeth, head for the gate," I said. "Favian is... not himself.
Tell the guards to restrain him and keep him from setting foot
outside the fae village."

Elspeth blinked, her sharp features at odds with the confusion on her face. "Favian?"

"Just head there. Surely, you heard that scream just now."

"I'd thought it odd..." She cocked her head.

Had she come to investigate? Perhaps my guards were a
touch cleverer than I gave them credit for.

"He's been scratched by the minotaur's hoof."

Her jaw dropped. "How?"

I brushed her away. "I must find Carac. I'll send him to join you."

Not waiting for her reply, I headed down the avenue, my gaze darting here and there to take in the activity of my people. What doors were open showed fae at leisure—enjoying warm meals, reading books, regaling their offspring with tales. Occasionally, I'd come across a human beating a rug or tending to a small garden, their offspring running giddily through the grass. Through Adelaide's open window, I spotted her latest burly human beating bread dough, Adelaide watching him eagerly from their kitchen table, her elbows propping up her head.

Whenever I drew an eye, smiles would vanish, backs would noticeably stiffen. The humans would bow or curtsy. The fae themselves hardly seemed to notice me.

At last, I reached the market, Borin's almost-continual songs from the square impossible to miss, despite how faint his voice was off in the distance.

The clang of steel on steel, though, that was what drew my attention.

The heat from the smithy was like a bubble, impossible to see but as real as the dirt beneath my feet as my face pushed up against it. Sparks flew near the forge in time with the crash of the hammer.

I approached the two figures shadowed by the orange glow of the molten fire. A human man hammering at a familiar sword—my grandfather's sword.

Carac, the other figure, turned around. His eyes shone as he stumbled back slightly. "Brecc. You're awake again. You look..."

He stopped himself as his gaze moved from my pointed ears to my presumably weary expression. "What happened to you?"

The blacksmith's husband didn't stop in his work, the burly man with wispy black-and-silver hair continuously pounding on the blade with a right arm more heavily muscled than the other. His attention was more focused on me than his work, though—until he caught me looking.

"Favian is... not well," I said, launching into an explanation of what the fae's own human wife had done to him. I couldn't help but notice the blacksmith's husband stiffen as I got to the part where Neela had run the hoof across her husband's face.

I understood my beloved's cousin's anger. Perhaps her punishment had been too great, but it had been the same as what he'd done to Edony's flesh and blood. But was it a sign of things to come?

Were other human spouses... unhappy? What kind of life had we been so eager to protect all of these years?

The clang of the hammer on my sword again snapped me back to the moment. We could worry about that later.

And I'd agonize over how my own people would handle such questions in due time, too. If Favian were any example, well, it wouldn't be a pleasant discussion.

"I should head to the gate," Carac said. He looked over his shoulder at the blacksmith's husband's work. "How much longer, do you think?"

The man didn't look up. "His Majesty's sword is almost finished—but it'll need time to cool."

"I won't need a sword against Favian," I pointed out. At least I knew where it was now—though I could hardly say I looked forward to having the thing in my hands again. It had felt so *useless* out there against a sentient maze willing to grab and shift and bar my way.

Carac nodded and we both turned. No sooner had we set foot outside of the smithy's heat bubble than the murmurs of a gathering drew my attention.

Fae filtered out from the square, some with human spouses beside them, others with fae friends and family on their own. All were in discussion, but strangely, not a single smile could be found amongst them.

Carac noticed I'd fallen behind and stopped. "Borin's music is ending early today?" he ventured.

Borin. If Kaylein was right, I needed to speak to him, too.

But ensuring Favian was safe took precedence.

A shrieking wail from the direction of the square made the decision for me.

It wasn't Favian's voice, though. It was high-pitched. A woman's.

I waved Carac on. "You check for Favian at the gates." He frowned, but I didn't wait for him to argue. I wove my way through the crowd and moved on.

A couple of fae women lingered in the back of the group, their conversation clear to my ears as I passed.

"What is *with* that human woman?" one said to the other.

"What is with that song, *I* want to know," her companion responded. They were both fair of hair and tanned in complexion. Sisters, if I remembered them right. "How depressing." Her eyes bulged as she saw me pass and she smiled—but I was in no mood for fae flirtations today or any day from now on.

In the middle of the square, Borin sat beside his human wife, both gently putting their instruments away in velvet-lined carrying cases designed to protect them, though their attention was almost entirely focused on Neela, the wailing human woman in question. Kaylein soothed her, patting her back with one hand, the other still clutching that accursed shorn hoof.

Neela batted it away. "Get that away from me! What have I done?"

"No more than he deserves, no doubt," Kaylein said.

I pulled up behind them, not saying a word.

"Majesty," Borin said softly, offering a half-bow. His wife, an elderly woman likely nearing the end of her natural lifespan, bowed deeper. I took note of the wince of pain on her face.

"Kaylein told me she spoke to you in my absence," I said. My eyes darted to Kaylein, who offered me a sullen glance. What were they doing here? Neela walked back and forth, tears on her face. When she spotted the book in my hand still, she darted forward and snatched it from me without ceremony.

Borin's wife gasped, but Neela flipped through the pages unabated.

"Here," she said. "What you sang.... It just didn't quite match what's written here."

Borin frowned and took the book from her. She let him, chewing on her nails as she watched him read. Despite his eyes roving over the pages, he spoke to me. "Kaylein has suggested twice now I sing a song I only somewhat remember," Borin explained. "I told her it would disappoint the crowd—and sure enough, it did."

"What song?" I asked.

"'The Slash of the Hoof,'" Kaylein explained.

All eyes but Borin's darted to what she kept clutched against her chest.

"How does it go?" I asked. There didn't seem to be a reason to ask why Kaylein found it relevant—though now I wondered if Neela had been the one who'd put her up to asking about it. Favian had insisted she'd stolen the book, after all.

Though no instrument played, Borin's human wife sang, her voice only slightly shaky with age.

"Immortal flesh, a monster's cry.

There be weakness in its eye.

But with a dagger, so black and foul,

Hide be pierced and darkness cowled.

So rode the King of Fae, the wise woman's gift

Tucked inside his grip to lift.

Sliced the hoof from arm.

Stopped the beast from doing harm.

But harm the hoof shall ever do.

Subjugating the flesh anew."

It was a tad... *graphic* for the general fae crowd, I supposed. But it wasn't as if Borin only sang jovial tunes. Almost all of the lyrics mired in history carried with them a sense of melancholy.

"So it's a special dagger," Neela said, wringing her hands as she began to pace. "That-That *thing* was lopped off the beast with a black and foul dagger, whatever that is."

I'd always imagined my grandfather wielding the sword he'd passed on to Father and then to me when he'd completed the task.

Where would we find a black dagger?

I knew of no such thing amidst the fae treasures.

But... I knew of a wise woman. The doe-like woman.

"But that's not the important part," Neela said.

"It's not?" I found myself saying. "The key to breaking the beast's flesh isn't the most important clue left to us by our ancestors in this song?"

Borin, still looking at the book, frowned. "'*Subjugating the flesh anew,*'" he said. "That line isn't in here. I always thought it meant…" He looked up at me, then the women around us. "Well, when a fae is refused at fete—"

"We know that part," Kaylein said hastily.

"Well, yes, but the line here is '*Bonding beauty and beast true.*'"

"That means the same thing, does it not?" his human wife offered. She shivered and squeezed her shawl tighter around her chest. Were Borin human, she'd look like his frail, old mother. She'd been here in our village a long, long time.

That fate awaited my Edony if I managed to help her survive even the next few days.

"It's less bleak," said Kaylein. "A bond between beast and 'beauty,' well, that's better than thinking of the human as subjugated to the creature's will. It's a two-way relationship."

"Not just human." Neela bit at her cuticles.

Favian, too.

Fae could be bonded just as easily.

"But there's more," Neela said.

Borin read from the book without adding melody to the words.

"*Bond will bind, body and mind.*
The creature will hunger for beauty's touch.
Only the bold should the hoof clutch.
Get close enough to smell its breath.

Be brave enough to risk death.

Do what King and King's Fae could not.

Stop the rot, stop the rot.

The son is saved, the maze's power caved."

"That sounds like instructions," I said, my mind whirling with possibilities.

"It sounds like blasphemy," said Borin's wife quietly.

Blasphemy.

Against the maze itself.

The ground began to rumble—something I'd only experienced outside of the safety of this village.

"What's going on?" Neela clutched Kaylein. Borin took hold of his wife, closing the book between them.

"The maze," I said. "It doesn't want to die."

"*Die?*" Kaylein ventured.

The shaking grew more violent. Off somewhere in the marketplace, shouts and screams joined in the rumble of the ground beneath our feet.

But loudest of all, somewhere beyond my sight, was the howl of the beast I knew too well.

"Is that...?" Kaylein asked.

"The minotaur." I nodded, steeling myself despite the unsteady terrain.

"But he's never come to the village," Borin protested. "Never."

"He's never had someone with his mark in his flesh in this village before today, either." My eyes caught Neela's.

Her cheeks darkened.

Could it be?

Was the beast at our door?

What could I do? I didn't know anything about this black dagger.

I didn't have time to unwind a riddle, either.

"Give it here." I snatched the shorn hoof from Kaylein, my voice barely audible over the wild and rumbling cacophony. Kaylein didn't have time to react or to try to stop me.

There was one thing I understood.

That monster wanted *my* beauty. Edony was bound to it—perhaps through her mother's blood. Perhaps through my own ardent desire for her.

But bound to it she was. That could not be denied.

And so I would be, too.

Gritting my teeth, I ran the sharp, jagged hoof across my face, the drip of blood across my left brow dripping over my vision.

FORTY-FOUR

EDONY

Overdue for a respite and with no idea what to do from here on out, we rested for a spell in the cold and airy decrepit Hall of the Obliterated. I found myself wandering around, seizing a bit of solitude.

Even without a plan, every minute we tarried was another moment the minotaur roamed free.

Only I had no idea now how to defeat it—even with the maze's help.

Wherever Lyra had produced that dagger, it was gone now. I couldn't rely on it.

Here I was in a ruined castle with those who'd challenged the beast—and lost.

But surely they at least knew *something*.

Who was I kidding? The dullahans couldn't talk—and neither could the ladydoves, though they scared me even more than the large, headless, fallen fae. And Mother, well, whatever she said could be taken with a grain of salt and would be delivered in a riddle.

My hand darted to my abdomen. Anything she said...

The flutter of wings drew my attention, a short chirrup drawing my eyes above me from where I sat on one of the only righted chairs in the room gathered around a fallen, rotting wooden table. Moonlight shone through the crumbling building, a little collection of pebbles falling from beneath the feet of one of the white birds. Her beady eyes stared down at me.

Behind me, the shuffle of stone scraping against stone overtook the silence.

A dullahan took a lumbering stride into the ruins of the room. Perhaps this place had once been a great hall, like the one at the castle that hosted the fete.

Had the fae once lived here?

Before the minotaur, before the maze?

And where did they live now? I supposed a part of me regretted not seeing the fae village at least once. At least I could comfort myself to know the place was never attacked. Neela and Brecc... They were safe there.

My stomach felt heavy, strange. But not an altogether unwelcome sensation.

The stone-on-stone echoes stopped, the grate of the dullahan dragging its stone sword against the ground ringing out into the silvery darkness.

Then it stared down at me—without eyes, but its head shifted and focused entirely in my direction. The ladydove flapped her wings and landed on the dullahan's head.

"Do my friends need me?" I asked, as if either creature might answer me. "Or... my mother?"

The creature's head moved slowly then, and it took two more steps toward me. The sword it had dragged behind it clattered to the floor, and then the creature got down on its knee, the ladydove chirping the whole time.

The dullahan's stone armor arms reached forward to embrace me.

"I love you. Mother loves you, too. Promise me. Promise me you will never seek a fae's favor."

But how...? Why would those last words from my father to me fill my head?

The dullahan pulled back, its stone grip cold yet somehow still comforting on my arms.

This was the dullahan with the oddly shaped helmet. The one Mother had stepped out from.

"Fa-Father...?" The guess passed my lips before I even thought too hard about it.

The dullahan's right hand caressed my cheek and I wept. This time, I threw my arms around him, the stone jutting into my damp shirt in all sorts of uncomfortable places, but I didn't want to let go.

"Father," I said. "I can't believe the maze let you come back amongst the fae." Leaning back, I wiped away the moisture coating my cheeks. "But you... didn't fight the minotaur, did you? I was told that Mother felled you. Her mind was clearly lost, but..." I trailed off.

The blocky, stone fingers of his gauntlet traced two lines across my face, hovering over it to never touch my skin.

The ladydove squawked, fluttering her wings, and the dullahan—Father—made the motion again.

"I don't understand," I admitted.

Mother's humming drew my attention from the dark hallway, the ladydove joining in with its shrieking cry.

"*Bond will bind, body and mind. Creature hungering for beauty's touch.*" The song she sung, whirling into the room as if this were just a jaunty tune, echoed morosely over the wide, empty room. "*Get close enough to smell his breath. Be brave enough to risk your death.*"

"She's been singing that off and on for the last hour," Gob grumbled as he stepped into the room behind her. Chip scampered beside him on four feet, a bounce to her step and her tail held high, though it seemed forced—her eyes darted wildly to the ladydove on my father's shoulder.

"The words keep changing a bit," said Chip, a slight waver in her voice. She sat down on her hind quarters like a cat and threw her shoulders back some. "But we think she's singing about her bond with the beast."

"Her bond with the...?" I ran my fingers across my face in echo of the movement Father had made.

In echo, I saw now, of the scars across Mother's face.

"You and Mother 'battled,'" I said, thinking out loud. "And that was the same as fighting the minotaur, like the other dullahans did?"

Father's stone helmet nodded brusquely once.

That had been enough for the maze to process his soul into these stone guardians?

To go up against one bound to the beast?

But that meant... "If we kill the creature, will Mother die too?"

"What are you going on about?" Gob asked.

I stood brusquely, wringing my hands. "Gob, Chip—I have

several things to tell you. Firstly, this is my father." I gestured at the dullahan beside me, who was in the process of slowly getting to his feet.

"Your *father*?" Chip wrinkled her nose. "But Lyra said..." She looked at my mother and tilted her head toward her, as if to imply the rest.

"She did. She must have killed him with that dagger—I doubt she knew who he was."

Almost as if to emphasize my point, Mother's song stopped and she began a lullaby, cradling her flat stomach. "There, there, child. It's almost time."

"And he became... one of them?" Gob shuddered. "They're dotted around this place like statues, I tell you. This is the first one I've seen wandering around. Always near her, I suppose." It was his turn to study my mother now as she turned over one of the fallen seats and settled into it.

"Perhaps the others are so ancient, they're practically statues—unless the minotaur nears here," I suggested.

"And this one, being new—and attached to your mother— is more apt to walk about?" Chip ventured.

The ladydove on Father's shoulder let out a squawk and Chip flinched, but she grit her teeth.

Gob stroked his chin. "The minotaur is after those marked by his hoof."

"And those born to people with the mark." I clutched my stomach again.

"But to say they're bound beyond that—the little Chipper stabbed the beast in the eye, didn't she?" Gob gestured a thumb at his cat-elf companion.

"Yeah, and you stabbed it in the arm!" Chip pointed out.

We all turned to look at my mother, humming as she rocked just slightly in her chair.

"And she bears no such wounds," I said.

So perhaps Mother wasn't in danger of dying when the minotaur did, after all?

But could I take such a risk?

I shook my head. It was irrelevant. The maze had tasked us with capturing the creature, keeping him away from the others in the labyrinth...

I looked around. If Mother weren't seeking sanctuary here, if that carved boundary weren't able to keep the creature away, this might have been a good place to keep the beast. If the maze could perhaps build a closed wall around it in one room.

"*The son is saved, the maze caved.*" Mother sang again, still staring at her stomach. Perhaps she thought there was a chance she was having a boy.

Having a king, like I might have been.

"Chip, Gob—there's something else I have to tell you. If I don't make it—"

"Come on now!" Chip shouted. "Don't talk like that!"

Gob held up a hand to hush her, his attention caught on me.

"Well, first off, I want the two of you to run. This isn't your fight," I said.

"It's not *your* fight, either," Chip said. "Any more than it is ours."

I shook my head. "But it is. My mother and father"—I looked at each in turn, two souls lost in starkly different ways —"are tied to the beast. I have been, too, since birth. And if it's true that I'm bearing a child, they will be too."

Chip's furry forehead furrowed. "But the Fae King—"

"I love the Fae King," I said—quickly and before I lost my nerve. "I'm sorry if I ever gave the impression otherwise."

Gob clucked his tongue and Chip let out a gasp. "But you said you were running from him—"

"I am," I said. "I have been." My palms grew clammy and I rubbed them against the thighs of my trousers. "But not because I fear him—because I fear what will happen when the two of us are together."

Gob and Chip held their tongues as I paced the cold room, launching into the story—the traditions of the human villages during fete, how someone like my mother could have been marked by the minotaur's hoof, my role as a chaperone and my brief but intense romance with Brecc. It spilled forth, like a release of all of my sins before the end. They'd traveled this far with me—we'd had each other's backs. They needed to know.

Chip shuffled forward on her back feet, walking like a human. She patted my calf. "Well, that's better than I thought, really. So I'm glad for you—still sad for you, but better this than what I *thought*."

"We saw each other but a few days past, the king and I." Had it really been so short a time? We'd been resting since we'd arrived here, stealing short naps and living off of berries and nuts and mushrooms and whatever else the birds brought back for my mother. Without the sun to rise and set, I couldn't be sure how long had passed. I just knew that every moment weighed heavily. "When you were sleeping—Lyra conspired to let me, er, speak with him again." My hand went tellingly to my stomach.

"Lyra conspired...?" Chip asked.

Gob grunted. "The tea. Thought I slept a bit too well. Chalked it up to all the *excitement.*" His eyes narrowed on me. "But what I don't get is—why you didn't tell us sooner."

I wrung my hands. "It felt like a distraction. I had to run from him. If we marry, the maze will collapse—"

"And that's a problem, *how*?" Gob asked sharply. "You knew. You *knew* I've been trying to get out of this place and you were the key to opening a path for me—for all the creatures here—all along!"

"I couldn't..." My mouth was dry. "I'll help you get out—the fae guards can lead you out—but I can't just... just let the walls fall. The world will end!"

"The *world*? Bit dramatic, isn't it? Weren't you the one who spoke of an aunt who travels to a land beyond the sea?" snapped Gob, crossing his arms tightly over his chest. "How could the fall of the maze affect even those there?" Somewhere in the distance, there was a deep, loud rumbling, but it wasn't reaching here. The maze wasn't punishing Gob for his traitorous thoughts. "If the maze were so keen on capturing the beast, it could wrap its stone walls around him like a box and leave the rest of us to fend for ourselves."

My mouth opened. Then shut. He had a point. The maze could trap the minotaur at any time. We'd seen with our own eyes stone walls appearing from beneath the soil.

"It wants us to... to trap it," I said. "And then, it'll let me be with Brecc—so long as we don't officially wed."

"Oh, well, that's just lovely for you," said Gob. "Meanwhile, the rest of us can go on feeding the maze, is it? Maybe you'll sneak me out—maybe not—but Chip here and her people and all the other creatures, even those other rotten trolls, they'll just go on letting the bleedin' stone feed off their life forces?"

Chip let out a sad little mew, her eyes darting tellingly away from the ladydove at my father's shoulder.

Father, who had stood stone-still throughout my tale, bent down to pick up his stone sword. He held it out to me, hilt first.

"Think he's saying to vanquish the beast," Gob muttered. "Not trap him—if that could even be done. You ask me, the maze sent us on a futile quest. If it wanted the thing trapped, it would have trapped him." He stared up at me, a hard glint to his eye. "I think the maze is afraid of you—Chip and me, maybe too. We're too outside of the norm. Wouldn't surprise me if Lyra knew that all along."

Chip gasped. "But Lyra's a good friend to the elves."

"Yeah, when they let matters be. She talks to the maze, don't she? And what kind of *good friend* puts you to sleep like that without asking?"

"But she gave us the dagger," I said. "She and the maze sent us—"

"Right into an ambush, didn't they? And failing that, a one-on-one encounter against the minotaur. We never had a chance." He grunted. "Face it, Edony. The maze wants you—and your baby if one's really about to form inside you—dead."

FORTY-FIVE

EDONY

"But the maze—it wants to keep the minotaur trapped. Not to kill me. To kill..."

I stopped myself from saying more. Mother, too, seemed to think capturing the minotaur was a foolhardy plan.

The maze wanted to live more than anything. Without the minotaur, its purpose was over. With Brecc taking a bride who no longer served the maze's magic—its fate would be sealed even before that of the minotaur's.

The maze wasn't offering a trade—a way for it to live and for me to be happy, too. It was simply trying to make me feel more confident to take on the beast, knowing full well I'd likely fail.

Brecc had been right. Defeating the creature was the only way.

But there was no way to defeat it.

"Huh," said Gob, looking back and forth. "The Hall of the Obliterated—"

"Heroes," I corrected.

Gob arched a brow but kept talking. "I'm saying a lot of traitorous things—*thinking* more of them, frankly—and all that rumbling we hear, it's off in the distance."

"But this place—it's still inside labyrinth walls," I explained. "And besides, it led us here. If this were some kind of sanctuary from the maze itself as well as the beast, then that would have been foolish of it to do—"

"Only it led the beast right to us, too, didn't it?" Chip said. Her thin lips downturned as she stared ahead of her, clearly thinking. "I don't trust the creatures here, but Gobble has a point."

My two companions stared at one another, both giving the other a reluctant nod.

"The maze probably hoped we'd die before we came across this place," Chip said. "It just dangled the Hall in front of us to keep us distracted with hope."

Gob scuffed one foot against the detritus-covered floor. "Only it was a false hope. What help can these lumbering things offer us? What good are these flappin' birds beyond picking off helpless little children?"

Chip's shoulders drooped.

Why were these birds here? Why did they do so much for my mother?

Father continued to hold his sword out in front of him.

I moved to take it, but as soon as I gripped the hilt between my hands, I knew it would be too much. It fell immediately to the ground, the tip dragging against the stone as the dullahans themselves often carried them.

If they could only lift the swords part of the time, what

hope did I have?

I shook my head and shoved the hilt back toward him. He took it and the ladydove on his shoulder flapped her wings.

Mother's humming drew my attention in the empty, chilling place.

"*The son is saved, the maze's power caved.*" She stroked her abdomen over and over.

"Why did the maze bring these warriors back to life at all?" I asked. "There have to be answers here."

Chip grunted. "If we'd fallen back there, taking on the beast, you think it would have fashioned Gob- and me-sized armors of stone?"

I started running around the room, looking for clues. "What was this place? A Hall of Heroes? Who named it that?" I didn't know what I was looking for, but I blew piles of dust away from every stone, kicked over every piece of debris.

"Well, the 'heroes' are the fae who tried to take on the minotaur long ago—before they got so rotten and lazy," Chip said. "I suppose."

"Before the maze even existed," I added. "The maze was the Fae King's last resort—built, I think, even after he cleaved the hoof off of the beast. When he found it hopeless to continue the fight."

"Which makes me wonder how *we*'re supposed to manage if they couldn't," Gob muttered.

Chip scurried around the room, joining me in my ransacking. The former dining hall couldn't look even worse than it had before.

"You told me." I turned to Gob. "Didn't you? That the minotaur could have been born of the fae. Somehow."

Chip shuddered. "What would a fae have to mate with to produce... that?"

Gob scratched behind his ear. "Maybe it's more a metaphorical birthing, you know? Magic can do strange things. Maybe it was more born of *feelings* than physical passion."

"*The son*—" Mother started singing. Then she stopped, looking up at us as if just realizing we were there. "What are you doing? Who are you?"

"It's fine, Mother—I mean, Aldreda," I said. "We're friends." I went over to pat her shoulders, staring over at my stone father, wondering how much of him could hear me now. He seemed able to communicate. In his simple way.

"'The son is saved,'" I repeated. "Could 'the son' be... the beast?"

"The son of fae?" Gob asked.

"Born of dark feelings, perhaps," I said. "Only I know nothing of how the fae were then. What could have led to such a thing?"

Gob grunted.

Chip's paw hesitated as it was about to knock an old, rusted goblet off the table. "I do. Well, I mean, my people and Lyra—they've all spoken of the fae. Now they're lethargic and self-centered, but they used to be self-centered and... more cruel."

"Cruel?" My throat caught.

"They're not exactly known for being kindly to others these days," Gob muttered. "Every time we go to trade with them—they look down at us with a sneer. That is, when they're bothering to deal with us themselves. Usually, they make those human spouses of theirs take care of business."

I frowned. No humans knew of the human spouses' fates. The families were well compensated, so we had to assume our lost loved ones were treated well, too.

But we had no evidence of that. My chest hurt. It was hard to imagine Brecc like that, but all I knew of him was this insatiable hunger that I felt as well—that gnawed me down to the bone.

"Yes, but back then, they roamed more wildly, visiting the rest of us inhabitants of the land whenever they pleased, taking whatever they wanted from us." Chip's front paws unsheathed their claws. "Mama told me they weren't like that anymore, though. That the cruelty had been ripped out of them as they found it hard to bear children with one another. That it had been *diluted* over time with human blood."

I laughed. "As if humans can't be cruel?"

"*You're* not." Gob rubbed his nose.

My cheeks flushed. I wouldn't have thought his high opinion would have meant so much to me.

Clearing my throat, I looked around us again. At the decayed home of... the fae? Perhaps it had stood long before the walls had.

"So where does that leave us?" I asked aloud. "What good does guessing at a past of horrors do us now?"

The ladydove on father's dullahan shoulder fluttered its wings and took to the air, circling up ahead in the bright moonlight before diving toward the ground. Only as she descended, she grew brighter—harder to look at. Blocking my eyes with my arm, I winced, but by the time the light around the edges had softened enough to take a look, I found another figure entirely.

A woman with a doe-like face, dressed in all white. Only it wasn't Lyra. Her brown coat was spotted with a pattern of white dots that curved like a crescent moon on one half of her face.

"Lyra...?" Gob asked. He hadn't noticed the difference yet.

"My name is Lenore," said the woman. The brightness around her had dulled somewhat.

Seated beneath me, Mother looked up and let out a little cry of joy. "A friendly face." She laughed.

Chip, shaking and frozen to the spot, got her wits about her and let out a cry that volleyed off of the crumbling walls around us. "You! You killed my brothers! I thought you were just a brutish animal, but if you-you're like Lyra, then—"

Lenore held up a hand. Human-like, as was Lyra's, though covered in fur. Beneath the white, flowing robes—reminiscent of Lyra's shoddier, unflattering outfit—poked out hooved feet.

"I apologize, sweet warrior. Not all of my sisters have retained their sanity after hundreds of years trapped alone in this place." Lenore swallowed visibly, then looked down at my mother. "They really were just trying to provide for our first companion who could speak in... I can't say how long."

Chip let out a hiss and I moved beside her, keeping my eyes cautiously on this new apparition.

"What are you?" I asked. "The other birds—they're like you?"

"They are." Lenore nodded. "Though they've forgotten how to change. When the Fae King, all those years ago, came upon us..." She sighed.

"The old Fae King," Gob said. "The one who 'birthed' the minotaur and created this maze?"

"It was not he who birthed it, exactly, but yes, he played a role." Lenore gestured to her stomach. "The Fae King... could not control his people's most base impulses. He had the idea that, well, the next Fae King should be different. Introduce new blood into the line."

"New blood. Like human?" I ventured. "But I thought the fae couldn't conceive, and that was what drove them to search for human spouses."

"Yes and no." Lenore's pointed ears fluttered. "They did struggle with fertility at times, but the primary motivation was different. The Fae King fell in love with a human woman, but he knew his people wouldn't accept her as their queen—not without a little intervention."

Mother hummed and went back to stroking her belly.

Father remained frozen, as still as a statue.

"He came to me," said Lenore, walking with slow, echoing footfalls around the room. "My people were the only not cowed by his. I agreed to help—my sister, Lyra, derided me for it. She left us—before she could be cursed, too, as it turned out."

"Cursed?" I asked. "The ladydoves?"

Lenore stopped her pacing behind Mother's chair and nodded. "It was not my intention, of course... I just... wanted the same thing the King did. The same thing he ached for with his little frail human."

"A kid?" Gob asked.

It couldn't be!

"The minotaur?" I said.

Lenore's large, round eyes grew glossy. "There are no males of our species. I did not require a man to lie with me, but I thought, well... The Fae King desired to whittle away at his people's cruelty, to allow them to embrace his prospects with a human bride. I knew I could absorb that dark essence from him —from his people—and use *that* to father my child. Yet I didn't expect my son to be so drenched in anger and self-right-eousness. Almost the moment he was born, he grew to great heights—and began his slaughter across the lands."

Chip hung her head heavily.

"Then we have *you* to thank," muttered Gob. "Even more than those wretched fae, apparently."

"My regrets go deeper than you know," she said. "To stop the beast, the Fae King had his best warriors take up arms—but they all fell one by one." She gestured at Father, at the dulla-han. Somewhere in these halls were eight more. "I crafted a small blade born from the same magic as my son, and that's when the Fae King sheared off his hoof." Lenore made a slicing motion across her own arm. "I wept. I couldn't help myself. I loved my child still."

Mother reached up and patted Lenore on her side. "My child will be born here," she said. "She'll keep him company. She'll save the son. No other human child has ever been born here." She hummed again, and her eyes darted toward me briefly—then she focused on me harder.

"Millicent," she said, calling me by my aunt's name again. "You look so like my husband..."

Lenore took a deep breath. "It was Lyra who created the labyrinth—not the Fae King. Lyra who took magic from all who live in these lands to feed her creation, to corner the beast and trap him." She gritted her teeth. "Only I could not let her finish her task—to kill my child. I felt her magic and I acted fast. I bound the maze's existence to my son's. When my son fell, the maze would, too. The maze wouldn't finish its task when it realized."

"No wonder Lyra can speak to it—and she has that shiny, nice place all to herself." Gob *tsked*. "Wise woman, my rear end."

"My magic backfired—I performed it here, in the Hall of Heroes, where the fae in their time of utmost glory once dwelled. My sisters, feeling my pain, all stood beside me." Lyra took up her pacing again, gesturing around the room as if to paint a picture. "The magic ricocheted. It bonded my son and the maze, but it started changing my sisters." She shook her head, and for a brief moment, I was certain her long muzzle transformed into a beak. "I did what I could to save them—to save the fae who, despite their sins, were no more sinners than I. If I could not raise *my* son, I would at least not deny the Fae King's wish for a half-human child. Not after all we'd gone through. After all we'd lost. What we'd done would mean *something*."

She stopped suddenly, her jaw grinding. "I twisted the wild magic and bound the fae to the maze, too. Sheltered them from its wrath, so long as they didn't seek to end its existence. I created a new castle for them, though I know now the Fae King spurned it. They kept it for formalities but used it less and less over time, preferring to retreat to the little alcove at the heart of the maze where the maze itself would leave them be."

She collapsed to the floor, letting out a hallow cry. "My magic was spent. Forever—and my sister Lyra's, too. To preserve our forms takes so much from us. We're safer as the doves." She clutched at her chest. "When the maze spit these warriors back at us, born from the very rocks themselves—I thought the labyrinth was showing us it was keeping the fae safe. But then with this one's appearance..." She looked up at my father.

"He 'battled' one bound to the minotaur," I suggested. "And then he fell."

"Yes," she said. "The humans bound to my son... He doesn't rest easy when they wander his home, this labyrinth. I couldn't save them. We'd carved a line where my child could not pass, for I feared he would return and seek us out, as he sought those others bound to him. When the dullahan brought this woman here, well, I vowed to keep her, at least, safe."

Mother looked up and smiled.

"She's not safe," I said, clenching my fist beside me. "She lost her mind—she killed my father—all because of you!"

Mother's face fell. "I didn't kill your father, dear. I've never... I've never..." Her eyes went wide as she looked from me to the dullahan I sensed to be my father.

She screamed and yanked at her red-and-silver hair. "No! *No!*"

"Calm yourself, child," Lenore said, putting her arms around my mother.

Mother knocked her away, her terrified gaze directed at me.

"Edony, run!" she said, calling me by my name for the first time in decades. "You're not safe here!"

Before I could even think, Chip bounded up the turned-over table and leaped up onto my shoulder, Gob tugging at my arm.

Lenore's arms extended outward and turned into giant wings. She shrieked.

"Not my child!" Mother shrieked. "Run! Run! Run!"

FORTY-SIX

BRECC

"Brecc, what have you done?"

Kaylein's mouth fell open as she stared at me, her arms pulling in as if afraid to come into contact with me.

"Oh, no. Oh, no..." Neela paced back and forth, her subsequent words as well as Borin's and his wife's lost to me.

My head pounded, but my senses felt heightened. My people were shouting—no one could miss that—but beyond the unfamiliar sounds of their cries, there was a heartbeat.

The maze's lifeblood.

The minotaur's heart.

Calling... Calling me to it.

"Brecc!" Kaylein grabbed me now, and I looked at her, slowly. She was there, but she seemed almost beyond my reach. As if I were observing her from somewhere else, talking to someone who wasn't me.

"Bond..." I said, trying to focus, to explain why I'd done what I had. "The brave bond to the beast—it's the only way."

I didn't know if that were true, but the heaviness in my gut drove me to that conclusion. No. It wasn't mere conjecture. After the song—seeing Favian's behavior... It all made sense.

I pushed past Kaylein, heading for the gate. The minotaur's heart thumped in my ear. There were people in front of me—fae, humans. Many of the fae clutched their humans to their sides, rushing toward their homes. My heart warmed, though the feeling was hollow. Part of me knew I liked this—to see my fae caring for their human spouses.

I cared for the human who would be my wife.

They cared. We did. Fae were capable of love.

My face itched, though. It *burned* in two jagged lines down my flesh.

I had a love out there, somewhere.

But my burning *need* for her was at war with something else.

Something's need for me.

Fae spoke in my ear, rushing past, their voices murmurs beneath the sorrowful cry of the beast. The recurrent shifting of the dirt below us made everyone's movements more difficult, but as though given no choice, I found my footing again and again, giving no apologies to the people around me seeking guidance.

A large part of me knew I was supposed to offer it—if ever there was a time for my title to mean anything, it was now.

But all I could do was run for the creature.

The air was warmer as I exited the market, fewer fae and

humans gathered in the outer avenues. The reason was clear enough.

I felt just like I had entering the smithy—pushing through a tangible, if invisible, bubble of hot air.

The brief thought of the smithy sent a prickling sensation of danger into the back of my head. I was plunging into this situation without a weapon of any kind.

Come, said a voice in my head. It wasn't the word, exactly, but the sensation, clearer than any the labyrinth itself had sent to me.

All thoughts of a weapon left me. I wouldn't need it. I was headed where I needed to be.

"Restrain him!" That was Carac's voice, a little unsteady in time with the shifting of the ground beneath our feet.

"We have bigger problems right now!" Elspeth. Anger laced her tone.

"He's summoning it!" Carac shouted.

"Then let him go out there!" Elspeth snapped back.

Two more of my guards were facing the gate, their swords hanging limply at their sides.

"We have nothing with which to restrain him," one said. He was short for a fae, his long, red hair whapping around his face as he shifted.

"We don't need to *restrain* people!" said the other. Her long, silver hair was tied back, her stance and her svelte figure a tad steadier than that of her companion on duty.

"Oh, open the door and be done with it!" shouted Elspeth. "If he goes out there, maybe it'll stop barking down the door!"

"You can't open the door!" shouted Carac. "It'll let that thing in!"

"It's never come to the village before!" said the red-haired fae guard.

"Well, it's here now!" shouted Carac back. He struggled to keep hold of Favian, the lither elf's elbow flying and jutting up against Carac's jaw.

The hot, breathy grunts of the minotaur echoed out from the other side of the wooden door. The door itself glowed, steam rising from every crevice.

Favian shook himself free of Carac's weak hold and flung himself against the door.

My feet picked up to join him.

"Fire!" shouted Carac.

The door had caught—there wasn't enough stone in this place to slow the molten power of the minotaur's hot breath. All that was stone were the walls surrounding us. The houses, the marketplace—everything—was made of wood, woven into trees. The entire place would light up if the flames spread inside.

"Brecc!" Carac screamed as I passed.

I turned back to look at him and he stumbled backward. "Your-Your face!"

My hand touched my cheek absentmindedly. The flesh stung and my fingers were dotted in blood.

"Leave us!" I shouted to him. My heart thundered, my mind growing heavy. There was something more I wanted from him. Some ardent wish to help me—to slay.... to slay...

But no. I would never want the beast to die.

Never.

He was as important to me as my Edony.

"Water!" I said. "Put out the flames!" I could wish for that much, for my guards to keep my people—my home—safe.

But Favian and I—we had other places to be. He and I exchanged a look. I could see myself reflected in his glossy eyes, observe the mussed hair, the wildness. The red lines dripping from brow to opposite cheek. We nodded and each took hold of the door.

It was hot—my hands wanted to tear away.

But they wouldn't. Beyond that door lay my destiny.

We pushed and the fiery gate opened, bits of ash and charred oak flittering down on us like falling rain.

The creature stood in the ever-darkness, the flame red from his nostrils lighting up his face.

He was injured. A long needle stuck out from one eye, which oozed with pus. A dagger protruded from his remaining arm. I looked down and realized I carried his cloven hoof with me even now.

My heart broke.

"Take it," I said, getting down on one knee and lifting the hoof with both hands above my head. "It's yours."

"Brecc!" Carac's voice seemed hollow now, far away.

The creature reached for it, that hideous dagger protruding from the flesh of his forearm. How could anything hurt my minotaur, my—

"Oh, labyrinth!" Favian shouted, tossing both arms aside. "Oh, labyrinth, take me! For I belong to the beast and.... and..." He blinked, staring in my direction.

My head snapped out of its haze, feeling wretched with nausea at myself, at the feelings coursing through me. I'd carved this bond—etched the proof of it within my flesh—for reasons other than to grovel and surrender.

As the minotaur's fae-like hand grabbed hold of the missing hoof, I leaped to my feet, taking hold of the dagger's hilt instead. Though the roar of the beast halted my movement for just a moment, thoughts of Edony brought me back to myself. I tore the dagger out, carving into the monster's flesh as I twisted, spinning around to give the movement more force.

The minotaur howled, tossing his mighty head back, and the darkness was alit by the flame of his cry.

In front of me fell not one old, molding hoof, but a second one, fresher than the other, the fae-like hand morphing into a cloven hoof as it fell.

"No!" shouted Favian, and before I could register his movements, he barreled into me, the dark dagger, which had felt heavy in my hands, skittering across the forest floor.

My shoulder ached as it took the brunt of the attack, and I didn't have time to do more than brace myself as we rolled through the fallen leaves.

Favian's first blow was unavoidable—unexpected, despite what he had just done. Grunting, I took the hit to my temple. His second hit, though—by then, I had my wits about me. Letting my open wound and sore cheek hit the rotting leaves with a sharp wince, I rolled once more and blocked Favian's blows with my forearm.

Favian straddled me, his hair hanging down so far, it glanced my arm and cheek. Drool dripped from his swollen lips as his wild, bloodshot eyes roved across my face. The minotaur's cries from behind Favian were bestial, and they could have just as easily come from this man.

From this friend consumed now by his own deed reflected back upon him.

"Favian," I said softly. "That dagger—it could be it. What we need to defeat him. He'll let us near now—or at least you, if he won't forgive me. We're bound to him."

"You hurt him," Favian snarled, his lips peeling back.

"I had to," I said. "Enough. Enough of this place. Enough of that *thing*. Favian, you did this to a woman once—can you not see how we were wrong? How we should never have made anyone suffer?"

"Favian!"

That voice. I turned as slightly as I could so as not to alarm the man holding me down.

It was Neela, standing in the open gate to the fae village, Kaylein and Carac holding her back by an arm each.

The door still burned on either side of them, but the fire was spreading on the outside of the wall—to the forest all around us. Perhaps the stone of the wall would keep my people safe.

"Favian, I'm sorry!" Neela cried. "I'm—" I couldn't hear what else she had to say.

Favian's rabid lips softened somewhat, just a glimmer of hesitance across his eyes as he turned to look at his bride.

"This madness," he whispered. "All I deserve and more—but I am sorry."

His hold on me loosed and he sat up. His gaze darted as well as mine to the dagger, its black tip seeming to smolder dark smoke from the pile of leaves in which it rested.

Favian leaped off of me and scrambled toward it.

I couldn't chance that he would retain his thoughts long enough. I scrambled up to grab for the dagger as well.

Only I lagged a few feet behind my oldest friend.

The beast's cloven feet advanced, crackling against the fallen leaves like little sparks of fire.

Just as Favian swept the dagger out from where it had fallen, the beast bolted past me, his breath making the air hot and sticky.

And the monster leaned down, using a jagged black horn with which to gore my friend—my brother.

FORTY-SEVEN

EDONY

"But Mother! Father!" I cried, my feet acting before my brain could, letting Gob drag me out through the Hall of Heroes.

"She told you to run!" Chip shouted.

Already, the stone echoed the chittering, harrowing cries of a swarm of ladydoves.

"Don't have to tell me twice," muttered Gob.

We were at the hallway leading to the front door now, a once-mighty gate that sat half-rusted, stuck open in the crystalline sands beyond it.

"I imagine all that lady's messing with magic sucked what life there was right out of this place," Gob said as our feet hit the cold sand. His hand dropped mine as he needed to swing his arms back and forth to make his way through the desert, which had slowed our steps on our way into this place.

At least if we were to die, we had some answers.

But answers were little solace when we were just pawns in a war between beings so much more powerful than ourselves.

"What danger did my mother warn us of? What was Lenore going to do with me?" I sent one wayward look over my shoulder.

As if the sounds of their flapping wings and harrowing song weren't clue enough, the stormy flock of white birds lifting up from the dilapidated building into a tunnel-cloud swarm made our retreat all the more urgent.

"I would guess it involves our deaths," said Chip, picking up speed and sending sand flying in her wake.

She had a point. Lenore, Lyra, Brecc's grandfather—the maze itself—they'd all had their own agendas.

All I'd done was fall in love—and dream of a life we might be able to build together.

Lenore might have shown pity for my mother. But if there was some way I, as the child of the labyrinth-bound, could help her son...

It was clear that despite it all, she wouldn't hesitate to use me.

I'd rested enough. My friends were counting on me. Though Chip's pace outmatched my own, Gob was starting to slow. Summoning all of my strength, I dashed forward and picked him up, throwing him over my shoulder like a sack of potatoes, and kept running.

"Come back, come back!" the birds seemed to call.

"Now they're talking?" Gob shouted. So he could hear it, too.

Ahead of us, Chip skittered to a halt right beyond the border the minotaur hadn't been able to cross.

She turned around, her nose twitching anxiously as I tried to catch up. Finding our scattered few remaining provisions, she gathered them up and waited, shouting for us.

"Incoming!" Gob yelled, his arm wrapping around the back of my head. I didn't dare stop to look, but I felt the sharp peck of a beak against my head.

"My... son's... sacrifice..." the bird seemed to say, her voice cracking and raw.

Me? She'd spared my mother, but I must have offered a new kind of sacrificial magic for Lenore to try.

"Get back, fiend!" Gob squirmed over my shoulder and I found my grip slacking. His hands pressed hard against me to raise his head up and—

With a crunch, his fangs dug into the bird's wings.

She shrieked and flew back, flittering her wings across my scalp again. I crossed past the line.

But just because it kept the minotaur on this side of the border, did that mean it also kept the ladydoves on the other?

I was counting on it.

Then I remembered. The birds had to have fetched those nuts and berries from somewhere—and the desert was unlikely to offer any.

"Keep going!" I shouted to my friends, bending to put Gob down and waiting for the onslaught. Instead, both Gob and Chip gathered at my feet, their backs to my calves as if to make a stand. I raised my arms up to protect my face—to offer minimal protection for us all.

The birds did pass the line, the symbols not lighting up on the scattered stones. Just before a swarm dive-bombed me, a bird-voice squawked at them, "Draw back! The heroes! Wait for the heroes!"

The ladydoves drew to a screeching halt. Half drove upward, the other half down, all darting left and right into two groups. Beyond them, far off yet, lumbered the nine dullahans, Father in the middle. Mother was nowhere in sight, unless she hid again in Father's empty shell.

Just at the edge of the etches marking the border, a sole ladydove flapped her wings, the feathers on the right wing drenched in red.

Gob spit a white feather dotted in blood onto the tiles beside the remnants of our earlier fire.

"We offered you rest. Food and succor." The bleeding lady-dove spoke without moving her beak, almost as if speaking through thoughts into our minds. "I didn't hope to hurt you. Your mother has been our companion all these years."

"'Hope to'?" Chip sneered. Gob strode over to her and accepted the satchel. The two worked seamlessly together, Chip handing it off without her gaze leaving Lenore's beady bird eyes once.

"My son is trapped," she said in that eerie voice. "You, human child, were born in this place—your life may belong to him."

"Born in...?" I looked around. Mother had mumbled about her child being born in the labyrinth, but I'd dismissed that as her rambling. Mother had come to the labyrinth many a time, more and more often before her final venture inside this place. But Grandmother, Father, Mother—no one had ever mentioned she'd *given birth* to me inside these walls.

My hand caught at my throat, breath difficult for me to snatch. But that...

That made things worse, surely?

Brecc was bade to marry someone born of one of the villages surrounding the maze. Someone the right age to be eligible for the fete—but that was beside the point. I hadn't even been born in one of the villages?

Had I ever been obligated to attend the fete?

"Edony's life belongs to no one but herself," said Chip, her eyes darting tellingly to my abdomen.

Myself first and foremost—but someday, perhaps, I would devote that life to this child.

This child. I believed it to be true now. I *felt* it.

And he would not have a life belonging to any monster or collection of stones.

The ground grew shaky beneath our feet.

"You ask me, you lot have had your chance already." Gob shifted the satchel over his back and nodded toward the approaching dullahans. "Feeding and feeding off the rest of us for ages? No, I think not. I think that ends now."

The dirt shifted, the walls a few yards in three directions sinking into the ground, popping up in different locations, the maze re-fashioning itself.

"The maze doesn't like what we're saying," I pointed out to my companions. My friends.

Gob wiped his mouth with his forearm and spit. "The maze can take its feelings and eat them, for all I care."

Chip scampered off to the remnants of our fire and snatched up a thick, charred branch. "Seconded." She snapped the stick against the ground, as if to take on the maze itself.

I laughed. I couldn't help it. The shrieks of the birds, the grinding of the stones as the dullahans approached, the rumble of the ground beneath us and the shifting of the stone walls—they made for sorry companions for laughter, but I felt giddy now.

We'd tried working with the maze. It had almost led us to disaster—twice, and countless times before that.

If there was no hope of working with it, what did it matter if there was little hope of beating it?

"Edony!" My name carried over the distance between us.

A blinding shot of light emerged from the line of dullahans and I looked away.

"No! Don't!" shouted Lenore in her strange mind-speak. "Keep her contained! You are *our* companions!"

When I looked back, the light was fading and Mother had crawled out of the dullahan with the strange-shaped helmet I knew in my heart to be my father.

Mother held Father's gauntlet that clutched his stone sword and helped—or at least guided—his sword into the air above him. She stared at him. Nodded.

And then stepped back as Father swung, faster than I would have thought possible for the stone soldier, his sword tracing an arc through the cloud of birds above him.

Three fowl fell to the sands.

"No!" shrieked Lenore again.

A furry paw on my wrist drew my attention. "We have to go."

The cloud of birds remaining swarmed up and collected together, about to dive down.

At my father—and my mother.

She looked toward me, and I couldn't hear everything she said.

"Go! Edony! Go!" was the most I could make out of it.

Her eyes were glossy and she mouthed something more.

"Edony, we have to go." Gob pointed past the stream, beyond the forest to what appeared to be a half-raised wall. As if the labyrinth had stopped in the middle of shifting.

Beyond even that, fire raged, smoke and embers crackling up into the endless night.

"But Mother." I swallowed. "She needs me—"

She was lost. Beyond the flock of birds, lost amidst a mess of sand and white feathers.

Chip hung her head. "They've got her, Edony. Like they got my brothers. She gave us the chance to get ahead of them."

"The maze is distracted! We have to go!" Gob added, tugging on my elbow.

"Goodbye, Mother. Father." I spoke quieter than I knew they could hear, quieter than anyone could hear. But I had to send the words out into the night air regardless.

The birds flew up, and I couldn't see my mother anymore. She may have lay amidst the dunes. Perhaps the sand had already sucked her up, though Lenore had led me to believe the maze couldn't extend its reach so far.

Something had happened to Chip's brothers in the sand, though.

But what surprised me more was to see the other eight dullahans fighting alongside my father—slower, too slow to be of any use against a larger opponent, but quick enough to cut ladydoves from the air.

"Come on!" Chip shouted from nearer the river. Though the

waters had slowed to a trickle, she couldn't get easily across without me.

A harrowing warbling song hit the air, the tune matching that of one my mother had sung earlier. *"Save the son."* I remembered those words especially.

Save the minotaur?

But that was what the ladydoves wanted.

Then with a high-pierced shriek, a single bird hovering nearby, her right wing drenched in red, collapsed to the sand.

"My poison." Gob grunted. "Bit slow-actin'. You, I thought you'd survive it—but her, in that smaller form of hers..."

The sands spit up as she collapsed into them, and from there, I could not tell what happened.

I turned and extended a forearm out for Chip to jump up on. Then, waiting for his nod for a go-ahead, I tucked Gob beneath my arm, the satchel—so light now on provisions—tucked at my side between us.

I stepped forward and waded through the water. It reached only my thighs, but it was cold and piercing nonetheless.

Gritting my teeth, I moved forward. This was nothing. Not compared to what we'd been through. Not compared to what lay ahead.

On the other side of the stream, I set my friends down and we approached the half-risen stone wall.

Chip scrambled ahead, poking at it with her charred stick, bits of ash crumbling off and landing at her feet.

"It's not moving." She shrugged in a very human-like manner and scrambled upward.

"Sorry about your ma," Gob said. "And your pop, too, if he was one of those things."

I shook off first one and then the other wet leg. "I didn't expect to find either of them again—in any form."

"Thanks to her, those 'wise women' who caused this mess might just be out of the picture," Gob said. "She had her bond with her dullahan—and he could probably convey their case to the rest." He sniffled and wiped under his nose with one finger. "I imagine if they were in their right minds enough to realize they had them birds to thank for all of this—their king, too, sure, but that man's already labyrinth-picked bones—maybe they weren't so keen to still be the ladies' companions."

"Well, they have you to thank, too," I pointed out, tapping the fang scars on my forearm. "Taking down their leader."

Gob's green cheeks darkened just slightly. "I wouldn't let her hurt you."

Digging my wet knees into the dirt, I hugged my friend. He jumped but soon accepted the gesture, patting my back in turn.

I stood, my heart full. "I'm glad I'm not alone," I admitted. Though I wished he and Chip were safe.

Gob grunted. "Me, too."

We both grinned.

"I won't let my parents' sacrifice be in vain," I said, as much to myself as to Gob. I patted my stomach and then steeled myself before the uneven wall, finding a foothold in a crack between stones and gripping two of the higher ones in order to launch myself over. Reaching a stone large enough to sit on at the top, I turned around and extended a hand out to Gob.

"It's like this over here, too!" Chip called.

Lowering Gob down across the other side of the wall, I jumped after, bending my knees to cushion the fall. It was just a few feet, but it still stung a bit at the ankles.

"This whole part of the maze looks unfinished," Gob said, waddling over to Chip to see what she'd been referring to.

Sure enough, the path ahead was a mess. Half-grown trees, crumbling stone walls—the faintest sign of a dirt path burrowing its way through the tall reeds and jagged bushes ahead.

The air stank of smoke, the charred remnants of a roast over fire.

"I take it that's where the beast has gone." Chip lowered her blackened stick to the ground and stared up at me. "So what do we do? His eyes were vulnerable, we saw that. Maybe we don't need a special dagger."

"With any luck, the beast might still have the dagger with him." Gob stroked his chin. "Though I have to wonder... if Lyra gave us the dagger—and gave it to your ma before that, which led to her stabbing your pop—should we even trust the thing?"

"It's the only thing known to cut the beast's hide," I said. "And blinding it alone isn't going to see to the end of the creature."

I braced myself for the shake of the ground, but there was none.

The maze really *was* distracted.

Chip took a deep breath and then started hacking. She looked at the satchel on Gob's back and nodded. "What say you we make some kerchiefs out of that so we can breathe better in the smoke? Drink the water and leave the rest behind." She looked over her shoulder. "We won't need supplies where we're going. It's now or never."

Gob hesitated, then looked at me.

I nodded.

He shifted out of his pack and passed around the remaining waterskins, getting to work ripping the cloth in three small pieces once he drank his own.

"There's something you should know," Gob said, handing me my cloth as I finished off my waterskin.

My stomach clenched at his words. What else could possibly have Gob so sullen?

Gob stared ahead at the plume of smoke and fire, reaching behind his cap to tie his cloth into place.

"That fire... is in the direction of the fae village."

I blinked, my heavy heart, burdened by leaving my mother and father behind, sinking further.

Neela.

Brecc.

CHAPTER

FORTY-EIGHT

EDONY

L ightened of the last of any of our burden, no longer impeded at every turn, the three of us made our way in the direction Gob led us. We had a routine for breaching the half-lowered walls when we encountered them, to climb over every fallen tree and overgrown thicket of brambles. Chip could scout ahead, give us a report, then I would use my height to help Gob over, following closely behind him.

We didn't stop for long at any point.

When the smoke grew so thick, it blotted out even the moonlight, we found ourselves flush against a wall that towered over me, no sign of a breach anywhere, no footholds for Chip to climb up.

The maze was focused here.

Coughing, Gob pointed ahead of us. "There should be a bend there," he said. "The path to the fae village gate."

Beyond the wall, what could only be the minotaur let out a mighty roar.

Chip flinched ever so slightly, but her paw gripped tighter on her stick. She was *determined* to put that in the monster's other eye, I was sure.

Gob vanished into the haze in front of us.

"Wait, Gob!" I shouted, holding my hand out to signal to Chip not to get too far ahead. She nodded and stuck around my ankles as we darted forward. When I almost tripped on her, I was struck by her barn-cat-like manner. They often wove around my ankles, too, looking for attention.

"I can't see!" Gob's voice rang out in the haze, followed by a series of coughs.

"Stay put!" Chip shouted. She tensed but waited for me to match her pace.

My eyes watered. They hurt to keep open, but I had to try to see.

Chip and Gob both let out a grunt as they collided, and I let out a quiet exhale of relief—only to start coughing myself, harder than I had before.

"I'm lost!" Gob threw up his hands.

Chip looked right and left. "I can't tell where the fire is strongest. And where are all the fae? Shouldn't they be evacuating?"

"To where?" Gob grunted. "Looks like the maze has them trapped in there."

Somewhere in the smog, a woman cried out—a word, not just a shriek. A name maybe.

But that wasn't as important as the fact that I recognized the voice as my cousin's. My sister's.

"Keep to the left!" I shouted, my mother's words echoing in

my head. *"Keep turning, left, and left, and left, and you won't be trapped in one place."*

My hand fumbled until I slapped my palm against the wall. "Follow me!"

Chip and Gob did as I did, stepping in behind me.

My eyes watering, the air filling with all of our coughs, we moved forward. The stone was warm, sometimes a bit painful to clutch, but I held on as if my life depended on it—because at this point, it probably did.

Neela was beyond this wall.

Brecc.

And all the other fae and human spouses, once comforted in the thought that the minotaur had never ventured here.

What could have changed the beast's course?

Was it something I'd done?

All the more reason to see this through.

It felt like forever as we pressed through the haze, the warm stone on our left hands and paw the only thing anchoring us to where we might have been.

And then I turned a corner.

And saw through the smoke.

Another wall a dozen yards away awaited, a wooden gate thrown open—the bulk of the blaze engulfing the door to ashes.

Figures hovered beyond the haze in that open doorway— and it looked like thatched roofs and wooden homes beyond it still remained unscathed from the blaze.

But between us and that gate was the beast himself, leaning his head back and yowling into the air.

And standing in front of him...

"Brecc!" I shouted.

Chip's and Gob's cries of my name fell on shuttered ears. I ran forward through the strewn leaves, the fallen branches, the cluttered grass, all smoldering with embers of flame.

Brecc's head turned toward mine—he was scarred.

Fresh gashes like my mother's were etched from his left brow across his nose and to the bottom of his right cheek. Dried blood sat in streaks below the lines.

"Stay back!" Brecc shouted, his eyes wild and glossy. Reminding me so of my mother's.

In his right hand he held the dagger I'd left lodged inside the minotaur's forearm. Only now, as I drew to a halt beside Brecc and spun around to face the creature, I noticed the beast was missing both arms.

Blood dripped off the dagger in Brecc's hand.

His arm shot out in front of me, as if that would be enough to separate me and the creature.

Gob and Chip, having taken a less direct path, drew up behind me, Chip growling and Gob breathing heavily.

Brecc spared them a glance but said nothing.

All of our focus was on the minotaur, who towered above us. The eye Chip had stabbed was swollen and oozing.

"What happened?" I screeched to Brecc. My hand reached up to touch the edge of his jaw, tipping his face to mine just slightly.

His wild eyes softened somewhat. "I bonded myself to the beast." He'd done that to *himself?* He grit his teeth and tipped his head toward a pile of leaves visible through the minotaur's bowed legs. "Favian was bonded first and drew the creature here—I decided to take a page from that book—a lyric book." He shook his head, his jaw tightening, as he stared the creature down again. "Bond myself to him—but the lure of the bond is harder to fight off than I expected it to be."

"Favian?" I asked, peering at the pile of leaves. A pale hand reached upward from within the pile.

Oh, no. He was dead?

I'd been angry at him, for doing what he'd done to Mother —for taking my cousin from me.

But this—this...

"Edony!"

Her voice again.

I spun around. Neela was visible just beyond the burning gates, two fae keeping her back, her legs kicking, as three others splashed buckets of water at the gate. Her face was scrunched up, tears gushing down her cheeks. She coughed, like the fae on either side of her, but she kept pushing against their grips.

"She did that to him," Brecc said. "Marked him. I doubt she imagined it would lead to this, but..."

So that had been my cousin's answer to finding out what her husband had done to her aunt?

Had that... been justice?

"He'll pay," Chip said from beside me. She didn't know the fae in question.

But she was right. The creature's reign of terror had lasted long enough.

As if he'd heard my thoughts, the beast stopped yowling. His head shifted and a single, beady eye leaned nearer, flames reflecting off it in spots like jagged glass. His breath was visible, the steam rising from his nostrils and the edges of his thick lips.

"No," said Brecc through gritted teeth.

I didn't know to whom he was talking—until I sensed the voice, in so many words, in my head, too.

"Kill. Him."

Was it the minotaur? Had he instructed Brecc to kill me, too?

"Obey me," the mind-speak conveyed to me. *"Revere me."*

I laughed harshly. "I don't belong to you."

Blood or scars—none of us needed to revere this beast. A small part of me felt sorry for him, knew he'd had no role in the way he'd been born—but he'd made too many suffer. He'd walked too long a time. It was our time now—the choices made by those long ago may have affected us, but they would not spell our doom.

We had a future to look forward to.

"Brecc," I whispered, pulling down the cloth covering my mouth and letting it dangle around my neck like the poorest excuse for finery. His eyes darted from the beast to me—roving wildly, like the creature was fighting to draw the Fae King back to him.

I took the hand in front of me, the one not holding the dagger, and placed it gently against my stomach.

"My king," I said softly. "Our future king lies within me."

Brecc blinked—hard. My words were the dam that broke his wavering resolve, his focus wholly on me.

He gripped my cheek and kissed me, sending, through the smoke and crackling of flames all around us, the wildest surge of hope through every pore in my body.

Gob cleared his throat from behind us. "Time for that kind of thing later."

I pulled back and noticed Chip's frown. They'd only just gotten used to the idea of me running *to* the Fae King.

But I wouldn't run away. No more running and hiding. I took Brecc's hand in mine and faced the beast. We died or he did—the labyrinth could do what it would with that.

"This blade will cut him," Brecc said.

"I know," I told him. "I was the one who lodged it in his flesh to begin with."

Brecc grinned at me wickedly, his lips warping some of the scars. It wasn't an altogether unattractive sight, though. Not here, facing the beast together as we did.

The minotaur threw his head back and yowled, telegraphing his intent to move forward, straight for Brecc and me.

Chip and Gob scattered in opposite directions, coming at the beast from the sides. Brecc gripped me around the waist and yanked me to one way, just as the minotaur charged forward.

"Yah!" screamed Chip, who leaped down from the tree above.

Only the minotaur seemed to expect her this time, rolling around so that her charred stick snapped as it hit against the beast's tough cheek skin, missing the eye entirely. My feet moved into action as Chip went flying. Reaching my arms above me, I just managed to catch her, but the force knocked us both back into a pile of leaves.

Chip groaned as we sat up, the sound of Brecc's and Gob's grunts almost as loud as the minotaur's.

Chip shrieked as she knocked aside a clump of long, white hair. Favian's pale face looked paler, his eyes devoid of life.

Clutching my abdomen, I got back to my feet. No more.

"Edony!"

Loud footfalls disturbed the scattered leaves all around me. Neela coughed, using one hand to cover her mouth as she extended the other down to me to lift me up. There were bags under her eyes, and her hair was wild, messy. She wore our golden family dress, which was smudged with soot and sagged off her thin frame.

I took her hand and stood in front of her. "You need to go back to the village."

The guards who'd been holding her back were now charging toward the beast, their swords extended.

Neela shook her head. "I'm not bound to that place anymore." She glanced downward as Chip scampered up my arm and to my shoulder. A whimper escaped the elf's lips and she burrowed her head against my neck.

"I did that to him. Marked him. When I learned what he did to Aunt Aldreda—I couldn't forgive him."

I patted her back, my focus drawn between her and the battle going on before my eyes. I was supposed to be there, in the thick of it. But doing what?

I still didn't know what I *could* do.

The ground shook beneath us, and the leaves beside us were swallowed up into it.

"Get back!" shouted Brecc over his shoulder at us.

Neela and I ran away from the hole swallowing up the pile of leaves, Chip jumping down from her perch and bounding past us at our ankles.

I watched as his white hair, his pale hand vanished down into the ground with the detritus. The labyrinth had swallowed Favian.

"I'm sorry," I said to Neela. For what it was worth, I was sure she'd loved him—I'd known Brecc just as long and I felt that to be true. "But please—you need to be safe."

It seemed to take her a moment to hear me. She stared down at the ground where Favian had been, replaced by nothing but dirt.

"I'm staying. You're fighting, too." Her damp eyes roved to Chip and widened slightly. We'd certainly never seen elves back home—and I knew they weren't allowed in the village. "And your friend?"

"Chipper," Chip said, nodding at her.

Neela stumbled back.

Gob—he who'd refused a weapon, who'd wanted nothing more than to leave this place—was proving especially valuable to Brecc and the two guards' assault, constantly getting the minotaur's attention by weaving around and through the towering creature's legs. Every time the creature moved to dodge one of the fae's attacks, he was drawn back to Gob slapping his calves, at one point, the beast's head lowering so close between his legs, the creature lost his balance.

Brecc used the opportunity to drive the dagger into the beast's shoulder blade, sliding up the creature's back until it got lodged in bone again.

The beast cried out and more smoke poured from his nostrils, spreading outward faster than the fire.

Chip, Neela, and I all coughed, and aside from the glowing

red nostrils of the beast, I couldn't see beyond the two standing with me.

"There's a song," said Neela between coughs. "When I learned you were out here and the minotaur was after you, I wanted to help. It spoke of 'saving the son'—"

"The minotaur." My throat scratched just to breathe. "He's the son."

Neela cocked her head slightly but didn't ask. "The bond between the beast and those marked by him. It's supposed to lead to his downfall."

"How?" I tried thinking back to the words Mother had sung.

"Well, it allows you to get close..." Neela frowned. "So that's why the Fae King marked himself, I think."

No sooner had she spoken than a woman's cry tore through the air and a dark form flew past us in the smoke, landing somewhere in the dirt. Neela ran after her—it had to be the female guard, who'd looked familiar, but who could say when I'd seen her at the fete, considering we'd all worn masks—and Chip raised her voice to be heard over the crackle of fire.

"Gob!"

We had to check on them.

I stepped forward, keeping my steps cautious if swift, and ran smack dab into a stone wall, the sounds of it grinding up from the ground into place just now reaching my ears after all the other raucous noise.

"That wasn't there before!" Chip bellowed, climbing up my arm to perch on me.

Of course the maze itself would work against us now. The only question was why it had waited so long.

Probably because it had hoped the minotaur would have taken care of us faster than this.

Now that it wanted to keep us apart—I wondered. Did we stand a chance?

Maybe not with walls burrowing through the haze.

"Brecc!" I shouted, slamming my palms against the stone. It was warm and it scalded my hands. I screamed but kept pounding. "Brecc!"

Chip twitched her nose and shook her rear end upon my shoulder. I stopped moving, but before I could ask her what she intended, she leaped up, her front claws digging into the top of the stones and her back legs scrambling for purchase.

"Chip!" I said, standing on my toes to offer a boost up.

"Hot, hot, hot!" she said, just barely keeping her balance somewhere atop the wall. It hadn't grown so high as to make her climbing it impossible yet. She scampered forward. "Over here!"

I followed the sound of her voice into the smoke, remembering to lift my makeshift kerchief over my mouth as I struggled to breathe.

"Brecc!" I shouted.

My name returned on his lips. "Edony!"

The sound of thumping against stone. He was there, just beyond the wall between us.

He was breathing at least, though his words were peppered with coughs.

"Gob!" Chip shouted, scampering farther down the wall. "He's all right," she shouted back at me. A tree rustled, and I hoped that was her leaping successfully to a perch.

Despite the warmth of the stone, the growl of the minotaur

somewhere deep in this place, I leaned my cheek as close as I could near the hot stone, longing to be near him.

"Brecc," I said, his panting more audible than mine. "How do we get married?"

"Married?" he echoed back, his voice thick with emotion. "You'd agree to be my bride? But what of your objections? Our union will cause the end of the world as we know it."

"I wasn't born in the villages," I said. "I was born here. In the maze."

He hesitated a moment. Somewhere in the distance, a sword clanged against stone. Likely from Brecc's remaining standing guard, who'd come to help him in battle.

Our time was limited. There could be no more fatalities today—not besides those of the beast and the stone that kept us all trapped inside it.

"I don't know if that would matter," he said. "It would just prove you were never eligible to be my bride, even when younger." He took in a sharp breath. "It wouldn't have mattered if I'd found you earlier. I would have married you without hesitation and then—"

"The maze would have collapsed regardless," I said. "That has to be why you never showed during my years of eligibility."

"You think the maze itself discouraged me?" He chuckled darkly. "I wouldn't put that kind of self-preservation conniving past it."

The ground rumbled beneath my feet, but I clutched on to the wall, my fingers scraping against the stone for purchase, as if I could claw my way through to him.

"Edony, will you be my bride?" Brecc asked.

For a moment, my mind couldn't catch up to what he was

asking. I'd said as much, hadn't I? That I would marry him. I just needed to know how—if we could manage to wed before it was too late.

But this *was* how. I'd witnessed Gloriana and her fae bride marrying—Lady Elspeth, I realized, the same guard who'd gone flying earlier.

"Yes," I said quickly. "I'll be your wife."

"Edony, my wife."

"Brecc, my husband."

"My queen."

"My king."

That was all it took. By fae precedent, we were married.

My hand clutched against the stone wall, my forehead grinding against the warm stone.

From deep within me, a surge of energy seemed to be rising, flowing outward from my core—my abdomen—and through to the wall.

The energy was tangible. Visible. The light shot out from my hands, as bright as the light from the dullahans.

I had to look away—but the sounds were overwhelming.

The roar of the ground, the shifting of the stone. The cry of the minotaur.

The stone crumbled beneath my skin.

"Edony!" Brecc screamed. And before I could even open my eyes, I felt his arms wrapped tightly around me.

His warmth was sweeter than the hot stones' had been. I burrowed my face against his chest, inhaled his woodsy scent mixed with char and ash. He took hold of my jaw and pressed his lips against mine.

The kiss made the world explode into thunderous sound.

The ground continued to rumble beneath me, but I was steady in his arms. Euphoric, I felt complete—all thoughts and worries pushed aside but for my Brecc.

My husband.

My eyes watering, I drew back, our gazes locked, the world bright and burning all around us.

He took my chin between his thumb and forefinger. "I was wrong," he said. "I should have never demanded you revere me. *I* revere you. My Edony. My brave, feisty queen."

"I do revere you," I said back. "My king."

The last thing audible, even beyond the crash of nearby burning trees, was the shriek of a woman, deep and sorrowful.

The smoke cleared, the fire lay in embers dying, and sunlight—bright, bright sunlight—fell all around us.

The horizon stretched on for ages. I could see the fae village in its entirety, missing its outer wall. Forests, streams, swamp—deadlands, desert. The Hall of Heroes—including my fallen parents.

The maze walls were gone.

A deep, snorting breath came from behind me and I spun, Brecc holding me tighter against him.

And the minotaur—his teeth grinding, his nostrils flaring—was free.

CHAPTER

FORTY-NINE

BRECC

My bride was in my arms. The sun—at its zenith—was shining. These lands had been set free. It should have been a dream.

Instead, the last vestige of our nightmare taunted us, the beast's beady eye fixed on us as one of his hooves scraped against the stone over and over.

"Seems like he's getting ready to run." The little green troll Edony had brought as a companion backed up with the diminutive furry elf. The elf's eyes were wide as she glanced up at the sunlit sky and my stomach pained at the thought of what my people had denied them. The trolls had encountered the daylight only when we'd let them near the gate for trade.

But for most of the maze's creatures, the sun had been entirely denied to them.

The troll tugged on the elf's furry arm and she turned to climb up a tree, but the nearest trunk was decimated, split in pieces, its top half fallen to the ground behind it. The two had nowhere to hide, not without passing in front of the beast first.

My eyes roved for signs of Carac and Elspeth, the only two guards to rush to my aid. But so be it. I wouldn't have the rest of my people—soft and so not ready for this new world—risk their lives against this beast.

Neela and Kaylein were seated some distance away beside a prone Elspeth, their jaws slack with shock and their eyes affixed to the beast.

Carac heaved and used his sword to support his weight where he crouched on one knee.

My grandfather's sword was still cooling in the smithy. Useless now as it had ever been.

And that dark dagger—it oozed mist from the minotaur's shoulder blade, but it didn't seem to slow the beast any more than the creature losing both his front hooves had.

"We should have gotten married right away." Edony picked at the open collar of my shirt, her eyes not leaving the beast. "If I'd known that the maze was never truly about keeping us safe—"

"Hush," I told her, squeezing her again. "We're married now. But we won't be for long if we don't manage to win this."

Reluctantly, I let her go and stepped between the monster and my wife—and our child.

The minotaur did not budge yet. I felt a sting across my fresh scars. The bond between us infuriated and confused us both.

Half the time, he could not decide whether or not to kill me.

"You fools!" The old doe-like wise woman appeared out of

nowhere, shuffling her tiny hooved feet across the leaves and ash. "You don't know what you've done!"

"She created the maze," said Edony from behind me. Her hand rested on my shoulder, and the simple touch was enough to give me the strength to move on.

I scoffed. "You'll have to explain that—later." The minotaur was moving closer, inch by careful inch, his mind screaming with a desire to take—or gore—Edony and me both.

"Feed to the stone," his mind speak seemed to say.

Edony must have heard it, too. "The labyrinth used to eat whatever died in this place." I knew by now that had happened to Favian. My friend. I'd have to wait to mourn him later. "He must not understand he's free."

Almost as soon as she spoke the words, the monster looked up and around him, his one glossy eye gazing out at the endless horizon. A sight he hadn't seen in ages.

"Edony!" shouted the little elf, scrambling up behind my wife, the troll not too far behind her. They braced themselves on either side of my beauty. "We need that dagger back."

Still lodged in the broad shoulder of the beast, the dagger hilt smoldered in the brightness of daylight, rising up to join the steam from the beast's nostrils.

"Carac!" I shouted as my guard got to his feet. "The dagger!"

He didn't have to be told more. We rushed the creature, Carac from the side, me from the front, our collective shouts enough to overpower even the ragged breaths of the beast.

"Brecc, wait!" my bride shouted.

The minotaur bent his head down, his horns pointed right

at me. Beyond Carac's own grunts, a woman's deep voice hit the air, in an incomprehensible sort of chant.

Just as the horns were about to reach me, I grabbed hold of them in both hands, letting out a groan as the force smacked hard against my palms.

My heels dug into the dirt as I clenched my jaw, the beast pushing me backward, dragging grooves into the ground with my feet.

The clang of Carac's sword against the beast's flesh was as fruitless as my own grandfather's sword against the stone wall.

A high-pitched battle cry sounded from behind me and after clutching my leg, then scrambling up my torso and to my shoulder, the elf reached my scalp and leaped off me straight at the beast's lowered head.

"Chip! Brecc!" Edony's footfalls joined the troll's.

"Stay back!" I shouted through gritted teeth.

Just as Carac's sword clanged down on the beast's side, causing him to yelp, Chip the elf leaped into the air, grabbing the hilt of the dagger, her back legs swinging wildly from side to side.

"Catch her!" Edony shouted.

Carac tossed his useless sword to the ground just as Chip pulled and went flying back, the dagger clenched between two front paws. Carac caught her, the both of them covered by the thick, dark smoke emitting from the dagger.

The minotaur yowled and lost some of his strength, giving me the advantage—enough to actually push back, though my legs burned with the effort of it.

"Don't hurt him!" Edony cried, and I was surprised to find her running toward the smoke as Chip let out a cry and bounded forward, the dagger, overly large for her, dragging behind her with one paw.

"Don't hurt?" Chip managed to say.

But whatever else passed between them was lost as the minotaur regained his strength, pushing back, my feet stumbling and pinning me beneath him.

His breath was hot as he leaned over me, holding himself up on two rotting stumps at the end of his arms. His breath stank of decay.

"Get close enough to smell its breath" or something like that, I remembered from that song. I laughed darkly. What good was that riddle? I was smelling it now. He and I were bonded. And yet... I had no hope. Was this to be the end of me?

I turned my head slightly. Edony. My beauty. My wife... For all of one moment.

That wise woman's strange chanting drowned out all other sounds.

"Don't let her bring the maze back!" The troll. Gob. I would never thank him for protecting my wife. I would never hear the tales of their travels.

I would never see my child's smile in the warm, omnipresent sun.

"Hush, hush," said Edony soothingly. She stepped forward, a blur of striped gray behind her, dragging behind it a plume of black smoke.

"Edony, run!" I said, choking on the foul odor of the beast.

The creature turned his head slightly, his focus on my Edony.

"*No*," I said, shifting up on my elbows, eager to draw his attention.

"Look at me," Edony said softly. And then she did something I never would have thought to do. Of all the ways to potentially stop this monster...

She took his snout in both hands, cradling him like a lover or a mother would.

The beast didn't fight the touch.

"The creature will hunger for beauty's touch." The songwriter had known. Somehow.

Edony, my brave, foolish beauty, leaned forward and placed her forehead on the top of the beast's nose, not wincing at the foul flesh of his rotten eye, the steam coming from his nostrils.

"She'll create the maze again!" shouted Gob.

Edony pulled back, tears streaming down her cheeks. A tear escaped the round, black eye of the minotaur, too.

"Banish the darkness!" Edony shouted, not tearing her gaze from the beast's. She leaned forward, putting her forehead to his again. "Let go, child of darkness and doe. Rest now. You're not alone."

The minotaur leaned back, freeing me from beneath him. I scrambled backward, getting to my knees to put steady hands on Edony's shoulders.

"Help them," she whispered, almost as if afraid to so much as move. "Stop Lyra."

I turned to the sounds of scurrying feet, the doe-like wise woman waving her arms and sending bursts of dirt flying from the ground to stop Gob and Chip's approach.

The troll held the smoking dagger now, though the elf was closer to the woman.

"Carac!" I shouted, and he stood beside me.

"My king." He held his sword aloft.

"The wise woman! She'll create the maze again!"

Carac blinked and looked around us. My beloved's cousin and Kaylein still sat beside Elspeth's prone form—but her still lying there might have meant she was still alive. Others from the village had gathered at the edge of town, where the labyrinth's wall had once been.

Looking around. Holding on to one another. The guards made their way to Neela, Kaylein, and Elspeth, but most others were drawn to the sight of my bride and the beast, forehead to forehead.

"Chip!" Gob cried, tossing the dagger into the air.

It rotated and flipped, but just as Chip was about to reach for it, Lyra swung her arms, her chanting ongoing, and a spurt of earth took the dagger away from the elf—and closer to the doe woman.

Carac and I made our charge, I without any weapon with which to arm myself.

A spout of earth spit up in front of us, but Carac swung his sword and chopped right through it.

I dove forward, shutting my eyes against the particles of dirt flying in every direction. I made it through and snatched the dagger's hilt mere seconds before Lyra's outstretched hand was able to do the same.

Her deer-like eyes widened, her muzzle parting.

"He shouldn't have been born," she whispered. "I only did what was right. His darkness can never be healed."

I raised the dagger above my head. "You don't know my wife."

Lyra closed her eyes and leaned back, muttering another spell-like prayer.

I hesitated.

"My sisters are gone," she said without opening her eyes. "That dagger, dipped in the essence of the darkness that birthed him—the darkness of your own people. Let it be the end of me. If you think your efforts will end him—then see it through."

"Stop the rot, stop the rot."

The song lyrics echoed in my head. She was the maze's power. To save the "son," she had to cave.

Still, my hand trembled.

"Watch out!" Chip cried.

"Majesty!" added Carac.

Gob's heavy breaths drew my attention to the side, but not for long before the pillar of dirt struck at me from behind.

Gob dove at my legs, sending me tumbling sideways.

Lyra peered out at us with one, large dark eye, a foul black mist exiting from her pores.

"Labyrinth, arise!" she shouted, waving her hands on either side of her.

"Not again." I stopped skidding, managing to stand on my two feet, even as the ground shook beneath us.

And then I moved forward, swirling around the pillars of dirt as if in a dance at the fete, stabbing the dark, cold dagger into the wise woman's chest.

She shrieked, a burst of white light shining through from the middle of the dark spots, at the wound at her heart.

And then she fell backward, and the world stopped shaking.

As she hit the ground, her body changed into white feathers, scattering into a wind that felt gentle and cool on my stinging cheek.

Gob heaved heavily on one side of me, Chip on the other.

"Majesty." Carac stood beside me, and I leaned on him as I turned around to join my Edony.

"Good-bye."

I'd recognize the sweet dulcet tone of her voice anywhere.

She was on the ground, holding tightly to the mutilated arm of the minotaur. The giant creature lay prone behind her, his snorting breaths growing light and wispy.

"Rest," she said. "The nightmare is over. Just rest."

As I neared, she reached forward and shut the beast's sole remaining eye.

His breath grew deep one last time and then his chest deflated.

The ground rumbled beneath him, the leaves and moss and dirt swallowing up the body of the beast that had tormented so many for so long.

Edony held on to his arm until the last moment. Nodding at Carac, I went stiffly to my knees and wrapped an arm around her shoulder just before the end.

Her fingers let go, and the ground stopped just short of opening beneath her legs, swallowing the last of the minotaur and this entire land's curse along with it.

Something warm but heavy lifted from inside me, fading away into a sense of freedom.

We were free. My people, my land. My queen and I.

No longer bound to monsters or walls or time itself. Unshackled from traditions.

Free.

CHAPTER

FIFTY

EDONY

"We brought you refreshments." The tray in my hands was piled high with breads, rolls, and other sweet and savory bakery items handcrafted by Gloriana, Lief, and all the Bakers who'd come to visit them, along with their spouses.

Gloriana had beamed when she'd told us Elspeth had been interested in learning the craft and had even leant a hand when it came to kneading the dough, despite only just recently coming out of recovery from her injuries.

Neela took her tray similarly teeming with goodies and handed them out to one side of the line of humans, fae, elves, and even trolls working on clearing the debris and building new roads connecting every village and colony, as well as the castle to one another. The castle would still host fetes, Brecc and I had decided, but for very different reasons.

To celebrate the demise of the maze once a year. And everyone—every creature of the maze—would be invited.

Our first celebration would be a little delayed this year, as we worked together to get the lands ready for easier trade and travel.

"Majesty." Carac offered a little bow before wiping his brow with the back of his arm.

"Please. Call me 'Edony.'"

He grinned. "Edony." He took a roll gratefully, and when Tea, Sully, and Bash scampered behind me with trays over their heads carrying wooden cups full of water, he took one of those cups, too, patting Tea on the head for his hard work.

I wove my way through the crowds and met up with Chip's parents.

"We can't thank you enough for what you did for Chip," said Brava.

"I didn't do anything." I handed her and Pluck some of the bread. "*She* saved me."

"You saved each other," said Pluck. He put down the little shovel with which he'd been working to snatch a roll and wrap his other forearm around his wife. "And after I asked you not to involve her..." He shook his head wistfully.

"We did save each other," I admitted. Another of the elf-cats came up and offered to take the tray from me to keep passing it around. Her thin lips curled widely into a smile; it was a refreshing change from when they'd once been so wary of me.

"We never should have trusted Lyra." Brava took a slow, small nibble of her bread.

"I don't blame you. You only knew her as a friend," I pointed out. "And I wouldn't have suspected her, either."

"Of being mother to the maze?" Pluck asked.

"Yeah... Though in a strange way, those rumors of the fae being parent to the minotaur were true." I looked out over the group spread out along the path leading to the fae village. Beyond the trees, I could see the smoking chimneys of the four human villages far off in four directions. I spotted Gob—pointedly ignoring the group of trolls lifting fallen branches behind him—hacking a fallen tree trunk with an ax.

"To think our Chip would help with the creation of a new world." Brava smiled up at her husband.

Pluck smiled back, though his face then fell. "And to get some more closure about the fate of our sons... We appreciate it."

I got down to my knees and hugged them both. "I'm sorry," I whispered. My mother had played an indirect role in that tragedy.

"We know," Brava said.

She leaned back and wiped her eye, finishing up her bread. "The kittens are so looking forward to fete," she said, clearly eager to change the subject.

"I can't wait for this project to be finished so we can all celebrate," I told her.

Excusing myself, I made my way over to Gob, pulling a special crab roll I'd put aside for him out of the pocket of my apron. As I moved, my hand brushed my stomach, slightly protruding, the presence there solid beneath my touch.

Our future king. Or queen. They would be born in a world so different than Brecc and I had been. A broader world—in which they would know so much more love.

"I'm glad you're staying through the first fete." My voice caused Gob to flinch, but he softened when he turned and saw me, letting his ax rest against the stump. I handed him the bread.

True to his name, he gobbled it up voraciously. One of his fangs caught the sunlight just right, as if to remind me that he'd gobbled into my flesh once with those things.

"You said you were going to reward me," he muttered.

I laughed. "Well, if it's just about the reward, you're welcome to coin at any time. Whatever you need to start your journey around the world."

Gob frowned, licking crumbs off his fingers one by one. "There's plenty of time for that. Want to make sure you're all set here in your new kingdom, don't I? Majesty." He offered a mocking bow.

I ruffled his red cap. "None of that." My gaze fell on Neela some distance away, chatting with some of the builders from Southwold who'd made their way here to help out. "My cousin has sworn to join her parents on a journey, too. Just like I always thought she would. Before..." I bit my lip.

Gob fixed his hat, but the irritation in his expression melted a bit as he studied me. "We couldn't save everyone."

He was right. We'd gone back to the Hall of Heroes as soon as we'd been able. The birds had been gone—no sign of their bodies—and so had Mother.

The dullahans had been nothing but piles of rocks in the sand.

Their lives, at least—though not mine, nor Brecc's, neither — had been tied to the minotaur's. Perhaps because it had been their second lives. And if Mother had been taken by ladydoves during that final assault, it made sense she might have dissolved into the ground, fed as magic to the labyrinth before it had fallen.

A scattering in the still-standing trees around us drew our attention. Chip's furry head hung down from a branch overhead. "Did you tell her yet?" She swung a bit, did a flip, and landed on top of the fallen tree trunk behind us.

"Tell me what?" I arched a brow.

"Obviously not," Gob muttered, avoiding eye contact with either of us.

Chip stood up on two hindlegs and put her foreleg on her hips. "I'm going with him!" She leaned down and wrapped one arm against him, pulling him toward her rather tightly. "Elf and troll—off to show the world what we can do together!" She gestured widely with her other front paw.

"All right, all right," Gob muttered, crossing his arms and pulling away. "Off to be the world's spectacle, rather, I venture. Not sure the other parts of the world have seen either troll or elf. Then again, once you've seen one *cat*..."

Chip didn't seem slighted. She jumped down.

I blinked, the news catching up with my brain. "Really? But what do your parents say, Chip?"

"Well, they're worried, sure." Chip rubbed the back of her head sheepishly. "But they know what I'm capable of now— and they know I won't be alone." She side-hugged Gob again, whose eyes widened, but he just took it. The two of them were bound to have a rather interesting time traveling together.

"I'm happy for you... But I'll miss you both," I admitted. My hand went to my stomach, but even without the future ruler to care for, I wasn't sure I shared that itch to go around the world like those around me seemed to. I had everything I could ever want right here.

"We'll be back!" Chip said. "Often, I should say! I want to tell everyone of our adventures, have the fae bard write up some songs about us."

"We've got one already in the works," Gob mumbled. He started humming, albeit off-tune, a song I knew Borin to be working on about the fall of the maze and the minotaur. "*An elf sought revenge, a troll did rebel, put aside their differences to send the beast to hell.*" He grinned at those words.

Chip *tsked*. "I wasn't *seeking revenge* for my brothers. More like justice—and the minotaur didn't even do anything to them."

"The maze did," Gob pointed out. "The whole bloody maze played a part."

She sighed. "So it did." She perked up. "But we'll give notes to the bard later—for now, we need to get this place cleaned up! The sooner we do, the sooner we have fete—and then we're off on our adventure." She sighed wistfully.

I smiled and gave her head a good pat.

"Grandmother!" The shriek was so loud, nearly every head in the vicinity turned to look.

I knew that voice, though. And for Neela to be calling that name...

"Grandmother!" I gasped. I'd seen her since the maze had fallen, but I'd never expected her to make the trek here herself.

"Excuse me," I said to Gob and Chip.

They knew my grandmother now, too. I'd invited them to dine with us back home a couple of times—though Brecc had accompanied us each time as well and we hadn't spent the night. Travel was so much easier without the giant maze to go around or get lost inside of. Horse-drawn carts would have an even easier time of it once a path was set and cleared.

"Give her my best," Chip called.

I ran over, gathering my skirt and apron up to have an easier time of running, especially with all of the mess still in the way.

Neela pulled back from giving Grandmother a hug and I slipped in right behind her. Grandmother's wavy, silver hair tickled my cheek before she pulled back and gave me a kiss on the brow.

"How are my girls?" she asked.

"What are you doing here?" My eyes darted to Kaylein, whom I realized I hadn't seen all day. Kaylein slipped her arm through Grandmother's.

"I've been telling her she needed to come to my village and see my workshop," Kaylein explained. She'd been Neela's guest when we'd gone back to visit. The two were good friends.

"But to walk all this way?" Neela's lips puckered.

"The path is almost entirely ready between Westbridge and here." Grandmother fluffed at the air. "We barely had to get off the cart to walk."

Kaylein started directing Grandmother through the remaining mess, toward the thatched roofs of the fae village. "I told her we were only about a week away from finishing, but she just couldn't wait."

"Everyone else is helping," Grandmother explained. "I thought the least I could do was help my granddaughters prepare for the fete."

"But what about the chores back home?" I asked.

Grandmother narrowed her eyes on me. "Oh, now you're concerned, eh? After my two granddaughters left me all on my own?" Her face brightened and she laughed. "I kid, I kid. But Kaylein did think..." She looked to the svelte elf, as if for permission to go on.

Kaylein grinned. "How about selling the old place and moving to the fae village, be nearer to her granddaughter queen, I suggested."

My jaw dropped. "And you *agreed* to that? I would have asked myself, but I never thought in a million years she'd *like* the idea."

"It's a new world, Edony." Grandmother patted Neela's shoulder as we all walked back. "And my traveling daughter and son-in-law and soon, my explorer granddaughter about to join them... I figured they wouldn't mind coming back to my new home amidst the fae between voyages on the great blue sea."

"Of course not." Neela squeezed Grandmother's arm, then threaded her other one through mine and hugged me as well. "My home will always be with the two of you. Three." She looked down at my stomach. "And counting."

I laughed, settling my hand on my stomach. "Let's just get to three first," I said. I offered Kaylein a grateful smile. "Though all the fae are family now."

"And all the humans are family, too—not servants to breed with." Kaylein shuddered.

Yes, that had been something of a point of contention in the aftermath. But Brecc had been surprisingly open to criticisms Neela and Kaylein had lobbied at him—he'd insisted he'd noticed as much, too.

Though not until he'd met me.

Fae were descended from warriors—barbaric ones, if Lenore's words had been true. They had the capability to be more than lofty lords. They were able to pitch in, too.

Everything had gone much faster when everyone who could had started to pitch in.

Though my future was filled with imminent partings—it was filled with happy reunions, too. Ebbing and flowing, coming and going, my loved ones would stop in and out of my life—but this place would anchor us, this new world we'd all built together.

Brecc's palm caressed the inside of my thigh as I sat bare naked on his lap. His thick, nude legs were warm, and they cupped either side of my buttocks, the hardness of his erection sliding through my folds making it hard for me to get a word out.

"Brecc," I gasped between deep, heavy breaths. "We have to get ready soon."

Off in the distance, down the halls, Borin and other fae and human musicians were playing soft music, the fete to celebrate the completion of the paths connecting our new world already underway.

Brecc grunted and brought the stroking hand down to the front of my folds, massaging my apex in rough circles with just the right amount of pressure.

"Let them wait for their heroine," he grumbled.

I cried out, grasping on to the poster at the foot of the bed in our room at the castle so I could stay upright. I was about to roll on the floor.

Not that Brecc would allow that to happen. His other hand lay flat against my stomach, guarding it warmly, gently.

My insides buzzed and my feet extended, my toes stretching out.

"We've already gone at it two times," I protested, but it was a weak protest. It practically came out as a mewl.

His lips nibbled at my earlobe. "And we'll go at it two more times before I'm satiated if you keep provoking me like this."

"Not fair," I whispered. "You're arousing me, too." I groaned.

He started rocking, his stiffness sliding down and up, his hand working to keep the blood pumping, pulsating right where he wanted it most.

My toes curled into the stone. "Brecc!"

"They can wait," he whispered, the tip of his girth nudging into my entrance.

I gasped, and he bent me forward just slightly—gently, his palm resting on my stomach, the other on my back—as he slid in deeper.

My walls fought, then collapsed, allowing his girth to fill me. An orgasmic melody floated past my lips.

He leaned me up slightly and his thighs bounced, taking me on his lap. I found myself bobbing in the rhythm, granting his thrusts more power—deeper, harder, the slap of our flesh coming together louder than the faint music, the heartbeat of our love.

And then he shook inside me, and we both stopped. I tumbled forward, gasping, and he took hold of me by the breasts—just enough to keep me steady, his thumbs and fore-fingers coming together to pinch my peaks.

He relaxed, his warm breath on my ear, our heavy breathing fading out.

"This has to be it." I panted. "We need to get out there—it's a farewell party for Neela, Gob, and Chip. I need to see my friends."

Brecc nibbled my earlobe once more. "I don't appreciate your tone, my queen."

I twisted my head to lean back and kiss him, my fingers darting over the stubble on his face. The scars were healing now, settling into their permanent grooves across his brow and nose and cheek. He looked just as handsome as always, his scars just proof of what we'd gone through. "There will be time for this later tonight. And every night in perpetuity."

"You speak as if you plan to live forever." His eyes grew hollow, all joviality in our banter lost.

At the thought of my shorter lifespan.

But to me... it would be an entire life. An entire life of joy and happiness.

"Wherever our souls go, we'll still be together," I promised him. I'd seen my father's soul accompanying my mother with my own eyes.

He sighed and kissed my temple, maneuvering to slide out completely and help me to my unsteady feet. My body still tingled from his touch.

"Forever," he said, swallowing. He slipped the blanket off the bed and wrapped it around my shoulders to keep me warm before I got dressed for the fete. "I promise you." Our eyes met and I believed his words. He'd told me of how his grandfather and father had acted after they'd lost their own human loves.

He moved to the washbasin at the vanity and picked up a cloth. I walked to the open window, through which streamed in the early evening moonlight, as I gave him space to get dressed first.

The landscape looked so different now. The hedge miniature maze at the back of the castle remained, but beyond that, endless landscape, our new roads driving paths through. Even the deadlands that had once been at the outer edges of the maze were clear now, the occasional hedge or bush planted to give the area a spark of life again, the roads taking up the bulk of the space.

I hummed to the sweet tune Borin's musicians played, the one I knew to be the final version of the tale of our quest *to save* the minotaur from the darkness and the cage.

And then I saw it—the dancing figure moving her arms high above her as her feet moved lithely over the stone path our people had lain.

"Mo-Mother?!" I gasped.

Brecc's feet padded quickly over to the window. "Your mother? Where?"

"There!" I pointed and the slight shimmer of her fiery-silver hair caught the light. She was just outside of the hedge maze. Mere moments from being back in my embrace.

"But how?" Brecc asked, playing with my hair as he shifted it aside to lay a kiss on my temple.

"There's magic in these lands," I said, turning around to slip my arms around him. Our mouths met, and then I pulled back. "That's answer enough for me."

He smiled, his lips carving a sort of roguish swagger into his two deep scars. "Let the bards sort out the details," he teased. "And leave hints for our grandchildren to unravel."

"'The Minotaur's Last Gift,'" I suggested, and as I spoke it, somehow I felt it to be true. Mother was back because the creature had willed it.

"I didn't realize he'd given us any other ones." Brecc shifted a lock of hair behind my shoulder.

"Without him, we never would have found each other." I pressed my forehead to his. "To love one another—for eternity."

"For eternity," he echoed. "Just promise me—no more running and hiding from me."

"Never," I said, getting down on my knees in front of him. My husband. My king.

My fingers worked at the waist of the pants he'd just pulled on and his hand ruffled my hair.

"What happened to 'we have to get going'?" he asked. "And your mother?"

"They'll wait," I said, laughing at myself. My lips smacked as I looked at the stiff erection I'd revealed before me.

We had all the time in the world. But I would seize every second of it.

THE SUCCUBUS SIRENS SERIES

Read sexy reverse harem stories set in the Succubus Sirens world of superpowered heroes, villains, and elves:

Succubus Lips – Succubus Heart – Mutiny's Rebellion – Succubus Soul: Veras Academy

These standalone, interconnected books can be picked up in any order, but if you want to avoid spoilers, it's best to read *Lips, Heart, Rebellion,* then *Soul.*

Praise for *Succubus Lips*:

"This is probably one of the most bizarre yet satisfyingly creative books I've ever read... If you're into kickass heroines and book boyfriends that make you swoon, this one is for you!" -The Lovely Books

"*Succubus Lips* is well-written and subversively funny, willing to toy with the reader's expectations and do the opposite... sexy without being tedious." -The Romance Reviews

Praise for *Succubus Heart*:

"This book kept my interest from the very beginning, and I enjoyed every scene. Absolutely recommended." ~The Romance Reviews

Praise for *Succubus Soul: Veras Academy*:

"With a great storyline, a bunch of brilliant characters (both main and supporting), plus some very steamy bits, this was a great book to read to while away the hours." ~The Romance Reviews

MY RACY REVERSE HAREM BOOK CLUB

STANDALONE CONTEMPORARY REVERSE HAREM

Nothing can keep Rose away from Romance Book Club at the library—not even the snowstorm of the century. Catching a

463

ride home through the storm with Lance, the stunningly attractive librarian who happens to be her neighbor, and Vaughn, his chiseled, alluring housemate, Rose takes them up on their invitation to drop by sometime and join them for their own book club. Rose gets more than she bargained for when she's introduced to Rafael, their magnetically charming third roommate, and the surprising genre of books they love to read and discuss. As the blizzard rages, Rose joins the Racy Reverse Harem Book Club, whose members are open to trying just about everything together to get warm.

A standalone novelette by Lina Jubilee, author of the reverse harem urban fantasy series Succubus Sirens.

ABOUT THE AUTHOR

Lina Jubilee loves reading, writing, drinking tea, and rooting for her favorite fictional romances. When not lost in a book, she cooks dinner at lunchtime, plans errands in fewer trips, and does everything she can to get back to romping through fictional worlds ASAP.

Ravenous readers, if you liked this book, please consider joining my Facebook street team! Connect with me:

Join My Mailing List (Get a Free Novelette!)

amazon.com/author/linajubilee

bookbub.com/profile/lina-jubilee

instagram.com/linajubilee

twitter.com/LinaJubilee

facebook.com/authorlinajubilee

Read More Hot Romances from Crimson Fox Publishing

A BEAUTIFUL RISK: LOVE AT LINCOLNFIELD BOOK 1

One stolen kiss. One wild fantasy. One big risk.

When a gorgeous Viking-like stranger plants a smoldering kiss on Passi in the thermal baths, she goes home with more than relaxation on her mind. The stranger sparks a fantasy hot enough to overcome the climax-killing side effects of her very necessary anti-depressants. When she walks into work to find the same devastatingly handsome man as the hospital's new risk manager, she frantically emails her best friend, detailing the fantasy starring her hot, new coworker. Only, instead of emailing her friend, she accidentally sends the X-rated message directly to *him*.

Insert leg in mouth. Quit job immediately. Or not...

Single dad Magnus is intrigued by the lovely woman he kissed at the baths who got away before he could learn her name. Even more so when he opens his email and discovers he was responsible for her breakthrough orgasm. But she's now his new HR director, and the reason she needs the medication means she won't date guys like him.

Exchanging risqué letters at work may be good, nail-biting fun, but the only way he can have her outside the realm of fantasy is to convince her to bend her rules and risk her heart on all that he has to offer.

A single dad, second chance, office romance, *A Beautiful Risk* is the first book in the Love at Lincolnfield series, heart-warming, hot page turners about the love lives of men and women who work at a Chicago hospital.

ALL IT TAKES

Megan Green has her whole life figured out. She's six months away from graduating uni, then she plans on backpacking around Europe for a year, before following her dream of becoming an interior designer.

What she doesn't account for is meeting local MMA fighter Kian Murphy.

With his athletic body and Irish charm, Kian has no trouble scoring with the ladies, and one night is all he's after.

But All It Takes is one night to change the rest of their lives.

After a chance meeting and passionate encounter, Megan finds herself pregnant with Kian's child. But with a womanizing reputation, and a temper that often leads him into trouble, Kian his hardly boyfriend material, let alone father material.

Now Megan and Kian must work out if they have All It Takes to turn their one-night-stand into a relationship that will connect them for a life-time.

All It Takes is a dual-POV, new-adult, contemporary-romance about responsibility, love and discovering who you are in life.